LONGING for a COWBOY CHRISTMAS

sourcebooks
casablanca

Cover and internal design © 2019 by Sourcebooks
Cover art by Gregg Gulbronson
Internal images © Lavandaart/Shutterstock
The publisher acknowledges the copyright holders of the individual works as follows:
A Fairy Tale Christmas © 1994, 2011, 2019 by Leigh Greenwood
Christmas in Paradise © 2019 by Rosanne Bittner
A Christmas Wedding © 2019 by Linda Broday
A Love Letter to Santa © 2019 by Margaret Brownley
One Snowy Christmas Eve © 2019 by Anna Schmidt
Through the Storm © 2019 by Amy Sandas

Published by Sourcebooks Casablanca, an imprint of Sourcebooks
P.O. Box 4410, Naperville, Illinois 60567-4410
(630) 961-3900
sourcebooks.com

Printed and bound in the United States of America.
OPM 10 9 8 7 6 5 4 3 2 1

Contents

A Fairy Tale
Christmas

—•◆•—

Leigh Greenwood

To my mother, for all those Christmases around the fire.

One

Shenandoah Valley, Virginia
1880

"It's too much work, Gertie," Nan said to the thin, middle-aged woman at her side. "And with Gideon not coming home this year, it just doesn't seem worth it."

Nan Carson stood with her farm manager's wife in the wide hall of her family home, Spruce Meadow. The dark oak floors gleamed with fresh wax. White wallpaper with tiny bunches of red poppies and blue cornflowers lightened the gloom created by the dark-stained oak doorways and the stairway that rose to a landing above. Pocket doors opened to reveal on one side an enormous formal parlor furnished with elegant Victorian furniture upholstered in wine-colored velvet and on the other a less formal gathering room furnished with dark leather, cotton prints, and overstuffed cushions.

"But Jake and Eli have already put a pile of cedar and holly on the back porch," Gertie replied.

"I'll tell somebody at the church to come get it. They can always use some extra."

"It won't seem right not seeing this place decorated," Gertie said, persevering. "Folks come all the way out here from town to look at it. Won't seem like Christmas to half of them. Gideon liked it, too."

"Well, if he'd wanted the decorations put up, he should have come home," Nan said.

She still hadn't gotten over the disappointment of

learning that Gideon was going to spend Christmas with his fiancée. It wasn't that Nan disliked Doris Morgan. She'd never met her. And Christmas was probably the best time for Gideon to visit his future in-laws, but this was the first year since their mother's death that Nan had been alone at Christmas, and she was finding it hard to keep her spirits up.

She was also finding it hard to accept the fact that her little brother was getting married while she seemed doomed to die an old maid. Not that thirty-one felt very old, but in Beaker's Bend she might as well be sixty. People got married by the time they were eighteen—or they moved away and never came back.

"Are you going to make cookies?" Gertie asked.

"Of course," Nan said, coming out of her abstraction. "Children get hungry every year."

"Then you'd better get started. Though how you have the patience to decorate so many I'll never understand, especially after taking care of this huge old house."

"It's no trouble. All I have to do is dust and make my bed. There's nobody to mess anything up."

Framed black-and-white pictures covered the walls in the hall, pictures of her father and mother, pictures of Gideon with his football and baseball teams.

There were none of her.

Nan pushed the loneliness aside. She was fortunate to live in a nice home, own the best farm in the valley, and have so many wonderful friends. So what if she wasn't going to have a husband and children? She shouldn't complain when she had so many other blessings.

She wasn't complaining exactly. It was just that there was an emptiness inside her that seemed to get a little bit deeper and wider each day. She felt like a pumpkin dusted with November frost, the last in the field. The outside was still firm and brightly colored, but the inside was slowly drying up.

"Maybe I'll make gingerbread people this winter," Nan said, giving her shawl a twitch and settling a smile on her lips. "I made the Christmas village last year."

"The children love your gingerbread." Gertie chuckled. "Only you got to be careful they don't look like nobody. Last time they took to calling one the preacher's wife. She got so mad she nearly disgraced herself right there in the church social hall."

Nan's smile owed more to her sense of mischief than to contrition. "Maybelle Hanks will be safe. I'll make certain there are no tall, spindly, sour-faced gingerbread women this year."

The butter hadn't had time to soften before the sharp, insistent ring of the doorbell brought Nan from the warm kitchen back into the chilly hall. "I'm coming," she muttered as she hurried along, her steps muffled by the runner.

The cut and beveled glass in the heavy front door distorted the world outside beyond recognition. Nan looked through the sidelights that flanked the door. On the porch, Wilmer Crider huddled into a heavy coat and cap, earflaps folded down. Nan picked up a wool shawl and wrapped it around her shoulders. A wintry blast whipped her skirts about her legs when she opened the door.

"What are you doing here?" Nan asked. "Who's at the inn?" She knew that Wilmer's wife, Lucy, had gone to stay with Ruby, her youngest daughter, through a difficult pregnancy. There wasn't anybody at the inn except Wilmer.

"L.P. and I got a sick fella out here." Wilmer pointed to the wagon just outside the front gate. "He walked through the door and fell down in a dead faint."

"What did Dr. Moore say?"

"Doc's with Ruby. She started having pains during the night."

Nan had a gift for healing, especially for making sick people feel comfortable and happy. Folks in the valley came to her when they needed help, some even when the doctor was available.

She heaved a sigh. "I'll take a look at him."

"You bundle up good," Gertie called from the back of the hall.

"I'm just going to the road."

"There's icicles hanging from the porch roof. You bundle up good."

Nan put on a heavy coat and wound a thick scarf around her neck.

"You can't go outside in those shoes," Gertie said, coming down the hall with a pair of sturdy shoes.

"I hope he's not very sick," Nan complained. "He could be dead before I get out the front door."

"I'll not have you down in the bed sick on Christmas," Gertie said.

The December air was frigid. The leaves of magnolias, hollies, and boxwood looked stiff, as if they would crack or break if they moved. Nan's breath billowed in white clouds before her, and the frozen ground crunched under her feet. The smell of a hickory and oak fire hung in the air. That would be Eli. He hated coal. Said it made the house smell bad. Nan pulled the rough wool of the scarf more securely around her neck.

The mountains that enclosed her valley rose in the distance, their tree-covered flanks dusted with a light covering of snow. Clouds heavy with snow filled the dull sky. Waiting. Threatening. The woolly worms had sported an especially thick coat this year.

The man lay almost buried in a pile of quilts in the back of Wilmer's wagon.

"I don't like the look of him," Wilmer said.

Nan didn't like the look of him either. He looked exhausted, glassy-eyed with fever. Chestnut-brown hair covered his head in waves. Several strands were matted to his damp forehead. His eyelids were only half open, almost obscuring the deep brown of his eyes. His face had lost all color, but it was clear and handsome and young. He was tall, so tall Wilmer had bent his legs to fit him in the wagon. His suit, starched shirt, and boiled collar announced that he was from a city. Probably somewhere up north. Nobody in the Shenandoah Valley dressed like that.

"Who is he?"

"Will Atkins. Comes from Boston."

"What's he doing down here?" Nan examined him carefully. "I'm sure he'll be all right once his fever breaks, but he'll need somebody to sit up with him tonight. Is there anybody with him?"

"His daughter."

"Good. I'll explain everything to her. Where is she?"

"There," Wilmer said, pointing to a person previously hidden by L.P.'s substantial bulk.

Nan's knees nearly went out from under her. A little girl of no more than four or five sat twisted around on the wagon seat. Her enormous, fear-widened brown eyes stared out from the most angelic face Nan had ever seen.

She was scared almost out of her wits.

Nan felt something clutch at her heart. This child was the image of the daughter she used to dream of having someday.

Nan wrenched her thoughts free of such fantasy.

She had no daughter, and this little girl was alone, frightened, tired, and probably hungry as well.

"Where's her mother?" Nan asked.

"There ain't no mother, just them two."

"She couldn't have come alone. Who looked after her?"

"Her father, I guess."

"Then she'll need someone to care for her until her father gets well."

"Don't look at me," Wilmer said. "I'm closing the inn. Got to go to Locust Hollow. Ruby's husband has come down with a fever, too. There's nobody to do the chores till he gets back on his feet."

"What are you going to do with this man?"

"I was hoping you'd take him in."

"I'm a maiden lady."

"Nobody's going to talk, especially not with him passed out cold as a trout and Gertie and Jake here to look after you. Besides, who's going to take care of her?" He pointed to the child.

Nan walked around to the other side of the wagon. The little girl was bundled up in a coat and mittens, staring out from a fur-lined hood. Her leggings and shoes were city clothes, too thin to protect her from the ice and snow of this mountain valley. She had to be cold all the way through. Even if her father hadn't been sick, Nan couldn't have abandoned her.

"Hi. My name is Nan Carson. What's your name?"

The child didn't answer, just stared back at her. Nan saw fear in her clenched hands, her ramrod-stiff posture, her anxious stare.

"Where are you going?"

Again, nothing.

"Do you know anybody here in Beaker's Bend?"

"You know they don't," Wilmer said, "not with them dressed like that."

"I guess not," Nan agreed, "but they've got to be going somewhere. Somebody must be expecting them."

"Well, they'll not be getting there today."

"Not for several days," Nan said, coming to a decision. "Bring Mr. Atkins inside. I'll take care of him until his fever breaks, but you've got to take him again after that."

"Sure," Wilmer said.

"You're going to stay at my house," Nan said to the little girl. She held out her hand, but the child didn't move. Tears welled up in the child's eyes and rolled down her cheeks.

"Please don't let my daddy die."

A lump formed in Nan's throat. She reached out, unclasped the child's hands, and took them in her own. "Your father's going to get well, I promise. I'm going to take very good care of him. And I'm going to fix you something good to eat and tuck you up in a nice, warm bed."

The little girl still looked fearful, but Nan felt her tiny hands relax and return her pressure. When Wilmer and L.P. lifted her father out of the wagon, the tears flowed faster and her hand squeezed tighter. Nan felt as if her heart would break. She put her arms around the child and drew her close. The tiny body felt frail, yet stiff with fear. Nan wanted desperately to comfort her, but she knew that only time would overcome her dread of being in an unfamiliar town surrounded by strangers, her father very ill. She must feel utterly alone. Abandoned.

Nan picked up the child. "I've never had a little girl of my own," she said. "For tonight, let's pretend I'm your mommy."

The child spoke unexpectedly. "My mommy's gone to heaven. Is Daddy going to heaven, too?"

Nan hugged the child a little closer. "No, your daddy's going to get well, and you're going to have the best Christmas ever."

The child put her arms around Nan's neck and held tight. Unwilling to break her hold, Nan carried her to the house down a rock-lined path past a bed of dead roses, an empty flower bed, and a half acre of brown, withered grass. She waited while Wilmer and L.P. struggled to carry Will Atkins up the steps. Gertie held the door open.

"Take him straight back," Nan told Wilmer.

"But that's your room," Gertie objected.

The big room, once Nan's parents', lay at the back of the house across the wide hall from the kitchen. Nan directed them to place Will on an oversized bed piled high with thick, soft mattresses. The room was filled with ornately carved, dark cherrywood furniture, but Nan's touches could be seen in the gingham bed cover and lace curtains at the window to let in the light.

"I'll sleep in my old room," Nan said.

She put the little girl down. The child wouldn't let go of Nan's hand, so Nan knelt beside her. "I'm going to take you to the kitchen while I see about your father." The child clutched tighter. "This is Gertie," Nan said, introducing her farm manager's wife. "She'll get you something to eat."

The child still clung to Nan. Nan choked up. How many times had she dreamed of holding her own child just like this? She didn't want to let go, but she knew she had to see to the father.

"You don't have to be afraid. I'll be right here."

Still she wouldn't let go. Nan didn't have the heart to force her to go with Gertie. Still kneeling, still holding the child's hand, she said to Gertie, "Bring some warm milk and bread and jam to the bedroom."

She turned to the child. "Would you like that?"

The girl didn't answer, but Nan thought she detected a brightness in her eyes. Nan led her into the bedroom, to a chair close to the bed. "Sit right here. You can watch everything that happens to your daddy. We're going to make him better. I'm going to light the fire. It'll soon be warm as toast." Nan lifted her into a chair. "I won't leave you, I promise. But I've got to make your father better. You want that, don't you?"

The child nodded.

"Then sit right here. I'll be back in a moment." The child looked scared, but determined to be brave.

Wilmer and L.P. had undressed Mr. Atkins and put

him into Nan's father's nightshirt. Nan put her hand to his forehead. He was burning up with fever. His pulse was calm and steady, but she would have to keep him warm. She took an extra quilt out of a tall wardrobe and asked L.P. to bring in more firewood for the woodbox. She went out and returned in a few minutes with a cool compress for her patient's forehead and a hot-water bottle for his feet. She would give him some hot herbal tea as soon as it was ready, but right now she was more concerned about keeping him warm.

She put another log on the fire and turned her attention to the child. Nan was pleased to see her take a bite out of a thick slice of whole-wheat bread covered with freshly churned butter and Concord grape jam.

Nan pulled up a chair next to her. "I wish you'd tell me your name."

The child wiggled a little, but she didn't look so scared. "Clara," she announced. She looked down at her shoes rather than at Nan.

"That's a lovely name. My name is Nan. I don't like it very much. I think Clara is much prettier."

Clara smiled rather nervously.

"When did your daddy get sick?"

"While he was sleeping. He wouldn't eat his breakfast."

Just as Nan had thought. Two people in Beaker's Bend had already come down with similar symptoms. Their fever remained high for about twenty-four hours, then it broke, leaving them weak but none the worse otherwise.

"He should be just fine in the morning. Do you want anything else to eat?"

The child shook her head.

"You can have more." Nan thought Clara was probably too frightened to be hungry tonight.

"No, thank you."

"Then I'm going to tuck you into a nice warm

bed," Nan said, wondering who had taught the child such beautiful manners. She acted older than her age. She must be an only child surrounded by adults. Nan wondered how long ago her mother had died. "When you wake up, your daddy will be all better."

Nan stood. Clara seemed reluctant to leave the fire and the comfort of her father's presence, but she slid out of the chair.

"I'm going to put you in the room I had when I was a little girl," Nan said. "You can sleep in the bed I slept in when I was your age."

Her mother had insisted they keep it for the time Nan's daughters would need it.

Wilmer had brought the bags in, and Gertie had taken Clara's bag upstairs to a small room with bright, flowered wallpaper. All the handmade furniture was half-size. Clara allowed herself to be undressed and put to bed. Nan marveled that a room that used to seem so friendly should seem so cold now.

"If you need anything, you just call," Nan told her. "I'm going to go downstairs to take care of your father, but I'll sleep in the room right next to you." She led her into the hall and showed her the right door. "I'll leave this open so I can hear you. All right?"

Clara nodded, but she seemed frightened again.

Nan hated to leave her, but Clara needed to go to sleep. She probably hadn't had any rest all day. After the trip and the scare of her father getting sick, she must be exhausted.

"Do you think it's okay to leave her up there by herself?" Nan asked Gertie when she came downstairs.

"I expect she'll sleep till morning. Poor thing looks worn to a frazzle. Now you come into the kitchen before your dinner gets cold."

"Bring it to the bedroom. I don't think I ought to leave Mr. Atkins that long."

"He'll be just fine."

"Nevertheless, I'll feel more comfortable if I sit with him."

Gertie went away grumbling under her breath, but Nan didn't pay her any mind. Gertie had never accepted the fact that Nan had grown up and was not the little girl she had been twenty-four years ago when Gertie married Jake Tanner and moved away from Beaker's Bend.

Will Atkins hadn't moved. Nan put her hand on his forehead, but she knew before she touched him that his fever hadn't broken. His skin was hot and dry. It felt tight. Nan had cared for many people, but no one had ever made her as nervous as this man did.

It's because he's Clara's father.

But she knew that wasn't it. She was nervous because he was a good-looking man. She couldn't help but be aware of it. She had felt something happen inside her the moment she set eyes on him. Almost as if she were sixteen again.

Don't be foolish. This man will be up and on his way in a couple of days, and you'll never see him again. He won't even remember your name by next Christmas.

Maybe, but she couldn't turn her eyes away from the handsome head that rested on her goose-down pillows. She couldn't help but wonder what had happened to his wife, and why he should be in the Shenandoah Valley at this time of year. She remembered his ready-to-wear wool suit and Clara's clothes that spoke of expensive shops in a big, eastern city. He wouldn't stay in Beaker's Bend any longer than necessary.

She had brushed his chestnut hair back from his brow, but not even his disordered hair and pallid skin detracted from his handsome face. She brushed the back of her fingers against his cheek. The skin was hot and taut, the cheeks gaunt from fever, but the clean line of his jaw and the finely etched nose complemented the fullness of his lips.

Nan made herself stand away from the bed when

Gertie came in to place her dinner on a table next to her chair.

"Jake's not easy in his mind about you having that man sleeping in your bed," Gertie said.

"I don't know why. I'm not sleeping in it, and Mr. Atkins is too sick to know where he is. If that's not enough, Jake can sleep at the foot of the bed."

Gertie looked affronted. Nan kissed the older woman's cheek. "You should be happy. Not an hour ago I was feeling down because Gideon wasn't going to be home for Christmas. Now we have company."

"They'll only be here a day or two," Gertie said. "It'll just be that much lonelier when they're gone."

Gertie was right. Nan would miss them. Odd. She didn't know anything about Will Atkins, but she felt drawn to him. But then, a handsome, helpless man offered an irresistible appeal to any woman. She was less able to explain her feeling for Clara. Already she felt a strong attachment to the little girl, almost as if she belonged to her.

It had to be the season and that she felt lonely because Gideon wasn't coming home. Next year she'd make sure she had so much to do that she wouldn't have time to be lonely. Maybe she'd go visit Gideon and Doris. She knew he'd invite her.

But it was too late for this year, and she was thankful for Mr. Atkins and his daughter.

❧

Nan twisted in her chair. She had forgotten how uncomfortable it was to sit up all night, even in a comfortable chair. She opened her eyes and glanced at the clock. Twenty-two minutes after midnight. She didn't get up. She had checked Will Atkins less than ten minutes ago.

Light from a single tongue of fire struggled to hold the darkness at bay. The pattern on the quilt, Will's shape in the bed, were crisscrossed with shadows cast by the posts at the end of the bed. The rest of the room lay in deep shadow.

Nan closed her eyes, but she remained restless. The floor creaked. Startled, she opened her eyes and sat up. Clara stood by her father's bedside.

Nan got up and knelt before the child. "You're supposed to be in bed."

"I couldn't sleep."

"You mean you've been lying up there all this time waiting for me to come to bed?"

Clara nodded.

"Didn't you sleep at all?"

The child shook her head.

"Then you can sleep down here," Nan said. She reached under the skirt of the bed and pulled out a trundle bed. "I'd almost forgotten this was here." It only took Nan a few minutes to make up the bed and retrieve the pillow and quilts from the bottom of the wardrobe. "Now, let's tuck you under."

Clara climbed between the sheets. "Are you going to stay here?"

Nan heard the fear in the child's voice.

"Yes," Nan replied.

Clara settled into the bed, but she didn't close her eyes.

"I'll be right back," Nan said.

She hurried upstairs, lifted the lid on a pine chest at the end of her old bed, and took out a large, handmade doll fashioned of heavy linen with clothes of bright gingham faded with time. She carried the nearly shapeless doll downstairs.

"Here's somebody to keep you company," she said as she slipped the doll under the covers next to Clara. "Her name is Betty. She's a little prickly because my brother Gideon tried to cut all her hair off. I gave Gideon a black eye. Papa was real mad, but Mama understood."

Clara giggled and pulled the doll close. "She only has one eye."

"The other one must have fallen off in the chest. We'll look for it tomorrow and sew it back on. Now you go to sleep. Your father ought to be better in the morning, and you'll want to be awake to keep him company."

"Aren't you going to keep him company, too?"

"Of course, but he'll especially want you."

"You're sure Daddy's going to be all right?"

"Positive. Now close your eyes. The sooner you go to sleep, the sooner you can wake up and find him well."

Clara obediently closed her eyes, the doll clutched in her arms, but Nan could tell she wasn't asleep.

"What's wrong, honey?"

"I'm cold."

"I'll get you another quilt."

But that wasn't the answer either.

"Would you like to sit in my lap for a minute?"

Nan didn't know why she asked that, but she had obviously said the right thing. Clara was out of the trundle bed and in her lap before Nan could change her mind.

Nan felt awkward. She had never held a child like this, but Clara didn't feel the least bit unsure. She pulled her knees up under her chin, rested her head on Nan's bosom, clutched the doll in a tight grasp, and closed her eyes. In less than a minute she was sound asleep. She didn't wake when Nan leaned over to get the quilt to cover her.

Nan didn't know what to do. She knew she should put Clara back in the trundle bed, but she was afraid she would waken her. The child might feel abandoned when she woke up.

It was some time before Nan drifted off to sleep again. She had a warm feeling inside that spread through her whole body. It made her feel good, contented. She felt almost like a married woman with a husband and a child to care for. She told herself not to be foolish, that only children indulged in make-believe, but she couldn't stop the feeling. Besides, she liked it. For the first time in a long while, she didn't feel as if the pageant of life had passed her by. It might be foolish, but it was only a small indulgence. It wouldn't matter. They'd be gone in a day or two.

Nan looked at the man in the bed and the little girl in her arms. She realized that she didn't want them to go.

Two

WILL OPENED HIS EYES. AS HIS VISION SLOWLY FOCUSED, he realized that he had no idea where he was. He felt terribly tired. He couldn't move. Then he remembered feeling sick. He must be at an inn. But where? He remembered a train conductor asking him how he felt, but he didn't recall anything after that.

Clara! What had happened to his daughter? He tried to sit up, but after barely lifting himself off the bed, he fell back. His vision went all blurry, and the ceiling dissolved into a pinwheel. But it soon cleared. With great effort, he turned onto his side. His gaze focused on the woman sleeping in a chair next to his bed; Clara lay asleep in her lap.

Where was he? Who was this woman? How had she gotten his shy daughter to trust her?

She had passed the first blush of youth, but she was still a lovely woman, her complexion creamy-smooth, the only color the pale blush of her cheeks and the deep rose of her lips. And the black of her lashes and eyebrows. Her nearly black hair had been parted in the middle and pulled into a knot on top of her head. It made her look too elegant even for this comfortable, well-furnished room. She wasn't beautiful, but in sleep she wore an expression of such serenity that he felt his anxiety ebb away. Whoever she was, she was kindness itself.

He was surprised that her husband had allowed her to sit with him. Even with his daughter to act as chaperone, men in the mountains were notoriously skittish about letting strangers near their women. He ought to know. He had grown up in the mountains.

Maybe it was because she'd been married for years. The way she held Clara—her arms holding her close, her chin resting on the child's head—showed she knew all about children. She must have several of her own.

He'd have to move to an inn as soon as possible. He didn't want to make any more work for her, or cause trouble between her and her husband.

But even as he told himself he ought to leave, his gaze was drawn back to the woman. Something about her appealed to him strongly. Maybe it was her kindness. He couldn't be imagining it. It must be terribly uncomfortable to have let Clara sleep in her lap all night, yet she looked perfectly content. No, she looked happy, as if she wanted to keep Clara close.

How could he not be drawn to a woman such as that? She had such a sweet, loving face.

He fell back, exhausted. He wondered how long he had been here. He hoped it hadn't been too long. Louise's parents were expecting him on the twentieth. They couldn't wait to get their hands on Clara. They'd been trying for years. Now they had succeeded, and they were impatient. After not forgiving him for taking their daughter away, they weren't likely to be pleased with him postponing their moment of triumph.

He thought of Louise's happiness when she'd learned she was pregnant, of how much she'd looked forward to having a half-dozen children. She had died before Clara's first birthday. The loss had almost destroyed him. Now he was going to lose Clara as well.

He drifted off to sleep wondering for the thousandth time if there were any way to avoid it.

∞

"Wake up, Nan. You had no business sleeping in this chair. Don't you know what it can do to your spine?"

Nan opened her eyes but didn't move. "Ssshhhh," she whispered. "You'll wake Clara and her father."

"Better I should wake them than you should be a cripple for life."

Nan glanced at the weak sunlight coming in the window. "I guess I'd better get up."

But she couldn't move. One arm and both legs had gone dead.

"Help me put her in the trundle bed." Nan allowed Gertie to lift Clara from her lap. While Gertie tucked the sleeping child into the small bed, Nan rubbed her arm to restore the circulation. The pinpricks of returning feeling were unpleasant, but she didn't mind. Looking at Clara as she slept peacefully made it worthwhile. Nan had brought help and comfort to many people, but nothing had ever touched her so deeply as Clara asleep in her arms. For one night she had been able to experience what it would have been like to have a child of her own.

Nan got to her feet. She felt stiff, her muscles slow to respond, her movements awkward. She walked around the bed to get a closer look at Will Atkins. "He looks better." She felt his forehead. "His fever has broken."

"I'll bet he's soaked the bed."

"Probably. Get some clean sheets. I'll get him a fresh nightshirt."

"You're not thinking of changing him, are you?" Gertie asked, scandalized.

Nan laughed softly. "Not that he would know the difference."

"You let Jake take care of him."

"Of course," Nan said. But she felt a tinge of regret. Being near this man infused her with an energy that made her more optimistic, more sensitive. She felt as though good news was on its way, as though something wonderful was about to happen.

∽∞∾

Will Atkins sat on the edge of the bed, his legs sticking out from a nightshirt that was much too short for him. "I can't face anybody looking like this," he said, rubbing his chin over a two-day growth of beard.

"That's Mr. Carson's nightshirt."

"I don't want to take his clothes. What's he going to wear?"

"Mr. Carson's dead."

"She's awfully young to be a widow."

"Who are you talking about?"

"The young woman who sat up with me."

Jake chuckled, a big grin on his face. "That's Nan, Mr. Carson's daughter. She ain't never married."

Will felt a muscle in his throat tighten. "What's wrong with the men around here?"

"There ain't any, leastways not any that ain't already married," Jake said as he poured the hot water into a basin and set it down on the stand next to the bed. "Old Mister Carson used to say she was too particular. Gertie says there weren't nobody good enough. I think she scared them off."

"What's wrong with her?"

"Nothing." Jake worked up a lather with the shaving brush. "It's just she's a real lady. A smart one, too. That's enough to put the fear of God into most men around here."

"In Boston, men would be standing in line to marry her," Will said, allowing Jake to lather his face. He would have preferred to shave himself—he'd never been able to afford the luxury of having someone do it for him—but he was too weak to hold the razor.

"Miss Nan don't hold with big cities," Jake said. "That's where Gideon went, and he ain't never come back."

"Gideon?" Will managed to mumble. He had to hold real still while Jake shaved his jaw.

"Her brother. He's marrying some city girl. That's why he ain't coming home for Christmas."

"But surely Miss Carson has more family." It was hard to talk when his upper lip was being shaved by a straight razor sharp enough to cut it off with a single slip of the hand.

"They're all dead."

"But this farm?"

"She owns it. Runs it herself, too. Well, actually Cliff Gilmer takes care of the cows, and Bert Layne sees after the crops. Me and Gertie help with everything else, but Miss Nan makes all the decisions."

As Jake lifted Will's chin to shave his neck, Will couldn't deny a feeling of relief. He had been nervous about facing a husband less than delighted to have his home invaded just before Christmas. He was also curious to learn more about a woman who could not only run her own farm but also be willing to take in a stranger who had fallen sick, who could win his daughter's trust enough for Clara to sleep in her lap, and whose kindness drew his thoughts back to her time and time again.

And not just her kindness. There was a sensuality about her, about the pucker of her full lips, the unblemished whiteness of her skin, the softness of her body's curves. He might be weak from fever, but he could feel a physical tug, the kind of pull he had felt very few times since his wife's death.

"Now you're to get back in bed," Jake said as he wiped the last bits of lather from Will's face. "Your breakfast will be in shortly."

"I'd like to see my daughter."

"She's getting dressed, but she'll be having her breakfast in here with you."

"And Miss Carson?"

"Her, too. The room'll be full to busting with all of you and Gertie bustling about to make sure you don't do nothing improper."

"I wouldn't think—"

"You can think all you want," Jake said, "as long as you don't do nothing."

No, Will wouldn't do anything, but his imagination wouldn't be nearly so obedient.

⁂

Will was so weak he could hardly hold his spoon steady. He found it hard to believe fever could drain so much of his strength in less than twenty-four hours, but he was determined that Nan wouldn't have to feed him. He didn't want to look helpless with Clara watching him.

"He's eating with a coming appetite," Gertie observed from the foot of the bed. "He'll be ready to go on his way by afternoon."

"Mr. Atkins is too weak to resume his journey for at least another day," Nan said. "Besides, Wilmer has closed the inn, so there's nothing for him to do but stay here until he regains his strength. You won't mind that, will you?" she asked Clara.

Clara shook her head happily.

Will would have been amused at Gertie's effort to protect her mistress if he hadn't been the one she was protecting her from. He had already asked about alternatives to the inn, but Jake had told him nobody was taking in strangers during the Christmas season. "They have enough to do worrying over their relations who moved to the city but always come home for the holidays."

"Then if he's so weak, you ought to let him get his rest," Gertie said, her hands on her hips.

"Let Clara stay with me," Will said. "You must have a lot to do to get ready for Christmas." He was surprised that Clara was so happy to sit next to Nan.

"Not all that much. Would you like to help me?" Nan asked Clara.

"I don't know how," Clara replied.

"What do you mean *you don't know how*?" Nan asked.

"She's never had a proper Christmas," Will explained. "The woman who's been keeping her doesn't celebrate Christmas."

"What kind of heathen doesn't celebrate Christmas?" Gertie demanded.

"Lots of people, especially people like me who don't have anybody to share it with," Nan said, hoping to stem Gertie's embarrassing questions. "Now please ask Jake to bring all the greenery on the back porch into the front hall."

"You said you wanted to give it to the church."

"I changed my mind. Clara and I are going to decorate the front hall. Hurry up. We can't get started without it."

Gertie didn't seem pleased to leave Nan unprotected, but she went off to find Jake. Apparently she thought keeping Nan out of Will's bedroom for the morning was worth the risk of a few unprotected moments.

"I apologize for Gertie," Nan said.

"Don't. A lovely young woman like you can't be too well protected. I'm surprised you don't have bars at the gate to keep the men out."

"The only bars we need in Beaker's Bend would be to keep the men in. Now Clara and I are going to leave you to your rest. We'll wake you for lunch."

"I won't sleep that long. I feel much better."

"We'll see. Clara, give your father a kiss."

"You sure she's not too much trouble?"

"I'll enjoy having her. Christmas is a difficult time when you're alone. But having lost your wife, I expect you know that."

Will didn't reply. Once again he felt the overwhelming guilt of not being able to stay at Louise's side when she was so sick. He hadn't even been in town when she died. He wasn't sure he could ever forgive himself for that.

That was one of the reasons he was taking Clara to live with her grandparents. He didn't want her to grow up staying with strangers, seeing her father only on weekends and not always then. She needed the kind of love, support, and comfort that could only be provided by someone who could be with her every day, sit with her when she was sick, share her happy moments. He might not like Louise's parents, but he knew they would take good care of Clara.

"Any time is difficult when you're alone," Will answered.

Nan looked surprised. "I'm not alone. I've got Gertie and Jake, the people who work for me—the whole town."

"You're alone when you're without a family."

Will didn't know why he'd said that. Maybe because he'd felt so alone during the five years since Louise died. He loved Clara with all his heart, but she couldn't fill the emptiness left by his wife's death.

"Well, I have a family today, don't I?"

Odd she should say that. He did feel almost like part of her family. Clara certainly seemed to. Just as inexplicably, the emptiness inside him didn't feel so overwhelming today. Maybe it was being in a real home with real people who cared. Even in the few hours he had been awake, he had felt more comfortable than he did in his apartment. It had been so long since he left the valley that he had forgotten how nice a real home could feel.

Louise had been just as anxious as he had been to leave the small town where they'd grown up as he was. Maybe more so. She'd probably worked harder to get ahead. Then she got sick and never recovered. It was as though giving life to Clara had completely used up her own.

He doubted that would happen to Nan Carson. He imagined she would glow with health. She was the kind of woman whose love and strength would never be exhausted. It would continually renew itself.

Will grew drowsy wondering why no one had claimed this woman. If he had been one of the village blades, he'd have camped on her doorstep. Just the thought of her lips, of the sweetness of her kiss, would have caused him to neglect any duties he might have.

He told himself he was too weak to get worked up over idle speculation, but he drifted off to sleep trying to imagine what it would be like to return each day to a home of Nan Carson's making.

⸻

"We won't be able to see out if we put anything else in that window," Nan said to Clara.

"But we've got all these branches left."

The room was littered with holly branches, pungent cedar, pyracantha heavy with clusters of dull red berries, pine boughs that filled the room with their fresh scent, magnolia branches with huge, shiny green leaves and brown seedpods filled with plump red seeds, and tiny sprigs of mistletoe, all on burlap sacks spread out to protect the carpets and floor. The broken pieces had been gathered up in a large wooden tub. Clara held a roll of red ribbon. Green and white lay just within reach.

They had decorated the parlor with spare good taste, but they had covered every corner of the gathering room. The deep brown of the walls and hardwood floor, the dark maroon of the leather chairs, the cheerful plaids and floral patterns were overwhelmed by green and red.

Each window held a wreath fashioned out of cedar branches and fastened together with bits of wire. Holly, bright with red berries, lay in each window seat. Branches of pine topped with magnolia circled every table in the room. More than a dozen candles stood in the windows and on the tables ready to be lighted.

"We need to save some for the wreath to go on the front door."

"Let's make that now."

"How about waiting until tomorrow," Nan said, laughing. "I think we ought to begin making the decorations for the Christmas tree."

"Can we have a real tree?" Clara asked.

"Of course."

"We never had a real tree. Mrs. Bartholomew doesn't like Christmas."

"Who's Mrs. Bartholomew?"

"The lady I stay with when Daddy's gone." Clara paused. "He's gone nearly all the time."

"Well, he's here this Christmas," a deep, masculine voice announced from the doorway. "Not in very good shape, but here nonetheless."

Nan looked up. She noticed how thin he was, as if he hadn't been eating well. But he was still very attractive. She wondered if Mrs. Bartholomew was a young woman.

Clara ran toward her father as he walked into the gathering room with careful steps.

"Easy, easy," he said when she seemed ready to throw herself into his arms. "You're liable to knock me over."

"He wouldn't eat the lunch I brought him," Gertie complained, entering the room on his heels. "He insisted on joining you."

"I'm punished for my disobedience," Will said, sinking into the only chair free of greenery. "I can't stand up long enough to hug my daughter."

"Of course not," Nan said, getting to her feet. "You ought to have eaten your lunch and gone straight back to sleep." She took a quilt from the sofa, unfolded it, and spread it over him.

"I seem to have slept away the better part of the day," he said. "Gertie tells me it's midafternoon. Have you eaten?"

"Hours ago," Clara said. "We had pork chops in gravy and lots of potatoes and—"

"Our lunch was too rich for your father. Bring his tray in here, Gertie. He can eat while we make the tree decorations."

"Eat in here?" Gertie asked, scandalized.

"Yes, in here," Nan repeated. "It's about time this room got used for something. Besides, it's no use decorating if nobody's going to look at it."

Gertie looked displeased, but she soon settled a tray in front of Will. "Don't spill anything," she said. "I don't have time for a lot of cleaning."

"Gertie!" Nan exclaimed.

"Well, I don't. Not with me doing all the cooking you haven't got time for now."

"Are we keeping you from—"

"You're not keeping me from a thing," Nan insisted, angry at Gertie. "There's more than enough time for the cooking I need to do."

Gertie sniffed in disagreement, but she left without saying anything more.

While Will ate his lunch of hot, clear soup, Nan showed Clara how to draw designs on colored paper and cut them out to make candy canes and other brightly colored ornaments. She showed the girl how to fold the colored paper to make boxes and pyramids. They glued narrow strips of gold and silver paper into shining garlands.

Nan couldn't remember when she had had more fun. The chance to show Clara a Christmas like none she'd ever experienced restored Nan's own excitement and anticipation. But one look at Will sitting in the chair watching his daughter with a rapt gaze made her realize that it wasn't just Clara. It was her father as well.

She had been acutely aware of his presence. His gaze followed her, his expression inscrutable. She felt as though he was trying to probe her mind and expose her thoughts. Nan had none except to make Clara happy. Well, she did wonder about him, his job, why he hadn't remarried.

She told herself it was silly to be curious about a man she had never seen before yesterday and wouldn't see again after tomorrow.

"Now it's time to string the popcorn," Nan said in a very businesslike manner when Gertie took away the lunch tray. She opened a box Gertie had brought in earlier, and immediately the smell of freshly roasted popcorn filled the air.

"That smells delicious," Will said.

Clara's eyes grew big.

Nan laughed as she handed Clara a needle threaded with a very long piece of string. "Don't eat too much. It takes a lot to decorate a big tree."

Gertie entered long enough to set a plate of golden yellow cookies on the table next to Will.

"Clara, show your father how I taught you to string the popcorn. While you do that, I'm going upstairs to bring down some very special decorations."

Nan returned several minutes later to find two chestnut heads together over a lengthening string of popcorn. Clara chose the kernels. Her father put them on the string. Then while Clara carefully pushed a fluffy white kernel to the end of the string, her father ate one of the golden cookies.

Nan couldn't help but notice how long and slender his fingers were. Her father's had been short and thick and powerful. Will's hands gave the impression of elegance. They didn't look as if they ever had a blister.

Forcing her mind back to her task, Nan cleared a broad hunt table, then covered it with cotton she unrolled in broad widths. "Let your father finish that," Nan said to Clara. "I want you to help me."

Clara came over to stare uncertainly at the cotton-covered table.

Nan knelt before the box and began to remove carved and painted wooden figures—men, women, children, dogs, a horse and sleigh, houses, trees, until she had an entire village.

"Ooooo, it's beautiful!" Clara cooed. "Where did you get it?"

"My father had it made for me when I was a little girl. Each year I got something else to add to it."

"Are you going to make a town?"

"No."

Clara's face fell.

"You're going to make it."

"Me?"

"Yes. All by yourself."

Clara regarded the figures with a questioning gaze.

"Are you sure?" her father asked.

"Positive," Nan replied as she came to sit in a chair next to him. "Setting up that village each year is one of my happiest childhood memories."

"Thank you for sharing it with Clara. She has so few happy memories of Christmas."

He'd never realized it before, but neither had he. Maybe that's why he had been anxious to leave his own home, why he hadn't thought it necessary to stay home with Clara. Nan, on the other hand, had experienced this happiness and was sharing this precious gift with two strangers.

He couldn't remember Clara ever being this happy, a joyfulness he had longed for without knowing it. Maybe that was why he felt so strongly drawn to Nan. Maybe it wasn't just her softness or her quiet allure.

"Forgive me if I'm prying, but don't you have any family?" Nan asked.

"Not really." Only Louise's parents, and they were about the last people he cared to see.

"You must have been going somewhere."

"To visit my wife's parents."

"Then you must resume your trip as quickly as possible. They must be anxiously awaiting—"

"My wife and I couldn't wait to leave home, especially Louise. We were so sure life would be better in the city. Any city."

"And was it?"

He reached for a cookie and ate slowly.

"Louise never regretted leaving, not even after she got sick."

He paused to watch Clara. She had made the first decision, where to place her church. She arranged several houses around it.

"I've had to work much harder since she died."

"So that's why you're never home."

Clara searched through the figures until she found what she wanted—a man, a woman, and a child. A family.

"Daddy," she called, "which is our house? The one we're going to live in when you get rich?"

"The big white one," Will said, pointing to the largest house in the set. "It's going to sit right across the street from the church."

"Where's your store going to be?"

"In the next block. Across from the bank."

They watched as Clara placed the two buildings, then chose the people to live in each one.

"So why did you come back?"

"I'm taking Clara to live with her grandparents."

Clara lifted a house out of the box that clearly belonged on a Southern plantation rather than in the Shenandoah Valley. "Daddy, who lives in this house?"

"Anybody you want, precious."

"I can't decide. You come help."

Will had difficulty getting up from the chair. He had difficulty getting down next to his daughter, too, but he was thankful for the interruption. He didn't want to have to explain to Nan his reasons for taking Clara to her grandparents. Or defend them. He didn't owe her an explanation for anything—he was doing the best he could for his daughter while honoring his promises to Louise—but he couldn't bear for her to keep looking at him like that.

"That's a mighty fancy house," he said as he watched Clara trying to decide where to place the house. "A mighty fancy lady ought to live there."

Clara giggled. "No. This is Nan's house."

"I agree. Now, where can we find a Nan?"

Once again two chestnut heads came together as father and daughter set about the task of populating their village.

Nan watched, her mind prey to fruitless speculation. It would never have occurred to her to give up her child, not even for a short time. There must be some terrible pressure on Will to force him to take such a drastic step. It was plain that he adored Clara.

Looking at him over his daughter's head, she could swear there were tears in his eyes. At least he was misty-eyed. No man who looked like that wanted to give up his daughter.

She noticed Will glance up at the plate of cookies, but they were too far away.

Nan got up and placed them on the floor next to him.

She hated to think of depriving grandparents of their grandchild, but it was even more terrible to think of separating a father from his daughter. There must be some way to keep them together. Right then Nan made up her mind to keep them at Spruce Meadow until she found a way.

Three

"YOU HAVE TO BUNDLE UP REAL GOOD," NAN TOLD Clara. "It's very cold outside." Breakfast had been eaten and everything washed up. They were going to look for a Christmas tree.

"It's cold at home, too," Clara said. She was so excited that Nan had to help her into her coat.

"But not as cold as here," Jake said. "You'll have icicles on your nose by the time we get back."

Clara giggled. "Will I?" she asked Nan.

"Not if you bundle up." Nan pulled a gaily decorated woolen cap over Clara's head. "Keep your gloves on."

"Why are you always trying to do things without me?"

The three turned to find Will Atkins standing in the doorway to his room. He was dressed in a suit with an overcoat and hat. Only his boots seemed sturdy enough to endure the hunt for a Christmas tree.

Clara giggled. "Daddy's not bundled up. He'll have icicles on his nose."

"This is all I have," Will said.

"You can't possibly go," Nan protested. "You're not strong enough to make it up the hills."

"I was hoping for a place in your wagon."

Nan looked undecided, but Clara took her father by the hand. "You can sit next to me."

"Okay," Nan said, giving in, "but you've got to let Jake lend you some clothes, and you've got to stay in the wagon. I won't have Jake trying to drag you out of the woods."

"You don't have a very good impression of me, do you?"

Nan didn't dare let him guess the impression she did have. She had lain awake half the night trying to think of ways to help him keep his daughter. But instead of thinking about his job and housekeepers to stay with Clara, she found herself wondering what he liked to eat, what made him laugh, what he liked to do for fun, where he had taken his wife when they were spooning.

"You've been very sick. You won't do Clara any good if you get sick again."

"Is that all you care about?"

His look made Nan uneasy. He was looking too deep, demanding an answer she didn't want to give. "What else should I care about?"

"Me."

Nan felt herself grow warm. Words stuck in her throat. Her thoughts came in hesitant fragments.

She felt foolish and utterly helpless to do anything about it. She was attracted to this man, more than to any other she had ever known, but that was no reason to be rendered brainless.

"I care about you, Daddy," Clara said.

"I'm concerned about your father, too," Nan managed to say. "But what kind of nurse would I be if I let him get sick again?"

"Let's go," Clara said, tired of standing around talking. "I want a big Christmas tree that goes all the way to the ceiling."

"We'll see," Nan said, using the diversion of bundling Clara up and putting on her own clothes to ease the tension with Will. "Jake has picked out one he's sure you'll like."

"Where is it?" Clara asked.

"You'll see," Nan said, scooting the child outside and into the wagon.

Soon they were on their way, Jake driving the team, Will and Nan seated on either side of Clara.

❦

"We got the biggest tree in the woods," Clara announced as she bounded up the steps and raced through the door Gertie held open. "It'll fill the whole room."

"Not quite that large," Nan said, "but it's the biggest Christmas tree we've ever had."

Will and Jake struggled up the steps and through the door with a holly tree heavy with berries.

"Take it into the gathering room," Nan said. "In front of the big window."

A fire popped noisily in the fireplace, providing cheer as well as warmth to the frostbitten quartet.

"I never thought a fire could feel so good," Will said. He dropped his end of the tree and backed up to the fireplace.

"You're taking all the room, Daddy," Clara complained, angling for her share of warmth.

Gertie came in, carrying a tray with three mugs and a heavy clay pitcher.

"Who wants hot cider?" Nan asked, rubbing her hands together.

The three warmed themselves in front of the fire, drank hot cider, and ate thick ham sandwiches while Jake attached the tree to a stand. Will helped him stand it up in front of the window.

"It doesn't touch the ceiling," Clara said, disappointment in her voice.

"It's all right," Nan said. "I've got something special to go on top."

"What is it?"

"I'll show you when we've finished decorating the tree."

Clara ran for the popcorn strings.

"Save them for later," Nan said. She opened another one of the many boxes Jake had brought down the day before. She reached inside and pulled a beautiful hand-painted glass ball from the depths of cotton. "Ask your father to help you tie this on the tree."

Clara stared at the ornament. "I might break it."

"I broke lots of them, but every year I got more."

With her father's help, Clara managed to tie the ball on the tree.

"How many more?" Will asked when Nan opened a third box. "My fingers are full of pricks already."

"Not many," Nan answered.

After they had tied on the last painted ball, Nan and Will helped Clara put the gold and silver chains on the tree. The six popcorn chains went on last.

"And now for the top," Nan said. She opened another box and pulled out a beautiful angel with long, flowing hair and a long, white dress. "It takes a ladder. Can you do it?" she asked Will.

"Sure," he said. He was a little unsteady, but Nan made herself concentrate on holding the ladder rather than on Will.

"There," he said, when he had settled the angel on the top of the tree.

He climbed down, and all three stepped back to admire their handiwork.

"You deserve a treat after all that work," Gertie said.

She set a plate of cookies on a small table. Will reached for one immediately.

"I only gave you five," Gertie told him. "Any more would spoil your dinner."

Will blushed slightly. "I didn't realize I had made such a pig of myself."

"Don't worry your head about it. Everybody in Beaker's Bend is crazy about Nan's shortbreads. They're the first thing to disappear every year." Gertie gave him a closer inspection. "You could use a little fattening up. Don't you eat regular?"

"It's hard, traveling all the time."

"Leave Mr. Atkins alone, Gertie," Nan said. "His eating habits are really none of our concern."

"Well, somebody ought to look after him. Everybody knows God never did make a man with sense enough to look after himself." Gertie turned to Clara. "I've got some hot chocolate in the kitchen. It's a lot better than that old cider."

"Go on," Nan said, when Clara cast her an inquiring look. "Gertie makes the best hot chocolate in the whole valley."

As she left the room, Gertie gave Nan such a pointed look that Nan felt herself blush. Gertie's change of attitude puzzled her. Just that morning she had acted as if she wanted Will out of the house at the earliest moment. Now, if her sly hints, head nods, and glances out of the corners of her eyes were any indication, she had decided Nan ought to marry him and take him in hand.

Nan suddenly felt weak. Marry him! That was what Gertie meant, but that wasn't what bothered her. She, too, had been thinking about marrying him. That bothered her a lot.

She didn't know anything about Will Atkins except that he traveled so much, he couldn't take proper care of his own daughter. That was the difference between men and women. If she had a child, she would never give it up, not even for the most successful business in the whole world. It was a choice only a man would make.

But she couldn't think Will was the kind of man to do that either, even though he had said he was going to. He loved his daughter too much. Nan didn't believe he could live without her.

"Gertie doesn't think much of men, does she?"

"Don't let her fool you. She spoils Jake something

awful. She'd take his boots off if he'd let her. Have some more cider. Jake says it's the best we've had in years."

Will looked as if he was going to say something else, but instead he reached for the cider, then another cookie.

"I have to eat my allotment before Gertie decides to take them back," he explained when Nan smiled at him.

"Eat all you want. They're very easy to make."

"And very rich."

"You keep eating like that, and you'll look like Santa Claus."

"Why isn't your brother coming home this Christmas?"

"He's spending it with his fiancée's family."

"Why don't you have a fiancé, or a family? How did a lovely woman like you escape being snapped up?"

Nan was tempted to tell him it was none of his business. "The time never seemed right. When the boys came courting, I was busy nursing my parents. After they died, nobody came anymore."

"You're content to remain here?"

"What do you expect me to do? Put an ad in the paper telling everybody the door's on the latch?"

"No, but you could move out of this valley. There are thousands of men who would move heaven and earth for a woman like you."

"They don't have to move anything but themselves."

"No one can find you here."

"My brother thinks I ought to leave. He says I'll never find a husband."

"Then why are you still here?"

"This is my home," Nan replied angrily. "These are my people. Besides, people who move out of the valley become changed so much they don't have time for their own daughters. I don't want anything like that to happen to me."

"You don't know anything about my situation," Will said. "I'm doing it because it's best for Clara."

Nan refused to apologize for her anger. She hadn't meant to hurt him, but he had hurt her, and she had struck back. He had no right to judge her, to tell her what to do, not when his own life was in such a tangle.

"You think sending Clara to live with her grandparents is so terrible?" Will asked.

"I think it's the most awful thing you could do."

"I agree with you."

"Then why are you doing it?" Nan asked, so surprised she didn't think to control her curiosity.

"Because there's nothing else I can do. Gertie's right. A man can't take care of himself. He's even worse at taking care of a child."

Clara came back into the room. She picked up her doll and climbed into the sofa. She leaned against one of the overstuffed cushions and stared at the Christmas tree. Will chose a cookie and moved back to the fire, but his gaze never left his daughter.

Nan got up to light the candles. She had been right. Will didn't want to lose his daughter. Her heart overflowed with compassion for a man forced by circumstances to give up the one person he loved most in the whole world.

"Are you sure you have to give her up?" Nan whispered as she came to stand next to him before the fire. The light from the candles played on the windows and the gleaming glass balls on the Christmas tree.

"I have no choice," Will replied. "I've tried, but I don't have time for both Clara and my business."

"Then why…"

"Why don't I do something else?"

Yes, she had been going to ask that.

"I'm a salesman. It's what I know, what I do best. It's really the only way I know to make a living. The business was Louise's dream. She wanted it for our children. She made me promise to do it for Clara."

Clara lay down on the cushion, eyes only half open.

"Do you think she cares?" Nan asked in a harsh undervoice.

"Not now, but when she's older, she'll—"

"She'll what? Want a lot of money she'll end up leaving to her children? She'd rather have you."

"Not everybody can make the choices they want."

"They can if they have the courage."

"What about you?"

"I haven't been offered any choices."

"You could leave."

"And go where? Do what? All I know how to do is run this farm."

"You could go with your brother."

"And be the old-maid sister, hanging on his sleeve, taking care of his children? No, thank you. I'd rather stay here and live my own life. If I'm going to take care of other people's children, I'd rather it be the people of Beaker's Bend. I've known them since I was born. We're all part of the same family. I'll never be truly alone as long as I'm here."

"But you'll never have a family of your own."

"There's always a chance."

"It looks like each of us is afraid to take a chance," Will said.

He looked down at his daughter, who had fallen asleep. "I never understand how children can fall asleep in the middle of a lighted room with people talking."

"Gertie would say it's because they have a clear conscience."

"I say it's because she hasn't stopped running all day. You shouldn't encourage her to be so much trouble."

"I don't mind. It's nice to have a child in the house. I'm going to miss her when she's gone."

"Speaking of that, we'll be leaving tomorrow."

Nan was shocked that he had made plans to leave

without talking to her; she was hurt that he wanted to leave so soon. "You can't. You're still not strong enough to travel."

"We'll stay at the inn for a day or so, then continue to Lexington."

"If it's only one day, you might as well stay here."

"We've caused you a lot of work. Besides, the neighbors will begin to talk soon. I lived in a small town long enough to know what gossip can be like."

"It won't make any difference. Everybody knows you're here by now."

"Thanks, but I think we'd better go."

Nan had expected to be a little dispirited when Will and Clara left, but she wasn't prepared for the feeling of desolation that weighed her down. Now, Christmas was going to seem gloomier than ever. The decorations, the tree, all the preparations would be a silent accusation that she didn't have the courage to leave Beaker's Bend and search for a new life.

Maybe Will and Gideon were right. Maybe she was foolish to stay here, waiting year after year for the man she feared would never come. It would be even more difficult now. Will Atkins and his daughter had filled her heart, and it would be hard for anyone to oust them. Not that anyone was looking to claim her hand.

No one had since Harve Adams.

∽∾∾

Will felt so tired that he barely had the energy to drop his clothes on the floor and crawl into bed. He had done his best to make Nan believe he had recovered his strength, but now that he was alone, he could admit that he was about to drop in his tracks. His clothes would be wrinkled in the morning, but he was too tired to care.

His body tightened into a ball in the cold bed. As he lay there, waiting for the bed to warm and his body to relax, he thought again that he didn't want to leave. It would be so easy to stay. And stay. But he needed to go before he became any more attracted to Nan. There was no future in becoming interested in a woman who would never be happy outside this remote valley.

Of course he couldn't consider coming back to live in the valley. He had made too many sacrifices for the life he and Louise had wanted, the life they had worked so hard to build and that he had clung to for five years.

Besides, there was nothing to come back to. These last days were unreal, a fairy tale. Christmas would pass and the magic would fade, leaving only the memory of yet another dream.

∞

Jake entered the front hall to take Will and Clara's luggage to the wagon. "I saw L.P. yesterday," he told Nan. "He hasn't heard from Wilmer since he left for Locust Hollow. The inn was still closed then."

"Maybe you should leave your luggage here," Nan said to Will. "Just in case Wilmer's not back."

"I think we should take it along," Will said.

"Do we have to go?" Clara asked. Her spirits had not recovered since her father told her they were leaving. She looked at Nan through teary eyes.

"I'm sure they'll have a Christmas tree in the inn," Will said.

"I want my tree. Not another one." Clara threw herself down on the sofa in tears.

Will sat down next to his daughter. "We'll be at your grandparents' house on Christmas. They'll have a Christmas tree, too."

∞

They rode to town in strained silence. When they reached the inn, they found it still shut up.

"Mr. Crider ain't come back," L.P. said. He looked at the leaden sky. "If he don't come back soon, he'll be snowed in up at that hollow." He paused. "Maybe he don't want to come back. He said he means to get shut of this place."

"You mean sell it?" Nan asked, incredulous. "He's run the inn for as long as I can remember."

"Ruby's been after him to move to the hollow. Besides, Wilmer's been wanting to take it easy. Says running an inn ain't no business for no old man."

"Can we go back to Nan's?" Clara asked. "Please, Daddy, say we can."

"Of course you can," Nan said, not waiting for Will to answer. "My feelings would be hurt if you stayed with anybody else."

Clara looked straight at Nan. "We don't know anybody else."

"Only for one more night," Will said. "Then we must be on our way. In fact, I ought to go to the train station to reserve our seats."

Nan took Clara into the general store while her father went to the train station. Rows of shelves bowed with the weight of their contents were barely illuminated by the light from two small kerosene lamps suspended from the ceiling.

Nan doubted that the potbellied stove turned out enough heat to keep molasses from freezing. She wasn't surprised the store was empty. It was too cold to linger. Even the floorboards creaked in protest as she moved about. Hurrying to make her purchases, she found Clara staring at the brightly colored sticks of candy Mr. Whitehall kept behind a glass cover.

"Would you like one?" Nan asked.

"Yes, please," Clara said.

"Is this the poor child of that man who's been staying with you?" Mrs. Whitehall asked.

"Yes," Nan answered, a little surprised at the way Paralee Whitehall had phrased her question and even more surprised by her judgmental attitude.

"When are they leaving?"

"They had planned to move to the inn today, but Wilmer's still away. They'll resume their journey tomorrow."

"I saw him heading toward the train station just now. He looked plenty recovered to me."

"I suppose that's why people ask me about doctoring and you about pork bellies," Nan said, a sting in her voice. "He's still weak from the fever. Let's go, Clara. We've got several other stops to make."

Miserable old busybody, Nan mumbled under her breath. *She'll have to sing a different tune if she wants any cookies from me this Christmas.*

"Why are you mad at that lady?" Clara asked.

Nan chastised herself for being so careless. She was so used to being alone that she had fallen into the habit of talking out loud to herself. That would never do around a curious child.

"Just annoyed. Now let's hurry. I want to see if they managed to decorate the church."

For the last seven years, Nan had been in charge of the Christmas decorations, but she had given it up this year. She just didn't have the heart. But now she was anxious to make certain it was done right. The lessons and carols service on Christmas Eve was an important evening for the whole town. Everybody would be there, from tots to grandparents.

Will found them just as they came out of the church.

"What took you so long?" Nan asked.

"I was looking around town. I hadn't seen anything of Beaker's Bend. I didn't realize it was this large."

"We have nearly a thousand people," Nan told him proudly. "We're the biggest town in the whole valley."

"I don't understand why you put up with Whitehall's mercantile," Will said. "You can't possibly find half the things you want in there."

Nan opened her mouth to contradict him, but realized that she had made the same complaint not twenty minutes earlier. Grady and Paralee Whitehall didn't make much attempt to cater to their customers. They stocked what Grady's father used to stock, and the people of Beaker's Bend were expected to make do with it.

"It is something of an irritation, but we can get anything we want sent in on the train."

"But you ought to be able to get it right here," Will insisted. "There's no reason why…" He stopped, looking a little apologetic. "I didn't mean to get wound up. That's one of the difficulties of liking your work. You can't stop thinking about it all the time."

"I don't suppose there's anything wrong with that as long as you don't ignore the really important things."

But he had already admitted he was unable to attend to the most important duty a man could have.

"I'm taking you to lunch," Will announced. "Don't worry, I already told Gertie. Where can we eat in this town?"

Nan laughed. She didn't know why, but she did. "Do you always invite people to eat without knowing where to go?"

"Sure. They always know the best places."

"The best place in Beaker's Bend is the drugstore. It's also the only place."

"Lead the way," Will said.

But they got sidetracked when Nan led him into the park in the center of town. A dozen trees, each more than a hundred years old, towered over numerous saplings of much more tender years. Through the center of this woodland glen a stream gurgled and splashed over a bed strewn with large stones. The creek took a sharp turn in the middle of the square and headed north toward the Shenandoah River.

"I'd been wondering how this town got its name," Will said, as they traversed the wooden bridge across the icy water. "I assume this is Beaker's Creek."

Nan nodded.

"I used to go fishing in a stream very much like this. I never considered it a successful day if I didn't come home with at least a half-dozen fish."

"The creek passes through the farm," Nan said. "Gideon used to go fishing all the time."

"Your own mountains, your own valley, your own town, and now your own fishing stream. I can see why you don't want to leave. I can't say I blame you."

They came out on the other side of the park to find another row of buildings facing them across a wide area that served as a road. It was sprinkled with enough trees to provide places for people to sit in the shade in summer.

"It gives the impression of the town being built in the middle of a forest," Will said.

"Every few years, when the leaves are deep and the snow stays under the trees for weeks, we have people wanting to cut them down. But then we remember how cool and delightful this is during the summer, and we decide we can put up with the snow and leaves a little longer."

They entered the drugstore and walked to one of the four wooden tables worn smooth with age and use. Six kerosene lamps made the interior bright and cheerful. A potbellied stove, glowing red, made it warm and cozy. On each side, rows of neatly shelved patent medicines rose to the ceiling. Pilfer-proof glass showcases contained jewelry, perfume, and enticing knickknacks.

"We're lucky it's Christmas and everybody has a house full of food to eat up. You can't find a seat here the rest of the year."

They sat down. A young girl in a starched, white apron set three bowls of steaming potato soup down before them. Pots of hot coffee and tea followed.

"Where's the menu?" Will asked.

"There is no menu," Nan told him. "Whatever Etta Mae cooks is what you get."

"What a darling little girl."

The booming voice caused Will to swallow his steaming soup too fast. He looked up through watering eyes to see a tall, blond woman towering over them. "Is this your daughter?" she asked Will.

"But of course she is," Etta Mae answered herself. "Nan keeps refusing all the fine young men so she doesn't have one of her own. I have something special for you, sugar, when you're done with your dinner. This could be your little girl if you weren't so picky," Etta Mae said, turning to Nan. "You tell her, Mister. It's not good for a woman to hide herself away on that farm."

Nan nearly choked. "Etta Mae! Mr. Atkins doesn't want to hear your opinions on what's good for me. And I've heard them too often already."

"Everybody agrees with me."

"I'm sure they do, but it would be more to the point if you would tell us what we're going to eat."

But Etta Mae hadn't said anything Will hadn't already been thinking. Nan would make a perfect mother for Clara. Already the child adored her, followed her around, quoted everything she said. She seemed to have a natural feeling for what to do and say to make Clara feel happy and secure. More than he did.

He knew Clara loved him, but sometimes he didn't know what to do for her. He became impatient.

But he couldn't think of Nan as Clara's mother without also thinking of Nan as his wife. That thought shocked him. She wouldn't fit into his life. Besides, he had never considered marrying again. He never expected to find a woman he could love after Louise. But Nan had shaken that assumption right down to the foundation.

Sitting across from her right now, nothing seemed more natural.

◈

"Why are you taking so long over your prayers?" Will asked his daughter. The fires had been allowed to go out for the night, and the house was getting cold.

"Jake said it was going to snow," Clara told him as she climbed in bed and let him pull the covers over her. "I wanted to remind God so he wouldn't forget."

"Why do you want snow so much?"

"Then we won't have to leave Nan."

It was some time before Will could get to sleep. He was haunted by the suspicion that in holding on to his attachment to Louise and his commitment to the future they had wanted, he had built a living tomb for himself, had locked himself in a past that was dry and empty.

He couldn't shake the conviction that life and love were here, now, in the valley, with Nan.

Four

As he got dressed, Will watched the snow come down so thick outside his bedroom window that he could hardly see the well less than thirty feet away. He couldn't see the barn or the smokehouse at all. He hadn't seen it snow like this since he was a boy. If it kept up, he wouldn't be able to leave today. If it snowed like this all night, the train wouldn't make it to Beaker's Bend inside a week.

He wasn't certain whether he was glad or frustrated. If he had left a day ago, he would have had regrets but no confusion. Now he didn't know what he felt, and he didn't know what he wanted to do about it. The snowstorm was going to force him to come up with some answers.

⁓

"Jake has already been to town this morning," Nan told Will when he entered the kitchen. "The passes to the north are closed. No trains in or out." She finished setting the table and turned to check the coffee.

"Does that mean we can stay here?" Clara asked. She had fallen into the habit of getting up with Nan. She was seated at the table, politely waiting for Gertie to finish cooking breakfast.

"Yes," Will said, giving his daughter a smile.

"Yippee!" Clara squealed. "Can we stay until Christmas?"

"I think you'll have to," Nan said.

Clara jumped up, ran over to Nan, grabbed her around the waist, and hugged her so hard that Nan grunted. Then she hugged her father. After that she hugged Gertie, which startled Gertie so much, she nearly spilled grits from the pot she was stirring.

"Sit down before you overturn something," her father said.

"Let's all sit down," Nan said. She didn't feel capable of standing much longer. The genuine warmth of Clara's hug had been a delightful surprise. But it was the look in her father's eye that made her feel weak in the knees.

She had been aware that since their lunch yesterday, he looked at her in a different manner. There was a new energy about him. Nan could almost feel it, as though something connected the two of them so that everything he felt touched her in some way.

Her skin burned. Her nerves seemed to be on end. The tension in the house had begun to escalate; she expected him to do or say something soul-shattering at any minute.

She was in love with Will Atkins, a man she knew virtually nothing about. Further, she didn't approve of what she did know.

How could she be in love with a man who would give away his child? She must be losing her mind. But it wasn't her alone. She could see something new in his eyes, hear it in his voice, feel it in his presence.

He felt it, too.

Gertie broke in on her thoughts. "I guess you'll have time to do your baking after all. With all this snow on the ground, you wouldn't be able to do much else."

"Yes," Nan said, reining in her galloping imagination. "Set out the butter so it can get soft."

"May I help?" Clara asked.

"Certainly."

"Are you trying to leave me out again?" Will asked.

"Can Daddy help make cookies?"

"Sure," Nan said, smiling, "if he thinks he can stand woman's work."

"It's got to be better than chopping wood, which is what I suspect Jake will have me doing if I don't luck into something easier."

But there wasn't enough to do for two extra people.

"The work would go twice as fast for half as many hands," Gertie muttered when she stumbled over Will for the dozenth time.

"But it wouldn't be half as much fun," Nan said.

"I got my own work to do," Gertie replied, wiping her hands. "I'll be back later." With that, she put on her coat and went out the back door.

"She does the Christmas cooking for her sister," Nan explained to Will. "She's never been very well, and she has seven children."

"That might be why she's never been very well," Will replied.

They soon forgot about Gertie and her family. Clara broke the eggs into a bowl, and Will beat them. Nan blended the sugar and butter together, then let Will beat in the eggs as Clara spooned them into the bowl. Will added the flour; Nan mixed it in.

Nan laughed. "You've got flour all over you."

Will looked down at the white dusting on his navy-blue vest. "So I have."

"Here, let me put an apron on you." Nan took a fresh apron out of a drawer. When Will bent down so she could loop it over his head, Nan almost froze. He was so close. His eyes. His lips. Her gaze locked on his mouth. She had never looked at him so closely before. His lips were full and firm, his chin slightly cleft, his nose chiseled and slightly rounded. Her gaze rose to his eyes. Deep brown. Wide and questioning.

Forcing herself to break eye contact, Nan looped the

apron over his head and stepped behind him to tie the strings. When she reached around to take hold of the strings, Clara started to giggle.

"You're hugging Daddy."

Nan was glad Will couldn't see the heat color her cheeks. She didn't know whether she imagined it, but he seemed to stiffen. Nan tied the apron quickly, picked up her spoon, and gripped the bowl.

She felt safe now, from herself and from Will.

"I'd hate for you to ruin your clothes," she said, choosing to ignore Clara's remark and to avoid looking into Will's eyes.

But the easy atmosphere was gone. As Will stood next to her, adding the flour a little at a time, she was intensely aware of his presence. She was relieved when he moved back to help Clara with the next batch of eggs. Nan took her time rolling out the dough. By the time she had finished, she felt more in control of her voice and body.

"Will, you can cut out the cookies. Clara, you decorate them. You can put a pecan half on each one, or a piece of red candy."

"I want more colors."

Nan set out everything she had. "There, do it any way you like."

Quiet settled over the kitchen. Will cut out the cookies and arranged them on cookie sheets, and Clara decorated them in a manner all her own. Nan added her own flour this time.

"Nobody will believe you made these," Will said, shaking his head over his daughter's fanciful decorations.

"It doesn't matter. If nobody wants them, I'll give them to Clara to take with her."

The thought of Clara and her father leaving was becoming more and more painful. In four days they had become a necessary part of Nan's life. She couldn't imagine having to face a day without them. Her mind told her that their presence was only temporary, that Will had to return to his business, that she would fall back into her old routine in just a few days.

But her heart would have none of it. The empty space deep inside her had been filled by this pair. She felt as close to them as to her brother.

Nan mixed the new batch of dough with more than her usual vigor. She had fallen in love with a man she expected to walk out of her life just as suddenly as he had walked into it. He might look at her as if she were his favorite cookie, but he had said nothing to indicate that his feelings were stronger than friendship.

She placed the dough on a marble-topped table and began to roll it out with a rolling pin.

This was silly. If Will's work was so important that he didn't have time for his daughter, he certainly wouldn't have time for a wife. Nan wasn't willing to give up one kind of loneliness for another. A life spent waiting for the man she loved to come home, knowing he could stay only a short time, would be worse than loneliness. It would be torture.

What if he had a normal job? Would she go with him wherever he went?

She didn't know. She had lived her whole life in Beaker's Bend. She knew the people. She had a place in the community. She wouldn't know what to do in a city. Any city. Even the thought of moving to Charlottesville or Richmond scared her.

Besides, she didn't know anything about being a mother to a five-year-old girl, and she wanted more children. She didn't think Will would want more, not when he didn't have time for the one he had.

"If you roll that dough any thinner, you'll be able to see through it," Will said.

His closeness shocked her. She had been so lost in thought that she hadn't seen him move to her side. Close enough for their elbows to brush. Close enough for her to smell his shaving lotion. Close enough for her hands to shake. She gripped the rolling pin to steady them.

"I guess I was daydreaming," Nan said. She rolled up the dough and started again. "Making cookies isn't very taxing," she said, petrified that he would ask what she'd been daydreaming about. "I've fallen into the habit of thinking over all sorts of plans."

With quick, practiced moves, she rolled the dough to the proper thickness, handed it to Will, and quickly started on another batch. She concentrated fiercely on the dough. She could feel Will looking at her. She didn't look up.

Suddenly Nan realized that the smells of baked cookies and vanilla flavoring were filling the kitchen. Smothering an exclamation of disgust, she dropped her rolling pin and grabbed a cloth. A blast of heat hit her in the face when she opened the oven.

"Watch out, they're hot!" she warned as she took the first tray of cookies from the oven. They were brown around the edges, but they hadn't burned. She felt like an idiot.

"They're all ruined," Clara exclaimed when she saw that the tiny pieces of candy she had used for decorations had melted and run together.

"They taste just as good," Nan reassured her, relieved to have something to divert attention from her lapse.

"Can I have one now?"

"In a minute. They're still too hot."

Clara went back to decorating more cookies, but Nan noticed that the child watched longingly each time she took out a tray. Her father watched with equal intensity.

"Now can I have one?" Clara asked when she finished her tray of cookies.

"Why don't you wait until we finish decorating all of them," Will said. "Then we can all have some together."

Clara looked a little disappointed, but Nan could tell she liked the idea of everyone eating cookies together. Poor child, she probably had to enjoy most of her treats alone. Nan knew from long experience that food tasted better when you had someone to share it with.

"Okay, these are the last cookies," Nan said as she closed the oven. Gertie came in the back door just as Nan handed Clara a plate of shortbreads. "Here, take these into the gathering room. Your father can put some more wood on the fire. Gertie will fix our lunch. I'll bring in the cups and hot chocolate."

"We're going to have hot chocolate?" Clara exclaimed.

"Yes, and I'm going to put a big piece of marshmallow in each one."

Clara slipped off her chair, grabbed the plate of cookies, and hurried to the gathering room.

"I don't know how you always manage to think of just the right thing," Will said.

"It's not hard. I just remember what I liked when I was a little girl."

"You must have been a very happy child."

"I was. You'd better go fix the fire. It's bound to be down to embers by now."

When Nan entered the gathering room, Will met her at the doorway and gave her a kiss.

"W-what—" Nan stammered, shocked. She could feel the heat rush to her face. All her thoughts from the kitchen came flooding back.

Clara giggled. "Daddy moved the mistletoe," she said, pointing to a sprig tacked over the doorway. "He said he could kiss a lady if she stood under the mistletoe."

"That's true," Nan said, too surprised to move.

"That was for letting Clara help with the cookies," Will said.

Nan hardly knew what demon prompted her to add, "I let you help as well."

"So you did." Will took her by the arms and kissed her again, rather more enthusiastically than before.

"Daddy's kissing Nan," Clara informed Gertie when she walked into the room.

"So I see," Gertie said. She eyed the pair critically. Nan had stepped back, confused at being caught. Will looked as though the results were surprising, pleasant but surprising.

"Does your father kiss a lot of females?"

"Gertie!" Nan exclaimed, scandalized.

"Daddy only kisses me," Clara declared.

Gertie regarded the pair once more. "Good." With that she turned and left the room.

Nan gasped, then stared at Will. Her mind was a blizzard of sensations; her body was too weak to take responsible action. She was petrified that he might take offense at Gertie's remark, but she thought she saw imps of amusement in his eyes. When his lips curved in a smile, she knew it.

They burst out laughing simultaneously.

"I apologize for Gertie. I don't know what's gotten into her."

"She's just protecting you. I would, too, if I were in her place."

Nan decided she'd better put the cups down before she dropped them. She had spent the better part of the last twenty-four hours convincing herself Will had no serious interest in her. His kisses had shattered that conviction. She had never been kissed like that by any man. More importantly, no kisses had ever had such an earth-shattering effect on her.

"Let's eat," Clara said.

"I'll pour the hot chocolate," Nan said, pulling herself together.

"I'll pass the cookies," Clara said. "Daddy might eat too many."

"He does like shortbreads," Nan said. "Maybe I'd better give you the recipe so you can make them when you go back home."

"I don't want to go back home," Clara announced. "I want to stay here with you."

"You have to go with your father."

"I want Daddy to stay, too."

"I have to work," Will said. "I need to make money to buy clothes and food and a house to live in."

"Nan has a house and lots of food. I don't need any more clothes. Let me stay with her. I don't want to stay with Grandmama and Grandpa."

Nan felt sorry for Will. It was difficult enough to have to give up his daughter, even if it wouldn't be for very long. But it must be even harder when Clara couldn't understand the reasons why he felt he had no other choice.

"It's very sweet of you to want to stay with me," Nan said, "but I'm sure you'll love your grandparents."

"Maybe they won't like me. They don't like Daddy."

Clara was threatening to work herself up to a real cry.

Nan took her in her arms and held her close. "You don't have to go anywhere right now. If the snow keeps coming down, you'll be here for days and days. Now why don't you go see if Gertie has lunch ready. It'll soon be time for your nap. You've had a very busy morning, and I have lots of things planned for later."

"Thank you," Will said to Nan when Clara went into the kitchen. "I don't know what to do when she gets upset."

"She's just frightened. It's hard for a child to face something new, especially when she has to face it alone."

"I know, but it's better that she be left with her grandparents than somebody who has no reason to love her."

"Are you sure her grandparents will?"

"Yes. They don't like me, but they'll love Clara because she's Louise's child."

"Why didn't you give her up when your wife died?"

"I kept hoping I'd figure out something else, that I wouldn't have to do it."

"Why did you give up?"

"Mrs. Bartholomew died. She was the second woman to keep Clara. I could see the list getting longer and longer. As Clara gets older, she's going to need somebody she can count on. If it can't be me, it ought to be her grandparents."

For a moment Nan could see depths of pain she had only suspected. Her heart went out to him.

"Isn't there anything else you can do?"

"Not unless you're willing to take her. I've racked my brain for two years, and there's no other way."

Nan had never considered taking Clara. The idea was unexpected, but she knew right away that was exactly what she wanted to do. "I'll be happy to take her."

Will stared at Nan. "I was just joking. I never meant to—"

A crash riveted their attention to the doorway. Clara threw herself at her father, a plate of sandwiches broken on the floor.

"Please, Daddy, can I stay with Nan? I don't want to go to Grandmama. I want to stay here. Please, can I?"

Will looked harassed. Nan knew men never liked to have their plans questioned or overset. "We can't impose on Nan like that."

"But she wants me to stay. I heard her say it."

"It's wonderful you like Nan so much, but your grandparents are expecting you," Will said. "Now you have to clean up the mess you made and apologize to Nan for throwing away your lunch."

"I didn't mean to," Clara said, barely managing to keep from bursting into tears.

"Don't worry about it," Nan said. "I'll clean up while your father takes you up for your nap. If it's stopped snowing when you get up, we'll go outside and build a snowman."

࿚

Will didn't go back downstairs after he put Clara to bed. For a long while he simply sat on the bed watching his daughter sleep. He was struck by her innocence and how much he loved her. He had never been gifted with words, but he had always taken his obligations to her very seriously. He didn't know how to show it except by working hard to provide for her future. That had been Louise's dream as well. But now he wasn't sure it was the best thing for Clara after all.

Nan had upset all his calculations.

Maybe Clara wouldn't care about money as long as she could go to sleep holding his hand every night. Maybe it was more important to her that he be around to sit in front of a fire and eat cookies. He thought of the lonely hotel rooms, the long trips, the weeks he didn't see her. He wondered if it was worth it. Right now it didn't feel as if it was. In all the times he had put her to bed, he'd never just sat, holding her hand, thinking back on all the little things they had done together during the day. It wasn't until he was marooned on a farm in the middle of the Shenandoah Valley that he found out what he was missing.

And all because of Nan Carson, a woman who represented everything he had walked away from.

She would be perfect for Clara. They already loved each other as mother and daughter. He doubted Louise's parents could love her as much. Besides, they were too old to have the care of a five-year-old. They had other grandchildren with prior claims on their affections, and they still cherished a lingering anger against him for taking Louise away.

If they had only known. Louise had been adamant

about leaving the mountains. She had been insistent that they build a business to insulate them against the poverty of her childhood. She had loved her daughter, but she had also resented the time the child took away from her work.

Nan found a way to include Clara in everything she did. She included both of them. They had gotten a lot done in the last three days. Clara had helped dust and straighten the house. They had helped clean up after meals. He had even filled the wood boxes and helped Jake with the milking. It hadn't been a chore. It had been something they had done together.

Will realized that it was something he had done because he wanted to be with Nan, to be a part of whatever she did. He wanted to be a part of it so much, he wouldn't mind staying here for the rest of his life.

The thought quite literally caused him to turn stiff with shock. He couldn't have fallen in love with Nan! Not in just three days!

No, he was in love with a dream, with this fairy-tale Christmas, with the seductive quality of a woman at once kind and generous, a woman who attracted him both physically and spiritually. The attraction was nearly irresistible—desire deepened by liking and caring—but it wasn't the kind of feeling to build a marriage on. Nan wasn't like Louise. She wouldn't fit into his world.

What a tangle.

He got up and walked over to the window. The snow was still coming down so heavily that it was hard to see the road to town. The farm looked beautiful, all white and silent. The house was warm and comforting. His new life in the city was wonderfully exciting, but how could he have failed to see the charm of the life he and Louise had left without a backward glance?

It had taken Nan to show him he had thrown away something very precious. He valued his new life, but now he knew it had come at a great price.

∞

Nan wasn't in the gathering room when he came down, but Gertie was. "I want to speak to you a minute," she said to Will.

"Do you think you should?" Jake asked.

Will thought he looked uncomfortable.

"With her parents dead and her brother more concerned with his own affairs than his sister, somebody's got to look after Nan."

"Is something wrong?" Will asked.

"That's what I'm about to ask you," Gertie countered.

Will looked blank.

"Nan just told me you might let Clara stay here."

"I mentioned it without thinking."

"Well, you'd better think about it right now. Nan has her heart set on keeping that child. Right now she's upstairs going through the attic looking for something she can give her for Christmas."

"We haven't even talked about it," Will protested.

"It's too late for talking. You take that child away now, and you'll break her heart."

"You'll break both their hearts," Jake added.

"She can't know what it's like to have a child around all the time. It's not the same as for a few days."

"I know that, and you know that, but Nan can only see the family she never had. She wouldn't care if that child were a little demon instead of the little angel she is." Gertie squared her shoulders and planted her hands on her hips. "Now I'd like to know what you mean to do."

"What do you mean?"

Gertie snorted in contempt. "She's in love with you, you daft man, and I want to know what you mean to do about it."

Five

WILL WAS SPEECHLESS, BUT WHETHER MORE AT GERTIE'S news or his reaction, he couldn't say. He felt as if the pins had been knocked out from under him. He couldn't believe Nan was in love with him. He hadn't tried to make her fall in love with him, and he didn't want the responsibility for her unhappiness when she discovered that he didn't love her.

He couldn't let Clara stay now. It would mean they would have to be in constant communication with each other. He liked Nan far too much to endure that.

"I don't mean to do anything about it," Will answered finally. "I don't see that I can."

"You made her fall in love with you," Gertie said, incensed. "You can't have yourself carried in here when you need help and then waltz out again when you don't."

"I had no hand in being brought here. I would have left that first morning if I had even suspected me being here would hurt Miss Carson."

"You can stop calling her *Miss Carson*," Gertie snapped. "It's not like you haven't been calling her Nan for days, coiling yourself around her like some weasel-eyed varmint. And it's too late to run away. The damage has already been done."

"What do you suggest I do?"

"Marry her."

"Marry her!" Will exclaimed. Gertie had to be crazy. Grown men didn't go around marrying women they'd known less than a week.

"You don't have to look like the idea is such a shock."

"I haven't thought of marrying anyone since my wife died."

"That was nearly five years ago. It's about time you thought about giving that precious little girl a mother, and you won't find a better one than Nan."

"Nan won't thank you for pushing her off on him like this," Jake said.

"She won't know if you don't tell her," Gertie shot back. "Besides, if I don't speak for her, who will? She won't say anything for herself. After Harve Adams left for Richmond, she gave up thinking any man would want her."

"That's crazy," Will said. "There ought to be dozens of men lining up to ask for her hand."

"There would be if she paid heed to every Tom, Dick, or Joe who hankered after her farm. But Nan wants a husband who will love her and give her lots of children. She doesn't deserve anything less."

"I agree with you," Will said. "But I can't marry her just because she thinks she's in love with me."

"She doesn't know it yet," Gertie stated, "but I do."

"It's impossible. I have to go back to Boston. She would never leave this valley."

"She would for the right man."

"But the right man wouldn't take her away from it."

"Maybe so."

"I'm sorry. I've never met a woman I admire more than Nan, but I don't love her."

"She wouldn't have to know."

"She'd know from the beginning. Besides, I like her too much to do that." Will looked out the window, but nothing had changed. If anything, it was snowing more heavily now than before.

"I doubt you could get to town in this blizzard," Jake said.

"Maybe Mr. Crider will reopen the inn."

"If he got caught in that hollow, he won't be back for a couple of weeks. Maybe more."

Will felt concerned. He also felt guilty. The best thing for Nan would be for him to take his daughter and leave immediately. The best thing for Clara would be to let Nan keep Clara.

And what about himself? What was best for him?

He didn't know. As late as yesterday, he would have answered a quick return to Boston. But Nan and the life here in her mountain valley had cast its spell over him. Maybe he had never lost his love for the mountains; maybe he had just needed a chance to do something else for a while, a chance to see what else he could become.

Now he knew. He had proved himself. He could afford the luxury of asking himself what he really wanted.

Nan.

The single word exploded on his mind. Maybe he didn't fully love her, but he wanted her as much as he had ever wanted any woman.

But not the same way she wanted him.

"Well?" Gertie prompted.

"I don't know," Will said, talking more to himself than to Gertie. "I just don't know."

He turned and left the kitchen.

"He don't seem to know his own mind," Jake said.

"Good," Gertie said, a slow smile beginning to spread over her lined face. "That's the best sign I've seen so far."

Will found Nan in the attic surrounded by piles of wrapping paper.

"What on earth are you doing?"

"Looking for a Christmas present for Clara. It was foolish of me not to have bought something when I was in town."

It was even more foolish of him not to have bought something. True, he hadn't known a blizzard was going to snow him in, but he did know he was heading toward his in-laws empty-handed. He had been counting on being able to complete his shopping in Lexington.

Even worse, he should have thought to buy Nan something. He would never be able to repay her for what she had done for him and Clara, but it was important that he try. Now she was worried about giving his daughter a present, with no thought for herself.

"You don't have to give her anything. You've given both of us far too much already."

"None of that will count on Christmas morning. You ought to know that."

He should, but he hadn't. Had he forgotten what it was like to be a child?

"I'll give her the dollhouse," Nan said, half to herself, not listening to him. "That and my princess doll."

"But those are your things."

"I know," Nan said, smiling as she turned toward him, "but I don't play with them anymore."

"I know that," Will said with an answering smile, "but you can't be giving away parts of your past."

"By the time you've finished building your business and Clara goes back to live with you, she'll be too big to want to take any of this with her." Nan turned back to her trunks. "I know I had more furniture than this."

Will took Nan by the arms and pulled her to her feet. "Listen to me. Maybe having Clara stay with you isn't a good idea after all. Maybe I ought to see if I can hire somebody's wagon to take us out of the valley."

"You couldn't get anywhere with a wagon. Why would you want to try?"

"I think you and Clara are becoming too attached to each other. Maybe it's better if—"

"Surely you're not afraid she'll come to love me more

than you? She adores you. Besides, I'd make sure she never forgot you for so much as a minute."

Her gaze was open, genuine.

"I know you would. You'd be wonderful for her, but I'm not sure she'd be so wonderful for you."

"Of course she would. I haven't had so much fun in years. I never thought I'd look into these trunks again, but I've been up here for hours. I can hardly wait to go through the rest. I can't believe I've forgotten so much."

Nan tried to turn back to her trunks, but Will wouldn't release her.

"I can't let you do this. It's not right. It's too much."

"But I want to."

"You've got to stop baking cookies and decorating trees and racking your brain for things to give her."

"We couldn't sit here for days doing nothing."

"Don't you see you're making it hard for me to take her away?"

Nan hadn't realized until now just how much she had come to depend on Clara's staying with her. The fear of losing Clara was as sharp as physical pain.

"I don't want you to go," she said.

"I've got to. We've both got to."

"Why?"

"Because if we stay much longer, we may not want to leave."

He knew. Somehow, he knew she loved him. She was glad. She would never have been able to tell him.

Nan lowered her eyes. "Would that be so terrible?"

"It would for you."

"Why?"

"Because you deserve so many things a man like me can never give you. You deserve a husband who loves your valley as much as you do, who wants a house full of children, who dreams of Christmas by the fireplace with candles in the windows and cookies and hot chocolate."

She looked straight at him, her gaze penetrating to his heart.

"Maybe I could learn to dream of something else."

"You would try, but it would take the heart out of you."

Her eyes clouded with hurt. "How do you know?"

"I know." Will leaned over and kissed her lightly. Then he took her in his arms and kissed her.

"There's no mistletoe up here," Nan said when she managed to catch her breath.

"I don't need mistletoe to want to kiss you. I'm terribly thankful for all you've done for Clara and me, and for all you want to do."

"Is that all?" She was looking at him in that way again.

"It's all there can be for us."

Nan had known that. She had told herself over and over again, but she had stubbornly continued to hope. Now he had told her, and she still didn't believe it.

I suppose you won't believe it until he walks out the door and takes his daughter with him.

Maybe not even then. A kind of magic entwined them. Will felt it, too. His kiss told her so. Oh, he didn't know it, not consciously, but it was stirring deep inside him. Otherwise he wouldn't be worried about her. He wouldn't have thought about the kind of husband she deserved. He wouldn't have thought about her marrying at all.

"I still think you should leave Clara here," Nan said. She had herself in hand now, her protective barriers in place once more. "I'll take her to visit her grandparents. I think she ought to get to know them. You go back to your work. Make all the money you want. When you're through, I'll bring Clara to you. I'll send her with Gertie if you'd rather."

"That woman would cut my throat."

Nan smiled. "No, she likes you. She didn't at first, but

she does now. She said you'd make some woman a fine husband if you could just stand still long enough."

"I thought I'd been doing little else since I got here."

"You've been restless ever since you found you couldn't move into the inn. You can't go anywhere until after the storm is over, so go back downstairs while I finish looking through the rest of these boxes. Christmas Eve will be here before you know it."

She needed time to go through the boxes before Clara got up from her nap, but she also needed time to think. She had to decide what she was willing to give up for Will. She wanted to be ready when he asked.

❧

Will stared at the snowy landscape. It represented everything he had worked so hard to avoid, everything he and Louise had fled. Yet now it called to him with an urgency he would not have believed possible as little as two days ago. He knew the strength of the call lay not in the land, the people, or the life. It was Nan. He had known that the moment he kissed her.

But had he gotten over Louise's death?

He turned away from the frosted window and paced the room. He didn't know. He hadn't wanted to see other women. He hadn't even thought of remarrying. Yet the idea planted in his mind by Gertie would not go away. Its hold seemed to grow stronger as the minutes passed, but he couldn't blame it on Gertie. She might have been the first to put the thought into words, but the fertile ground was of his providing. His attraction to Nan was more than thankfulness for her kindness or simple appreciation of an attractive woman. He was strongly attracted to her as a woman whose company he enjoyed, whom he admired, whose nearness aroused feelings in him that had lain dormant for years.

He had begun to think of her as a part of his day,

as part of the pattern of his existence. It didn't matter whether he left Clara with Nan or with her grandparents. He couldn't just go back to Boston and forget Nan.

Louise is dead. Nan is alive.

Will stopped and stared out the window again. The scene was more beautiful than a painting. Limbs of spruce, pine, and magnolia trees bent low under the weight of snow piled high on their branches. A white ribbon of snow topped miles of split-rail fences, limbs of oaks, and maples like icing on a cake. It covered the entire earth—the blacks, browns, and greens—with a pristine mantle of white. The scene was softened by the heavy fall of snow as it floated to earth in large, fluffy flakes.

He wished he could leave now. Every moment spent with Nan in this comfortable house, in this idyllic setting, sapped his strength and reduced his resolution.

Only clinging to a dead past will make you go back to Boston. Nan loves Clara. Clara loves Nan.

You love Nan.

He turned away. Everything about these last few days was so unreal, so dreamlike, it distorted his sense of reality. It made him think that somehow he could find a way to have Nan, this idyllic valley, his business, *and* his daughter. His mind told him it wasn't possible. His heart convinced him not to give up hope.

❧

The rest of the day was somewhat awkward. Jake and Gertie didn't come up to the house for dinner, so the three of them ate in the kitchen.

"Let's have snow cream for dessert," Nan suggested.

"What's that?" Clara asked.

"You live in Boston, and you don't know what snow cream is?"

"No."

"Shame on you," Nan said to Will as she folded

her napkin and got to her feet. "You get the snow. I'll prepare the mix."

Nan beat two eggs into some heavy cream. Then she added a dash of vanilla flavoring. "Do you like apples?" she asked Clara. The child nodded. "Then we shall have apple ice cream. We'll add cider. Don't tell your father, but I'm going to add a good bit of apple brandy to his share."

The back door opened. A blast of biting cold air invaded the warm kitchen, followed by Will. Clara burst out laughing.

"Daddy, you look like a snowman."

"A few more minutes out there, and I'd have been an ice man," Will said, shaking the snow from his clothes.

"Take him into the gathering room and make sure he gets warm," Nan said to Clara. "I'll be in with the ice cream in just a minute."

When Nan entered the room, Clara and her father were seated on the rug before the fire. Clara leaned against her father, his arm around her, both of them staring into the flames.

Nan's heart filled to overflowing. She almost hated to interrupt them. She wondered how many times they had been able to enjoy such a moment together. If Will could only realize that moments such as this, days such as they had enjoyed, were far more important to Clara than a large inheritance.

But maybe it was important to Will. Maybe his feeling of self-worth depended on his success.

She remembered that her father had never been so happy as when he had a good year with the farm or when one of his business ventures turned out particularly well. The same had been true of her mother. She seemed to equate her self-worth with her success with the house or the community.

They were all guilty of using senseless measures of

self-evaluation. Probably the whole world worked that way, but she wasn't going to do it any longer. Nan was worthy of love because she had so much love to give, and she was going to start acting like it.

∽∞∽

"Have you ever considered living somewhere other than this valley?" Will asked.

Clara had been put to bed, and they were seated in chairs drawn up to the fire. Nan had blown out all the lights except a night lamp on a table across the room. The firelight cast dancing shadows along the walls and caused Will's expression to change constantly.

"Yes."

"Where?"

"The question of a particular place never came up."

Nan knew what he was asking, but she didn't know how to answer. She had always wanted to stay in the valley, but she had also assumed she would go with her husband.

Only now she wasn't sure she could ever be completely happy away from the people and the places she had grown to love. She knew that no matter where they lived, she couldn't be happy with Will if he remained so deeply absorbed in his business.

"Would you still consider it?"

"I couldn't say until I was asked."

"Well, suppose some man like me wanted you to marry him and move to Boston."

She wasn't going to let him hide behind anonymous pronouns. If he wanted to find out how she felt, he was going to have to ask her point-blank.

"I'm not likely to meet a man like you in the valley. The farthest anyone here would be likely to move would be Richmond."

"Well, suppose someone did."

"I can't answer about 'someone.'"

Will stared into the fire. The shadows cast by the firelight danced across his face like so many devils.

"Suppose I asked you to marry me and move to Boston. Would you consider it?"

"Yes."

"Well?"

"Well, what?"

"What would you decide?"

"It would depend on whether you loved me."

"Of course I would love you."

She noticed the tense. She wondered if he had. "You haven't said it."

"I didn't mean that... I wasn't talking about... This is insane!" he muttered as he got to his feet. He paced before the fire, his fingers digging in his hair. Suddenly, he turned to face Nan. "I'm not acting like myself. Maybe it's the snow or the season. Maybe I'm still delirious. Maybe I've been seduced by three of the most wonderful days in my life. But I'm in love with you, and I want to marry you."

Nan had only received one proposal, and though it had come with conditions, it hadn't been anything like this. She wasn't about to marry a man who thought he had to be delirious to love her.

Nan stood up. "Then I suggest you go to bed. Maybe the fever or delusion will pass."

Will virtually jumped in front of her.

"I didn't mean it like that. It's just that I don't know how I could have fallen in love with you so fast. I hardly know you."

"Sorry, but I don't feel like providing you with a character study."

"I'm doing this all wrong."

"Yes, you are."

"You're a lovely, kind, wonderful woman, and I'm making you feel like I don't like being in love with you."

"Do you?"

"I hardly know. I hadn't even thought about it until Gertie said I ought—"

"Gertie! What did she say?"

He looked like a man who had stepped into a trap and only realized it the split second he put his foot down.

"She said it was going to be mighty quiet around here after Clara left."

Nan knew Gertie hadn't said any such thing, but there'd be plenty of time later to find out exactly what she had said.

"That has nothing to do with marrying you."

"I wouldn't leave her here if you didn't want to marry me. Knowing she would be with you all the time and I couldn't be would drive me crazy."

He seemed to have a particularly strong association between loving her and insanity. Nan decided that didn't bode well for a stable marriage.

"If I were to consider marrying you, I'd have to know I was going to be more important than your business. You can't send me to my grandparents when you don't have time for me."

"That's a cruel thing to say."

"Sending Clara away is cruel."

"I don't have any choice."

"Yes, you do. Sending Clara away is a consequence of other choices."

"You wouldn't marry a man who could do that?"

"No."

"Even if you loved him?"

"Not even then."

"But you do love him, don't you?"

"I… Don't you think…"

"Answer me. It's all I have left."

Without warning, Will took her in his arms and kissed her passionately. "Tell me, please."

"I love you," Nan whispered. "I think I always will."

Six

NAN SLEPT LATE THE NEXT MORNING. SHE WAS SHOCKED to find when she looked at the clock that it was close to eleven.

She threw back the bedcovers, and her bare feet hit the ice-cold floor. Stifling a strong desire to climb back into the warmth of her bed, Nan dressed quickly. She didn't understand how she could have slept so late, not even after lying awake half the night thinking about what Will had said.

Yes, she loved him, enough to follow him anywhere. She'd probably never love anyone else. But as long as his business or his success—she didn't know which—was more important than anything else, she couldn't marry him. She had thought about it until dawn, but the answer always came out the same.

She wanted a husband and children and a home of her own. She would work with her husband, she would support him in every way she could, but she and their family had to be the most important thing in his life. On that there could be no compromise.

But reaching that decision made Nan feel even more miserable than before. She looked around. She had spent her girlhood in this room. She had hoped and dreamed and built her castles in the air here. Now it seemed they were all going to fall down in the same place.

Well, there was no use getting maudlin over it. She'd had two chances. She had chosen not to take either of them. She couldn't blame anybody but herself. It was foolish to pine over decisions she wouldn't change if she had the opportunity.

Harve hadn't been the right man for her, and she had known that. She wouldn't have married him even if her mother hadn't been too sick for her to leave.

Will wasn't the right man, either, even though she loved him so much she thought her heart would break.

Nan washed her face with cold water, then hurried downstairs. Clara sat in the gathering room rearranging her village for at least the sixth time.

"Where's Will?" Nan asked Gertie as she accepted a cup of coffee.

"He saddled a horse and rode off to the village the minute the snow slacked off," Jake said.

The snow had stopped completely, and the sun glistened with blinding intensity on the pure white of the virgin snow.

"Did he say why?"

"No, just that he had business to attend to."

The faint hope that remained splintered and shattered. If his business was important enough to draw him out in all this snow, he'd never change. It would be better for her if he left as soon as possible.

Nan put down her coffee and marched into the gathering room. "Have you ever built a snowman?" she asked Clara.

"What's a snowman?"

"Get your coat. I'll show you."

"I can hardly see," Clara complained after she had been bundled into a heavy coat, gloves, a scarf, and boots.

"It's very cold outside," said Nan, who was just as thoroughly covered. "And it takes a long time to build a good snowman. Now let me see, we need a hat and scarf and coal for the buttons and eyes. I wonder if Gertie has any carrots. Of course we could use a parsnip."

"What do you need all that for?"

"I'll show you," Nan said, infusing her voice with gaiety she didn't feel. "We're going to build the biggest snowman in Beaker's Bend."

Clara didn't seem to be having much fun at first. The snow was so deep, she had trouble walking even when she followed in Nan's footsteps. It was also bitterly cold. But by the time Nan had rolled the first ball about a foot thick, Clara caught the spirit. She rolled the ball all over the yard while Nan started on the second. They laughed and shrieked and had so much fun, they got the balls too big. They had to get Jake to lift one on top of the other.

"It's a good thing you didn't make them any bigger," Jake said. "I wouldn't be able to put the hat on his head."

Clara rolled the third ball all by herself. Her nose was bright red and her gloves were covered with snow, but she didn't utter a word of complaint.

"Now we have to make his face," Nan said when Jake balanced the third ball of snow on top. "That's why I brought the coal." Nan chose two big pieces for his eyes and several little pieces for his mouth. "Now you do his nose." Nan handed Clara the parsnip.

"I can't reach it," she said.

Nan lifted her up. Clara jammed the parsnip into the snowman's face with such vigor that his head fell off.

Jake put it back on and shoved a long, narrow stick through the middle to hold it in place.

This time Clara put the nose in place with great care.

"Now," Nan said, "we have to do his buttons. I'll do the top ones, and you do those on the bottom."

"People don't have buttons on their bottom," Clara said.

"Snowmen do," Nan insisted.

That was good enough for Clara. She happily placed six pieces of coal on the bottom ball of snow. Nan only had two left for the middle. She wrapped the scarf around his neck.

"Now for the hat. Do you think you can reach that high?"

"I can if you hold me."

"It'll have to be Jake. I'm not that tall."

But Will was. Why wasn't he here? What could he be doing in town that was taking so long? He should have helped his daughter roll the balls of snow. He should be holding her up so she could put the hat on the snowman. It was a hunting hat with flaps that folded down. It wasn't an elegant hat, but it was the only kind of hat Nan's father ever wore.

"There, it's all finished," Nan said as she stepped back to admire their work.

Clara looked around. "We messed up the yard."

Nan decided that Mrs. Bartholomew must never have let Clara make a mess when she played. The snowy perfection of the large yard had been seriously marred by the numerous tracks they made rolling the balls, but Nan didn't mind. They had a wonderful snowman, and the trees were still gorgeous.

"I'll race you to the house," Nan said. "I'll bet Gertie has lunch ready."

Clara didn't move. "I wish Daddy was here," she said. "I want to show him our snowman."

Nan wished he were here, too, but she was also angry that he should deny Clara the pleasure of sharing her first snowman with him. She was even more angry that he had never taken the time to build a snowman with his daughter. If she married him, she was going to make some major changes in his life.

But she had already decided she wouldn't marry him. There was no use thinking of it. It would only take the hurt longer to go away.

"He'll be back before long. You can show him then."

"It might melt."

"Not today."

"Are you sure?"

"Positive. Now let's get inside before we turn into snowmen as well."

"I can't be a snowman," Clara said as she struggled through a snowdrift piled up against a buried bush. "I'll be a snow girl."

"And I'll be a snow woman," Nan said. She picked Clara up and carried her to the steps.

"Can we build a snow horse and a snow cow?"

"You'll have to talk to your father about that. I'm not good enough. Anyway, it's too cold to stay out here anymore today."

They warmed their feet and hands in front of the fire, but Will didn't return. They ate hot beef and gravy on thick slices of toasted bread and had hot baked apples spiced with cinnamon and cloves for dessert. Still Will didn't return. Clara went to bed for her nap, and Nan baked six loaves of Christmas bread to take to church that night. No Will. He stayed away so long that the wild thought occurred to Nan that he might have gone back to Boston without telling her. She dismissed it immediately, but she was completely out of patience when he returned barely in time for dinner.

"Where have you been?" she demanded. "Clara's been worried sick about you." Nan didn't let the fact that Clara had only asked once trouble her conscience. The child had probably become so used to her father's absence that she accepted it without thinking.

"I had some business to take care of." No apology, no nothing. In fact, he looked very pleased with himself. She guessed he looked so happy because he'd been able to get in touch with his office in Boston. He'd probably tied up the telegraph all day.

Nan tried to tell herself that what Will Atkins did didn't concern her in the least, but she failed miserably. She saw him slipping further and further away. No matter what her mind said, her heart had not given up all hope. She might know she was being foolish, but she couldn't help it.

"You'll have to hurry if you're to get dressed before dinner."

"Dressed? What for?"

"We're going to church for the Christmas Eve service."

"Did I know that?"

"You would have if you'd been home today." Good God! She sounded like a nagging wife, and she wasn't even married to the man. She wouldn't be surprised if he tried to sneak away in the middle of the night. "I was going to tell you, but I slept too late."

"No problem. I'll be down in a jiffy."

Nan would have held dinner back if it had been possible, but it didn't matter. Will was back in five minutes. At least, living out of a suitcase had taught him to concentrate on the essentials.

⚬⚬⚬

"We have to hurry," Nan said as she got up from the table. "We'll have dessert when we get back."

"How are we going?" Will asked. "I doubt a wagon can get through all those drifts."

"You'll see. Just make sure you bundle up."

When they stepped outside, Jake was waiting with a long-legged white horse harnessed to a sleigh. The harness bells jingled as the horse pranced expectantly.

"A sleigh!" Clara squealed and dashed down the steps. She stumbled in the deep snow, but she got to her feet and climbed into the sleigh before either Nan or her father could reach her.

"Sit between us," Nan advised as she covered Clara with a fur robe. "It's going to be awfully cold."

But Clara was too excited to feel the cold. The

bells jingled merrily as the sleigh moved smoothly over the snow. Moonlight reflected off the pristine surface, making the night almost as light as day. They hadn't gone far before Clara bounced up in her seat, pointed, and shouted, "There's another one."

In front of them, a sleigh pulled onto the road from a farm lane.

"You may see more before we reach town."

Clara saw three more, and she waved and called out to each one. They all waved back, laughed, and called to each other. At the church, however, everyone hurried inside out of the cold with no more than a few hurried greetings.

Will felt as though he had stepped into a different world.

A small pipe organ played Bach softly in the distance. Candles seated in beds of greenery illuminated each stained-glass window. Running cedar had been wound around the end of each pew. Two enormous white candles on the altar and two branches of smaller candles on each side caused the brass and silver to glisten and gleam. Above the altar was a scene of Christ surrounded by children.

As Will followed Nan into the Carson family pew and knelt to offer his prayer, he felt at peace with himself for the first time in a long while.

The service of lessons and carols lasted less than an hour. Will had heard better choirs and seen bigger organs, but this service moved him as others never had. He felt a chill up and down his spine when the children's choir came down the aisle, their youthful voices—some sweet, some hopelessly out of tune—raised in song. Their white smocks and freshly scrubbed faces made them seem like angels.

The young people and the adults followed. Will guessed each family in the community must be represented by at least one member in the choir. He wasn't much of a singer. His deep bass voice always seemed to be an octave below where it should be. But Nan sang with a light, clear voice. Much to his surprise, Clara did as well.

He had never heard his daughter sing. He didn't know until now that her voice was as pure and sweet as any in the choir. His vision became misty, and he reached over to put his arm around her shoulder. They would sing together again. Soon.

After the service, everyone repaired to the social hall for hot drinks and the bounty of the Christmas season. Will had forgotten how much food could appear at a country gathering. He could have eaten dinner all over again. He contented himself with hot, spicy punch and about a half-dozen of Nan's shortbreads. Clara did her best to sample every kind of cake and cookie in the room.

By the time they headed for their sleigh, Will was certain he'd been introduced to every person within ten miles of Beaker's Bend. Clara exchanged shouted good-byes with several new friends she met in the social hall.

"Can I go to Peggy's house tomorrow?" she asked her father even before she snuggled under the fur robe.

"Tomorrow's Christmas," Will said. "I doubt that's a very good time."

"Peggy asked me most especially to come."

"I think you'd better discuss it with Nan, but we'll talk about it tomorrow," Will added when Clara turned to Nan, ready to ask her right then. "It's a beautiful night," he said, changing the subject. "It's a shame it's so cold."

It was also a shame Clara wasn't home in bed. He would have liked the opportunity to ride home alone with Nan. He slid his arm along the back of the seat until his fingers reached Nan's shoulder. He felt her stiffen, but she didn't pull away. He gently rubbed her shoulders.

Her muscles tightened, then gradually relaxed. He let his hand rest on her shoulder, his thumb moving gently against the nape of her neck.

Will didn't think he'd ever seen a more beautiful night. As the other sleighs turned off into their lanes, the silence deepened until they had the night to themselves. Even the forest animals had fallen silent. A full moon bathed the world in a bluish light. It seemed almost as bright as day but was much more intimate. Snow-covered trees and endless fences cast inky-black shadows across their path, causing the horse to shy now and then. Only the steady jingle of the harness bells broke the silence.

With sudden and unmistakable clarity, Will realized that he had become a different person from the man who left Boston a week earlier. These last days had removed a kind of crust, an artificial overlay, gradually developed during the last fourteen years. Something inside him had now reached back to a time he had lost, or forgotten. In doing so, it had pulled the present into focus. He saw himself clearly now—no cloudy spots, no shadowy corners.

The life he and Louise had built in Boston had become his past. He had to let go of it in order to live in the present, in order to build a future for those he held most dear.

He understood all this because of Nan, this quiet miracle of a woman who had invaded his life and transformed it in a twinkling. He wanted to tell her how much that meant to him, how much she meant to him. How much he loved her.

He would. He would never stop telling her.

The drive ended much too soon. Clara had fallen asleep against him. He carried her upstairs. Nan undressed her while he turned back the bed and took her wet clothes downstairs. When he came back into the room, she called, "Daddy," in a sleepy voice and held out her arms to him.

Nan slipped out, leaving Will alone with his daughter.

He sat down on the bed and put his arms around Clara. She hugged his neck.

"I want you to stay with me always. Nan, too," she added sleepily.

"I will, darling. Maybe Nan will, too."

"Talk to her, Daddy. Make her stay."

"I will, sweetheart. Now it's time to go to sleep. It'll be Christmas when you wake up."

∞

Nan was struggling with the dollhouse when he closed the door to Clara's room.

"Since you seem determined to give away your childhood, let me carry that for you." The dollhouse was sturdy and quite heavy.

"Set it here on this table." Nan had set up a table clearly made to hold the dollhouse. "Now we get to put everything inside."

"*You* get to put it inside," Will said. "I wouldn't know where to begin."

"Then you can bring down the rest of the things on my bed."

Nan had apparently emptied her attic. There were two dolls, a baby crib, a stroller, a sturdy winter coat and mittens, and an assortment of candy. There were also two dresses, a pair of shiny black shoes, and enough ribbons and bows for Clara to wear a different one every day for weeks. Will was embarrassed by the bounty.

"Clara is never going to want to leave after this."

Nan paused. "I hadn't thought about that. If you think—"

"I didn't mean it like that. It's just that I never know what to get her. I keep putting it off until it's too late, and I end up not getting anything."

"Which is all the more reason you should leave her with me," Nan said, getting to her feet. She turned around to find herself face-to-face with Will. His arms closed around her.

"Do you really want a daughter badly enough to take Clara?"

"I wouldn't be *taking* Clara, just taking care of her for a while."

"Don't you want children of your own?"

"Yes, but—"

"Wouldn't you need a husband for all of that?"

"Of course, but what—"

"Do you still love me?"

"Will Atkins, I answered that question last night. I'm not so fickle as to change my mind today."

Will kissed her soundly.

"And you're certain you couldn't marry a man callous enough to give up his daughter."

"That's not exactly what I said, but the answer is still the same."

Nan tried to wriggle out of his embrace, but Will grinned and held her tighter. "I was just making sure."

"Are you certain you didn't take a nip from that bottle Homer Knight had hidden under his jacket?"

Will laughed. "No, I didn't sample Homer's white lightning, or whatever it was. But I'm feeling tipsy just the same."

Nan didn't understand. He seemed to be delighted that she wasn't going to marry him. Yet he held her in his arms and had kissed her several times. That didn't make sense. She would have been hurt that he was so happy if she hadn't been convinced he was talking about something else all the while.

"Maybe you'd better go to bed until you get over it. You're not making any sense."

"I'm not ever going to get over you." He kissed her again. "Now I'm going to go to bed because I can't wait for Christmas morning."

He waltzed her over to the mistletoe. "Ever since I was a little boy, I've wanted to kiss the woman I loved under the mistletoe on Christmas Eve."

"It's time to stop this nonsense," Nan said. She was finding it difficult to keep her spirits up. Will seemed to be having a good time, but she just wanted to go to her room and cry. "I don't know what kind of silly game you're playing, but—"

"I'm not playing a game. I'm deadly earnest. The only thing silly is that I didn't have enough sense to know what to do earlier."

"I don't understand—"

"Don't try to understand. Just believe."

"Believe what?"

"That I love you."

Then he kissed her. Nan started to draw back; she felt certain she ought to, but she couldn't. She didn't want to. She had been allowed a small window of time to taste some of the joy life could have given her. She didn't know why she should be restricted to just a taste, but she decided to take every bit she could get. It would come to an end soon enough.

Nan wound her arms around Will's neck and leaned into the kiss. Quite suddenly, she wanted to be as close to him as possible. She wanted to feel the warmth of his body against her own, the pressure of his chest against her breast, the security of his arms around her. For one brief moment she wanted to forget leaving home, motherless daughters, the pressure of business. Just once she wanted to feel prized above all worldly possessions.

She wanted to feel that Will loved her for herself alone.

Only two other men had kissed Nan. The memory of their chaste kisses was obliterated by Will's passionate embrace. He stunned her when he forced his tongue between her lips. She went weak in the knees. She thought she would faint when she felt the heat of his desire pressed against her abdomen.

Nan had never been so close to unchecked emotion, to raw need. It both frightened and excited her.

Will broke their kiss. He looked visibly shaken.

"I think it's time I went to bed," he said.

"That was more than a stolen kiss under the mistletoe," Nan said.

"Too much, and not nearly enough."

"I don't understand."

"You will," Will said, and kissed her on the nose. "I promise you will."

Seven

Nan was surprised to find she wasn't the first one in the kitchen on Christmas morning.

"What are you doing here?" she asked Gertie. "Why aren't you enjoying your own Christmas?" Eggs, biscuits, sausage, grits, ham and gravy, jellies, butter—everything was ready for an enormous breakfast.

"Christmas is no fun for two old people. Jake and I wanted to watch Clara. He's lighting the fire right now. You go tell Clara and her father they've got fifteen minutes. After that, we start without them."

But it didn't take Clara that long. In exactly twenty-one seconds she was out of bed, into her robe and slippers, and downstairs wanting to know why the door to the gathering room was closed. Will wasn't far behind. He had taken time to comb his hair and brush his teeth, but everything else was left for later.

"When do we get to open our presents?" Clara asked for the fifth time.

"After you finish your breakfast," Nan said.

"But I'm not hungry."

"You have to eat something," Will said. "Gertie has worked very hard to fix a nice breakfast."

It was apparent to all four adults that while Clara might appreciate Gertie's effort, she wished she had saved it for some other time. She toyed with her food, barely tasting what was put on her plate. She ate only half of a hot biscuit covered with butter and grape jelly.

"I think it's time to open the presents," Nan announced.

Clara was out of her chair and at the door like a flash.

"Close your eyes," Nan said.

Clara slammed her eyes shut and put her hands over them.

"Don't open them until I say so," Nan said. She guided Clara out of the kitchen, down the hall, and into the gathering room. "Now open your eyes."

Clara dropped her hands. She looked around at the many gifts. "Which one is mine?"

"All of them," Nan said.

Clara's eyes grew wider and wider. "Everything?"

Nan smiled and nodded.

"Can I, Daddy?"

Will nodded.

There were two dolls, one a beautiful, blond princess doll dressed in a lovely white gown, the second a country doll with pink cheeks and freckles on the end of her nose. She wore a calico dress with an apron, a sunbonnet on her unruly red hair, and black boots on her feet. Clara walked straight to the second doll, picked her up, and hugged her close.

"You have to give both your dolls names," Gertie said.

"This is Peggy," Clara said.

"The little girl she met at church last night," Nan whispered to Will when he looked totally at sea.

"And the other?" Gertie prompted.

"That's Nan," Clara said.

"I don't look a thing like—"

"I think that's a perfect name," Will said. "Now before you get busy with your other presents, Daddy has something for you."

Will produced a package from behind one of the chairs. Clara tore the paper off to reveal a pretty white Sunday dress and a new pair of shiny, black patent-leather shoes. Clara couldn't wait to try them on. She kicked off her slippers, shrugged off her robe, and pulled her nightgown over her head.

"Where did you get that?" Nan asked in an undervoice.

"I told him about it," Gertie said. "I saw it at the mercantile."

"It was the only thing in the place I'd buy," Will said.

Clara put her shoes on bare feet and stood up and adjusted her dress.

"You look beautiful," Nan said. "I think you ought to give your father a great big kiss."

Clara ran over and gave her father a big hug and kiss. "Now I'll look at the rest of my presents."

Nan picked up a package wrapped in plain paper and handed it to Will. "It's not much, but I thought you might like it."

"Shortbreads!" Will crowed with laughter. "I'm never going to live this down, am I?"

"I'm afraid not. If I forget, Gertie's bound to remember."

Gertie and Jake were exchanging presents. They weren't aware of anybody else just then.

"I've got a present for you," Will said. "It's a little strange, but I hope you'll like it. Actually, I've got more than one, but open this one first."

Puzzled, Nan accepted the envelope Will handed her. Inside she found a folded piece of paper. When she opened it up, she found a crude picture of a store with *Atkins Mercantile* written across the front.

"Now this one," Will said, handing her a second envelope.

Inside, Nan found a second piece of paper. This time, *Atkins Hotel* was written across the front of a building that looked more like a country inn than a hotel.

"I don't understand," Nan said.

"You'll never make an artist," Gertie said, looking at the pictures with a critical eye. "Not if you can't draw Wilmer's inn or Grady's mercantile any better than that."

Nan grabbed the pictures and looked at them again. Then she looked up at Will and back at the pictures.

"You didn't... You couldn't... I didn't know..."

"For goodness' sake," Gertie said, "they aren't that bad."

"It isn't that," Nan said. "Don't you see? His name is on them."

"I'm not blind," Gertie replied. "Though why he'd want to put his name on those buildings is more than I can understand."

"You bought them, didn't you?" Nan said, turning to Will.

He nodded.

"You're not going to take Clara to her grandparents?"

He shook his head.

"You're not going back to Boston?"

"No."

"Will someone tell me what's going on?" Gertie demanded.

"Where am I going to live?" Clara asked.

"Right here, darling," Nan said. She gave the child a hug, but her eyes never left Will.

"Where's Daddy going to live?"

"That depends on whether Nan likes my last gift," Will said.

He took a small box out of his pocket and opened it. A diamond ring nestled in a bed of deep-blue velvet. Nan looked at the ring, then at Will.

"I would have gone with you. You know that, don't you?"

"Yes, but I discovered I didn't want to go. It's ironic, but I discovered my new life was hollow, an illusion. Everything that's real and lasting is right here."

Will took the ring out of the box. His eyes never left Nan's face, but somehow he managed to slip it on her finger. They stood there, holding hands, staring into each other's eyes.

"Where's Daddy going to live?" Clara asked again.

"Right here," Gertie answered. "Now why don't we go into the kitchen? Nan and your father have a lot to talk about."

"But they're not saying anything."

"Yes, they are. You just can't hear it."

"Are they going to do that a lot?"

"Probably."

❧

"So that's what you did yesterday." They were seated on the sofa, Nan nestled in Will's arms. "I knew Wilmer wanted to sell, but what about Grady? His family has owned the mercantile for a hundred years."

"Maybe, but Paralee wants to join her son and daughter in Charlottesville. And when a woman wants something—"

"I know. Daddy used to say, 'When a stubborn woman wants something, a wise man lets her have it.' Is that how you felt about me?"

"You helped me to see what I wanted most. Once I knew that, the rest was easy."

"Truly? You won't regret it in a few years?"

"I haven't changed what I want to do, just where I want to do it. I plan to build a business empire from one end of the valley to the other."

"But you'll come home every night?"

"Every night."

"And you won't be away at Christmas."

"Never again."

"And Clara can have some brothers and sisters?"

"As many as she wants. When can we get started?"

❧

"What's that funny sound?" Clara asked Gertie.

"I think it's Nan saying yes."

"It doesn't sound like yes to me."

"It will when you're old enough to understand the question."

About the Author

Leigh Greenwood is the award-winning author of over fifty books, many of which have appeared on the *USA Today* bestseller list. Leigh lives in Charlotte, North Carolina. Please visit his website at leigh-greenwood.com.

CHRISTMAS IN PARADISE

---◆-◦-◆---

Rosanne Bittner

One

Wyoming Territory
August 1886

MAGGIE RESTED HER FATHER'S OLD SHARPS ON A ROCK, taking steady aim. She couldn't hold the big, heavy rifle on her own long enough to keep it steady. To this day, she wasn't sure how she'd once managed to hold it long enough to shoot a grizzly. Pure desperation, she supposed, since the bear was attacking the man she loved.

That was almost four months ago. Right now, she was aiming the old but dependable rifle at the biggest buck she'd ever seen, even in these wild Wyoming foothills. The only thing bigger would be an elk...or another grizzly.

Please don't move. She lined up the rear sight with the sight at the end of the barrel. She squeezed the rear trigger to set the load, then moved her finger to the front trigger...and fired.

She winced when the butt of the rifle punched her shoulder, but she'd been prepared for the kick, her feet straddled and well planted. The buck fell, and Maggie let out a war whoop. She eagerly turned from her hiding place behind the rock and shoved the Sharps into its straps, then mounted her horse, a two-year-old buckskin mare she called Missy. "Let's go, girl!" She kicked the horse's sides and rode the roughly one hundred yards to where the buck had fallen. She hated to see any animal suffer, and she wasn't sure enough of her aim to be confident she'd put this beautiful animal down instantly, rather than just wounding him.

She dismounted and quickly tied her horse to a small shrub, then carefully walked around the buck. She saw no movement, and her heart filled with pride at her kill. This was her way of proving she was a true rancher's wife and loved this land and this life, showing her husband of only two months that he'd made the right choice in marrying her. God knew he'd had his heart broken bad enough by his first wife, who'd hated life here in Paradise Valley—hated the remoteness of it, hated getting her hands dirty, hated common chores and hard work.

Not me, she thought. *I love every inch of this land. My hands were never clean back on Pa's farm in Missouri, and I worked as hard as any man. I can handle ranching.* She looked around, drinking in the Wyoming landscape… the mountains…the grasslands. *Most of all, I love the man who owns all of this!*

The trouble was, that man's first wife was the most educated, sophisticated, beautiful woman Maggie had ever met. She could never come close to any of that, so in her mind she figured she had to prove herself in other ways. She had to make Sage love her for her abilities as a rancher's wife. Such a life wasn't easy, but she'd been brought up hard back in Missouri, treated far more like a boy than a girl by her abusive father.

She could hold up to ranch life, but it also took determination and grit to be married to a man like Sage Lightfoot. He was all man, all power, all sureness, and capable of brutality against those who would harm those he loved. He had a temper no one wanted to mess with, though he never turned it against her. Not Sage. For a man of his size and strength, he could be surprisingly gentle.

She heard the pounding of horses' hooves then. Here on Paradise Valley Ranch, a gunshot brought men running. She'd seen this big buck out her kitchen window more than once. When she spotted him again this morning, she quickly threw on coat and boots and grabbed Missy from where someone had left the mare, saddled, near the barn. She could only hope the buck would still be in sight when she reached a place close enough to shoot it.

The trouble was, Sage often preached about the dangers of a woman going out alone in this country. After what she'd been through when she first met Sage, she well understood his concern. She'd promised her husband that she would always let him or one of the men know if she intended to go riding. Now she'd broken that promise, and Sage would be worried, but there hadn't been time to let anyone know what she was doing.

She touched her belly. The child she carried was an even bigger reason she felt she had to prove herself. Always, she feared Sage would change his mind about accepting a baby that wasn't his, a baby whose father was unknown. She hated the word people used for such a child...*bastard*. She would never think of her precious baby that way, but she knew others would if they knew the truth.

Right now, only Sage knew. He'd told the ranch hands that the baby was his, but they all knew what she'd been through when Sage first found her out on the plains—alone—digging her husband's grave after a gruesome attack by outlaws that had left her wishing she was dead. The ranch hands probably all wondered what the real truth was, but they were good men. Sage loved her and had married her, so the men who worked for him also loved her and were kind to her.

She smiled when she heard whistles and shouts. She appreciated how the crew at Paradise Valley looked out for her, protected her, praised her cooking, and respected her as the wife of the owner of this sixty-thousand-acre spread. Most of them were ex-outlaws, although the "ex" was questionable at times when it came to their fierce protection of Sage and this ranch and anyone Sage loved. They were solid and dependable. Sage himself once led an outlaw life, practically forced into it by the terrible hurt of being reviled by his own family because of his Indian blood.

But that was in the past. Maggie was determined to make sure it stayed there, determined to show Sage Lightfoot more love than he'd ever known and give him the family he'd always wanted. Some would think it strange that they had married so quickly, thinking it was only because she was carrying. Out here, people made decisions out of necessity and survival, but no matter what others thought, she'd married purely for love.

She recognized the three men riding toward her—Bill Summers, Hank Toller, and her husband, who had a concerned look on his face, but she didn't care if he was upset that she'd come out here alone. She'd just shot the biggest buck in Paradise Valley, which would provide a lot of meat for all the ranch hands. She'd proven her value as Sage Lightfoot's new wife.

Two

"LOOK THERE, SAGE! THAT WOMAN OF YOURS HAS SAND in her gizzard, I'll say!" A hefty Hank Toller dismounted and, as usual, spit tobacco juice, making sure to aim it away from everyone. "Maggie, did you count the points on that beast?"

"I didn't even think to count them!" Maggie answered excitedly. "I was just so happy to get him with one shot!" She looked up at Sage, not quite able to read his eyes. "I'll bet this is the biggest buck anybody on this ranch ever shot," she told him, smiling.

Sage just shook his head. "I expect it is."

"Ain't no man on this ranch ever shot one bigger," Bill verified. "I'm guessin' that creature weighs two hundred fifty pounds, probably more." He winked at Maggie. "I'll be lookin' forward to some venison steaks for the men right soon."

Maggie laughed. "I'll make sure every man gets a good meal out of this. We need to celebrate a successful roundup and the good price Sage got for those cattle you men herded to Cheyenne a couple weeks ago."

Sage dismounted and walked over to inspect the deer. "You sure he's dead? Wild animals have a way of suddenly rearing up after they lay there a bit. Be careful, Hank."

Hank was counting the points. "Twelve!" He stood up, his stomach jiggling as he laughed. "Twelve points! Sage, we gotta keep the head of this thing for a souvenir. That's some woman you have there!"

Sage looked Maggie over appreciatively, a sly grin

finally making its way to his lips. "Oh, I already know that." He walked closer to Maggie. "Step back, Maggie. If you're going to go hunt an animal like this, don't take it for granted he's dead just because he's down. A good kick from an animal that size could kill you, or the baby." He gently took her arm and pushed her farther away. "Slit his throat, Hank. If he still has any life in him, we don't want him to suffer."

"Sure, Sage."

Maggie winced a little when Hank took a big hunting knife from his belt and deftly ran it across the buck's throat. She couldn't help wondering if Hank had used that knife on a human being before, but she was sure if he had, it was for good reason. Hank was one of the friendliest men in Paradise Valley. Maggie didn't know his sins and didn't care to judge him, just as she didn't care about Sage's misdeeds. They were all good men at heart.

"You two get that buck down to the slaughtering shed and bleed it out and gut it," Sage told Bill and Hank. "And I agree we should save the head and those antlers. Do what you have to do for that."

"Joe Cable knows how to clean and dry out what needs to be," Bill answered. "He could make a living at taxidermy, but he'd rather be outside ridin' the range, like most of us." He proceeded to help Hank tie the legs of the buck.

"Hang it over Maggie's horse," Sage told them. "Maggie can ride back to the house with me."

"Sure enough." Hank threw a blanket over Maggie's saddle, and Sage helped both men tie the deer onto her horse. Hank and Bill rode off, carting the buck behind them. Sage turned to Maggie, who eyed him warily.

"Are you mad at me?" she asked, stepping back a little as he came closer, towering over her with a loving but somewhat chastising look on his handsome face.

Sage sighed and folded his arms. "Maggie, when are you going to stop looking at me like I might beat you or something? I'm not your father, and I'm not those men who killed your first husband and abused you."

Maggie shrugged. "It's hard for a person to get over how they were raised. Every time I made my pa mad, he found a way to punish me, and it was always more than just a scolding."

"Have I ever laid a hand on you that way?"

Maggie grinned. "Of course not. But you're my husband, and I've seen the mean side of you against men who crossed you. Husbands have rights."

"*No* man has rights like that, especially not a father or a husband. And you know what my first wife did to me. She's the only woman I was ever truly angry with, but for God's sake, I never hit her. You know me better by now, but damn it, Maggie, you have to tell me or one of the men if you're going to ride off alone. What if Missy stumbled or threw you off? Or what if that buck kicked you? You could lie hidden in this tall grass for hours before we'd find you. You do happen to be carrying, you know."

Maggie walked closer and threw her arms around him, resting her head against his chest. "I know. But there wasn't time to tell anybody, Sage. I had to hurry after I saw him out here again."

Sage's strong arms came around her, and he kissed the top of her head. "Just keep your promise about not going off alone. This ranch might be well guarded, but seven or eight men can't scan a whole sixty thousand acres day and night or all at once. You're lucky Hank and Bill and I were already back from the east range when we heard your gunshot and were able to get here as fast as we did."

"But I was okay."

"How could we know that?" Sage squeezed her closer. "Maggie, I went through enough hell rescuing you from those men on the Outlaw Trail. I'm still not quite over it, and I know you aren't either. And I know why you came out here and shot that deer."

Maggie frowned, looking up at him. "What do you mean?"

Sage moved away slightly and cupped her chin in his hand. He leaned down to kiss her softly. "I mean you don't have to keep proving your worth to me. You think that because you're carrying another man's baby, I'm going to eventually stop loving you. Or that I'll never be able to love that kid in your belly. And you're still comparing yourself to Joanna."

Maggie turned away. "She is so beautiful, and educated and all lady and—"

"And she was out for nothing but my money," Sage reminded her, "which is why I divorced her. Her kind of betrayal was as bad as cheating on me with another man. You, on the other hand, are the most blatantly honest and generous woman I've ever known. There's a lot more to a woman worthy of love than education and sophistication, Maggie, and you're it. And you're damn beautiful in your own right. You're all the reasons a man wants a woman in his life forever."

Maggie looked up at him. "I love when you tell me things like that, Sage."

Sage chuckled and leaned down to kiss her forehead. "You damn well know that I'm not a man to speak my feelings easily. I wouldn't have told you I love you and I wouldn't have married you if what I just said wasn't true. What more do I need to do to prove how I feel about you?"

Maggie's eyes teared. "Nothing at all. It's just me being scared of losing you, Sage, because I love you so much and I love this life and this ranch." Her smile faded. "If this baby at least belonged to James, it would be different. He was my legal husband. But those men shot him down, and now I'm carrying a baby fathered by one of them."

"And I made sure they're all dead. Through it all, I

fell in love with you. Have you ever once heard me call that child a bastard?"

Maggie quickly wiped at her tears. "No. But I can't help wondering if you've *thought* it."

"And what did I tell you about that baby when I told you I wanted to marry you?"

Maggie faced him. "That you would love it like your own, and he or she would inherit part of this ranch like they had your own blood."

"Am I a liar?"

Maggie sniffed and wiped at her nose with her sleeve. "No. Joe Cable once told me you're as honest as what a man sees in a looking glass, and that's why he likes working for you—your honesty and your loyalty."

"Then why are you doubting my word? And why do you think you have to find ways to make sure I *keep* loving you?"

Maggie looked out at the heavenly colors and glorious beauty of Paradise Valley. The beautiful log home she lived in sat peacefully below, beyond a half mile of yellow grass that rippled from a soft wind. Pockets of cattle and horses dotted the landscape, along with two cabins, a large bunkhouse, two big barns, a chicken coop, and storage sheds. She'd never loved anything as much in her life as she loved Wyoming and this ranch and the man who owned it. "It's just me, I guess. You're all man and so sure of yourself, and some men don't want kids at all, let alone when they aren't their own."

Sage pulled her back into his arms. "Well, I *do* want kids. You know that. For one thing, I'll need them to help run this ranch, and I'll take in the one you're carrying and love it because I love his or her mother. You already had to bury a baby girl back in Missouri, and I know you've been yearning ever since for another baby. Maybe this one is a gift from God because of what you went through. I don't know. I'm not much of one to talk about things like that.

"I just know I've found the perfect woman to share this ranch with me. And as far as anyone other than you and me knows, that baby you're carrying *is* mine. Everybody knows we spent quite a while together searching for those bastards who took you, so no one will doubt we could have fallen in love and answered each other's needs on the trail. Hell, that *is* what happened."

Maggie snuggled against him, breathing in his scent, all leather and fresh air and man. "How could any woman *not* fall in love with you?"

Sage gave a light laugh. "There are plenty who would find that difficult. You already know I'm not always easy to live with."

Maggie stood on her toes and managed to reach his lips for a quick kiss. "Are you proud of me for shooting that buck?"

"You know I am—just as proud and grateful as I was when you shot that grizzly that was trying to tear me to pieces back when I first found you." He leaned down and returned her kiss, deeper, hungrier. "And right now I could lay you down in this grass and have at you." He pressed a hand against her bottom. "But some of the other men will be riding this way soon with some fencing, so I'd better get you back to the house."

He lifted her in his arms, and Maggie reached around his neck when he kissed her again, a long, slow kiss of promise for things to come later. He finally left her lips and kissed her neck as he carried her to his horse. "Damn it, Maggie, I have chores. You have completely disrupted my day, and now I don't even want to go back out once I get you to the house."

"Well, I have some bread dough rising, and it needs to be punched down and kneaded again, so we *both* have chores."

"Then I'd better get you back." Lifting her as though she weighed nothing, Sage plunked her on his horse, then mounted up behind her, wrapping his arms around her and taking the reins. "Maggie girl, as a hunter, you are beginning to make me look bad."

Maggie rested against his solid chest as Sage urged his horse into a gentle trot toward their log home. "That would be impossible," she answered. "You're the bravest, most able man I've ever known. I'd be dead or living some kind of horror if not for you. And you most certainly would have brought down that buck with one shot and done it easily. I just got lucky."

"Don't underestimate yourself."

Maggie smiled at her husband's words of love and pride, and his reassuring arms around her. She was safe and loved in his embrace. "I love you, Sage."

"Then keep your promises, Mrs. Lightfoot, or I *will* have to punish you."

"And how would you do that?"

Sage grinned. "Let's just say that I'm having fun thinking about it." He ran a big hand over her belly. "But you need to start taking better care of yourself. Don't be riding around so much on horseback, and I'm going to have Rosa start helping with more of your chores around the house."

"I can do them."

"Stop arguing with me."

"Yes, sir." Maggie knew the difference between a teasing Sage and one who meant business—and he meant business with his last statement, which was fine. It meant he cared. No man had cared about her like Sage did—not her demanding and unforgiving father, and not her first husband, who'd only used her for sex and chores and knew nothing about how to love or how to *make* love. Those were two things Sage Lightfoot was damn good at.

Three

"I DON'T LIKE THIS DROUGHT." SAGE REMOVED HIS BOOTS and socks while Maggie brushed her hair vigorously, always finding it difficult to pull a brush easily through the thick mass of red curls.

"We have plenty of water in South Creek," Maggie reminded him.

"For now. And every time we get a storm with lightning, I worry about a prairie fire. We need a lot more than a couple of storms and a little rain to avoid that danger."

Maggie set down the brush. "And you were wise enough to preserve the northeast ten thousand acres for an emergency. You shipped off fifteen hundred head of cattle last month, Sage, and so far, the rest are still grazing on the southwest section."

Sage removed his shirt and pants. "What's there is fast drying up. One good fire will devour all that's left and move this way. It could consume this house and all the outbuildings. The canyon between here and the grass in the northeast will save that section. Sully Creek runs through there, and so far that keeps it green. But getting the cattle across that canyon wouldn't be an easy task. My plan was to cut the grass there for winter feed, not graze it. In the meantime, it won't take long for hungry beef to graze out those eight thousand acres, let alone lap up what's left of South Creek if we don't get some rain." He laid his clothes over a chair and removed the top half of his long johns. "The biggest problem is we didn't get enough snow this past winter. The mountain runoff is done with."

In the mirror, Maggie had watched him undress. His physique always moved her in womanly ways. Sage Lightfoot was tall and broad and muscled. He knew his way around men of every type, with guns and fists. He'd lived with the worst of them. Power and bravery emanated from his very being, and she loved every inch of him, to his heart and soul. He'd worked hard to build up what he now owned, but he always worried about losing it. He'd known too much hurtful rejection, from his adoptive family to his first wife. Now he feared losing all he had worked for to drought and fire.

"Sage, you'll be okay. There's always open range."

"That's not something I can depend on anymore. The damn government is cracking down on grazing on government land, and they own too much of Wyoming. Now we're forced to compete with other ranchers for open range, especially in time of drought. And that's not even taking into account the sheep men. These conditions can lead to range wars."

Maggie rose from her dressing table and walked over to hug her husband around the middle, resting her face against his bare chest. In spite of wearing a flannel gown that should be too warm for the hot August night, she shivered—not from the night air that came through an open window, but from Sage's suggestion of a range war.

"I hate that kind of talk. I know you, Sage, and if there is any kind of fighting over grazing land, you'll be right in the middle of it. That won't mean just other men trying to take what isn't theirs, but it would also mean the law coming to take care of things, maybe even the federal government. You and the law don't exactly get along."

Sage moved his arms around her. "I didn't mean to upset you. I'm just trying to look ahead and find ways to stave off any trouble. The best thing that could happen is about a week of hard rain, and that's not likely this time of year."

Maggie looked up at him. "Maybe the men could dig some fire barriers now—do a controlled burn or something in the south or the west that might prevent a fire from going too far."

Sage grinned, holding her face in his hands. "Along thousands of acres? I'd have to hire a hundred more men, which I can't afford. And who knows where a fire might start? Lightning can strike anywhere. It's a damn big country, you know."

"Yes, it is, and I love all of it!" Maggie grasped his wrists. "And I love the man who runs it all. You have to stop worrying about what *might* happen, Sage."

Sage leaned down to kiss her, and Maggie reached up and put her arms around his neck, returning his kiss with a soft "Mmmmm." She pulled away with a smile. "Let's only talk about these things at the table or something—not here in the bedroom. I prefer to talk about things that make me happy when we're in here."

Sage grinned and lifted her into his arms. "You mean you prefer to *do* things that make you happy when we're in here."

Maggie laughed. "That's exactly what I mean."

Sage laid her on the bed, and Maggie moved under a quilt. Sage crawled in beside her, then moved on top of her. He kissed her deeply as he ran a hand along her leg and over her bottom. "You should be too tired from your big hunting expedition this morning and all the baking you did today to want your husband's attention tonight."

"I'm *never* too tired for you," Maggie answered, shivering with desire as Sage nuzzled her neck.

"You little vixen. You left off your drawers."

Maggie smiled slyly. "I was hoping you'd do enough searching to notice once we got into bed. I'm just making things easier on you."

Sage ran a hand over her belly. "Your belly is growing. Our baby is getting bigger."

"He or she certainly is, and faster than I expected for only four months along." Maggie frowned. "When I get really big, it won't bother you, will it?"

Sage chuckled. "It only accents that you're all woman. You're beautiful and so full of life."

Maggie's smile faded. "You'll love this one just as much as any babies we have in the future, won't you?"

Sage studied her eyes as he ran a gentle hand over her belly. "We've had this conversation too many times, Maggie. You know I will. I want a whole passel of kids starting with *this one*, as long as you're healthy enough for it and you want them, too."

Maggie reached up to push some of his thick, dark hair behind one ear. "I do. I intend to give you as many children as you want. You deserve a loving family."

"And I'll always love the small but damn strong woman who gives me that big family. I love her fiery-red hair and her eyes green as grass and the freckles across her nose and cheeks and the way she handles a Sharps rifle."

Maggie laughed lightly. "There was a time when I threatened to use that rifle on *you*, if you will remember. I'm so glad I didn't kill you when you found me out on the plains alone. I'd have missed out on all of this."

Sage met her mouth again in a hungry kiss. He worked his magic with hands and kisses and pure manliness. There was no more to be said, no doubt about his love for her. Maggie opened herself to him, forcing back thoughts of fire and a possible range war. Here in this bed there should be only good thoughts, only fulfilling passion…only this…Sage Lightfoot making love to her in the beautiful way he had of making sure she knew she belonged only to him. With his fingers, he explored secret places, stirring the silken juices that made her whimper with desire and finally whisper his name in a sweet climax.

Sage moved between her legs and pushed himself inside her. He groaned with pleasure, which only made Maggie want him more. She loved knowing she was pleasing him. She sighed and whimpered in return, his rhythmic thrusts always bringing her to something beyond ecstasy, a sweet fulfillment she'd never known until this man showed her what making love was really about. Sage seemed to naturally understand what a woman needed. He never took her just because he felt he had husbandly rights. Maggie knew that even as his wife, if she told him no, he would leave her alone.

She groaned as she arched her body to take in every inch of him. When she was lost under him this way, she *never* wanted to say no. She was totally at his command, eager to do whatever pleased Sage Lightfoot. He'd taken away the ugliness of the attack that had created the child she carried, and he'd said he would love the baby and raise it as his own. How could she not love and respect him for that?

They moved in glorious rhythm, feeding each other's needs while reveling in the ecstasy of mating. Maggie ran her hands over his muscled arms and solid chest and shoulders, returning his heated kisses with fervor as his thrusts grew deeper and faster. Sage was all power, yet all gentleness.

Life couldn't be any better than this. But sometimes past disappointments and heartache caused both of them to fear that something—or someone—would take all this away. She prayed to God every night that would never happen.

Four

SAGE RODE STORM HARD, RACING TO KEEP UP WITH A sleek, wild black mare he'd broken out of the herd of mustangs the rest of the men were helping chase down. This mare in particular was the perfect size for Maggie, and she was beautiful…like Maggie. He wanted to gift something to his new wife. She deserved it for all she'd been through, and for being the best wife he could ask for.

He kicked Storm's sides and urged the horse on until he was close enough to lasso the mare. He threw his rope, letting out nothing short of a war whoop when the loop fell over her neck. He supposed this was how elated his Cheyenne ancestors must have felt chasing down wild horses and buffalo. He quickly wrapped the other end of the rope around the pommel of his saddle and slowed Storm. "Hold her steady, boy," he told the horse, patting Storm's neck. "You're a little lathered, I know. We'll take a rest."

Storm planted all four hooves solidly and refused to buckle under the wild mare's attempts to escape. She whinnied and reared with fear and confusion, yanking hard at the rope but not getting one inch of relief. Sage dismounted and walked closer to his catch. "Calm down, girl. You're going to live a good life once we get you broken in."

The mare whinnied and bucked again, her eyes wide and wild. She tossed her head and snorted when Sage came a little closer. He stayed out of reach long enough to light a cigarette and step out his match. He took a long drag on the smoke as he studied the vast valley below, where his men chased and herded what looked like a good fifteen or twenty mustangs. They headed east, toward home base and the corrals that would hold the fresh horses for breaking and branding.

Sage couldn't help feeling pride at knowing everywhere he looked, the land belonged to him. Paradise Valley couldn't be a more fitting name. Most of this land was part of a sprawling valley in the foothills of the Rockies, and each season brought a wild array of colors, from wildflowers to grasses of a hundred shades of green and yellow. The gray and purple mountains to the west were speckled with dark-green pine and the white trunks of aspen, which displayed bright-green leaves that glittered when they rippled in the wind.

For the first time in his life, he felt true peace. Having Maggie come into his life had helped. She was everything his first wife wasn't—unselfish, hard-working, brave, and able, good with her father's rifle, willing to put up with the loneliness and hardship of living in the wilds of Wyoming. Maggie didn't care about fancy things, and she was a damn good cook.

The best part was, she'd love him and do whatever it took to help him even if he didn't have a dime…and it didn't matter to her that he carried Cheyenne blood…or that he'd once ridden with and lived the life of outlaws. She knew he'd started this ranch with cattle he'd bought from another man along the Outlaw Trail—cattle that man had stolen. But he'd built a huge herd of his own from those first few. He didn't know a damn thing about where some of his men came from or what they'd done in the past—and he didn't care. Neither did Maggie. She never once looked down on any of them, and they all loved her and respected her.

He'd built a beautiful home for Joanna, but she'd thrown it all in his face. Maggie, on the other hand, loved it, and to her, their big log home might as well be a castle. And in bed… He grinned, feeling the manly urge he always felt at the thought of Maggie taking him with great passion every time they made love—and they made love often.

He could hardly wait to show her this black mare. The horse had a white patch on her chest and around all four legs at the bottom. He smiled, knowing how excited Maggie would be with the gift.

The mare had calmed as Sage stood there smoking, then suddenly jerked and whinnied again when he turned to walk closer to her. He paused to sniff the air as he studied the horizon in all directions, glad he didn't smell any smoke other than that of his own cigarette. He still worried about fire, and about the fact that streams and watering holes were drying up, as well as the grass itself. It wouldn't be long before he'd be forced to herd the cattle to the northeast section of grass he'd been saving. He'd even posted men there to guard it, fearing a neighboring rancher would try to sneak his own cattle onto the still-green grass.

He finished the cigarette, then stepped it out in a patch of gravel, smashing it good and hard with his boot and watching the spot to make sure the stub was definitely out. He walked even closer to the mare, and she tossed her head again, eyeing him with obvious distrust.

"Settle down, girl." Sage reached up and touched the horse's neck. "See there? I'm only here to give you an even better life—a good barn that's warm in winter, plenty of oats, and a rider who's so lightweight that you'll hardly know you're being ridden. She's small and beautiful, and she knows and loves horses. You'll never have to work hard, and you'll never be ridden hard."

The horse snorted, as though to say she didn't believe him. Sage patted her neck again, then walked back to Storm. The big Appaloosa grunted and shook his mane hard, sending sweat flying.

"I know, boy. Let's get you back to your stall and rub you down. We can ride easy on the way." Sage remounted Storm and turned him to head to the house. The wild herd his men had rounded up was already over a rise and had disappeared in the direction of home, but Sage could still see their dust. He frowned when he spotted something else headed that way…a fancy buggy pulled by a sleek, black horse. The animal's perfect cadence bespoke an expensive steed, trained only for pulling buggies and not for riding.

Sage couldn't see from his position who was driving the buggy, but he did recognize two other horses riding beside it—an Appaloosa and a roan-colored gelding. They belonged to two of his ranch hands, big Joe Cable and the Mexican Julio Martinez. They had apparently seen the unknown visitor coming and decided to accompany them. It wasn't often that strangers made it into Paradise Valley without being spotted and questioned.

"Who the hell could that be?" Sage muttered to no one. He kicked Storm into motion, heading in the direction of the visitors, tugging the mare along behind. He hoped this unknown visitor had nothing to do with Joanna. The last time she'd come to visit and beg for money, he'd sent her packing with plenty of cash and orders to never come back to Paradise Valley. The expensive rig below must belong to someone else… someone with even more money than Joanna had, unless she'd found another rich husband. He damn well intended to catch up with the rig and question whoever was in it before they reached the house.

Five

JULIO AND JOE SAW SAGE COMING AND SLOWED THEIR horses, shouting to the driver of the buggy to stop and wait for Sage to catch up. Keeping Storm at a slow pace because of the horse's recent hard run, Sage finally reached the carriage and halted Storm beside it. A dark-green canopy trimmed with gold-colored fringe sheltered both the driver and his passenger from the hot Wyoming sun.

Sage did not recognize the driver, nor did he recognize the stern-looking older woman who made her appearance when she rolled up dark-green canvas shades at each side of the back seat. Once the shades were opened, Sage could see padded seats covered with soft green velvet. The skinny wooden carriage wheels were painted yellow, with bright red trim. Any man could see the rig was high-end, and the older woman who likely owned it radiated wealth, both in her clothing and her demeanor. Her feathered hat nearly touched the roof of the buggy, and her blue velvet dress looked as though it was tailored just for her buxom figure. Sage thought how she might be attractive if not for the dark, judgmental look in her eyes. Her lips were tightly pressed, and her eyes reminded him of black clouds.

The bearded carriage driver wore a silk top hat and a black frock coat. He was burly, with dark eyes that glared as though he was God Himself, eyeing all the men with the hand of judgment, as though they should all be condemned to hell.

Sage turned his attention to Joe. "What's going on here?"

"They are unarmed, Sage. We didn't figure there was any harm in bringing them in. They asked about you and about Maggie."

"*Maggie?*" Sage turned his attention to the driver. "Who the hell are you, and what do you want here?"

The driver held his chin high, his black eyes looking ready to burst into flames. "I am Reverend Billy Parker, and this lady is a member of the Church of Judgment and Salvation, so you will not curse or blaspheme in her presence."

Sage looked at Joe. The man shrugged and grinned a little. "They won't tell me what they want—just to see you and Maggie."

A disgruntled Sage leaned on his saddle horn and frowned at the preacher. "Well, here I am, and I'll speak any way I want. This is my land, and so far you are trespassing. Are you here to judge me or save me? Whichever it is, I'm not interested."

"You're Sage Lightfoot? The outlaw?" the reverend asked. "The murderer? There is no salvation for such a man, especially one who I am told carries Indian blood."

Sage straightened. "Mister, you got the name right. And you got it right that I'm part Indian. You even got the outlaw right, but I'm no damn murderer. Any sonofabitch I ever killed was in self-defense or defending someone else!"

The woman in the back seat gasped and finally spoke up. "Dear God! He is a sinner beyond redemption, Reverend! We must get the child out of here!"

"*What* child?" Sage asked, now beginning to bristle. "I don't care to be called names by someone I have never met! You two had better explain yourselves damn quick, or these men will accompany you off this ranch!"

"We prefer to first meet a Mrs. Maggie Tucker before we explain," the reverend told Sage.

"She's Mrs. Maggie Lightfoot now, not Maggie Tucker. She's my *wife*! *I'll* decide whether or not you get to meet her. And I'll not have her insulted the way you just insulted me. More talk like that, Reverend, and I'll drag you right off that buggy and give you a sound wallop! I don't like your attitude."

The reverend refused to meet Sage's gaze. "Whether the name is Tucker or Lightfoot, it does not change why we are here. The woman with me is Mrs. Elvira Hart, and she has good reason to meet your wife. We mean no harm. This involves Mrs. Hart's son. She needs some questions answered, and only this woman named Maggie can answer them! If you do not allow us to speak with your wife, we will come back with the *law*." He finally faced Sage. "I don't think a man like you, or those who work for you, care to have the law come riding in here asking questions about how you built this ranch, Sage Lightfoot!"

"And *I* don't like being threatened! Law or not, any men who come onto my land unwelcomed will get chased right back off! And I'll not take you to see Maggie until I know what this is about."

"It's about my *son*!" the old woman yelled. "Jimmy Hart!" She raised her chin and sniffed as though victorious in some kind of combat.

Sage was taken aback. Jimmy Hart was one of the three men who'd raped Maggie after murdering Maggie's husband…one of the three men who weeks later stole Maggie away after she and Sage fell in love…one of the three men Sage killed to get her back.

"What *about* your son?" Sage asked. "He's dead. Is *that* what you're here to find out? It was me that killed him, and he damn well deserved it! He murdered Maggie's first husband, and he and two of his friends raped Maggie. What the hell *else* do you want to know?"

The stout Elvira Hart stiffened, her bosom heaving with deep breaths of frustration. She glared at Sage so fiercely that he felt he'd just been stabbed. "I want to know if she is carrying my *grand*son," the woman declared. "If she is, I intend to take the child and raise it!"

Sage's fury knew no bounds. He'd never been more tempted to wrap his hands around a woman's throat. Not even Joanna had ever made him this angry. He unwrapped the rope from around his saddle horn and handed it over to Julio, then dismounted. "Take this mare on home, Julio. And don't pay any attention to what that woman just said."

"*Sí, señor*," Julio answered.

"And get off your horse," Sage added. "Storm has been ridden hard. I need you to ride him to the barn—slowly—and brush him down. See that the mare is penned—separate from the other horses. She might be in heat, and I don't want any stallions getting to her. I'll ride back on your horse. When Maggie sees you on Storm, she'll be worried about me, so just tell her we traded horses because I was going out after more horses and Storm was worn out. And don't say a word to her about these visitors, understand?"

"*Sí, Señor Boss*." Julio dismounted, handing his horse's reins to Sage. The two men exchanged a look that said it all. All the ranch hands knew what had happened to Maggie, and all of them knew Sage claimed to be the father of her child. None of them knew if that was true or not, and none of them cared. They all adored Maggie, and she belonged to Sage, which meant to question the situation in front of Sage would likely get them fired... and likely not without a beating.

Julio mounted Storm and rode off with the mare.

"What do you want to do, Sage?" Joe asked him.

"I'll handle it," Sage answered. "Just don't say a word to the rest of the men about this."

"You know I won't," Joe answered.

Sage mounted Julio's roan gelding. "Wait till this is

over," he told Joe, his best friend and a man he trusted with his life. "I'll be wanting these two escorted off Paradise Valley, and I need you to go along to make sure that happens."

Joe nodded. Sage urged Julio's horse closer to the reverend, who still sat glaring at Sage. "How dare you keep this fine woman waiting in this heat!" he declared.

"Do you think I give a damn?" Sage answered. "She's the one who chose to come here." He turned his attention to the woman.

"How in hell did all this start?" he asked. "Jimmy Hart was a murderer and a rapist. He was living on the Outlaw Trail with men as bad or worse than he was, and they all died, most of them at my hand! How in God's name did you know anything about *any* of that? You certainly aren't the type to hang around men in places like that."

Elvira Hart stared straight ahead. "I am a woman of considerable wealth," she answered. "Whatever I need to know, I can hire men who will find out for me. As far as how this started, Jimmy knew he'd not get his share of my fortune until he was twenty-five years old, or I was dead—whichever came first. He wanted it sooner, so he robbed a local bank in Omaha to get what he wanted. He thought I would pay it back out of my own money. Instead, I sent men to arrest Jimmy for his sin, but he ran off. I hired men to track him, and they learned he'd taken up with thugs and was committing other crimes. They traced him to a place called Hole-in-the-Wall, where they—"

The woman sniffed and choked up, quickly dabbing at her eyes with a lace-trimmed handkerchief. "Where they learned he'd been killed," she continued. "Other men there talked. They told the men I hired that my Jimmy was shot down by a man named Sage Lightfoot, who owned a ranch called Paradise Valley. And they said...they said it was over a woman named Maggie Tucker... That in all the shouting, they heard men say she was pregnant with a bastard child…and that *you* rode off with her after killing my Jimmy and the men he rode with—and in a very brutal way, I might add!"

"They were brutal men," Sage answered. "I did what needed doing. They'd taken an innocent woman—a woman who was carrying *my* baby—understand? *Mine!*" He turned to the reverend. "Now, turn this rig around and get the hell off my land!"

"Not without talking to Maggie Tucker!" the reverend demanded. "Mrs. Hart wants to hear from her own lips that the child she carries is not Jimmy's. It is possible Jimmy was the only man who had his way with her, and not all three men. Mrs. Hart is very well off. She will take the child and raise it properly. The child will want for nothing."

"Except the love of its real mother," Sage growled. "I told you the baby is *mine*, and Maggie is my wife now! I'll not let you put her through the humiliation of the kind of questions you'd ask her, so get the hell out of Paradise Valley. I'll not take you to see Maggie!"

"You *must!*" Mrs. Hart insisted.

"I don't have to do one damn thing I don't want to do. Get off my land!"

"But…my grandson…"

"Lady, that baby is mine, so you have no rights to the child." Sage turned his attention to the preacher. "Get the hell back to wherever you call home."

"You, Mr. Lightfoot, are a sinner of the worst sort," the preacher answered. "I feel sorry for what you are going to suffer upon your death!"

Sage looked at Joe and grinned.

"Sage, I hope we both go at the same time, so we can have each other's backs when we get to hell," Joe joked.

Sage nodded. "I'll be proud to have you at my side." He turned his attention back to the preacher, his smile fading. "You've had your last warning, Reverend." He rode closer and grabbed the bridle to the sleek horse that pulled the rig, forcing the horse to turn. "Get moving, or I'll take the reins from your hands and my men will lead this horse out of here whether you like it or not. You've pushed my patience as far as it will go. If you want to come back here with the law, just try it and see what happens!"

"If the baby your wife is carrying is a bastard, or if you impregnated that whore out of wedlock, you will find something is wrong with the child once it is born, because it is *cursed*!" Reverend Parker declared.

"And any man who would declare a curse on an unborn baby is the one who will end up in hell!" Sage leaned down and slapped the rear of the horse pulling the buggy and shouted for it to get going. "That baby is going to be just fine," he shouted as the animal reared slightly and charged away, causing Mrs. Hart to let out a little scream when the buggy turned sharply, nearly throwing her out of her seat.

The reverend scrambled to reach down and get hold of the reins as the rig clattered and jostled across the open valley.

Sage trotted Julio's horse up to Joe, stopping to light another cigarette. "Make sure they get all the way off Paradise Valley."

"I will."

Sage looked at the man darkly. "The kid is mine, Joe."

Joe nodded. "Sage, whether that kid is yours or not, there ain't a man on this ranch who would judge either way, and you know it. We all love Maggie and know what happened to her. If we could have been part of killin' those men, we would have gladly taken part. But no matter what, Maggie and that baby will be fine, and no man will ever disavow it's yours. Somethin' happens to you, Maggie and the kid have plenty of men to look out for both of them."

Sage looked away, taking a long drag on his cigarette. His head ached from suppressing the rage he felt toward the reverend and toward Elvira Hart. "Thanks, Joe. I'm just glad Maggie didn't hear any of that."

"Me too." Joe grinned. "Sage, that's the most control over your temper I've ever seen you manage," he joked. "There was a time when you'd have dragged that reverend out of his buggy and made him wish he'd never come here. Maggie must be workin' the meanness out of you."

Sage turned and glowered at him. "Just get going and make sure they are well off my land before you come back home, or you'll find out just how mean I still am."

Joe tipped his hat and chuckled. "Yes, sir." He rode off after the buggy.

Sage turned Julio's horse and headed for the house, anxious to see Maggie and show her the beautiful mare he'd captured for her.

His eyes teared at the thought of how hurt Maggie would have been to hear Elvira Hart's words. She would probably even start doubting his love for her and his willingness to accept her baby. He didn't want that to ever happen.

His fists tightened in anger. Joe was right. His handling of the Reverend Billy Parker and Elvira Hart had been far too gentle compared to what he *really* wanted to do. The old Sage would have made sure the reverend never even left Paradise Valley!

Six

SAGE RODE JULIO'S HORSE TO THE HOUSE AND DISMOUNTED, handing the reins over to Julio's fifteen-year-old son, Jorje. "Put your father's horse up, will you?" he asked the handsome young man.

"*Sí, señor,*" Jorje answered. "I saw my father ride in earlier with a wild mare. He said you are the one who caught her."

Sage nodded. "I did. She's a gift for my wife."

Jorje nodded excitedly. "She is beautiful, *señor*—the horse, I mean." He put a hand over his eyes. "I mean, so is your wife." He turned away. "I mean that in a good way, *señor.*"

Sage chuckled. "I know what you meant."

The young man looked up at him. "Will you let my brother break in the mare?"

Sage nodded. "Probably. Go take care of this one for now."

"*Sí.*" Jorje walked off with his father's horse. The young man's brother, Roland, was becoming one of the best bronco busters on the ranch. Sage had already decided Roland would be the one to break the mare. The young man had a gentle way with wild horses. He seemed to understand each and every horse's personality, which ones would be ornery and which ones would turn out sweet and gentle.

Sage walked up the steps of the veranda and stomped dust and gravel from his boots, then brushed off his clothes before going inside. Maggie liked a clean house,

and with Rosa Martinez's help, she kept it that way.
Julio's wife was a round, short woman who always
carried a smile and enjoyed helping her boss's pregnant
wife. It was obvious the woman liked Maggie much
better than she'd ever liked Joanna, who'd ordered Rosa
around like a slave and looked down on her as "that fat,
little Mexican woman."

It was Rosa who greeted Sage with the expected
smile. "*Señor,* I was just leaving. There are several loaves
of fresh bread on the table. The *señora* and I baked today.
She said I could take two loaves home to Julio." She held
up the loaves as though to make sure he didn't think she
was stealing them. "I hope you do not mind."

Sage grinned. "Of course not. I don't know what
we'd do without you, Rosa—or Julio, for that matter.
And those sons of yours are becoming two of my best
hands."

"Oh, *sí,* they are good boys!"

Rosa hurried out, and Sage sat down in a nearby chair
to remove his boots. Maggie came out from one of the
bedrooms, carrying a few of his dirty shirts over her arm.
"Wash day tomorrow," she told Sage. She laid the shirts
over a chair and walked closer. "You look like you could
use a bath."

"I could. You going to give me one?" Sage asked with
a sly smile.

Maggie folded her arms. "It's still light out, Sage
Lightfoot. Someone could come in. Besides, you haven't
had any supper yet."

"I'm not that hungry, and we can lock the door."

"Oh, no we won't. Those men out there come up
with too many reasons to come knocking, and I would
be embarrassed beyond recovery. If I help you bathe,
we'll end up doing much more than that."

"You bet we would." Sage set his boots aside and
rose, putting his hands on either side of her face. He

leaned down to kiss her hair. "Have I told you lately that I love you?"

"Yes. Just this morning before you left the house to go after wild horses." Maggie frowned. "And I saw Julio ride back here with a beautiful black mare but riding your horse. Why wasn't he on his own? And where have *you* been?"

Sage studied her green eyes, trying to hide his lingering anger over what the preacher and Mrs. Hart had said. "I rode Storm hard to chase that animal down. I got hung up with something else and couldn't come right back, but I wanted Storm to cool down, so I told Julio to bring him back here for a good rubdown. I also wanted that mare corralled right away. She was pretty worked up. So, I traded horses with Julio."

Maggie grasped his wrists. "And you are as tense as a rope about to snap. What's *really* wrong, Sage? What kept you?"

"I was just tired and decided to have a smoke and take a few minutes to drink in some of the beauty of this land. You know this country. It won't be long before we're buried in snow. It could be sixty degrees today and ten tomorrow."

Maggie offered her mouth up to him, and he kissed her gently. She stepped away then. "You're a bad liar, Sage. You told me yourself once that you never lie, and now I know why. You *can't* lie, not without it showing in your eyes. Go wash up and I'll make supper, after which you can tell me the *real* reason you got back later than the others."

Sage let out a deep sigh. "Don't worry about it. Just make that supper. I'm hungry as a bear that just woke up from a long winter's nap." He kissed her once more and headed down the hallway to the room they kept for bathing.

"I left two buckets of hot water back there," Maggie

called to him, her heart heavy with worry. "And bring me your dirty clothes when you're done."

Something was wrong. Sage Lightfoot was such an honest man that she could tell by the look in his eyes when he was holding out on her.

Anger. That's what she saw there. He couldn't hide it, no matter how hard he tried. And if Sage was the one who'd captured the mare, he would definitely have been the one to bring her in, out of pure pride. Whatever had kept him was serious. His excuse of getting "hung up" on something else made no sense. From the window over the kitchen sink she could see every man as he rode in, and Joe Cable wasn't back yet. Whatever kept him must have to do with the reason Julio came back with Storm and the mare.

Maggie stirred a mixture of rabbit meat, potatoes, and onions, then sliced some of the freshly baked bread. A hot bath and a full stomach should help calm Sage down. What bothered her the most was that when he was angry, Sage always told her why. The only reason he wouldn't was if he thought it would upset her, and knowing that *did* upset her.

You can't hide it for long, Sage, she thought. *You wear your emotions right smack on your sleeve for everyone to see. Once that stomach is full and you're relaxed and I look you straight in the eyes, you'll tell me the truth.*

She turned to look out the kitchen window again, straining to see the black mare Julio had brought back. She was corralled alone in a distant pen, and she was beautiful. There was no way Sage would normally have let someone else bring her in.

Seven

MAGGIE WAITED AS SAGE CLIMBED INTO BED, WEARING only his long johns. He settled his head against his pillow, and Maggie snuggled against him, laying her head on his shoulder. "You smell so good," she told him. "All soapy clean."

A deep chuckle came from somewhere in Sage's throat. "Only a woman would talk that way. And 'soapy clean' isn't a term you can use very often for me—not after working with horses all day."

"You always smell good. Even without a bath you smell like leather and the outdoors."

"And one thing I love about you, Maggie girl, is you always try to look on the bright side of things." He turned on his side and stroked her hair. "I love when your hair is brushed out long. I wish you'd wear it like this all the time."

"Well, it's not very practical for chores," Maggie answered. "I can just see it dangling into chicken droppings when I go into the henhouse to gather eggs, or see it catching fire when I bend over the hearth."

"And you wouldn't have to worry about that if you used that fancy cookstove we have for cooking."

Maggie kissed his neck. "I know. But then I have to mess with dirty coal. I'm too used to using the fireplace. It's mostly Rosa who uses that stove. I'll admit it's handy for big gatherings where more than one oven is needed, but I'm fine with the fireplace for everyday cooking. Besides, you bought that stove for Joanna. Using it reminds me of your perfect, beautiful, prim and proper first wife."

Sage pulled her closer, kissing her forehead. "You know better than to think like that. Joanna was selfish, and worthless as a ranch wife." He grinned. "But I love your jealousy. It makes you more passionate when we make love." He met her mouth in a gentle kiss.

Maggie studied his dark eyes. He'd hardly spoken all through supper, other than general conversation about the hunt for mustangs. *You should have heard the cuss words that came out of Bill's mouth when one of the mares bit him on the ass,* he'd joked. Maggie could tell he was trying to keep things light and not talk about what was really bothering him.

"Sage." Maggie ran her fingers into his shoulder-length hair. "What happened out there today?"

He closed his eyes and leaned down to kiss her throat. "It doesn't matter."

"Yes, it does, because it affected your mood. I've seen you really, really angry, Sage Lightfoot, and it usually ends up with someone wishing they hadn't crossed you. And I know when you're trying to bury that anger. You could have a heart attack or something."

That brought out a loud laugh. "You do know how to help get rid of my anger," he told her. "Jesus, Maggie, I'm only thirty, and as far as I know, I'm healthy as a horse."

"I don't care. I don't remember where I heard it, but someone once told me it's bad for a man to hold in his anger. You, Mr. Lightfoot, usually let it all out in an explosion of yelling or fists or sometimes a gun. Maybe you already did that. I'm asking you again what happened out there. And if you don't tell me, I will go sleep in a different bedroom."

He ran a big but gentle hand over her belly, feeling the swell of her baby, then on over her full breasts, squeezing lightly, then to her neck, the side of her face. He leaned in and kissed her again. "Do you really think I'd *let* you out of this bed?"

Maggie sighed in resignation. "Well, I guess you *are* a little stronger than I am."

"A *little*?"

"But then all I would have to do is ask, and you'd never force me to stay here."

Sage grinned. "Pretty sure of that, aren't you?"

Maggie kissed his chest. "Yes. Now, tell me what happened."

Sage sobered, studying her eyes. "I love you," he told her. "And I love this baby. Understand?"

Maggie frowned with concern. "Yes. Did someone *say* something about the baby?"

Sage pressed her closer. "How in hell can you know me so well when we've not even been together five months yet?"

His remark reminded Maggie of that very fact. Only in this wild, untamed country could two people still practically strangers in some ways find intimacy and love and marriage so quickly. That's what caused some of her doubts and anxiety. This had all happened so fast. Maybe *too* fast. Would Sage later regret his decision of taking her for his wife so soon after they met?

"I'm learning that when a woman truly loves a man, she can sense his every mood," she answered, "and you're a man who can't hide his feelings. I think that's why men who challenge you usually back off. They can tell you mean exactly what you say, and they're afraid to test you." Maggie kissed his neck. "The short time we've been together scares me sometimes, Sage. I can tell that today's events had something to do with me, or you wouldn't be so hesitant to tell me. And I'm scared that whatever went on might have made you regret marrying me so quick."

Sage frowned and shook his head. "That will never

happen." He stroked her cheek with the back of his fingers. "Look, someone came visiting that I didn't care for. That's all."

"Oh, there was much more to it than that. You didn't *shoot* someone, did you?"

"No, but I dearly wanted to." Sage kissed her hair and kept her close. "You listen to me, Maggie. About this nonsense of us knowing each other only a few months… Don't forget that I knew Joanna since we were teenagers, but it turned out I didn't know her at all, so you stop worrying about the short time we've been together. I suspected deep inside that Joanna wasn't right for me, but I went against my better judgment *because* I had known her so long.

"The way we were torn apart when her family sent her away, and then seeing her again years later and hearing her lies about how much she loved me… I guess I just wanted to believe it all. I felt responsible to make her happy and to give her everything she wanted. But all those years meant nothing to her." He sighed deeply and turned onto his back, keeping an arm around Maggie so she rested into his shoulder. "It's all different with you. You're the kind of woman a man doesn't *need* to know for a long time. Sometimes you just know when you've found the right woman. I love you, and I'm happier than I've ever been in my life, so I don't want to hear that you doubt that…ever. Understand?"

"I think so. What I don't understand is what all this has to do with whatever happened today."

Sage laid there quietly. Maggie could tell he didn't want to say whatever it was she was forcing him to tell her. "Sage?"

With a deep sigh, he finally answered. "I'd roped that black mare you saw Julio ride in with. I was bringing her in when I saw someone heading for the house in a fancy buggy. Julio and Joe were accompanying them. I rode down to catch up with them, and that's when I gave Julio the mare and had him bring it in with Storm."

Maggie ran a hand over his bare chest. "Who was in the buggy?"

Sage stroked her hair for several more silent seconds before answering. "A preacher, and a bitch of an old woman named Elvira Hart." He paused. "She was Jimmy Hart's mother," he finally admitted.

Maggie stiffened and pulled away slightly. "Dear Lord! What on earth did she want?"

Sage studied her lovingly and forced her back into his embrace. He told her what happened, leaving out the worst of the names Mrs. Hart and the reverend had called Maggie. Maggie couldn't help the tears that filled her eyes. She tried to rise.

"You stay right where you are." Sage told her. "And you listen to *me*. We've been over this too many times, Maggie. I didn't want to tell you because it would remind you of those men and what happened. I sent her and that damn preacher out of Paradise Valley. I had Joe go with them to make sure they were well off the ranch."

"They said all that in front of Joe?"

"Don't be worrying about that. Joe loves you practically as much as I do. *All* the men love you, and just like me, they think of the kid in your belly as *mine*! It doesn't matter to any of them if it's true or not, and there isn't a man on this ranch who would ever speak otherwise. Joe doesn't think a damn thing about what those people said, and all the men know what happened to you and why you went with me to find those men. I wanted you to go so you could identify them…"

Maggie felt his whole body tense up.

"…before I blew them away!" he finished.

"But Mrs. Hart heard all this from someone who was up at Hole-in-the-Wall, which means all those men were talking about it."

"Let them talk! Jesus, Maggie, we'll never see any of them again."

A tear slipped down one side of Maggie's face. "But I'm your *wife*. You have to hate knowing men are talking that way about me."

"Not any of *my* men, and that's all that matters. Joe won't say one word about what was said out there, and I made sure that so-called preacher knows not to come back here. If Mrs. Hart wasn't a woman, I would have landed my fist in her face for the things she said. And if I didn't love you and this baby like I do, why would I defend you so fiercely? Tell me you trust in my love, Maggie Lightfoot."

Maggie moved her head back and looked into his eyes…eyes that could not lie.

"I trust you."

"Do you trust that I love that baby you're carrying?"

"Yes. I just wish so much it was yours, Sage."

"It *is* mine, just like the babies after this one will *sure* as hell be mine. I'm claiming this baby as my own, Maggie, not just in words, but legally. He or she will carry my name, and that's the end of it. No more discussion."

Maggie leaned closer again and reached around his neck. "I love you so much."

"Yeah?" Sage moved on top of her. "How about showing me? Nothing calms me down more than being right here in this bed with you, especially when you're underneath me."

Maggie smiled through tears as he met her mouth in a deep kiss that told her everything she needed to know. She closed her eyes as Sage moved down and nuzzled her breasts through her soft flannel gown. He moved a hand up her leg, pushing her gown up as he did so. Maggie rose up and let him pull off her drawers.

"You okay with this?" he asked. "You worked hard today, too. And now I've upset you."

"I'm just upset over you having to hear what those people said," Maggie answered softly.

Sage grinned, sadness in his eyes at the same time. "I'm part Indian, Maggie girl, found abandoned in the desert and raised in a wealthy neighborhood in San Francisco by Christian people who I thought loved me… till I dared to kiss a white girl. I've seen and heard it all. Nothing could hurt me more than what my own family and that white girl did to me." He kissed her eyes. "I know the goodness of your soul, so nothing anyone says about you can hurt me. The only thing that could hurt me is not having you in this bed every night. And I'll always protect you against people like the ones I chased out of here today."

Another deep kiss erased it all as Sage again worked his magic, making Maggie ache to take this man who always filled her every need.

For the next stretch of time, she was lost beneath him, breathing in his kisses while he pushed deep inside her, branding her, sealing their love. She pressed her fingers against hard muscle, bracing herself by keeping hold of his arms while she offered herself to him like a royal feast to a king. This man had risked his life hunting down those who had so horribly abused her, and now he loved her and had accepted the child she carried.

She realized he well understood how it felt to be adopted and supposedly loved, only to be cruelly rejected later. The sudden revelation of why he'd vowed to love her baby as his own brought a wave of relief to her heart. Sage Lightfoot would never treat a child he accepted as his own the way he'd been treated. He'd been rejected because of his Indian blood. He would never allow her baby to be rejected for not knowing who his father was. He wouldn't allow her baby to suffer that kind of hurt.

The sheets were damp by the time they finished. Sage

stayed on top of her, grasping her face in his hands. "I almost forgot… I have a wedding gift for you."

"A *wedding* gift? Sage, you didn't need—"

"Yes, I did. We had such a simple wedding, with a preacher coming here and just the men to witness."

"But living here in Paradise Valley is the most wonderful gift a woman could ask for, especially in this big, beautiful home you built. I'm perfectly happy, Sage. *You* are my wedding gift. Your love—accepting my baby."

He kissed her lightly. "A woman should have a true wedding gift. I got you something I know a woman like you will appreciate much more than a house and fancy dishes, something that's truly all your own."

Maggie smiled, getting excited. She scooted back and pulled a sheet over herself. "What is it?"

"Did you like the looks of that black mare Julio brought in?"

"Oh, she's beautiful! She's one of the prettiest—" Maggie hesitated. "The *mare*?"

"The mare. I'll have Roland break her in for you, but I can already tell it won't take much. She seems pretty gentle, even in her wild state."

"Oh, Sage, thank you! It's a wonderful gift! As soon as we get up in the morning, I want to go out and see her!"

"Just be careful. You *are* carrying, you know. I don't want you on that horse until Roland has her fully broken in. Even then, I want him or me to be there the first time you ride her. Promise me that. I know how stubborn you can be."

"I promise."

Sage pulled her close again. "I'll let you name that mare whatever you want…the baby, too." He furrowed his brow. "When in hell do you think you are you due, anyway? I just realized we haven't talked about that."

Maggie counted—hating the fact that she had to start

with that awful night in mid-May. She hoped once she held the baby in her arms, it would help her forget the horror of how he or she was conceived. "Sometime in February," she answered.

"Dead of winter," Sage said, looking concerned. "Heavy snows could make it hard to get a doctor here. I think I'll hire the doctor from Cheyenne to come here to live the first or second week of February, just to be sure someone is here who knows what the hell he's doing if anything goes wrong." He pushed a red curl behind her ear. "I don't want to lose the best thing that ever happened to me."

"I'm healthy, far as I know. My first birth went just fine, in spite of how young I was." Maggie's heart tightened at the memory of burying her little one-year-old daughter, who'd died from fever back in Missouri. It seemed as though she'd already lived a lifetime in the twenty years she'd lived. At fifteen she'd practically been sold by her drunken father to James, a neighbor who wanted a wife. James was decent to her, but not a truly loving husband. She was pregnant by sixteen, had her baby at seventeen, and buried her at eighteen. When she was nineteen, James, fifteen years older than her, decided to head west. She turned twenty before they reached Wyoming, where outlaws murdered James and had their way with her.

Then Sage came along and taught her what being loved was supposed to be like. Yes, it was possible to fall in love at first sight...first touch. "This baby has to live, Sage. I don't know what I'll do if I have to bury another child."

"That's why I intend to make sure a doctor is here." He kissed her forehead. "And not just for the baby's sake, but for you, too. I don't know what I would do without you in my life." Another kiss. "But let's not think about bad things, Maggie. Let's think about that mare and what you want to name her."

Maggie smiled. "I have to see her close up first." She ran a hand over his arm and shoulder. "Thank you for wanting to give me a gift, Sage. It only shows how much you love me."

"You bet." He settled beside her and pulled the covers over them. Even in summer, the evenings were cool in high Wyoming country.

Big country, Maggie thought. *Filled with big men that fit it.* She couldn't be more in love, and she loved every man on this ranch for accepting and loving her as Sage Lightfoot's woman. She loved that term—not just his wife, but his woman. The man owned her, heart and soul…and body, and that was fine with her. But oh, how it hurt to think of the things that preacher and the woman with him had said to Sage, and in front of Joe.

"I'm so sorry, Sage, for what those people said."

He settled next to her. "Don't be sorry, Maggie—not ever. Sorry is for people who've done something wrong, and you've never done anything wrong in your whole life. Men like me, *we're* the ones who have things to be sorry for. I don't deserve something as loving and generous as you. The only thing more perfect is that baby you're carrying." He ran a hand over her belly again. "This kid had no choice in how he or she was conceived, so no man has a right to ever judge or refuse to love him or her, especially not that snooty Mrs. Hart or that hypocrite of a preacher who drove her out here. I'd better not see either of them again. I might not be able to hold my temper the next time."

Eight

MAGGIE RODE PATCHES AT A GENTLE PACE. SHE'D NEVER loved a horse more than this beautiful gift from Sage. The white patches on the mare's chest and forehead and around all four hooves had prompted the name Maggie gave her. The markings were distinctive and different from any of the other horses. Even the horse's black tail and mane were mixed with white hairs.

Bill Summers rode beside her as she pulled Patches to a halt at the top of what she liked to call Lavender Hill. Intensely purple flowers bloomed in the valley below during late summer and early fall. "It feels good to get out of the house and enjoy some cool, fresh air," Maggie told Bill. "It won't be long before the snows will be too deep to do this—at least that's what Sage tells me. This will be my first Wyoming winter."

Bill pushed his hat back a little. "Well, ma'am, you'll be surprised how cold it gets here, and how deep the snow piles up. I can already smell snow in the air, and you've seen new snow on the tops of the mountains. We always worry about how many cattle we'll lose to blizzards and such. You'll be *wantin'* to stay in that house for sure. We generally tie ropes from the house to the barns and from the barns to the bunkhouse—somethin' we can hang on to and find our way when it's snowin' so hard you can hardly see your hand in front of you. Men have been known to die out here just a few feet from their own front door. You can get confused real fast in a heavy snowstorm."

"My goodness!" Maggie sighed. "I expect by then I'll stay inside anyway because of the baby." She studied the valley below. "But for today I'll enjoy this crisp, clear weather. I just wish things weren't still so dry."

"Well, ma'am, it's like that all over—everything dry as a bone. We actually pray we *do* get some snow cover soon. We moved the cattle to that northeast quarter about three weeks ago. It's all that's left. We saw signs of other cattle grazin' there, but we didn't catch who was doin' it. Sage is there now, figurin' how we can protect what's there."

"It cost Sage a lot of money to order all those extra oats and hay from Omaha," Maggie told him. "I feel so sorry for him."

Bill, a rather short, slender man who'd never revealed anything about his past, glanced over at her. "I expect if he hadn't given another wad of money to that damned first wife of his last spring, it wouldn't be so bad. You sure are a breath of fresh air compared to her."

Maggie smiled and pulled her sheepskin-lined corduroy jacket closer around her neck. "Thank you, Bill." She took another deep breath and realized Bill was right. She, too, smelled snow in the air. Such weather came early to the mountains and high plains.

"You sure you should be out here ridin' all over the place in your condition?" Bill asked with a frown.

Maggie shifted in her saddle. She didn't want to let on to a ranch hand, but she seemed to be bigger than she should be for only about five months along. She'd thrown a blanket over her lap and legs for warmth and to help hide her belly. "I'm fine. Men seem to think a woman should go to bed as soon as she knows she's carrying and stay there until the baby comes. It's not like that at all. I can do all the things I normally do." She smiled at Bill. "Thank you for taking your day off to ride with me. I just had to get out and enjoy this beautiful valley before the snow gets too deep for it."

"You know Sage. If I let you ride off alone, he'd tan my hide."

"And I wouldn't hear the end of it for a week," Maggie added. "But I can handle Sage Lightfoot."

They both laughed. "That's more than any of *us* can do," Bill told her. He lit a thin cigar. "I'm told Indian women do all their hard chores right up till the baby comes, then just stop and have the kid and keep goin'."

Maggie sniffed. "I've already had one child, Bill Summers, and I can assure you, no woman just sits down and has a baby and then keeps going. It's a pain no man would ever understand, but it's soon forgotten once a woman holds that baby in her arms."

Bill looked away.

"Shit," Maggie heard him mutter. "I'm sorry, Maggie. I didn't mean to remind you of the one you lost."

"It's okay. I'll soon have another baby to hold."

They both remained quiet for several minutes. Maggie wondered if Bill was thinking about how this baby came to be. None of the men ever mentioned it, and none seemed bothered by it. "I think I'll make another big batch of that chicken stew you and the men like," she told Bill. "A great big pot that Julio can take to the bunkhouse for all of you to share."

Bill chuckled. "You know how much we all like that stew. It's a lot of work makin' so much of it, though. Maybe you shouldn't bother."

"It's not so bad. I'll just need Rosa to help me boil and pluck the chickens and peel the potatoes. Once everything is in the pot, there isn't much to do but keep stirring it and let it simmer for a good, long time. The longer it cooks, the better it tastes." Maggie noticed Bill stiffen a little as he gazed across the valley. "What is it?" she asked.

"'Couple of the men are comin', ridin' hard." He looked at her with a frown. "You stay right here, no matter what, understand?"

"Yes, but—"

"Right here. No hard ridin'. Somethin' happens to you, I'm responsible, and I don't intend to answer to Sage for it."

"I'll stay."

"I'm ridin' out there to see what's goin' on. They wouldn't be ridin' that hard unless there was some kind of trouble."

Bill charged down the massive hill into the valley to meet up with the riders. Maggie could hear shouting but not exact words. All three men galloped their horses up the hill then, and Maggie watched Julio and Hank charge past her toward the ranch, both glancing at her with deep concern on their faces. Bill returned and took hold of Patches's bridle.

"What are you doing?" Maggie asked.

"Makin' sure you go right to the house and stay there," he answered. "There's some shootin' goin' on out at the northeast quarter—drovers from the Grayson ranch tryin' to horn in on Sage's grass."

Maggie gasped. "But Sage is out there!"

"That's right—and some of the other men. Don't you be worryin' about Sage. You know damn well he can take care of himself. Julio and Hank came back to get more men and ammunition."

"But I should help! I could ride out there—"

"No, you *couldn't*! And I ain't lettin' you ride hard back to the house neither. We'll just keep it at a gentle lope. Hank and Julio can take care of things."

"But Sage could get hurt!"

"I'm takin' you back to the house where you'll wait for him, you hear me? *Wait* for him! If he *were* to get hurt, the last thing he would need is to worry about you, or for you to lose that kid and bleed to death or somethin'. He'd need you to be okay so's to help him heal, understand? That's the best way to help him."

"Are you saying he's already hurt?"

Bill didn't answer.

"Bill Summers, tell me the *truth*!"

"Just a flesh wound," Bill said. "Sage stayed out there, which means he's good enough to keep up the fight. They're just goin' for more men."

"I should be with him!"

"Do what I said, Maggie. Sage is proud of how you handle life out here. Obeyin' his orders is part of it. *Not* obeyin' could make things worse, so you wait at the house."

"Oh dear God!" Maggie fought to see through the tears that welled in her eyes. She clung to the saddle horn as Bill led Patches at a very gentle run back to the ranch house, which took a good half hour. Hank and Julio and both of Julio's sons and two other men passed them on the way, all well armed and all riding hard.

Maggie's heart fell at the sight. Sage was hurt! Men were shooting at each other!

They reached the house, and Bill helped Maggie dismount. "You do like I said and wait here," he told her. He remounted his own horse and charged away.

Maggie watched after him. *Please let Sage be all right*, she prayed.

Rosa came out of the house and walked up to her, moving an arm around Maggie's back. "Julio told me," she said. "They will be fine, *señora*. Sage has good men with him, and he is a man who can handle himself."

"I can't lose him, Rosa."

"You won't." She urged Maggie toward the front door. "Come inside. Sit down and rest while you wait. Sage will need you when he comes back."

"Rosa, if I wasn't carrying, I'd be riding out there with the rest of them."

"And your husband knows this, *señora*. And just knowing it is all he needs. But in your condition, he would be very worried if you did not stay here and wait. Do not forget your promises. Waiting here will help him more than trying to go there and help. *This* is how you can help him."

Maggie followed Rosa inside and reluctantly sat down to wait...and pray.

Nine

MAGGIE RUSHED OUT THE DOOR WHEN HANK, JOE, AND Sage rode in after dark. She noticed Sage stumble a little after dismounting. "You're hurt!" she called out, coming down the steps to take his arm.

"Just grazed my side," Sage answered. "Lost some blood is all."

"*All?* A wound is a wound, Sage Lightfoot! It could get infected. What happened out there?"

Sage grimaced as he climbed the steps to the veranda. "I'm okay, Maggie, but there is a lot of blood on my shirt and pants." He pushed her a little to the side. "I don't want to get blood on your dress."

It wasn't until they walked inside the house where there was more light that Maggie saw what he was talking about. "My God, Sage, are you still bleeding?"

"I don't think so."

"Rosa, bring some hot water and some towels!" Maggie told the woman. "Sage, come down to the bedroom and get those filthy clothes off. And don't worry about my dress. We have to get that wound cleaned up and bandaged." She walked down the hall with him. Once they reached the bedroom, she helped him get everything off other than his long johns. She winced at the sight of a deep, ugly cut across Sage's left side. "My God, Sage, a few inches to the left and you'd be suffering a gut wound—the worst kind!"

"Well, that didn't happen, so you keep calm. I don't want you losing that baby over this."

Maggie quickly spread an old blanket over the bed quilt so Sage could lie down without getting blood on the covers. Rosa rushed in with a flask of whiskey in one hand, a pot of hot water in the other, and two towels over her arm. She handed Maggie the whiskey, then poured the hot water into a washbowl on a stand near the bed. She set down the pot and handed the towels to Maggie. "*Señor* Lightfoot, is my Julio all right? And my sons?" she asked.

Sage put a hand over his eyes. "They are all fine, Rosa. I think things are settled, but I left Julio and a few other men out there to keep an eye on that section for a couple more days. Your sons are on their way back."

Rosa heaved a sigh of relief as Maggie wet a small towel and began washing dried blood from around Sage's wound. She fought tears at the thought that he could have been killed today. "This should be stitched up," she told him. "It's awfully deep."

"The bleeding has already slowed, and I've seen stitches lead to infection too many times. Just pour some whiskey on it and wrap it tight."

"Rosa, go get some gauze," Maggie told the woman. "*Sí.*"

Rosa hurried out, and Maggie paused to study Sage's angry eyes. "What is going on?" she asked. "What happened out there?"

Sage sighed deeply. "Just get this wound cleaned up." He reached out and lightly touched her fast-growing belly. "How's that baby doing?"

"He or she is doing just fine." Maggie frowned and began washing off more blood. "And you deliberately avoided my question. I asked you what happened. Why did you answer by asking how the baby is?"

Sage glanced at Rosa, who came in just then with the gauze. "Rosa, you should leave for a bit. I need to talk to Maggie. Thanks for bringing everything."

"*Sí, señor.*" Rosa put a hand on Maggie's shoulder. "If you need my help, I will be in the kitchen."

"Thank you, Rosa."

Frowning with concern, Rosa left, closing the door behind her.

Maggie washed off more blood, then moved to sit on the edge of the bed beside Sage. She took a clean towel and pressed it against the wound. "Tell me what's going on while I make sure all the bleeding has stopped," she told Sage.

He studied her lovingly, obviously hesitant to say what he had to say. "Give me a swallow of that whiskey first. I could use it, and not just for the pain."

Frowning, Maggie took the flask from where she'd laid it on the bed and handed it to Sage. He uncorked it and raised it, taking a long swallow. "Pour some of this on the wound, and then press the towel against it again."

Maggie obeyed, feeling sorry for the way Sage jumped and grunted when the alcohol stung his side. She recorked the flask and pressed the towel against the wound again. "Why do I have a feeling this involves me and the baby again?" she asked Sage.

He grasped her arm gently. "I'm afraid it does."

Maggie closed her eyes and looked away.

"Don't do that, Maggie. It's just a fact." He squeezed her arm. "Remember those visitors who came by about a month ago—that damn preacher and that woman who claimed to be Jimmy Hart's mother? You never met them, but I told you about them the day I caught that mare."

Maggie met his gaze. "This has something to do with *them*?"

Sage pushed some of his hair off his forehead. "Yeah. They came back, this time with men they claimed to be the law—said that northeast section didn't belong to me legally, and they were going to open it to public grazing because of the drought. They even brought some of Grayson's men and cattle with them to let them graze on my land."

Maggie hesitated. "Can they *do* that?"

"Not in *my* book! And not when they are lying. It took me about one minute to figure it was a hoax. I recognized one of the men with them. He was there that day—up at Hole-in-the-Wall the day I rescued you. I don't even know his name. I just remembered his face, and I put it all together real quick. He's apparently the one who told Elvira Hart about the shoot-out that day—and that I killed Jimmy up there. He saw an opportunity for him and his outlaw friends to steal some of my cattle off that section and claim the *law* was removing them. Elvira Hart must have cooked up the whole plan to try to bully me into bringing her to see you—said the law would leave me alone if I cooperated."

Maggie closed her eyes and struggled against tears. "Oh, Sage, all this has caused you so much trouble."

"You and the baby are innocent of *all* of this, Maggie, and you are my *wife*. You aren't the one causing trouble. It's other people, people who think that just because of how this baby was conceived, you should be willing to give it away with no feelings. They don't know how we both feel."

Maggie couldn't stop the tear that slipped down her cheek. "I don't understand how a man like you, who is so rough around the edges and built this place with a bunch of outlaws...I mean...men who don't generally care much about babies and all that...how you can take in this baby like it's your own."

"Stop it, Maggie!" Sage moved a little and winced with pain again. "We've had this conversation more than once. You know damn well I'll never let another kid feel like I did when I was made an outcast. And *this* baby belongs to the woman I *love*, which makes it even more important that I protect it...*and* protect Paradise Valley. Our baby will bear my name and everything that goes with it."

Maggie smiled through her tears. *Our baby.* What better assurance could she have that Sage would always think of him or her as his own? She pulled the towel away to see the blood from the wound was coagulating. "Sit up so I can wrap this wound," she told him as she got off the bed and reached out to help him up.

Sage obeyed, grimacing with pain as he managed to move to the edge of the bed. "Who shot you?" Maggie asked. "Was anyone else hurt?"

"No one but the man I'd recognized from Hole-in-the-Wall. He's dead."

Maggie met his gaze. "You?"

Sage grunted as he scooted farther back on the bed. "Who else? Once he knew I recognized him, he went for his gun. I pulled mine and shot him, but he shot wildly as he went down, and it grazed my side. One other man started to draw, but Joe Cable warned him it was a bad idea. My men had them surrounded, rifles and guns drawn. And in spite of being shot, I landed into that preacher, something I sorely wanted to do the first time he came around. I guess my anger overcame my concern over being shot and the fact I was bleeding like a stuck pig. It felt damn good to land a fist into that sonofabitch's face! He didn't look too good by the time I finished with him, and I told that fake bastard that if he comes back here one more time, he'll be having throat trouble, if you know what I mean."

"Sage, you'd *hang* him?"

Her husband shrugged. "Doesn't hurt for him to *think* I would. Besides, I'm not so sure Joe and Bill and the rest of the men wouldn't do it *for* me. They're as mad as I was. That preacher and Mrs. Hart and the others left, taking the first man's dead body with them. I still don't know what his name was."

Maggie shook her head. Only Sage Lightfoot would shoot a man he didn't even know and not regret it one bit. She faced him, terrified this might not be the end of it. "What if they do come back, Sage, with the *law* next time?"

Sage reached up and made her sit down beside him. "Don't be worrying about that. They won't come back, especially not with the law. They *broke* the law, coming here and thinking they'd let those outlaws steal my cattle! If they truly *could* have come lawfully, they would have done it. That means they couldn't find one damn judge or lawman who agreed with them. Mrs. Hart can't win because no one can prove *who* that baby's father is. Only God knows. Besides, that preacher is too afraid I really *will* hang him."

Maggie quickly wiped at unwanted tears. Sage put an arm around her and kissed her hair. "It's over, Maggie. All there is to do now is settle in for the winter and wait for our son or daughter to be born."

Maggie nodded, hoping he was right. "Just promise me there won't be any more fighting and killing over this innocent child," she asked.

She met Sage's gaze and saw only love and promises. "There won't. I put an end to it today."

Maggie wondered if she could love anything more than she loved Sage Lightfoot right now. He'd actually risked his life to protect her and her baby's reputations. "Thank you, Sage."

He closed his eyes and shook his head. "Maggie, a woman doesn't thank her husband and the father of her child for risking his life to protect them. That's what any man would do."

Maggie felt a weight lifted from her shoulders, realizing she'd been looking at this man all wrong, still thinking he'd leave her if he got tired of all of this. "You really do love me," she said.

"Don't tell me you still doubt that."

"Not really. I guess I was just afraid to fully accept the fact that you love me, because I know it was hard at first for you to accept the baby, Sage. You can't deny it. That day at Hole-in-the-Wall, I saw the look in your eyes when that man who had hold of me yelled out that I was carrying. I saw that little bit of surprise and doubt in your eyes. You knew you loved me, but could you accept my child? I don't blame you for wondering. But after today…what you did out there…" Maggie rose and grabbed the roll of gauze from the side table. "I'd better get that wound wrapped."

She reached around Sage's middle and started winding gauze around the wound. She met his gaze as she did so, and Sage caught her face between his big hands. "It's over, Maggie. They won't be back. And when word gets out, no one within a hundred miles of here will ever doubt who that baby belongs to. No one is going to come snooping around here when the snows come. And once this baby is born, it will have my name. When you hold that kid in your arms, and I see the love in your eyes, I won't have any trouble loving it, too."

Maggie finished wrapping the wound and tied off the gauze. She leaned forward and kissed Sage's cheek, not minding the dust and sweat there. She was just glad he was alive.

When she'd first met Sage Lightfoot, she'd thought he was a man not to be trusted, a man who wanted only what most men wanted. But he'd turned out to be so much more. He was all bluster and sometimes meanness and anger on the outside, but on the inside, he was that little boy who just wanted to be loved. The family who'd found and raised him had hurt him in the worst way. He wanted love and a family as much as any man would, in spite of the rugged, angry, uncaring demeanor he showed on the outside. Sage Lightfoot had a heart as big as the Wyoming landscape, and she wanted this baby as much for Sage as for herself.

Ten

MAGGIE STOOD BACK AND EXAMINED THE HUGE PINE TREE Joe and Hank and Julio had brought in from the foothills. Building a wooden stand for it and getting the tree into the house and safely secured had been a real comedy of errors, along with arguments and not a few cuss words. Once the tree was up, the men apologized for their impatience.

It was a magnificent tree, perfect for her and Sage's first Christmas together. She and Rosa popped corn half the day just to make a long enough string to wrap around the tree fully, and Maggie spent the rest of the day tying colorful ribbons on the ends of branches. She'd made a straw doll with a red velvet dress to secure at the top of the tree for an angel. She thought how, if she had another baby girl, she would save the doll for her and tell her it came from Mommy and Daddy's first Christmas. Just the thought of it made her love Sage beyond what she thought possible.

She'd decided not to use any candles on the tree, too fearful of fire. Memories of the horrible fires that visited the ranch just two months ago were still too fresh. It wasn't long after the incident over the northeast section that it happened...a freak thunderstorm at a time when there should have been snow. Lightning had set fire to what was left of the dry grass, and high winds caused the fire to move so fast that there was nothing the men could do to stop it. The raging inferno took thousands of acres as it crept closer to the homestead, then consumed a supply shed and one of the barns, along with the precious winter feed stored inside. A sudden downpour helped save everything else, including the log home Maggie so loved.

Sage had been right. It was going to be a long, cold winter, and now an expensive one. He'd been forced to order more winter feed from Omaha, as well as lumber and supplies to replace the barn, which the men managed to frantically build before the dead of winter. It needed some finishing touches inside, but that would have to wait until spring. Sage needed a place to keep his best horses out of the worst of the wind and cold, including her own beautiful Patches.

The rest of the horses were doubled up in the remaining barn, making it a lot more work keeping stalls cleaned out and feed in the feeding troughs. On the days the winds calmed and sunshine warmed things at least a little, the horses were let out for exercise, but now the winds were high and the snows deep. The only good thing about the extra-deep snow was that it meant a lot of moisture in the ground for the next year. And sometimes a burn-off brought better, thicker grass the next spring. In that respect, the fires could be considered a blessing. Sage's biggest worry now was if he'd be able to get a doctor from Cheyenne to the homestead by the end of January, in time for the baby's birth.

Maggie touched her belly, which still seemed too big for being only seven months along. Was she going to have twins? Her belly was getting so big that she feared this child would come sooner than she thought, and if it came too soon, it would die.

She shook away the thought. It was better to think about the beautiful Christmas tree and the red shirt she was making for Sage. He would look so handsome in red. He looked good in *anything*, but red accented his dark hair and eyes and skin. She couldn't imagine why Joanna would throw away such a good man for a fancier life in a big city like San Francisco.

Some people just aren't cut out for this life, Sage had told her once. She supposed he was right. It was a hard life, that was sure, but it was worth it just to be in Sage Lightfoot's arms at night, where she felt only safety and love. Thank God his wound had healed with no problems. There was nothing to do now but look forward to spring and better grass...and the baby.

Sage came inside, interrupting her thoughts as he quickly closed the door against a savage wind. He stomped the snow from his boots and pants onto a braided rug at the door, then knocked more snow off his hat and hung it on a hook before removing his heavy sheepskin jacket.

"It's damn wicked out there," he told her, walking over to the fireplace and rubbing his hands together. "I don't want you going out at all—not for anything, understand? Not in your condition."

"I won't." Maggie walked closer. "You actually have little pieces of ice stuck to the ends of your hair," she told him, smiling as she reached up to pull some of it off.

"I *feel* like ice all over," he answered, rubbing vigorously at his arms. "I'm really worried about the cattle scattered all over the place out there."

"You're the one who said we'd be fine even if we lose several head," she answered.

"I know what I said, but I still hate the thought of it."

"We'll be all right. I have to believe that." Maggie leaned in to hug him. "And you know I'll do everything I can to help in the spring."

"You'll be tending a new baby in the spring." Sage stroked her hair. "How are you? I need to send for that doctor, even if he has to literally live with us for the next month or two. I'll pay him whatever it takes."

"Sage Lightfoot, you're half-broke already." Maggie looked up at him. "And there *are* other people who might need him. I'll be fine. Having babies is a natural thing. Rosa can help me. And for heaven's sake, how many calves and colts have you helped birth? Most of them come all on their own, and mother and baby are just fine."

Sage gently pushed her away. "And sometimes things don't go right, and mother and baby are *not* okay. And losing a cow or a mare is a whole different thing from losing the woman I love." He bent down to kiss her forehead.

Maggie sobered. "Sage, promise me you will take this child in and love it even if something happens to me. No matter how he or she was conceived, they will be a part of me."

"Let's hope that's something we won't have to worry about. Either way, you know I will, and I'm a man of my word."

"And that's one of the things I love about you."

He embraced her fully. "Right now I'm getting a little anxious to be able to hold you extra close again. Something keeps getting in the way."

Maggie smiled and hugged him again as best she could. "I want the same thing, but for now you will have to settle for a slightly fatter wife. I hate to think of how big I'll be after another six or eight weeks."

"Fat is fine with me as long as you're healthy." Sage kissed her hair again. "And what do I smell? Is that pie baking?"

Maggie pulled away and took his hand. "Yes. Rosa and I will be baking pies for the next two days so we have plenty for the men on Christmas Day. We're also going to cook all three wild turkeys the men shot for Christmas dinner."

"I'm hungry already, but for now I'll take the venison stew. Cold weather brings out a man's appetite."

"Then come to the table, and I'll fix you a big bowl of stew and slice some fresh bread."

They walked to the kitchen end of the great room,

and Maggie took a heavy china bowl from the cupboard and a dipper from a hook at the side of the fireplace hearth. She swung the chimney crane toward her and dipped some stew into the bowl.

"Still refusing to use the coal stove, I see," Sage teased.

Maggie set the bowl of stew in front of him. "I'll use the coal stove Christmas Eve and Christmas Day because of all the cooking Rosa and I will be doing."

"Just don't *over*do it. The men will understand if you can't fix an entire dinner. Turkey and pie will please them just fine."

"I'll be careful." Maggie turned to spoon some stew into a bowl for herself, then hesitated when a deep, gnawing pain gripped her abdomen. *No!* she thought. *It can't be!* She paused, waiting for the pain to go away, then turned and sat down with the bowl of stew. She reached out to grasp a loaf of bread and was starting to slice a piece for Sage when it hit her again. She couldn't help wincing and letting out a little gasp from the deep pain, unable to hide it from Sage.

Sage set down his spoon. "Maggie? What is it?"

"I think just some kind of indigestion." She picked up her spoon. "Eat your stew."

"Don't lie to me. Was that a contraction?"

"No. That would be impossible this soon."

The pain came again, and she dropped her spoon into the bowl and grasped her belly. "No!"

"Shit!" Sage got up from his chair and walked around to hers. "Please don't tell me the baby is coming."

"I don't... Maybe..." Another pain hit her then. "It can't be!" she said before bending over a little. "Sage, it's too soon! Oh God! Too soon! The baby will die!"

Sage quickly picked her up. "I'm taking you to the bedroom, and I'll go get Rosa."

"Sage, it can't be the baby yet! I can't be more than seven months along!"

"I damn well know that! And I planned on having a doctor here for this!" He carried her down the hallway and laid her on their bed. "Hang on, Maggie girl. I'll get Rosa!"

"No! Stay with me!"

"Maggie, this isn't something I can do. You need Rosa. I'll be back as fast as I can get here!"

"Use the ropes, Sage! Use the ropes! Don't get lost out there!"

"I won't," he called out as he hurried down the hallway. "Stay in that bed!"

Maggie heard him shuffling around to get his boots and coat back on, heard the door open and slam shut, then lay there listening to the howling wind outside. "God, not now!" she groaned. The day after tomorrow would be Christmas. Would Sage spend it trying to figure out how to bury their baby in the cold, frozen ground?

Another gripping pain clawed at her insides. There was no doubt about it. This baby was coming, early or not. And it couldn't possibly survive.

Eleven

SAGE PACED...AND PACED. HE SMOKED ONE CIGARETTE after another.

"Somehow this will work out, Sage." Joe Cable sat at the kitchen table drinking coffee, grimacing when another scream came from the bedroom.

"I don't see how," Sage lamented. He sat down in his big, leather chair, running a hand through his hair. "The baby is too early, and if there are other complications, I could lose Maggie and the baby *both*. I don't think Rosa will know what to do. Maggie needs a *doctor*!" He put his head in his hands. "Jesus, Joe, what will I do if this goes bad? Maggie is the best thing that ever happened to me." He looked at Joe, unable to hide the tears in his eyes. "God wouldn't punish a woman like Maggie, would He?"

Joe rose to pour himself yet another cup of coffee. "Punish her for what?" He stoked the fire under another hanging pot of hot water in case Rosa might need more.

"I don't know. I mean, she couldn't help what happened to her. That damn bitch who came here with that preacher tried to say what happened to her was a sin, even on Maggie's part. That preacher said the baby is cursed."

"That's just that sonofabitch runnin' off at the mouth, and you know it. Jesus, Sage, you aren't a man to listen to that kind of horseshit. Neither one of us knows much about God and religion and all that, but I think I know enough that God would never cause bad things to happen to somebody like Maggie, and He would never see what happened to her as a sin. Ain't a man on this place who would see it that way."

Another scream, followed almost immediately by yet another. Maggie's labor had been going on for twelve hours—since supper last night. Sage's now-cold and uneaten bowl of stew still sat on the table. Outside, the wind howled.

"Maggie said her first birth went fine," Sage told Joe. "She didn't think she'd have any problems." He rose and started pacing again. "Goddamn weather!" he grumbled. "There isn't a man on this ranch who wouldn't be risking his life going after the doctor in this shit. It's impossible to get through to Cheyenne." He walked to a front window, unable to even see any of the outbuildings because of blowing snow. "There must be drifts six feet deep out there. God only knows how many cattle we'll lose on top of everything else." He ran a hand over his eyes. "I don't even care. I'd give *all* of them up if it meant saving that baby."

Joe nodded. "I'm with you there. You want some coffee, Sage?"

Sage shook his head. "No. I just want this to be over with."

Joe sat back down and lit a cigarette. "Ain't it a bitch? All the men on this ranch who are able to chase down wild horses and hog-tie a damn bull…ram a brand on a cow's rump, break a buckin' bronc, and yes, even help deliver calves that are turned around wrong, shoot wild game, wrestle with barbed wire, live outside in the worst weather—you name it, we've all done it. But ain't none of us knows what to do about a woman givin' birth or about a tiny little baby that ain't full growed. I've never felt so damn helpless in my life."

"Neither have I." Sage turned from the window. "I've shot men down and rustled cattle. When I was a kid, I was wounded at Sand Creek, one of the worst massacres of Indians in history—lived through that—got kicked out on my own in my teens, ran with the worst of them on the Outlaw Trail, outlaws and whores alike. I never dreamed I'd have a ranch like this someday…or care about a woman like I do now."

Another scream.

Sage closed his eyes. "Jesus. I'm sure Rosa knows about giving birth, but I doubt she knows what to do with a premature baby."

"You already said that, Sage. Rosa is a good woman, and she's had four kids, two of them still little, so she fresh understands what Maggie is goin' through, and you know she'll do all she can."

Sage sighed deeply, pacing again. "I know that, but she only knows about births that go right. When I took Rosa more towels a few hours ago, the ones she handed me were so damn bloody, it scared the hell out of me. Maggie could bleed to death. Anything could happen!"

"And you have to stop imagining the worst, Sage. Maggie is little, but she's a real strong woman."

Sage sat down and put his head in his hands again. "I'm not sure she's strong enough to have to bury another child. That would take all the spirit out of her."

Things seemed to grow quiet then…too quiet. Sage raised his head and looked at Joe. The two men exchanged what they knew was the same thought. Had Sage lost both his wife *and* the baby?

They finally heard a baby's cry—a surprisingly strong one. Sage jumped up from the chair and walked down the hallway. "Rosa?"

"*Un momento, señor,*" the woman shouted from the bedroom.

There came several long, agonizing minutes of waiting. Sage could hear the women's muffled voices, but he couldn't make out what they were saying. The baby continued crying at the top of its lungs.

Sage looked at Joe, who'd followed him to the door. "That doesn't sound like any premature baby, does it?" Sage asked. "I mean, shouldn't it be kind of a weak cry? It's two months early. That little kid shouldn't even be alive."

Joe grinned. "One thing is sure. That ain't no ailin' baby, Sage. Soon as you find out what's goin' on in there, let me know and I'll go out to the bunkhouse and give the men the news."

"Just be sure to hang on to the guide rope. I don't want to lose my best man."

"You won't." Joe grinned wider. "And I won't tell the rest of the men you called me your *best* man. I don't want to get in no fist fight once I get over there."

The two men shared a grin, but then Sage sobered, looking toward the door again. "Rosa! What's going on? I hear the baby, but is Maggie all right?"

"She is fine, *señor*. I need a little more time. Joe can go tell the men that the baby and the mother are both well. We just need a few more minutes."

Sage looked at Joe again, frowning. "I can't believe it."

"Well, whatever happened in there, it sounds like everything is okay." Joe put out his hand. "Congratulations, Boss."

They shook hands, and Joe headed down the hallway, leaving a stunned Sage waiting at the bedroom door. Joe suddenly stopped and looked back. "Jesus, Sage, ask Rosa what she had. Is it a boy, or a girl?"

Sage glanced at the bedroom door. "I'm so surprised by the sound of that crying that I didn't even think to ask." He ran a hand through his hair again and then knocked on the door. "Rosa! What is it? Boy or girl?" He actually heard light laughter from both women.

"It is a boy, *señor*," Rosa answered. "And wait until you see him!"

Sage glanced at Joe.

"I heard," Joe told him. "I'll go tell the men." He walked into the great room to put on his boots and coat.

Sage heard more groans from the bedroom. "Rosa, what's wrong? Can I come in? I'm going crazy out here."

"Just a few more minutes. I have to make sure to get all the afterbirth so there is no infection, *señor*. Be patient."

Sage heard the front door close as Joe left, and suddenly he felt more alone than he ever had in his life. He sighed and paced up and down the hallway until finally the bedroom door opened and Rosa came out carrying a basket full of bloody towels. "She is all cleaned up now, *señor*. You can see Maggie and the baby." She actually giggled. "You will be surprised!" She hurried past him, and Sage stood there a moment, not sure what to expect.

"Sage, you can come in now," Maggie called from the bedroom.

Not sure what to expect because of Rosa's remark, Sage hurried inside. Maggie lay there with her tumble of red hair spread out on the pillow. She looked pale and tired, her hair damp, circles under her eyes…and small… She looked so small. But she was smiling…a bigger smile than he'd ever seen on her face.

"Come and look!" she told him.

Sage walked closer, cautiously peering at the newborn boy as Maggie pulled a blanket away from him. The child's fists flailed in the air, looking whole and strong. His crying finally turned to tiny squeals, and Sage thought he looked much too big to be premature.

"Sage, you have a son," Maggie told him. "A fully matured baby boy, strong as any!"

Frowning, Sage just stood there staring.

"Sage, it's okay. The baby is fine…and *I'm* fine."

Sage shook his head. "I…don't understand." He grabbed a wooden chair from nearby and set it beside the bed.

Maggie moved the baby slightly and pulled the blanket farther off the boy so Sage could see everything was there—fingers and toes, tender, still-red skin. "Rosa and I need to wash him off better," she told Sage. "Rosa is preparing a fresh pan of hot water and a clean washrag for that."

Sage leaned closer, reaching out to gently stroke the baby's thick, black hair. "I still don't understand, Maggie. He's so big."

"I know!" Maggie leaned close to kiss the baby's cheek. "Sage, he's a full-term baby!"

Sage frowned. "But when you first realized you were carrying, you said—"

"I know, Sage. I said that because of the hard journey, James and I were both too tired to be intimate. But when I saw my baby, I realized he had to be full-term. And then I remembered…you know…about two months *before* the night those men attacked us, James and I *did* have relations. I remember because I didn't feel well, but James was… He'd been drinking. After that, I had my time of month, lighter than usual but still there, so I thought it meant I couldn't possibly be carrying when those men attacked me." She reached out and touched Sage's hand.

"I guess I don't know my own body as good as I thought. Apparently, I got fooled. I must have already been carrying when those men came along. How I managed to hang on to the baby through all that—and then all that happened after that when you found me, and we went after those men—I'll never know." Maggie couldn't help her tears of joy as she kissed her baby's head. "To me, it's a Christmas miracle, Sage. That's the only explanation for why he's so big and strong, like James. Now that awful woman can't come along and try to take him away."

Sage touched the baby's fist as Maggie covered him

again. "I would never have let that happen, Maggie." The child grabbed hold of Sage's finger and hung on tight. "He's strong. That's for sure."

Maggie smiled, her whole face lighting up. "God has given us a real miracle, Sage. Tomorrow is Christmas, and look at the wonderful Christmas present He has given us!" Maggie kissed the baby again. "He's so beautiful and perfect. And I'm so happy, for *both* of us." She grasped Sage's hand. "I want to name him James, if that's all right with you. James Tucker Lightfoot."

Sage nodded. "That's fine with me. It's only right to name him after the man who fathered him. I'm glad you're *my* wife now, but it's too bad your husband never lived to know he had a son."

"I think he does know. He wasn't the greatest husband, but he wasn't a bad man, either, Sage. I think he's in heaven, and he knows about his son."

Sage nodded. "I hope you're right." He moved to sit on the edge of the bed, leaning over mother and baby. "I'm feeling proud but a little intimidated," he told Maggie. "I'm actually a father now."

"And you'll be the best father this little guy could ask for. I know you will, Sage. And we'll have more—lots more—enough ranch hands that you won't even have to hire extra help."

"Whoa! Slow down there, woman." Sage studied her tired eyes and pushed more of her damp hair away from her face. "Let's not move too fast. I want you strong and healthy before you go through this again. And I'm going to see about bringing in another woman to help you for a while. Rosa has a husband and family of her own to tend to."

"I can manage."

"No, ma'am. I won't allow you to do too much. I intend to spoil you rotten. You deserve it." He leaned close and kissed her lightly. "You sure you're all right?

Don't lie to me about anything, Maggie. I couldn't bear to lose you now."

"I'm okay. Just a little weak. And I'm hungry. Have Rosa heat up that stew neither one of us got to eat." She moved away from the baby a little more. "Here. You hold him."

Sage shook his head. "I wouldn't know how."

"Then get used to it, Sage Lightfoot. Hold your son."

Sage smiled and gently moved his hands under the baby. He deftly lifted the boy, holding him in his lap for a moment. The baby kicked, and his mouth turned into a little *o* as he stared at the big man holding him.

"Merry Christmas," Maggie told him.

Sage smiled and laid the boy back beside his mother. He studied Maggie for a moment, smiling. "And Merry Christmas to you. I love you, Maggie."

"And I love you." She put a hand on his arm. "Things will be good now. These heavy winter snows will mean thick, tall spring grass and swollen streams—plenty of water. You and the men can get new barns built, and little James will grow and get stronger. We're going to have a good life here, Sage. I'm the happiest I've been in my whole life. What woman could ask for more than a healthy son, a handsome, loving husband, and to live on the most beautiful piece of property in Wyoming? Tomorrow is Christmas…Christmas in Paradise!"

Sage put a big hand to the side of her face and kissed her again. "*You're* my paradise, Maggie. Coming across you out on the plains last spring was the best thing that ever happened to me." He stood up and moved around to the other side of the bed, then carefully lay down beside her, pulling both Maggie and the baby into his arms.

Outside, the wind continued to howl and moan over Paradise Valley. Tomorrow was Christmas. It would most certainly be a white one. More than that, it would be their first together.

In spite of the howling blizzard winds, they could hear the faint sound of shouts of celebration coming from the bunkhouse. James Lightfoot had finally arrived, and he wasn't just Sage and Maggie's son. He belonged to Paradise Valley, and to every man who helped run it.

About the Author

Award-winning novelist Rosanne Bittner is highly acclaimed for her thrilling love stories and historical authenticity. Her epic romances span the West—from Canada to Mexico, Missouri to California—and are often based on personal visits to each setting. She lives in Michigan with her husband, Larry, and near her two sons, Brock and Brian, and three grandsons, Brennan, Connor, and Blake. You can learn much more about Rosanne and her books through her website at rosannebittner.com and her blog at rosannebittner.blogspot.com. Be sure to visit Rosanne on Facebook and Twitter!

Author's Note

This Christmas story stems from my novel, Paradise Valley *(Sourcebooks, 2013). I wrote* Paradise Valley *with no outline and no plan of what would happen in the story or how it would end. I simply sat down and started the book with Maggie alone on the Wyoming plains, digging a grave for her husband, who'd been murdered by outlaws. I hope you will read* Paradise Valley *and learn how the beautiful love story of Maggie and Sage Lightfoot began, and what they went through before ending up devoted to each other by the end of the book.*

Because Paradise Valley *ended with Maggie carrying a baby whose father was unknown, I felt my readers deserved to know what happened with that baby. That in turn led to writing this Christmas story and finding a "Christmas miracle" ending for Sage and Maggie.*

As of the publication of Christmas in Paradise, *I have been writing thirty-six years, with sixty-nine books in print. Visit my website (rosannebittner.com) to learn about more books to come and for my latest news! I am also on Facebook, Goodreads, Twitter, and Instagram, and I have a blog at rosannebittner.blogspot.com.*

Merry Christmas—every Christmas—to my readers!

A CHRISTMAS
WEDDING

———— •••• ————

Linda Broday

One

A BRUTAL NORTH WIND HOWLED AND SWIRLED DOWN THE side of the canyon into the town of Hope's Crossing as if determined to crush the smallest sign of holiday cheer.

The storm seemed to take special aim at Rebel Avery's little sod house. Inside, Rebel pulled her shawl closer, huddling in the soft, woolen folds. Chewing on her bottom lip, she shoved the curtain aside to peer out. No snow yet.

No one was moving in the town that barely boasted sixty residents, give or take a few. They'd probably all hunkered down to ride out the November squall that had swooped upon them with little warning. School had been dismissed early, so her children, Jenny and Ely, were safe and warm with her.

A sniffle diverted her attention to another matter, this one of greater worry. Rebel went for another wet cloth to replace the one already in use. She took the bloody one from Ely's nose and gently pressed the clean one into place and sat down next to him.

"What did you and Billy Truman fight about this time? Mr. Denver said he's had enough, and so have I." The schoolmaster had mentioned taking drastic measures if the boys didn't settle their differences. Whatever that meant, it sounded ominous. Maybe kick Ely and Billy out of school?

Ely shoved back a hank of sandy hair and gave an

angry huff. "He called me a dummard and said I don't have the brains God gave an ant. He's right. I cain't cipher, cain't hardly read, cain't do anything."

"Well, you're not stupid." Rebel lifted his drooping chin with a finger. "Some things may come harder for you, but you'll get them with work. I promise. We'll do it together."

She pushed back her chair and started to rise.

"Billy called me and Jenny throwaways," Ely said softly, sniffling. "Said we don't have no ma or pa, and nobody wants us."

The words stung Rebel, and she could only imagine what they did to a sensitive nine-year-old like Ely. She was tempted to go have a talk with Billy's mother, but Martha Truman was in no shape for that, huge as she was with another baby—her eleventh child. All to date were rambunctious boys called the Truman Ten and were known to strike terror into not only children, but adults.

Rebel sat slowly, her anger rising. "*I* want you. And I'm not giving you up."

Four-year-old Jenny rose from the rug where she was playing with her rag doll. She propped one elbow on the table edge. "I want you, too, Ely. Billy is so mean."

"Stay out of this, Jenny." Ely jerked the wet cloth from his nose. "This is my fight."

"Ely! Be nice to your sister. Neither of you needs to fight." Rebel wished she knew the source of all this anger. Ely had been slow to trust and open up—understandable given where they'd been—but things were escalating instead of fading and had spilled over to Jenny.

"Sorry." Ely glanced up with a glum face. "That wasn't all Billy said, Miss Rebel."

Jenny crawled into Rebel's lap and snuggled close. Rebel took Ely's hand. "Tell me everything. It helps to get it out."

The boy stared into the flames of the small fireplace. The fire cracked and popped in the quiet.

Finally, he shifted his gaze back to Rebel. His voice

trembled. "Billy said Mr. Travis is a no-account killer, and the judge might hang him. They won't, will they?"

Fear shredded the last of Rebel's calm. "No, honey."

But she wasn't so sure. A bounty hunter had ridden into the town seven months ago and captured Travis Lassiter. Rebel had only gotten one letter from him in all this time. Travis had spoken of his love for her and the children but said to put him out of their lives and go on. Months without another letter made her fear that he was dead.

How could she stop wishing for the arms of the man she loved?

She cried herself to sleep each night, thinking of their plans to marry. Travis had seemed eager to help raise Jenny and Ely after the town founder, Clay Colby and his wife Tally, had rescued them along with a group of women from the Creedmore Lunatic Asylum, and now here she was, a single mother for the foreseeable future.

Like most of the men in Hope's Crossing, Travis was an outlaw. Actually, Rebel had been told the town was a hideout before Clay, Travis, and the other men stopped their criminal enterprises and decided to become respectable. She hadn't asked what Travis had done in the past.

His hope for the future was what interested her.

He was a fine man with a good heart, and she didn't care what anyone said.

Billy Truman had poked Ely with the sharpest stick he could find and dug around in the boy's already fertile ground of insecurity. The wind battered the house like Billy's fists had battered Ely. There was little justice in the world for small children who had no one but a former saloon girl to care for them.

"I know what we should do," Rebel declared. "Let's bake some tea cookies. And while we do, I'll tell you about my favorite Christmas."

"I like cookies." Jenny patted Rebel's face. "What's Christmas?"

The question stunned Rebel. It seemed inconceivable that the girl wouldn't know the magic of Christmas. But then, she and Ely had been locked away for two years where no holidays existed, inside the walls of Creedmore Lunatic Asylum.

"It's the happiest time of the whole year, and it'll be here in a little over four weeks." Rebel struggled to put on a happy face for the siblings when she felt anything but.

"I don't believe in Christmas!" Ely scooted back his chair and stalked to the ladder that led to the tiny loft where he slept.

Rebel sighed, her heart heavy, wishing she knew how to soothe him. But she didn't know any magic words to make him forget the darkness he and his sister had endured. She couldn't even put happiness in her own heart, so why did she think she could fix Ely?

They needed something, anything, to lift their sagging spirits.

With Jenny's eager help, Rebel stirred up the cookie dough and told the girl of the time when she'd lived with her parents in Missouri—the year she learned about Advent and the calendar that marked off the special days leading up to it.

The time before she'd learned the darkness inside one man's heart.

She'd been seven then and safe from the evil of the world.

"My mother would start baking three weeks beforehand, and the house would smell like cinnamon and nutmeg. We'd hang a pretty wreath of pine boughs on the door, and my father would butcher a hog for Christmas Day. Excitement filled the air, and I'd pray to get a new doll. My brothers would hope for a new sled or skates." Rebel rolled out the cookie dough and let memories of home sweep her away. "On Christmas Eve, Father would chop down a tree, and we'd have such fun decorating it."

"Can we have a tree?" Jenny asked.

The question jarred Rebel. She'd given no thought to a tree. Even if she had, where would she get one? Trees were scarce in this part of Texas. But she didn't hesitate. "Yes, we'll have a tree." Of some sort. Even if she had to decorate a tumbleweed.

An image of a homemade wooden ornament with the name *Abigail* carved into it flashed into her head. Rebel's chest squeezed. Abigail Marie Quinn didn't fit inside dingy, smoke-filled saloons and back rooms.

Remembering the holiday awakened such a longing inside Rebel that she could scarcely stand it. Oh, to go back to that innocent time!

The small treats each day.

The Advent candle they lit each Sunday before Christmas.

The excitement of making gifts and hiding them under the tree.

She angrily dashed away her tears. There was no going back. Those days were dead, gone, and buried. Best to not think about them.

Jenny patted her arm. "Why are you sad?"

Rebel forced a smile. "I'm sad that our cookies can't feed all the children. But we're going to enjoy these, and maybe next time we can bake more. Now let's get them in the oven."

While the cookies baked, Jenny went off to play with her doll, and Rebel's thoughts turned back to Travis. Oh, to feel his strength, his arms around her, his lips on hers!

After all her years working in saloons, she didn't have much to offer any man, but Travis never saw her as less. He said he'd be proud to take her just as she was. You couldn't ask any more from a man than that.

The relentless wind battered the small sod house harder and drew Rebel's concern. She'd seen it blow like this before but not in the winter. She prayed it would stop soon.

A sudden gust hurled something against the window, shattering it, and glass flew inside. Rebel jumped and gave a loud cry. Jenny screamed and hurtled from her bed. Rebel glanced around for a piece of wood to cover the window but saw nothing that would work.

Ely appeared at her elbow, staring at the glass. "What are we going to do?"

Good question. She put her arm around Jenny, who clung to her dress as helplessness washed over her. For a moment Rebel wanted to throw up her hands and scream. But she couldn't afford to give in to desperation.

She straightened her shoulders and grabbed a wool coat and scarf. "I don't exactly know, Ely." She'd have to figure it out.

Afraid the cookies would burn, she tried to pull them from the oven, but in her haste, dropped the pan on the floor. She was drowning in problems.

Sucking in a bracing breath to keep from bursting into tears in front of the children, she bent and scooped the hot dough back onto the pan. "I'm going out to try to fix the window. Both of you stay inside where it's warm." She pulled on a pair of gloves.

"I can help." Ely opened the door for her.

"Not this time. Please, I don't want to argue. Stay inside."

The wind pushed her back, but Rebel gathered her strength and moved into the storm, pulling the door shut behind her. It was all she could do to stay upright.

Outside, she noticed Clay Colby walking toward her, his dog Bullet at his side. She yelled into the gale, but there was no way he could hear over the storm.

As he got closer, she got his attention. "My window broke. Can you help me?"

"Sure. I'll have to go for some wood," he yelled over the wind. "Go back inside."

When he and the dog returned, she hurried out to

hold the piece in place while Clay hammered and soon had the broken pane covered. Bullet and Scout, a hound that belonged to the Bowdres, scampered around them, drawing a smile. Oh, to be so carefree.

"Thank you, Clay. I don't know what I would've done."

"Don't mention it. In this town, we all help each other." Clay smiled and patted her shoulder. "You're not alone, Rebel."

Then why did it feel that way? "Care to come inside for a cup of coffee?"

"No, thanks. I was on my way to meet the stage. It's late. Come on, Bullet! Let's go."

They said goodbye, and Rebel returned to the warmth of the house.

Jenny came running, her sobs cutting into Rebel. "What's wrong?"

"My dolly's broken. Everything's broken." She thrust her doll's arm into Rebel's hand and ran crying to her bed.

Something had to be done to lift their spirits. To lose one of their own so abruptly with hardly a word since had plunged them into despair, leaving everyone wondering who would be next. A posse of lawmen could swoop in at any time. Christmas should be full of hope and optimism, not this cloud of worry. The memories of past Christmases gave Rebel an idea. She pulled her coat back around herself and retied her woolen scarf. "I won't be long. Stay inside and, Ely, watch your sister."

Rebel fought the wind all the way to the Bowdre house.

Nora opened the door, wiping her hands on her apron. "Rebel, come inside before you freeze to death."

"Thank you. This storm's something. It broke one of my windows." Rebel untied her scarf. "Clay put a piece of wood over it for now. But everything is wrong."

"What do you mean—everything?" Nora led her into the small parlor.

"Ely has all this anger inside. He fought with Billy Truman again today. Came home with a bloody nose." Rebel sighed and sank into a chair. "And Jenny's doll's arm came off, and she sobbed that everything was broken. It does seem to be the case. Then the pan of cookies I was baking ended up on the floor."

The beauty and warmth of the home surrounded her. Nora was a mail-order bride and had come to marry Jack Bowdre seven months ago. She was a plump, no-nonsense woman who jumped in with both feet to make the house a home—from the pretty rose wallpaper to the pictures of the surrounding landscape to the artful curtains on the windows. No sod here. This home was made of wood.

"Some days are like that." The teakettle whistled, and Nora rose. "How about a nice cup of tea? That will make everything better."

"That sounds lovely."

Nora left the room and soon returned with a tray laden with tea, cups, and little cookies. They sat with steaming cups in front of the fire while baby Willow, a child the couple had found next to her dead mother and taken in, crawled around them. Rebel liked the woman who sat across from her and her boundless love for not only Willow, but also a nine-year-old orphan named Sawyer whom Nora and Jack had rescued from a mean outlaw. The woman had the kind of strength Rebel wished for. Nothing seemed to get her friend down. Not even snakes scared her. She'd picked one up that had curled on her husband's chest while he was unconscious. If not for that, he'd have died. The curvy, blond-haired woman had courage in spades.

Rebel eyed the cookies. "Would you mind if I take one of these to the children?"

"Not at all. Take three or four apiece," Nora urged. "I'll wrap them up when we're done."

"Thanks." Rebel took a sip of tea. "I have an idea, and I want to see what you think of it."

"If it's a way to dispel this gloom and make everyone get along, I'm all for it."

"I want to have an Advent calendar—only the whole town will be the calendar."

Two

"OH, YES! I ALWAYS LOVED THE CHEER ADVENT ADDED to my holidays when I was a child." Nora's brown eyes twinkled. "Tell me more."

"We'll have to somehow fashion a large calendar with a little door on each day." Rebel took a sip of tea, her mind whirling.

Nora bit into a cookie. "We'll make it out of sturdy wood so this infernal wind won't blow it over. Yes, that would be best."

Baby Willow tugged on Rebel's skirt and she picked her up, closing her arms around the child, inhaling the sweet scent. With effort, she brought her thoughts back to her plan. "Inside each little door will be a name for the person who has treats that day. The children will go to that house."

"Yes! Yes! And on each Sunday leading up to Christmas, we'll light one of the four Advent candles."

"Great idea. I wonder if Skeet Malloy will make us a holder. That blacksmith can make anything. When this storm passes, I'll ask him. We can get candles from the mercantile." Rebel carefully untangled black strands of her hair from Willow's little hand. "We'll get the children involved. I know, maybe we'll have them draw for a chance to be the one who lights the candle in church each Sunday."

"If they fight or misbehave, they'll have their name removed." Nora reached for the teapot. "More, Rebel?"

"Yes, thank you." Rebel moved her cup closer.

"Unless I miss my guess, this will teach them to get along better, and I think it'll fill the town with the Christmas spirit."

"Absolutely."

They sipped their tea and discussed the finer details. The more Rebel thought about the idea, the more excited she got. In a way, this would re-create her old Christmases before her life turned dark and ugly.

"Have you seen Martha Truman lately?" Nora asked. "I swear, if that woman gets any bigger, I think she might pop."

"I'm rooting for a girl for her this time." Nora sighed. "She has to break the cycle somehow. Ten boys is enough. And boys don't help their mother like girls do. Lord knows, she can use all the help she can get with Sid gone so much."

"The other day, Martha confided that she'll just cry if she has another boy." Rebel could understand that. She was ready to cry at the drop of a hat anyway.

"It seems like Sid should find a different job besides driving the stagecoach. He needs to be home to corral those rambunctious boys."

"I agree." Rebel's thoughts turned back to Ely's most recent trouble. "Nora, I don't know what to do about Ely. He has all this anger inside, and it seems to get more explosive each day. He thinks Travis hung the moon, and when Billy called Travis a no-account, it sent him over the edge."

"I can imagine. Someone needs to take Billy to task."

"The boy is taking advantage of Martha's inability to ride herd over her brood. If we can give all the children projects to accomplish in addition to the Advent calendar, it might help tamp down this urge to be spiteful."

"What are you thinking about? Drawing, coloring, making something simple?"

"That's it! They can make each other a gift. There

are fourteen children in all. That would be fourteen gifts they each have to make." Rebel smiled. "I'd say that will keep them too busy to jump on each other with their fists."

"The boys' gifts will be easy, but what can they make Violet and Jenny?" Nora asked.

"We should pull in Tally and the other women for input. How about in the morning once we get the kids to school?" The baby squirmed, and Rebel sat her on the rug. "But one idea would be making Jenny and Violet each an ornament for the tree."

The door opened, and Jack stomped in. Nora went to greet her husband. Rebel always thought Jack was a handsome man with his long brown hair and gray eyes. But what impressed her most was that he treated people with kindness and respect and never looked down on her for having worked in a saloon. Willow squealed and crawled as fast as she could to him. Jack scooped the baby up in his big hands and nuzzled her neck, which made her giggle.

He glanced up and smiled. "Miss Rebel, good to see you."

"You too, Jack."

Nora helped him with his coat and hat, and then he came into the warm parlor. "A bad storm out there, but I got the cattle fed and broke the ice on the water."

"Sweetheart, Rebel has come up with a brilliant idea." Nora sat down next to him on the sofa and told him about the Advent calendar.

"We're still working out the details," Rebel added.

"I love it." He untangled Willow's fingers from his mustache. "I never celebrated Advent when I was a boy, but I think it's a fine thing to teach these kids. I'll speak to Malloy and see if he can make a holder for the candles from his forge."

Excitement built inside Rebel. "Thank you, Jack.

We'll also need a large wooden calendar with a little door marking each day that's big enough for a tiny slip of paper."

Nora leaned forward, excited. "That sounds like something right up Tobias January's alley."

"He loves working with wood and is very good at it." Rebel loved the jolly old man with his snow-white beard. He and his wife, Belle, had brought Rebel to Hope's Crossing in their wagon and were like family to her. Both were getting up in years but were determined to do whatever they could to help out and never let age hold them back.

Jack nodded. "Tobias will do an excellent job."

Rebel stood. "I should get back to Jenny and Ely. Nora, will you open your home for a meeting in the morning? Mine is a bit small, but we can use it if need be."

"No, here's fine." Nora handed Rebel her coat, scarf, and gloves. "Be careful going home."

"I will." She kissed Nora's cheek. "Thanks for the tea and the ear."

Jack stood. "With luck, this storm will pass soon. Tomorrow should be better."

Which storm did he have on his mind? The one outside or the one inside?

"I hope so." Rebel drew her bottom lip into her mouth and asked the question that came so often to her lips. "Have you heard anything from Travis? I'm so worried."

"No, I'm sorry." Jack's gray eyes met hers. "I'm sure he's all right. Try to stay positive."

Rebel nodded and stepped out into the ferocious wind that cut through her clothes like a sharp knife. She pulled her coat closer around herself and kept a tight grip on her scarf. Bits of sleet stung her face and took her breath. She could barely see the tall windmill on the left through the haze. Gathering her strength, she aimed herself toward the sod house that crouched in a row with six others at the right of the line of four small businesses.

She'd barely made it six steps when the wind whipped her scarf off. Releasing one of the curses she rarely uttered since leaving the Cimarron saloon, Rebel chased after it, careful not to crumble Nora's cookies. She couldn't afford to lose a single thing. It took everything she had to provide for the children. Sobs burst from her mouth, and she stumbled, almost going to her knees.

She fell against the low fence around the church that doubled as a school. When she looked up, a tall man in a Stetson came toward her through the haze. Travis? Her heart leaped into her throat, and her pulse raced. Was it possible?

He reached for her, but before she took his hand, he vanished into the gray, swirling storm.

Thick despair choked her. On top of everything else, she was now seeing things.

Three

REBEL SWALLOWED HER DISAPPOINTMENT AND RUSHED inside her gloomy soddy, closing the door against the storm. She forced a cheery smile and hollered to the children. "I brought a treat for you while I cook supper."

Jenny came running. "Goody."

"Gingerbread or raisin?"

"Both."

It took all her willpower to deny those pleading eyes. "Sorry, just one for now. You can have more for dessert after supper." She glanced toward the ladder to the loft. "Ely, come down, please."

Jenny squinched her eyes together and sighed. "I'll take gingerbread."

Ely dragged himself down from the loft. "What?"

"Would you like one of Mrs. Bowdre's cookies?" His sullen eyes crushed her.

"They're delicious," Jenny mumbled around a full mouth.

"Not hungry." Ely turned away.

"Maybe later, then." Rebel put the remainder on a small plate. "Ely, would you like to read a story to your sister?"

"I guess."

The sod house was extra dark with the boarded-up window adding to the gloom smothering Rebel. The trick her eyes had played on her still shook her to the depths of her soul. He'd seemed so real she could smell the scent of leather and shaving soap. If only she could hear from him, get word of some kind to help her go on. Hearing nothing put all kinds of bad thoughts in her head—the kind that living with an outlaw often turned into reality.

She closed her eyes and let the memory of him sweep over her for a minute, then went about the business of preparing supper.

The children's silence and Travis's empty chair filled every corner and crevice of the house with loneliness.

Later, as Rebel sat by the fire sewing the arm back on Jenny's doll, a knock sounded on the door.

She wiped her hands on her apron and went to open it. Darkness had fallen, and Martha Truman leaned against the side of the door, breathing hard, her face red from the cold.

"Martha! What's wrong? Is it the baby?" Rebel ushered her inside, and Ely pushed a chair forward.

Martha's dark-brown strands hung down her face, and her amber eyes held worry. She brushed back the tangled mess and put a hand on her swollen belly, collapsing onto the seat of the chair with a big sigh. The dimples in her cheeks were nowhere to be seen. "It's not the baby. It's Henry. I can't find the boy anywhere. He didn't come home for supper, and I've been all over this town searching for him."

Rebel reached for her scarf and coat hanging on a nail next to the door. "Don't you worry, Martha. I'll round up some men to help search. You stay here and rest."

"He's my son. I should be out there with you," Martha protested.

"Please, let us do this one thing for you."

"All right. You're a good friend."

Ely and Jenny crowded around Rebel, their eyes big. "Ely, do you know where Henry might've gone?"

The Truman boy was three years older than Ely and the oldest of his brothers. Henry resented having to ride herd on his siblings and had been known to hide from his mother before.

"I saw him take off after school by himself," Ely mumbled.

Martha leaned closer. "Where?"

"Last I saw he was going out of town the back way."

Rebel's breath caught. The men had blasted the back entrance shut to make the town easier to defend. There was now only one way in and out. Each time the stagecoach came, the driver had to make a wide turnaround in the middle of the town and go back out the same way. Henry would've had to scale a pile of huge rocks and rubble that stood eight men high. Everyone knew the heap was unstable, and when it rained, huge rocks shifted and rolled down.

The rowdy twelve-year-old could be lying horribly injured. Or worse, he could be buried beneath the pile.

"Good Lord!" Martha's face drained of color. "I told him time and again to stay away from there. Oh dear!"

Rebel patted her hand. "We'll find him. Try to stay calm. I'm sure he'll be fine. Kids are tough." Especially Martha's. Again, Rebel wished Sid Truman would take the boys in hand. "When will Sid be home?"

"Not for a few days. The stage lines gave him the run down south. I sure do miss that man. Others shouldn't have to help. Our boys are Sid's and my responsibility." Martha sighed. "Speaking of, what did Billy and Ely fight about this time?"

Rebel lowered her voice. "We'll talk more later. I should get moving."

She put the scarf over her head, thrust her arms into the coat sleeves, and grabbed a wool blanket.

"You're easy to talk to, Rebel. Will you stand in for me and talk to Henry—if you find him?"

She'd made a living listening—and pretending. Lonely cowboys in the saloon needed someone to share their troubles with, and she'd discovered they often were willing to pay for a bit of softness. She was glad to put those skills to use with true friends and no longer have to pretend how she felt.

"He'll turn up soon. I just know it." But what kind of shape would he be in?

∽

Rebel lit a lantern and pounded on doors, ending up with six volunteers. The two dogs—Bullet and the hound Scout—seemed eager to climb. Jack held Scout firmly. The dog might prove her worth this night.

"Miss Rebel, why don't you go wait with Martha and keep her calm," Clay gently suggested. "Let us handle this."

"I appreciate your concern, but I have to go. Henry might need a soft touch, and I gave Martha my word I'd stand in for her."

"Then let's get to it." Ridge Steele, the town mayor, tugged a wool scarf tighter around his neck. "Henry won't survive long out here. Damn, it's colder than hell with the furnace out."

"I won't be surprised if he's lying hurt somewhere." Jack raised his lantern higher, pulling his coat tighter. His hound raised her head to bay. "Come on, Scout. Let's find Henry."

They hurried to the blocked back entrance they'd dynamited, calling out to Henry. They found the boy's satchel on some rocks. Rebel's stomach clenched, but she worked faster climbing the pile of boulders and rubble, conscious of more weather coming in, announced by the sleet in her face. She and the men kept calling out every so often but otherwise kept silent, moving upward, picking a path, careful not to fall to the bottom. The dogs stayed next to them. It was a painstaking chore, and Rebel kept thinking that it could be Ely out in the cold.

A sudden misstep sent her tumbling backward, and she landed hard on her arm. Pain shot through her, and she let out a cry, but even with frozen fingers, she didn't let go of the lantern. The pile of blasted rock was treacherous enough in the daytime but deadly at night.

"You all right, Rebel?" Jack called from behind.

"Yeah." She collected herself and resumed the climb. Time passed slowly in the frigid air, her breath fogging with each exhale.

A sudden weak cry reached her. "Stop. I think I hear something. Henry! Call out!"

"Over here." The boy's voice came from the right.

Jack let his hound go, and the dog picked her way over the rocks toward the sound.

"Henry, are you hurt?" Rebel called.

"Yes."

"We're coming!" She wished it wasn't forty to freezing and black as a witch's hat.

After climbing, sliding, and a great deal of cussing, they reached Henry. His leg was trapped by a large rock. Rebel wrapped the blanket around the boy. The hound licked his face with her long tongue.

"We need a lever. It's the only way to lift the boulder." Clay looked around at the pile of rocks.

There were no trees or hefty branches.

"Let's try to roll it off," Ridge suggested. "There are plenty of us."

"Guess we have no choice." Jack scanned the group and singled out the reverend. "Pastor Paul, why don't you go back and see if you can find a pole, in case we can't manage this."

"Good idea." The reverend offered a short prayer and turned back toward the town.

"Be careful," Clay warned.

The men strained and pushed, but the rock barely moved before falling right back into place, causing the kid more pain. Over and over, they gave it all they had—to no avail.

Rebel's hands, feet, and body froze in the cold wind. She tried to put the feeling from her mind and knelt next to Henry. Conversation might keep the boy from thinking how miserable he was. "You know, I ran away from home once. I got mad at my father for refusing to let me go to a party, so I thought I'd be by myself where there were no rules. But you know what?"

"What?"

"I never knew exactly how scary and dark the night could be. Or how warm my father's arms were. I found out how much he truly loved me. I think you will, too."

Then years later, she'd run away again—all the way to New Mexico Territory—and never saw her father again. Lessons she learned the hard way. But she didn't tell Martha's oldest any of this.

A lock of red hair blew in Henry's face, and he shoved it aside. "I just want to go home."

"You will soon. Is your leg hurting badly?"

"I think it froze. I can't feel it anymore."

That was probably fortunate, or he'd be in tremendous pain. Rebel kept her questions gentle. "Where were you going? What were you running from?"

"Just wanted to get away," Henry mumbled. "Needed quiet, someplace where I don't have to sit on top of one of my brothers."

"I understand that. Sometimes a body yearns to be alone, but you worried your poor mama."

"Sorry, I didn't mean to worry her. Guess she's mad."

"No, just terribly worried." Rebel rested a hand on Henry's shoulder. "She'll be relieved to have you safe."

"Reckon so." Henry wiped his nose on his sleeve. "I miss my pa. He's always gone."

"Yeah, I'm sure he misses you and your brothers, too."

"Then why don't he stay with us?"

"He has to work," Clay said quietly. "He's got a lot of mouths to feed."

"Yeah." Henry shivered in the wool blanket. "I just want to be a kid again, you know?"

Poor kid. It wasn't fair to have to be the man of the house at twelve.

The lantern showed Henry's pale face smudged with dirt and tears. His hair stood in spikes. "Why did you risk your lives to come save me when I've brought nothing but trouble?"

Rebel took his hand. "You and the rest of the children are our hope for the future of this town.

"We've all taken our lives down the wrong road," she added. "It's too late for many of us to turn things around, but you and the others are just starting. If this town survives, it will do so under your care, so we're going to work as hard as we can to protect and guide you."

"I never thought of things that way," Henry said, a smile transforming his face. "I'm going to try harder, and I'll make sure the others do, too."

"That'll be a start." Clay ruffled the boy's hair. "This land is changing, and we have to change with it. Like Rebel said, our time is about done, but yours is just beginning. Don't forget that."

Henry's smile widened. "I'm hope for the future."

"Yes, you are." Rebel put her arm around his shoulders. "Hang in there, Henry. Things are bound to get better." Jack rose and gave the boulder another try, only to have it fall back on the inch it gave.

Clay joined the other men and they huddled, blowing on their gloved hands, waiting.

Pastor Paul finally returned with a hefty six-foot pole. They wedged it beneath the rock, and each man put his full weight on the thick piece of wood that looked to be the tongue of a wagon. The boulder lifted just enough for Henry to yank his leg out.

Screams came next as blood began to flow back into his crushed appendage. He lay sobbing and shuddering on the rubble.

Ridge and Jack brought their lanterns closer so Clay could check for broken bones. "Don't feel a fracture."

"See if you can put your weight on it," Rebel urged. But the minute Henry did, he gave a sharp cry and would've fallen if they hadn't held him upright. "We'll have to take turns carrying him."

The trip down was agonizingly slow, but they finally reached the bottom. A crowd had gathered, word having spread.

Martha rushed forward. "Henry!"

"I'm fine, Mama," the boy protested, glancing around sheepishly. It was clear he didn't want to be seen as a mama's boy. He clutched the blanket tighter. "Thanks for keeping me company, Miss Rebel."

"I'm glad I could. Think about what we said." Happy she could help, Rebel turned toward home and a warm fire.

Four

THE BOWDRE PARLOR WAS A HOTBED OF NOISE AND activity when Rebel and Jenny arrived for the meeting the next morning. She went straight to Martha and asked about Henry.

"His leg was broken, and Doc Mary says he may limp the rest of his life." Martha had bags under her eyes, and Rebel knew the reason why.

"He's lucky the ordeal didn't kill him."

Martha gave her a sad smile. "I'm sorry you had to go out in that storm, but Henry was very grateful and talks about your kindness."

"Think nothing of it, Martha. I'm happy to help anytime you need it."

"Funny thing. I don't know what you and the men said to Henry on that pile of blasted rocks, but he's changed."

"How so?"

"He lined the boys up, looked at them real stern, and said he didn't want any more trouble out of them. If they gave him grief, he'd set them straight in no time."

Would wonders never cease! It seemed Henry had turned over a new leaf, and it was long past due. Rebel found a seat near where Jenny was playing with Nora's Willow and Tally's baby, Dillon, a six-month-old darling.

As wife of the town founder, Tally Colby took charge. "Thank you all for coming. We owe Rebel a debt of gratitude for her brilliant idea for the Advent celebration. Hope's Crossing needs something like this."

Everyone started talking at once, their eyes on Rebel.

"I haven't celebrated Advent in the last ten years." Belle January slid her hand inside Tobias's, and their gazes met.

Rebel glanced down at Jenny, on the floor playing with Willow. "It's been longer than that for me, Belle. I was just a child."

"All right, we have a lot to discuss." Tally glanced at a sheet of paper. "Tobias, since you'll be making the wooden calendar, tell us what you'll need and how long it might take to build. It needs to be finished by Monday. Advent officially begins this Sunday with the lighting of the first of four candles."

Tobias stood, his long, white beard flowing down his chest. Although he had to be over seventy, his eyes twinkled like a young boy's. Rebel could see his delight. "I'm honored. Advent always used to be an important part of the holidays for me and Belle. We have plenty of wood left over from the various buildings, so that won't be a problem. I'll start on it today. Making all the little doors will take the most time." He held up a drawing. "Pass this around, and tell me where I need to make changes."

After everyone in attendance had seen the sketch, Tally glanced around the room. "Does anyone have anything to say?"

Martha Truman struggled to her feet with considerable effort, wiping away tears. "My boys have never celebrated Advent, and I think us doing so will make a difference in their lives. They need to know that Christmas is about more than one day and why. I know they've been unruly, and I apologize. Especially to Rebel. Billy has been unkind to Ely, but I pray this will make him consider his actions."

Rebel stood. "As I pray it does for Ely too, Martha. That's one reason I thought of this."

"Amen," Tally murmured.

"If no one has any suggestions for me, I'll get busy." Tobias put his hat on. "I need every minute between now and Monday."

"Thank you, Tobias." Tally turned to the rest. "Now, let's make a list of names to go inside the doors of the calendar. We need twenty-five volunteers."

Women around the parlor began raising their hands and signing up.

"I'll take Sunday, the 19th," Rebel said, knowing Sundays would be hardest to get taken.

One by one, they filled every day except for December 24th. Tally scanned the group. "Will someone take Christmas Eve?"

The silence dragged on for several moments.

Then a whisper came from the corner. "I will."

Rebel craned her neck, surprised to see Eleanor Crump slowly rise. The woman kept apart from the rest as though they had the plague or something. No one knew much about her. As usual, the woman's matted hair, stooped shoulders, and strange bug-like eyes made Rebel shiver. All of the children were frightened of Eleanor and refused to walk near her home, which was little more than a lean-to. Who knew her age? Eleanor could be anywhere between thirty and seventy.

"I'll take Christmas Eve," Eleanor repeated softly.

Stark quiet descended, and Rebel imagined everyone was wondering how they'd get the children to go to her house for the treat on December 24th. Or even what the odd woman would give out.

But Rebel felt her pain. "I'm happy you took a day, Eleanor. I'll be glad to help if you need it."

"So will I," Tally declared, along with a roomful of murmured reinforcement.

The woman gave them what appeared a nod and hurried her bent frame out the door. Rebel's heart broke. She had to find a way to make Eleanor feel useful and wanted. And she'd have a talk with Ely and Jenny about being kind to the older woman—lots of talks.

They were going to learn about the true spirit of Christmas and acceptance of all.

⌒∽⌒

A weak sun came out that afternoon, but the cold continued to seep into Rebel's bones. Jack and Clay put in a new windowpane to replace the broken one in her kitchen, and the light lifted her spirits a little.

She decided to decorate the soddy for Christmas and took down the jar that held a few coins her washing, ironing, and sewing took in—forty cents in all. Some colorful paper would be cheap enough, and Ely and Jenny could cut pretty shapes to hang with string.

It wouldn't be as nice as a tree, but it would be something.

Rebel grabbed her scarf and coat and headed to the mercantile. On the way, she passed the outdoor firepit where the men liked to gather. A man she knew only by name joined them. Tait Trinity had built quite a reputation and had the largest price on his head of all of them, but she liked the honesty and fairness in the outlaw's eyes. Yet, Rebel suspected that anyone who dared to cross him would find themselves in a bad situation in the time it took to breathe.

Jack warmed his hands. "I hate to change the subject, but what are we going to do about a Christmas tree? There's nothing in this part of the country except scrub oak and juniper. The children need a real tree."

That they did. Rebel paused to listen.

"Anyone volunteer to ride to Cimarron after a tall pine and haul it back?" Clay asked.

"I'll go." That came from a man she only knew as Drew.

"You just got out of the calaboose," Jack said. "Alice and the kids would throw a fit."

Tait Trinity straightened. "I'll go after it."

"I'll ride along to keep you company," Ridge Steele offered.

Rebel smiled and continued on to the mercantile. One large tree would do. Everything pretty much was a community effort, and she liked that. Sharing made it easy for everyone to enjoy the same thing without the expense or effort falling to one person.

Flakes of snow hit her face, and she glanced up. Now, it felt like Christmas.

But thoughts of Travis that were never very far away muted the joy.

❧

Supper that night was simple but filling, perfect for a cold winter evening.

Rebel turned the conversation to Advent and told the children Eleanor Crump had taken Christmas Eve.

"Well, I'm not going to her house," Ely declared. "She's scary. I think she might be a witch. Billy Truman says so. He says she eats kids."

"And that makes it gospel?" Rebel asked. "I will not have you being rude."

"But—"

She fixed Ely with a stare. "We have manners and compassion in this house. You'll act accordingly."

Ely ducked his head. "Yes, ma'am."

"Good." Rebel pushed back her chair and rose to pour herself another cup of coffee.

After they did the dishes, she helped the children cut pretty snowflakes and other designs from the colored paper. Then she put string on them, and soon they hung from every portion of the soddy, adding a bit of cheer to their lives.

The glow of a warm fire with snow softly swishing against the windowpanes brought thankfulness to Rebel's heart. Only one person would make it better, but she didn't know where he was or if she'd see him again in this lifetime.

Five

THE FOLLOWING DAY AFTER GETTING ELY TO SCHOOL, Rebel opened her trunk and took out yards of red satin fabric that she'd saved in hope of using it for a wedding dress one day. Underneath lay yards of red lace. She had no use for either now, but the fabric would make a nice gift for Eleanor Crump. It might bring some joy and put a smile on the woman's face, and that would be worth everything.

After holding the fabric to her face for a long, wistful moment, she put it away and met Nora and Tally. With snow drifting about them, they dove into decorating the town with streamers and ribbon from the mercantile. Other women joined them, and soon red ribbons and greenery hung from every house, pole, and business. A few of the men rode out and came back with sacks of mistletoe that hung in the mesquite and scrub oak. The women added the clumps of live beauty to the decorations fluttering everywhere, and the place was transformed.

By afternoon, the town looked festive and bright, and the mist in the air that fogged their breath added to the holiday spirit. Rebel almost burst with joy, and laughter bubbled over. She flung her arms wide, her face tilted to the heavens.

Tally nudged her. "I'm glad to see you so happy."

"I'm alive and raising two orphans, and that's reason to celebrate." Rebel's attention shifted to the children walking from school. Nora took two Truman boys in tow, aiming them toward the windmill with arms full of big, red bows. Then she grabbed her son, Sawyer, and Ely, putting brooms in their hands. They swept off the boardwalk in front of the businesses with hardly a grumble.

"Amazing," Rebel marveled. "They're even smiling."

Tally moved closer to whisper. "Did you see the candy canes she sneaked to them?"

"Good heavens. Whatever works, though, I always say." Rebel turned to a different subject and told the women about gifting the red satin fabric to Eleanor Crump. "I want to make her life better. She seems to have so little."

"Your big heart is what I love most about you, Rebel," Nora answered.

Rebel smiled. "You don't think it'll make her retreat further?"

Tally hugged her. "Follow your instincts. Maybe your kindness will make a difference. I'll make more of an effort myself. But are you certain you want to part with that fabric? Weren't you saving it for a wedding dress?"

"Yes, but I won't need it without a groom, and it's time I faced facts. Travis isn't coming back." Rebel took a deep breath to still the unease inside her and changed the subject. "Do either of you know why Eleanor keeps herself apart from us?"

"Clay said she used to be married to an outlaw, but he died in a shoot-out," Tally volunteered. "That's all I know."

"Maybe losing her husband threw her into deep despair." Nora wound red ribbon around a wooden candy cane. "I'm ashamed that I haven't reached out."

"Me too. I'll bake some apple cinnamon bread to take as well." Rebel mentally went over the ingredients. She'd need to pick up some sugar.

First, she went to check on the children, who were busy making gifts for each other. Clay was patiently helping ten-year-old Violet paint a spinning top for one of the boys. Rebel admired the blind girl's courage and attitude. Just then, Jenny dropped her top on her green dress, leaving a streak of blue paint. Rebel sighed and heaped praise on her. It was all right.

Twilight found the rough outlaw town looking like a magical fairyland. Red and green streamers blew gently in the breeze, and juniper branches and mistletoe hung from every corner and over every doorway.

Rebel went to the mercantile for sugar and baked two loaves of apple cinnamon bread. She'd take one to Eleanor Crump after church the next day.

Thoughts of tomorrow's lighting of the first Advent candle that would kick off the season sent excitement through Rebel. She just knew this was going to be a Christmas to remember.

Maybe it wouldn't be perfect, but doing things for others filled her heart with such joy, and that was the most important thing.

◆◇◆

Before the Sunday sermon, Rebel and the women gathered the children in the vestibule and let them draw a number from a hat. The child with a number one would light the first candle.

Henry was there on crutches with his leg splinted. He seemed to take no joy in the drawing, standing glumly at the side.

His brother Billy pushed several of the kids, and Rebel took him aside for a scolding. "Straighten up, Billy, or I'll be forced to tell your father."

A grin split the boy's face. "He's gone."

"He'll be back, and you can bet he'll get an earful." Rebel was satisfied to watch the boy squirm.

Before she knew it, Henry was there, his hand on Billy's arm. "Remember what I told you?"

Billy swallowed hard. "I'm sorry, Miss Rebel."

Whatever Henry had said had made quite an impression. But then, Martha herself had testified to the change in her oldest.

"That's fine, Billy. Now get back in line and behave yourself. Act like you have half a lick of sense."

"Yes, ma'am."

Henry returned to his place against the wall, and the drawing went smoothly. Pretty little Violet got number one.

"I'll help you light it, honey," Tally said, smiling. She glanced out at the sanctuary all aglow. "The holder is beautiful, and the candle is waiting to be lit."

"I'm so excited, Mama." Violet fumbled for her mother's hand and took it.

Rebel worked to swallow the lump in her throat, then took Jenny and Ely to their pew.

She didn't feel very well. Her face was quite warm, and cold seemed to have invaded deep down into her bones. She pulled her shawl closer around herself, determined to stay.

The heartwarming service was filled with beauty, and Pastor Paul gave a wonderful sermon about forgiveness. It seemed appropriate for a church full of outlaws, yet Rebel saw their misdeeds as justice. When there was little law to be had, a man had to take it for himself.

Her thoughts went to Travis, and she prayed he was warm and fed, not lying dead somewhere.

Tomorrow, Rebel would open the first door of the large wooden Advent calendar, and the children would go to the selected home and collect their treat. The schoolmaster had declared school out until after Christmas, so Ely and Jenny would gather with the other children and resume making gifts for one another.

After cooking lunch, Rebel gathered her loaf of apple cinnamon bread and the red fabric and hurried toward

Eleanor Crump's house. The woman hadn't attended church, and Rebel hoped she wasn't ill.

Speaking of that, Rebel felt a bit light-headed, but she pushed it aside and went on. Nothing to make a fuss over.

The house was little more than a lean-to with slanting walls and a grass roof. It blended into the brambles so well that Rebel almost didn't see it. She didn't know how anyone could live there.

Eleanor opened the door a crack, looking none too happy. "What do you want?"

"I brought you something and made some bread. I thought you might like a loaf. And I wanted to thank you for volunteering to take Christmas Eve on the Advent calendar. That was really nice of you."

"I don't gen'rally welcome visitors." Eleanor's gaze was riveted on the apple cinnamon bread. "Maybe just this once." She held the door open wider.

Rebel handed the fragrant loaf to her and stepped inside. A tiny cot stood next to one wall with a woodstove across from it. Eleanor Crump barely existed. Yet everything was neat.

That surprised her. Taking in Eleanor's appearance, she'd expected a pigsty.

She nodded to the woman, meeting her sad, mud-brown eyes. Up close, Eleanor didn't appear that old. Rebel held out the red fabric. "I also brought this. I hope you like it."

At first, she thought the woman would refuse, but then she accepted it, running her gnarled fingers across the silky length, her eyes shining.

"Thank you, Rebel."

"I've never had an opportunity to get acquainted, and I'm sorry."

"Thank you for the bread. It smells good."

"I came here with the Januarys two years ago. I used

to live in Cimarron and worked in the Wildcat Saloon." Rebel watched the woman's eyes closely but saw no flicker of shock.

"I know."

The simple statement jolted Rebel. Maybe she was the talk of the town.

"Then you understand that I have no call to think I'm better than you. I've done things I'm not proud of. Everyone here in Hope's Crossing has, but we do our best to live good, decent lives from this point forward." Rebel gave her a smile and talked about the town's decorations. "You won't recognize it. Everything sparkles, and the smell of juniper hangs in the air, filling the town with freshness." Rebel laughed. "I've never seen the children so excited. This is like one of my early Christmases."

"I haven't celebrated the holiday in a very long time. No reason to." Eleanor's words dripped with sadness.

"What happened to make you lose your way?" Rebel asked softly.

Eleanor stiffened. "Maybe you'd best go."

"I'll be back to visit soon."

Rebel said goodbye, and as she moved toward the town, her steps got slower and slower. Thoughts of how easily tragedy could strike and steal the ones she loved occupied her. She as well as all the women could certainly attest to the swift changes life could bring, and living in an outlaw town made the possibility even more likely.

Danger continued to surround the town, and the fact that lawmen could swoop in at any given moment kept everyone wary. A bounty hunter had ridden in and taken Travis. Clay had been pardoned by the governor not long ago, but most of the men still had prices on their heads.

Rebel turned her gaze toward the church, and her feet followed. Soon she stood at the front where some prayer candles burned. She picked up a long, thin match and lit a wick for Travis.

Boot heels struck the floor behind her, but she barely heard them so intent was she on her prayer.

A large hand touched her shoulder. A man cleared his throat. "Hello, darlin'."

Rebel whirled and threw her arms around his neck. Was he real or nothing more than a figment of her imagination? She touched his cheek and jaw, his hair. He seemed real.

"I waited so long." Tears slid down her face. Nothing had ever felt as good as his arms around her, holding her. "Don't ever let me go, Travis."

"Don't worry. I don't plan on it." Travis held Rebel against him, and the wild heartbeat of the woman he'd walk a million miles to claim raced against his chest.

She laughed and tilted her face toward him. So vibrant and alive, she took his breath. He tumbled into the depths of her beautiful green eyes that glittered in the light streaming in through the windows. His breath catching in his throat, he lifted a dark strand of hair curling about her shoulders. How had he gotten so lucky? The husky sound of her voice tethered her to him like strips of rawhide.

He pulled his lady close for a long kiss, and for a moment, everything seemed right in the world.

How long they stood there, wrapped in the warmth of their love, he didn't know.

Travis thought of nothing but the woman in his arms.

He slanted another kiss across her lips and took a long drink of the sweet nectar he'd missed all these months. God, he loved the taste of her. Loved kissing her. She was everything he wanted.

But she was pale and thinner. Had she caught something?

"I told you to forget me and go on with your life, but I'm mighty glad you waited."

"I had nothing to go on for." She laid a hand on his face. "You're all I wanted."

He was home, and Rebel was in his arms. She was the woman he'd give up everything he owned to spend one more night with. Two years ago, she'd first captured his attention in the Wildcat Saloon in Cimarron, and he'd been unable to take his eyes off her. Her flashing green eyes and lush, midnight waterfall of dark hair had filled his dreams then, and her bold kisses sent fire to his belly now. She excited him in ways no other woman ever had.

Finally, he raised his head. "Let's get out of here. I have a lot to tell you."

He tucked her securely at his side, but they were besieged the moment they stepped outside. It seemed everyone in town had gathered. They clapped, then Clay strode to hug him. "Welcome home, brother."

When Clay stepped aside, Jack took his place, then Ridge, and one by one, the other men and women told him how worried they'd been, and how nice it was to have him back.

Travis laughed and winked at Rebel. "You'd think I was a prodigal child and had taken off of my own volition to wander aimlessly."

A child's yells split the air, and Jenny came running with Ely beside her. "Mr. Travis!"

He scooped Jenny up. The two orphaned siblings had endured more in their short lives than most adults. He wanted to give them everything they'd been denied. Come hell or high water, this Christmas would be the best he could possibly make it.

"God, I've missed all of you!" His gaze moved from the children to Rebel, and he reached for her hand. "Let's find some privacy."

Six

THE SODDY LOOKED LIKE THE BEST THING TRAVIS HAD seen in months. He knocked the snow off his boots and stepped inside. He removed his hat and hung it with his coat, then moved to the table where Rebel told him about the storm and the broken window while she scurried around making coffee. Her flushed face and heated glances told him she had some time to make up in mind. He propped his elbows on the smooth wood, his eyes on the woman who filled his world.

Her hair curled over her shoulders and spilled down her back, hanging to her slim waist. He was finally home.

Jenny patted his arm. "Mr. Travis, we missed you real bad."

"I missed you too, honey." He lifted her into his lap. "Tell me what's been happening."

"Well, Billy Truman is an old meanie, and he fights with Ely."

Travis ruffled Ely's hair. A slow grin crossed the boy's face. "That true?" Travis asked quietly.

Ely sat silent, running a finger across the wood grains of the table.

"That mean, ol' Billy Truman called you a no-account killer, Mr. Travis," Jenny huffed, evidently tired of waiting for her brother to reply.

"That true, Ely?"

"Yeah." The boy uttered the word so softly that it was difficult to hear.

Travis's stomach clenched. He'd always known this

was coming but hadn't expected to bring his sorry past to bear on these kids so soon.

"Listen, Ely. You don't have to defend me. I can do that myself." Travis put a hand on his shoulder. "Fighting isn't any way to settle a score. You beat an opponent by outthinking and outsmarting him, not with your fists. Words hurt sometimes, but words are all they are, all they'll ever be, unless you give them power by using your fists."

Ely glanced up. "Did you ever get so mad you had to hit something?"

"I used to fight a lot until a wise old man took me aside. You know what he said?"

"No."

"He said never to wrestle with a pig. It'll only get you dirty, and besides, the pig likes a fight. I think this Billy enjoys tussling."

A tiny smile tried to curve Ely's mouth. "Yeah, that's because his brothers always make him eat a lot of dirt. Thanks, Mr. Travis."

"I don't like big pigs." Jenny wrinkled her freckled nose. "I only like the cute babies."

"You know, I like the babies, too. They're cuddly." Travis kissed her cheek. "Like you."

Jenny leaned back to look up. "Are we throwaways?"

The question caught Travis off guard. "No, honey, of course not."

"Billy said we were." Jenny's eyes filled with tears. "I don't wanna be thrown away."

Clearly, Billy Truman was a troublemaker who liked to jab, opening wounds.

Travis wiped Jenny's eyes. These children were starved for attention. He meant to give them all they could stand in the coming days. "Don't worry. It'll never happen as long as I'm alive."

Jenny snuggled against him. "And Billy called Ely a dummard, too, and made Ely real mad."

A muscle in Travis's jaw worked. "Why did Billy say that?"

Anger crossed Ely's face. "'Cause I'm dumb. Arithmetic is hard. I just can't do it."

"I'll work with you on that. All right? You're not dumb. You just need a little more time to catch on and someone to help you figure it out. I'm here now, and we'll get it."

"I hate school."

"I didn't especially like it either when I was your age," Travis confessed. "But I'm glad I toughed it out and learned how to get by in the world. It's bad when you can't. I've seen grown men unable to write their name, and it embarrasses the heck out of them."

Rebel had a bout of coughing that worried Travis. "Are you all right?"

"It's nothing." She waved her hands as though shooing it away. "I'm fine."

Maybe he was making more out of it than it was, but that was because he loved her so much.

A few minutes later, she slid a steaming cup of coffee in front of him. Travis relished the brush of her hand against his. After seven long months, the sparks still sizzled.

Her lazy smile held a promise of soft sheets and long wintry nights.

He grinned over the cup. "What about you, Miss Rebel? Any news?"

She sat and, with his hand in hers, told him about needing Christmas spirit and the wooden Advent calendar Tobias was making. "We lit the first candle in church today, and we open the first door of the calendar tomorrow. I hope the children will stop fighting."

"Sometimes they just need an outlet for worry and making sense of things." Travis tucked a strand of beautiful hair behind her ear.

After soaking up his fill of male companionship for the moment, Ely went back to his loft. The boy seemed better settled. Travis's heart went out to him. Ely had a lot to overcome.

A few moments later, Jenny got down from his lap and wandered off, leaving Travis alone with his love.

Rebel caressed his jaw. "I've been out of my mind imagining all sorts of things. I thought they surely must've hung you. Do I need to hide you?"

"Nope." He kissed her fingers. "I'm free. At least for the crime of stage robbery. Funny thing, the one they charged me with was one I didn't do. I had the damnedest lawyer, though. He put on a real show in the courtroom. Pulled his gun and fired into the ceiling a couple of times. Scared the jurors, and they dove under their chairs. The judge, too." He nuzzled her neck.

She tipped her head back to give him greater access. "He sounds like a character."

"For a fact. He scared the witnesses so bad that they all left town, and the judge had no option but to dismiss the case."

"That's wonderful." Rebel frowned. "But will they come to drag you back later?"

"Nope." Travis grinned. "You want to hear something funny? For a while, they thought I was Brushy Tom Oliver. It seemed in my best interest to play the part, since Brushy only had one charge against him, but they got that straightened out pretty quick." He pushed back her hair and kissed behind her ear. "You don't know how often I dreamed of you in the dead of night, thinking of being back here, kissing you, making love. I missed you, pretty lady."

"I ached for you with every fiber of my being." Rebel's voice trembled with emotion, and he knew what a toll this waiting had taken on her.

"I've had a lot of time to think sitting in my cell, and I have something in mind."

"What?"

"Let's get married on Christmas Day."

Shock rippled across her face. "Married? You still want to marry me?"

"Is that so farfetched?"

"Oh, Travis!" Rebel jerked from her chair and landed in his lap, her arms around his neck. "You don't know how happy this makes me." Her breasts pressed against his chest, and she planted a kiss on his lips.

A second later, she drew back to stare. "But that's just a little over four weeks off! And I gave Eleanor Crump the red satin fabric I'd been saving. I don't have anything to make a dress."

"Don't sound so flustered, darlin'. I don't care if you wear a sack. I just want to make you my wife."

"I'd just as soon stand before the preacher tomorrow." She pouted. "I don't want to wait."

"Nope, Christmas. Anticipation will make it all the sweeter." He tweaked the tip of her nose.

Rebel sighed. "You drive a very hard bargain, but I see a glimmer of gold at the end."

"When did Hope's Crossing get a church? I thought I was seeing things."

"Right after the bounty hunter took you, a man of the cloth named Pastor Paul rode into town along with a schoolmaster, Todd Denver. After the lumber arrived, it took no time to build the church, which doubles as a school." Rebel lowered her eyes. "I wasn't sure they'd welcome someone like me."

"They damn sure better, or I'll have something to say," Travis growled.

She put two fingers on his lips. "Let me finish, sweetheart. No one said a word. They don't treat me any different from the other women. It's this town. We all come from a stained past. You and the other men are outlaws. Some of the women are a product of an asylum, and others like me made a living in smoke-filled saloons and dingy rooms. No one is better than anyone else."

"Except apparently this Billy Truman. Maybe I should speak to his parents."

Rebel shook her head. "The Trumans are good, decent people." She told him about the family of ten boys and how they were running wild these days. "Martha, bless her heart, doesn't feel up to chasing after them, and Sid is gone all the time."

"Then it's up to us men to fill in." He scratched his stubbled jaw in thought.

"We hope having the children make gifts for one another will help."

Travis gave her a look of admiration. One thing he loved about Rebel was her quick mind. Maybe that came from the hard life she'd lived in the rough town of Cimarron, where killings were a daily occurrence. He wanted to make her forget all that and put new memories in her pretty head.

Nothing about her was ordinary or would ever be. He hadn't thought much of his chances with her, being younger and all, but they'd hit it off. Rebel Avery had a lot more experience in everything, while he only knew one thing well—how to draw and shoot in a split second. Nothing else. Way he saw it, the beauty was way too good for someone like him.

Another thing. While most of the women wore high-necked dresses, she left hers unbuttoned above the swell of her breast. His heart beat faster. Tonight, he'd take his time showing her how much she meant to him and how lost and alone he'd be without her.

She was the woman he loved for now and forever.

He brought his thoughts back to the Truman boys. "I think us men might have a few ideas of our own. We'll keep those kids so busy they won't have time to wipe their noses or think about causing hell. You say there's ten of them?"

"Yes, but sometimes it seems more like double that.

They range in age from twelve to two, and Martha has another baby just about due. We're all praying she gets her girl."

Travis chuckled softly. "I can see why."

Rebel rose to get the pot and refilled his cup. He was afraid to blink for fear this was all a dream.

Rebel soaked up the sight of Travis. She loved the corded muscles along his forearms and the cleft in his chin that deepened when he smiled, but it was his blue eyes, the shade of deep, still water that never failed to set her blood pumping. Some might not think him a handsome man, and maybe he wasn't the best-looking with his hard, angular jawline and high cheekbones. But she'd seen his caring, his commitment, and real love shining on his face. He was perfect in her eyes.

They were going to be married on Christmas Day! Her stomach flipped over.

She leaned forward and ran her fingertips over the stubble marking his jaw. Heat darkened his eyes, and his breathing roughened.

"You don't know how much I want you, Rebel."

"Kiss me, Travis."

He reached for her and, with the ease of a man used to working with his hands, lifted her onto his lap and claimed her lips. His touch sent her thoughts whirling and hunger overpowering her senses.

Rebel slid an arm around his neck, her fingers tangling in his dark-blond hair. She lost all track of time and space.

The man she loved was home, and loneliness and worry would no longer hammer her night and day.

The sound of the children moving about in the other room finally penetrated her senses, and she stood, straightening her hair. "Goodness, look at the time. I have supper to get."

The clear hunger for something more than food shining in Travis's eyes made her stomach quicken. "I wouldn't mind missing it to keep holding you."

"I think the children might protest." She put her hands on his shoulders. "Now, let me cook."

"Not just yet." He called the children, and they sat at the table. "Miss Rebel and I have some news—we're going to get married."

"For true?" Ely asked.

Rebel laughed. "Yes, on Christmas Day."

Jenny squealed and scrambled into Travis's lap. "We can be a fam'ly?"

"Yes. A real family." Travis hugged the four-year-old.

Ely sat silent, watching.

"What's the matter? Aren't you happy, Ely?" Rebel asked.

"Does this mean our last name will be Lassiter?"

Rebel met Travis's troubled gaze and imagined he was wondering what grief he'd saddle the children with. "How would you feel about that, sweetheart?"

"I'd like it just fine, but I reckon the kids can choose whatever name they want." Travis's gaze swung to Ely. "Would you like to take my name, son?"

The boy's forehead wrinkled. "I don't want to be Carver anymore. Our daddy threw us away because he didn't want us, so I reckon we'll throw him away. I'll be Ely Lassiter now."

"An' I'll be Jenny Lass'ter." The child twisted her hair. "Is that hard to spell?"

"I'll teach you, pretty girl," Travis assured her.

This was all well and good, but Rebel didn't know how one went about changing a name. Did it cost money? The nearest lawyer would probably be in Tascosa or Springer. She'd do anything, make any sacrifice to give these children a happier future. Lord knows, the Carver name had brought nothing but horror and despair.

"Good. Now that that's settled, I'll start supper."

And what a meal she prepared with her limited larder! They celebrated Travis's return, and even the snow stopped. The four of them sat around the table talking long after she finished the supper dishes. Travis told about his adventures as a boy in the swamps of Louisiana, but no mention was made of time spent recently in a Texas jail.

After they'd eaten, a knock came on the door. Rebel opened it. "Nora, how nice to see you. Come in."

Nora stepped inside. "I just wanted to see if you'd like me to keep Jenny and Ely overnight. You two have some…talking…to do."

Rebel laughed at the underlying meaning. "Yes, we do. I'll get them ready. Thank you."

It didn't take long. She told them she'd see them tomorrow.

Finally, she had a chance to be alone with Travis. He put another piece of wood in the potbelly stove, then turned and wrapped his arms around her. She laid her cheek against his chest and nuzzled against his leather vest. The scent of the brisk winter air lingered on his clothes.

"I couldn't wait for this moment." She glanced up, mesmerized by the clear blue of his eyes.

Wanting shimmered, darkening his eyes, making his deep voice raspy. "Lady, I'm going to strip off your clothes and have my way with you."

A delicious shiver raced up her spine. She gave a throaty chuckle. "You are, huh? Is that a threat, my love, or a promise?"

"Oh, that's definitely a promise." His voice was low, silky. He crushed her to him, pressing his lips to hers in a kiss that could've stripped the barbed wire from ten miles of fence line. The depth of desire sent her senses reeling. She wanted to hang out a sign that said he belonged to her, then take her time in finding the source of the heat and this all-encompassing hunger that flooded over her. She yearned to be the kind of wife that a man like Travis deserved. A man who always saw the good in her and overlooked her shortcomings.

Her heart pounded against her ribs as she yanked his shirt from his trousers and ran her hands underneath the fabric and over the muscles of his back.

"Lady, you don't know what you do to me. You're nothing but temptation." He nibbled his way across the seam of her mouth before settling his lips firmly on hers.

This kiss was raw and deep with passion. Rebel sighed and melted against him, tucking his love around her like a warm blanket. Travis ended the kiss all too soon for her liking.

She toyed with the ends of his hair. "What if something happens and we can't marry on Christmas Day?"

"It won't." He winked. "I have faith."

"Then I'd best see about a dress." There was not a second to waste.

"Not tonight." He stood, scooped her into his arms, and headed for the bedroom.

They took their time undressing each other. Then Travis propped himself on one elbow, admiring her willowy curves as she turned down the wick on the lamp.

Damn, she was a sexy woman!

"Come here, lady." He pulled her down beside him and ran his fingers across her silky skin. "I've waited a long time for this and wondered if I'd ever see you again. I can't imagine how hard it was on you with the kids."

Her green eyes were large and mysterious. "Let's not talk about the past. It's over. Our future is just beginning."

"I agree." He captured her bottom lip lightly with his

teeth and sucked it into his mouth, seeming to draw her inside him as well. He wished he could. He could protect her a lot better.

Rebel slid her hand between their bodies and closed a fist around him. He tensed and fought the reaction that would send him tumbling over the edge before he was ready.

"You don't play fair, lady."

She laughed. "I know. But you love me anyway." Her eyes darkened. "You complete me, sweetheart. Without you, I'm half a person."

"I'm no good without you either." He shifted his focus on her generous curves and lavished much attention on her breasts.

When their bodies were well caressed and they feared the slightest movement would end what they'd had such fun building, he slid inside her tight warmth. The frantic pace he set left Rebel gasping, gripping his back, trying to draw more of him into her.

As if he held anything back. Travis gave her everything he had, and she took it all.

Although they'd made love many times in the past, this was different. It seemed like their very first joining.

He waited, pacing himself, and when Rebel reached for the stars, so did he.

Together. As things were meant to be.

Seven

THE NEXT MORNING, UNDER ELY'S AND JENNY'S DIREC-
tion, Travis helped Tobias carry the six-foot-tall calendar
and set it up outside the mercantile under the overhang
that would protect it from the weather. The heavy piece
of wood fit into a sturdy stand Clay had made. They
shouldn't have a problem even if the wind raised holy
hell, as it was wont to do sometimes.

Folks kept interrupting so often to say how happy
they were Travis was back until he finally shrugged his
shoulders at Tobias and just chatted until they moved
on. It was nice to be missed though, and their concern
and happiness filled a part of him that had been parched.

They almost treated him like a celebrity, and he
expected a band to come marching by any second. It
would certainly fit in with the beautiful ribbons and
greenery hanging everywhere.

Christmas spirit was alive and well in Hope's Crossing.

Rebel would have the best one ever, or Travis would
bust a gut trying. Lord knows she'd seen far too much
disappointment, too many hard times.

She'd developed a persistent cough during the night
which drew concern, but she'd kissed him and said he
was making a mountain out of a molehill. Nevertheless,
this morning with the onset of fever, he'd insisted on her
seeing the town's doctor, a petite woman named Mary
Cuvier. The woman wore a necklace made of bullet
fragments she'd dug from her patients. A little odd, if
you asked him.

"Rebel has influenza, and she's contagious. Best to stay away."

Travis had spread his legs in a wide stance. "You'll have to shoot me first."

Dr. Mary shook her head like he was one bullet shy of a box of ammunition, but he'd taken Jenny and Ely back to the Bowdres for now. The kids were scared half out of their minds, but Travis tried to downplay the seriousness, insisting Rebel was only tired.

Clay wandered by the mercantile as he and Tobias were finishing. "Join me and the men to talk. We want to know how you worked a miracle."

While he really wanted to go check on Rebel, he stood with the men at the outdoor firepit and told them about the bounty hunter, the jail, the trial. "I owe my lawyer a huge debt. If he hadn't come unhinged and shot up the courtroom, I'd probably be in prison or a graveyard now. Those witnesses fled, and the sheriff said they never stopped running."

Chuckles went through the group. "Just shows to never give up." Jack slapped Travis's back. "Great to have you home."

"I want you to hear the news. Rebel and I are going to be married on Christmas Day. You're all invited."

Jack let out a whoop. "You got a good woman in Rebel. She's done a lot for this town." He glanced toward home. "Nora's got some chores for me so I'd best go."

"Me too. Congratulations, Travis." Clay moved toward the corral, and the rest scattered.

The stage rolled in, and Travis went to meet it. Thank God, Sid Truman was back. Travis introduced himself, then paused to watch the passengers stepping down. One woman glanced at the pretty decorations, her eyes lighting up. Rebel would be pleased.

Angry voices pulled him from his thoughts. "I had that first!" Billy Truman yelled.

"No, you didn't!" Ely screamed back.

"Give it to me!"

"Make me," Ely dared.

Before Travis could move, the boys were tangled up, fists swinging. "Stop that!" He sprinted for them and arrived on the heels of Sid Truman. Each grabbed a boy and pulled them apart.

"What's the meaning of this?" Sid demanded.

Both boys launched into an argument, and soon they had a ring of kids around them.

Travis glanced at Sid. "Let's go someplace quiet to sort this out. It's past time."

"I'm glad I drove the stage in when I did," Sid said. "Martha's been telling me about Billy."

They grabbed their sons and stalked to the windmill. The boys were sullen and quiet.

Travis glared. "Start talking, Ely. We're not leaving until you tell me what you're so all-fired mad at. I don't care if we have to stay here all night."

"Nothing. Nothing's wrong."

"Something is. What's got you so all-fired mad? Talk."

"Billy, you too. Why are you always looking for trouble?" Sid gave his son a shake. "Why? You have a roof over your head and food in your belly. I'm working as hard as I can to make sure you and your brothers have everything you need."

Both boys sat there in stony silence, their gazes lowered.

Finally, Billy spoke. "It's you, Pa. You're always gone. It's like you don't care about us anymore. You never take me fishing or help me with my sums. You don't hear Ma crying after we go to bed. Little Jonesy don't even know you're his pa. He's started calling Clay Pa."

Sid stared, his face a mask of pain. He pulled Billy up and wrapped his arms around his son. "I've never stopped caring. I hate being gone all the time, but I don't know how else to earn a living."

"I fight with Ely because he has what I want," Billy mumbled. "Miss Rebel loves him, really loves him, and Mr. Travis, too. Heck, they're always doing things with them."

Travis prodded Ely. "What do you have to say? What's your excuse?"

Ely glanced up with tears in his eyes, his chin quivering. "My pa threw me and Jenny away like trash, so maybe we are."

"Well, you're not," Travis said firmly.

"Pa said we were too much bother and took us to Creedmore. It was dark, and there were big rats everywhere. Those men were real mean, and they didn't feed us or nothing. Billy said nobody can love us." Ely wiped his nose on his sleeve. "Sometimes I get real scared and think you and Miss Rebel are going to throw us away, too."

"Son, that's the furthest thing from the truth." Travis pulled him into a hug. "You and Jenny will always be our children. Forever."

Billy sniffed, his eyes filled with tears. "I'm sorry, Ely. I didn't know." He reached for Ely's hand and shook it. "Friends?"

"Friends." Ely wiped his hands on his pants. "Want to go back with the others? I'll make you something."

"Sure."

Travis watched the two boys race each other. "I think we made a lot of progress." He glanced at Sid. "I've been trying to think of a way for you to stay here."

"I ran a café in Tascosa until it burned. That and driving a stagecoach are all I know."

A café. That was it. Jack had often bemoaned the fact that Hope's Crossing had no eating place and that his son, Sawyer, loved to cook.

"What do you think about us opening one here and letting the children work a few hours each day? It would teach them to work together, and they'd earn a little money. But you'd run it and do the bulk of the work."

Sid's gray eyes lit up. "You know, that sounds like the answer to a prayer. Except I have no money to buy lumber, a cookstove, tables, chairs, dishes, or supplies."

"What if we all chip in? And we have lumber left over from the other buildings."

"I don't know what Clay, Jack, and the others will say."

"It won't take long to ask."

"Thanks, Travis. I have to find a way to stay home. Martha has too much on her shoulders, and the children need me."

Yes, they did for a fact. Travis and Sid went to speak to Clay.

Clay grinned. "I've been thinking of building a café next. We really need one, but I held back because we didn't have anyone to run it. Love the idea of the kids working a few hours a day if they want. Builds character."

"Thank you, Clay." Sid shook his hand. "I'll even build it if you'll feed my family."

"Deal."

"Let's go open the first door of the calendar and kick this Advent off." Travis moved to the wooden apparatus, and folks gathered around. "All right, you've all probably heard that Rebel has taken sick and is unable to be here. I ask Mrs. Colby to come up to start this holiday celebration. But first I want to thank Tobias January for building such a calendar on short notice. Tobias, did you sleep the last few days?"

"Dang little." The breeze ruffled Tobias's long, white beard, but his grin was unmistakable.

"Please give him a round of applause, everyone." Once the clapping died down, Travis turned the affair over to Tally.

She opened the little door on December 1st with a flourish and took out the small piece of paper. "Children, Nora and Jack Bowdre are the first to offer treats, so go visit their home."

The Truman Ten ran shrieking toward their treat with Jenny in the middle of the pack and the dogs barking and jumping around them. Travis watched, holding his breath for fear she'd get trampled. Jack and Nora's son, Sawyer, and Ely each got on one side of Violet and led her. Travis smiled, his chest swelling to see Ely making sure the sweet, blind girl was seen to first. The boy's heart was in the right place.

His throat tightened at how excited the children were, wishing Rebel could see them. This was her dream, her idea, and she should be here.

Travis wove through the onlookers and their pats of sympathy to Rebel's little soddy. Her deep, croupy cough stopped his heart. It sounded even worse than before.

Belle January came to meet him. "Her fever is raging, and she can't breathe. I've seen this before, and unless we do something, she might die."

Over his dead body.

He jerked off his coat and strode to the bed. If he hadn't known who lay there, he wouldn't have recognized her. He sat on the bed and gathered her in his arms, pulling the quilt tight around her. Chills racked her body.

"I'm so cold," she said weakly. "Please get me w-warm."

"You got it." He laid her down and reached for another heavy quilt, tucking it close to hold in the heat. She couldn't stop shaking and coughing.

The door opened, and the tinkling of Dr. Mary's necklace preceded her. She carried a bucket of water and cloths. "You shouldn't be here, Travis."

He glared up. "I'm not leaving. Shoot me, and at least you'll have another bullet for your necklace there."

The doctor glared. "You're an ornery cuss. You know that? Move over. I need to bathe her in cold water and try to get that fever down."

Travis settled Rebel back on the pillow and took the water and cloths from the doctor. "Whatever needs doing, I'll do. Rebel is my whole life, and I aim to get her well. We *will* be married on Christmas Day."

Dr. Mary exhaled loudly. "I hate to burst your bubble, but it's not going to happen."

"I have faith it will. I'll call if I need you or there's a change. You and Belle have other things to do." Travis took a soft cloth and dipped it in the water as the door of the soddy softly closed.

He talked to Rebel as he bathed her face, neck, and arms. "I never told you about the time I got cornered by a pack of coyotes and stayed awake fighting them off one night. I knew if I went to sleep, they'd tear into me and my horse."

Although she didn't speak, her sunken eyes followed his every movement. He recounted other tales, and she slept. He removed the quilts and her nightgown and kept bathing her while the hours passed, blending together into a patchwork quilt of time where squares met and lives crossed in this desperate struggle to save the woman who filled his dreams and gave him hope. She was his future, just as the children were the future of the town.

If Rebel died, so would he.

The next few days passed in a blur. He got Rebel to drink many cups of hot tea laced with whiskey and honey and continued the cold baths against her protests. He finally pulled the quilts over her and let her sleep a while.

Belle brought a hot dinner of potatoes and fried rabbit, and they talked while Travis ate.

"We had influenza sweep through Tascosa a few years back," Belle said. "It was bad. That's why the doctor wants to keep this contained. We can't afford an epidemic here with the town still so young. But we do have two more cases."

"How are they doing?"

"They're not as sick as Rebel and should be fine in a week or so."

"Good. Rebel is the woman I'm going to marry, and I won't leave her." His voice trembled, and he turned away.

Belle laid a wrinkled, gnarled hand on his arm. "Love is a powerful thing. Tobias and I have been married for fifty-three years. Treasure the time you have with Rebel."

"Everyone keeps saying she won't make it, but she will. I have faith. I'm only an outlaw, but some things a man knows deep in his heart."

And this was one of them. Rebel was going to marry him in whatever dress they could find, and they were going to make a good home for Ely and Jenny. Mark his words.

Rebel had a coughing fit, interrupting their conversation. By the time Travis got to her, she'd lost her breath. He wiped the thick mucus from her chin and placed a wet cloth on her forehead. She coughed until she couldn't get air into her lungs.

The closing door told him Belle had left. Travis pulled Rebel up and rubbed her back. Her fever had returned. She railed, out of her head, her eyes glassy, calling him a name that made him cringe. He reminded himself that she didn't know what she was saying.

Something his mother had done a long time ago crossed his mind. He laid Rebel back down and hurried to the small kitchen area, yanking open drawers and boxes until he found the mustard. He mixed it with a little water until it formed a thick paste, then spread it on two of the clean, heated cloths.

By the time he got back to the bed, Rebel had fallen into a deep sleep. Or maybe it was unconsciousness. She didn't open her eyes when he sat her up and wrapped the mustard plaster around her back and chest.

Deep coughs continued to rack her body over the next few hours. Those and moans were the only signs she was alive.

Dr. Mary returned that night. She approved of the mustard plaster and asked him why he thought of it.

"My mother made these when I was a boy. I used to hate when she put them on me, but I loved the result."

The doctor tsked him. "I pity your poor mother. She had her hands full with you."

"You said a mouthful. She's gone now, but I still hear her on occasion."

"I don't think I ever asked about your family."

Travis abruptly turned. "I should check on Rebel. What else do I need to be doing?"

"Praying."

"I'm doing that, Doctor." Or as much as he knew how. He'd never been a churchgoer.

Rebel was asleep again. Deciding it was time to take advantage of the small break, he swung around. "Would you mind staying for a little while, Dr. Mary? There's something I need to do."

"I'll be glad to. Just be sure to not touch anyone while you're out."

With a nod, Travis opened the trunk at the foot of the bed and pulled out the yards of red lace, then got Rebel's Sunday dress of rich purple. Putting on his coat, hat, and gloves, he went out into the cold.

Light snow fell, and the Christmas streamers decorating the town looked like children's forgotten playthings, fluttering and twisting in the slight breeze. The mistletoe caught his eye. What he wouldn't give to catch Rebel underneath a clump and kiss the daylights out of her.

His heart aching, he shook himself and went about his business, soon knocking on Nora's door.

She opened it, smiling. "Travis, come in. How is Rebel?"

"I really just have a moment. She's very sick, and I don't want to leave her alone too long." He held out the dress and lace. "Would you spruce this up for our wedding? I want to surprise her. She worried about having something nice."

Nora gently touched his arm. "I'll do anything for her. Tally too. But Eleanor dropped by during the night and left Rebel's red satin fabric on my porch with a note that said we should make her a wedding dress from it."

"Eleanor Crump?" He remembered how skittish the woman was around people and how pitiful she looked with her wild hair. "How did she get the material?"

"Rebel gave it to her as a gift. She cares a lot for Eleanor."

That's how special his lady was. No one had a bigger heart.

"I'm happy to hear about that." He glanced at the purple dress. "It wouldn't have worked, but it was the best option I had at the time."

"No, it wouldn't have. Tally and I will make a wedding dress and put the red lace on it. We know Rebel's style. I'll keep this one, though, for her measurements. But are you sure the wedding will happen this soon?"

"We're going to be married on Christmas Day. I have faith, you see."

And he wanted Rebel to be prepared for the wedding in case she didn't have time enough when she recovered.

Eight

IN THE PASSING WEEK, EXCITEMENT OVER ADVENT pervaded the small town. Children were smiling and happy with nary a cross word. Sid began work on the café, with the men helping when they could. Friends constantly stopped by Rebel's soddy to leave food, inquire about her, and tell Travis how much of a difference her idea made to the holiday season. He always met them at the door with something covering his mouth like the doctor had said. A warm glow filled him at the thought that her need for a Christmas like she used to celebrate had spawned all this in a town filled with outlaws.

That morning, Rebel had the worst coughing fit she'd ever had, coughing up green phlegm until she couldn't catch her breath. The loud wheezing scared Travis. He held her in his arms, wishing he could take her place. He was strong and healthy and could fight harder.

Frustrated, he released a string of silent curses and tenderly wiped her mouth.

She looked at him through sunken eyes, her voice faint. "I'm not going to make it, Travis. Let me go."

Shock raced through him, her words freezing his blood. "I can't. I can do anything but that. You're going to get well, and we'll have our wedding. I believe that with all my heart."

"Shhh, listen." Rebel fought for air to speak. Finally she went on. "Promise to raise Ely and Jenny. Change their names to Lassiter, be the father they want." Coughs, deep and terrifying, sprang from her.

Travis held her close, rubbing her back, watching her face turn blue, unable to do a damn thing.

When Rebel could speak, she whispered, "Don't let those children grow up unloved and unwanted. Promise."

How could he think of doing anything—much less living—without the woman he loved? His heart was shattering.

After a sleepless night sitting by Rebel's side, watching the rise and fall of her chest, fearing the next breath would be her last, Travis opened the door the next morning to find Ely and Jenny. "Hey there. I wish I could hug you, but Dr. Mary is very strict."

"How is Miss Rebel?" Ely asked. "Does she ask about us?"

Travis couldn't tell him that she rarely woke and was getting weaker by the minute. She'd eaten very little and had lost so much weight that her cheeks were sunken, her cough constant. No, he couldn't worry these kids.

"Miss Rebel is going to be just fine. Wait and see. She asks me all the time how you're doing and if you're minding the Bowdres."

"They're real nice, but they're not you and Miss Rebel." Jenny sighed. "I'm lonely. Ely goes off with Sawyer playing, and I just have my doll or baby Willow. Even Violet is too busy."

Sadness dimmed the four-year-old's bright eyes and brought tightness to Travis's chest.

"Honey, you're outnumbered, but there's nothing anyone can do about that. Ely, can you pay more attention to your sister?"

"I'll try, but Jenny isn't as much fun as Sawyer. He knows how to make traps and fishing lures and everything."

After a little more conversation, they left, and Travis went to make another mustard plaster and tempt Rebel with a bite of milk toast.

But despite everything that kept him busy, her words echoed in his head.

I'm not going to make it, Travis. Please let me go.

How was he supposed to do that? And where to begin?

No, she had to live. That's all there was to it. He'd accept nothing else.

Tally appeared at the door to ask about Rebel and leave some soup.

He stood for a moment, trying to get the woman's words to make sense in his brain. Finally, he managed a smile. "We're taking this a minute at a time."

"The dress is coming along well, and I think Rebel will be pleased. The fabric and lace are just so beautiful." Tears welled in Tally's eyes. "I pray she makes it. Rebel is the dearest friend I have. She was supposed to hand out treats to the children on Sunday, but I'll take her day."

"Thank you. I'll tell her you called, but I won't mention the dress. That's our secret."

Another week passed, and with each day Rebel got weaker and weaker.

She seemed to be waiting on his blessing to die. Selfish bastard that he was, he couldn't give that.

Outside the door, he often heard the children laughing and playing, and one night, Dallas Hawk brought his fiddle and played soft Christmas music in front of the house. Travis sat in the dark, in despair with his head in his hands, more alone than he'd ever been in his life.

The good news was that he'd heard the other two with influenza had recovered, for which he gave thanks. But still his angel showed no sign of turning the corner.

A week later, Dr. Mary came in the evening to check on her patient. Rebel struggled to breathe even in her sleep, her mouth gaping open. The fever had dried and cracked her lips. The doctor put an ointment on them and gave it to Travis to continue.

He watched her check Rebel's feet, saw her lips set

in a tight line and the hopelessness in her eyes. "What is it, Doctor?"

"Signs. Travis, I don't think you're going to get your wedding." Her voice was soft and held a quality he'd never heard before.

A hand seemed to reach inside his chest and squeeze his heart. "No, she's going to live."

"I'll send the pastor. You need someone to talk to."

Anger sharpened his tone. "Keep him away. I don't have time for naysayers. I'll have to ask you to leave now."

Sadness dripped from her face. "I wish I could give you what you want. If you need me…" She went to the door and out into the night.

After Doc Mary left, Travis lifted Rebel's weak, almost lifeless form inside her quilts and carried her to the sofa. He sat down, holding her tight. He smoothed back her hair and kissed her cracked lips. Her heart was barely beating. His eyes filled with tears.

"I fell in love the first time I saw you dancing on the table in that saloon in Cimarron. You were the most exciting, flashy woman I'd ever seen, and I couldn't take my eyes off you. I knew what you did for a living, but it didn't make one bit of difference." His voice broke, and he had to stop for several long moments.

After gathering himself, he went on. "I noticed the caring and compassion inside you. I once saw you take food to a woman and children living in a hovel. And you spent several days at a miner's bedside, nursing him back to health. You hid that compassion from others, but I saw the real woman you were beneath the face paint and too-bright smile.

"I wish I could let you go, but I just can't." He broke down in heaving sobs, burying his face in her dark hair. "I love you too much."

The clock on the mantel ticked loudly, and the snow whispered against the windowpane.

Everything was continuing as normal—except Travis's heart.

"I never told you about my life. I had a brother named Mason. He was eaten up with greed, always wanting what other people had. It came to a point when he started taking whatever he wanted and shooting anyone who objected. I began going along to try to keep him out of trouble, but he kept dragging me deeper and deeper into his mess. One day, Mason tried to rob the bank and got shot for his trouble. I whirled and killed the bank guard on pure instinct, and that's how it all started. That incident put me on the run."

Travis stopped to check if she was still breathing and found it barely noticeable.

"I'll do my best with the children, but I'll make a piss-poor father. I'm nothing but an outlaw, a man who's killed, and the only softness I know is what you taught me. I need you, darlin'. How I'll survive without you, I haven't a clue."

He could draw and shoot in the blink of an eye, but he didn't know how to live without the woman who'd seen the man he wanted to become.

❧

Travis sat holding her long past midnight and finally dozed off. He woke to sunlight streaming through the window. His arm was numb, but it matched the rest of him. Rebel's eyes were closed, and her breathing didn't seem as labored. But that was only wishful thinking.

He didn't know what day it was, but the church bell tolling was a clue that it was Sunday. They'd light another Advent candle. By his estimation, it would be the fourth. Christmas was a week away—his and Rebel's wedding day.

Letting out a sigh, he carried Rebel to the bed and covered her. Then he put on a fresh shirt that Belle had brought.

A knock came at the door. Dr. Mary stood smoking her pipe. "I wanted to check on our patient. Hope I'm not too early."

"Not at all. In fact, if you could stay with her for a bit, I'd appreciate it. I have something to take care of."

The doctor tamped out her pipe and left it on the stoop. "Don't ever smoke, Travis."

"Don't intend to." He reached for his hat and hurried out, thankful for the wide brim that shielded his eyes against the glare of the snow and the sunlight bouncing off it. His boots crunched, making a loud sound. He'd lived in the silence of the soddy for what seemed like forever, so the smallest noise seemed jarring.

"Mr. Travis!" Jenny saw him and came running. "Can you come to church?"

"As a matter of fact, that's exactly where I was going." Travis glanced at Ely. "You got a haircut. Looks good."

The boy grinned. "Thanks. Mrs. Bowdre cut it."

They walked to the church, and Travis left them in a pew to speak to the reverend. "I promised Rebel I'd change the children's last name to Lassiter. Can you tell me what's involved?"

Pastor Paul's eyes twinkled through his spectacles, and his wavy hair was neatly combed. His white clerical collar was a little askew as though rebellious. "I've heard their story—their father gave up his rights. Until you can draw up legal documents, I'll perform a ceremony in front of the congregation. I do think it will give the children a sense of belonging."

Travis held his hat with both hands. "Can you do it today?"

"I'll be happy to. How is Rebel?"

Travis inhaled a shaky breath. "Not much change. Just a matter of time, according to the doctor." And then his world would crash around him, and he didn't know how he'd go on without the woman who'd seen the best in him.

The reverend rested a palm on Travis's arm. "I'll keep her in my prayers."

The service commenced, and the fourth candle of Advent was lit. Following the singing, Pastor Paul went to the pulpit. "Today is a special time for two children who have been buffeted by uncertainty and sorrow. We're going to have a little ceremony for Jenny and Ely Carver to give them the permanence and stability they need in their lives. Will Travis and the children come forward?"

Ely glanced at Travis in wonder. "Is this going to make us yours?"

"Yes. You and Jenny will officially belong to me—and Miss Rebel. You'll be ours."

Pastor Paul faced them. "Is it true you wish to take the last name of Lassiter?"

"Yes!" Ely answered.

Jenny wiped her eyes. "Uh-huh!"

Everyone laughed at their enthusiasm.

Pastor Paul asked Travis to take the children's hands. "Do you promise to care for and love Ely and Jenny and help them grow into a strong man and woman?"

Travis pledged his love and support. Then the reverend turned to the children and asked, "Do you promise to obey and love your new father?" He glanced at Travis, who nodded, then added, "And mother."

More yeses followed.

"I pronounce you Ely Lassiter and Jenny Lassiter forever and always."

The kids turned and hurled themselves into Travis's arms.

"Can we call you Papa now?" Ely asked.

Tears filled Travis's eyes. "Absolutely."

The lost children had been found, and this Christmas

had become full of wonder and security for them. Travis just wished Rebel could've been there.

After church, he stood with his son and daughter, getting in a little more conversation, when Billy Truman sprinted to the crowd, announcing that his mother was about to have her baby.

"I wonder if it'll be a girl." Ely sighed. "If it is, she'd better be tough."

Jenny hopped up and down, flicking her hands. "A real baby that cries and everything."

"Imagine that." Travis picked her up and gave her a long hug. "I need to go see about your new mama."

"Tell her about the baby." Jenny kissed his cheek.

"I will, honey." If she woke up. He'd done what Rebel had asked.

The excitement was over. As the siblings walked toward the Bowdres' house, Travis turned to look at them, his throat tightening. He now had a son and a daughter.

If Rebel would only fight hard to come back to him and the children, he'd be complete.

Nine

REBEL OPENED HER EYES AND TOOK IN FAMILIAR surroundings. Her fever, her aches were gone, and her head was clear. She lifted a feeble hand that seemed to weigh a ton and laid it over her eyes.

What day was it? How long had she been sick?

A man—Travis, she thought, squinting—was rattling around in the kitchen. One thing about a soddy…all the rooms were together. She tried to call to him but couldn't make a sound. She was so tired, but she didn't want to sleep until she'd asked some questions.

At last, he finally came closer to her bed, and she took in the sight she'd never expected to see again. The cleft in Travis's chin appeared deeper, his eyes bluer.

When he saw her staring, he did a double take, then hurried to her side. "You're awake. You're really awake. I'm not dreaming, am I?"

Rebel worked her tongue and got out one word. "Water."

A big grin stretched across his face. He strode to the kitchen in that long, smooth way of his and returned. He gently lifted her and held the cup to her mouth. "Sleeping Beauty, you sure know how to worry a man. I have a lot to tell you."

The cold water soothed her parched mouth and throat. It was as though she sipped from a mountain stream. She drank her fill and lay back on the pillow. "How long have I been sick?"

"Three weeks all together, but lingering near death's

door for seven days." The bed sagged when he sat down beside her. "We had a service yesterday, and I gave Jenny and Ely my name. I wish now that I'd waited. Only Dr. Mary kept telling me you wouldn't make it."

"No, I'm glad you went ahead." Her voice came barely louder than a whisper.

"Darlin', your idea of this Advent is a huge success. It's really made a big difference in the children and adults, too. I'm just sorry you missed most of it. Oh, Tally said to tell you that she took your day on the calendar."

"That's good."

He smoothed back her hair and tenderly kissed her. "I don't know why God granted my request. I'm only glad He did." Travis chuckled. "Maybe he'd never heard such a pitiful outlaw's strange prayers. But here you are, alive and feeling better than you have in weeks. I'm a lucky, lucky man."

"Did I miss the wedding?" she asked, her voice faint.

"Nope. Christmas is in five days. I just don't think you'll be up to the ceremony."

Rebel's mulish chin raised just a hair. "I'll be there. But I won't have a dress."

Travis rose and went to the nail where her few dresses hung. Maybe he was going to pick one out. "I found this old thing hanging at the back the other day when I was snooping around. Do you think it'll work?"

What one could he possibly be talking about? He spread it on the bed, and Rebel's breath caught. The red satin she'd saved for so long had created the most beautiful dress she'd ever seen.

Tears threatened. She ran her fingertips across the fabric. "Oh, Travis! But how? I gave this fabric to Eleanor Crump."

"And she gave it back saying she wanted to see you get married in it. Nora and Tally finished two days ago when you were at your worst and it appeared I'd lose you for sure." He lifted her hand to his lips. "Promise you won't worry me that much again."

"I'll try not." Rebel swallowed hard and stared into the face of the man she loved. "You had the dress made even when it appeared we wouldn't need one."

"Call me crazy. Everyone kept saying the wedding wouldn't happen, and I kept telling them that I had faith it would, though I wavered a bit when I thought your next breath would be your last. I didn't see how you could survive."

"I fooled everyone."

"That you did. Oh, I have news. Martha had her baby yesterday, and Sid was here for the event. Mother and baby are doing well, I'm told."

"And?" Rebel saw the teasing glint in Travis's eyes and knew he was stringing her along on purpose.

"She finally had a girl."

"Hallelujah!"

The bed shifted when Travis stood. "I'm sure you're starving. I'll heat up some soup, then I'm going to bring our son and daughter home."

"Good. I need to see them."

∽∾

Jenny squealed and Ely grinned when Travis told them to gather their things. He thanked Nora and Jack and they left, talking all the way home.

The children ran ahead hollering, "Mama! Mama!" They disappeared into the soddy, leaving Travis to follow.

Jenny was talking a mile a minute when he strolled in. "And Mrs. Truman had a girl. I was so happy. We don't have enough girls here. There's jus' me an' Violet, then baby Willow an' the new one. That's all."

"It'll even out one of these days," Rebel said calmly.

"Guess what the new baby's name is."

"I don't know. What?"

"Noelle."

"Honey, that's so pretty. Now let your brother talk, please."

"I thought I'd never get a turn." Ely propped his elbows on the bed. "My name is Ely Lassiter now. I like Lassiter because I know you and Papa will never stop loving me and Jenny. When I get big, I want to be just like my papa. No one tries to hurt him because he's tough and will scare them."

Rebel glanced at Travis leaning against the wall. He lifted innocent eyebrows at her.

"Your father will indeed scare people who try to harm us." Rebel pulled Ely close and kissed his hair.

After several more minutes, Travis pushed away from the wall. "That's enough, kids. Let your mama rest. She's tired."

With a happy sigh, Rebel burrowed into the covers, loving this man who watched over her, doing everything to see she gained her strength for the wedding that almost wasn't.

❧

The days flew by in a flurry of excitement. Though shy, Eleanor came to visit Rebel, which pleased her to no end. This was Eleanor's start to finding her way back.

A big snow on Christmas Eve left everything all white and glistening like thousands of diamonds. Eleanor opened her door and gave out pretty, little, bite-size decorated cakes she'd made. The kids loved them and said she made the best treats of anyone.

"She didn't look that scary, and she can sure cook," Ely had reported.

Rebel remained very weak and unable to be up long at a time, but she wasn't going to miss another day of her children's lives if she could help it. Travis hovered over her as though she was going to break until she sent him to go spend some time with Clay and Jack. Just as he started out, a wagon lumbered to a stop hauling a big Christmas tree, and Tait and Ridge jumped down.

In all the flurry, she hadn't given the tree a thought. Ely and Jenny ran out of the soddy like a couple of banshees. Rebel wrapped her shawl closer and went to look, holding on to the few pieces of furniture for support.

Christmas was almost perfect.

But she didn't have any gifts for the children. Or Travis. Even if she hurried, she couldn't make anything in time. She went to her trunk and raised the lid. At the very bottom in the corner, she found a watch chain—her only remembrance of her father—and slipped it into her pocket. After digging through the contents, she found nothing suitable to give Jenny and Ely.

With a heavy heart she lay on the bed.

∽∾

Travis entered the quiet house to find Rebel napping, teardrops clinging to the tips of her long lashes. As he turned to go, the toe of his boot caught the open trunk and made a racket.

Rebel raised herself on an elbow. "You're back."

"Sorry I woke you. We got the tree unloaded and up in the center of town. The children are decorating it under the ladies' watchful eyes."

He sat beside her on the bed and wiped her tears. "What's wrong?"

She moved into his arms and laid her head on his shoulder. He held her tenderly as she bemoaned, "I don't have any gifts for Ely and Jenny. What kind of mother am I?"

"The best kind. I got you covered, darlin'."

She leaned back to look at him. "What do you mean?"

"I bought a pocketknife for Ely and a new doll for Jenny—one with glass eyes and real arms. You're no longer alone and having to figure things out by yourself. We're a team, and we'll handle problems together."

"It's hard to realize that after all these years of being on my own." She brushed her fingers across his cheek and jaw. "I love you so much."

He placed a hand around her neck and pulled her forward until his lips met hers. The kiss was long and deep. Rebel melted against him and he savored the chance they'd been given.

Thankfulness for the wish granted and love for this remarkable woman wound through Travis like a life-giving river. He prayed he'd never have to learn to live without her. She was all he ever wanted and all he'd ever need, and he couldn't wait to make it official.

He broke the kiss and lay down beside her, pulling her close, lacing his fingers through hers. "We need to make some decisions."

"Like what?"

"Where we're going to live for starters. This soddy is too small for four people, and mine is practically uninhab-itable. What do you say to us building a new house?"

A soft gasp left her. "How? With what? Do you have money?"

"I have a little I saved up over the years. I never needed much, so I put aside everything I earned. We're not destitute by any means."

"That's good to know."

"But I received a proposition that I want to run by you." He brought her hand to his mouth and kissed her fingers. "Owen Vaughn over at the mercantile is having to leave for a while."

"That's old news. I heard he's going to settle his father's estate and expects to be gone for at least six months—or so Tally says."

Travis stared at her. She was sick and bedridden for weeks. How could she know this? "I guess I'm a little behind on the grapevine. Anyway, he asked me to take over in his absence."

"That's wonderful!"

"Not only that, but he has that big house and offered it to us while he's gone." He drew lazy circles on Rebel's arm. "I figure we can build our house in that length of time."

Rebel was quiet for so long he thought she'd drifted off. Finally, she sniffled. "I don't know what to say. It's too generous. The people here truly are amazing. They open their hearts and let you walk in."

"Yes, they do. I take it that's a yes on accepting?"

"A very positive yes."

"I hope you're ready to work because it's not going to be easy."

"As long as you're with me, I can do anything."

Ten

REBEL WOKE EARLY ON HER WEDDING DAY TO AN EMPTY bed and stretched. This was it. This was the day she'd waited for her whole life.

She rose and dressed. Though still weak, she was making progress. Each day saw more and more improvement. She glanced out the window, and the snow falling softly didn't even spoil her mood. Whatever happened didn't make any difference and wasn't going to ruin her plans.

Thankfully, Travis had brought in a good supply of wood and had the stove going. She hummed a happy tune. From now until eternity, they'd be together in the same bed with his strong arms around her.

"Mornin', Mama." Jenny wandered to the kitchen area to hug Rebel.

The word *mama* made her breath catch. "Did you sleep well, sweetheart?"

"I dreamed you were wearing angel wings."

"Angel wings?" Rebel laughed. "Honey, I doubt that'll ever happen."

"You were so pretty, and you said you loved me."

Rebel pulled out a chair at the table and sat Jenny in her lap. "I love you more than you'll ever, ever know, and I'll never stop."

"I'm glad."

Ely climbed from the loft. "Mama, I can't find my best shirt to wear to the wedding."

Again, the word *mama* brought unexpected happiness.

"I'll find it, honey. What would you like for breakfast?"

The meal passed in a blur. She and Travis gave Ely and Jenny each their one gift. The children tore into them in record time and grinned at the unexpected treasures.

Rebel pulled a small box from her pocket and handed it to Travis. "Merry Christmas."

His eyes met hers. "We never talked about exchanging gifts."

"It's something of my father's, and I want you to have it. Open it."

He flipped the lid up and removed the gold watch chain. "This is really nice. Are you sure you want to part with an heirloom?"

"I do. It'll finally replace that old piece of frayed leather. Besides, it's still in the family."

"I'll look like a banker with this hanging from my watch pocket." He grinned and kissed her, then reached behind him for a small package. "This is for you."

Rebel tore open the paper and gasped at a tortoise-shell hair comb adorned with sparkly crystals on one end. "I've never seen anything so pretty. This is the perfect touch for my dress. I love you, Travis Lassiter."

"I'm glad you like it, darlin'."

They attended church and lit the last Advent candle, then had the lunch that Nora and Tally had prepared. Finally, that afternoon, Nora and Tally shooed Travis out and locked the door. They assisted Rebel with her wedding dress and declared her the most beautiful bride they'd ever seen. Tally fixed her hair, arranging it up high with loose tendrils of dark hair trailing down and framing her face. The crowning touch was the hair comb Travis had given her.

Before she knew it, her friends had left and Travis stood at the door looking like a prosperous business-man or lawyer. Gone were his worn shirt and trousers, replaced by a new three-piece dark suit, the gold watch chain hanging from his pocket, his hair curling possessively around his collar. This was probably the first time she'd ever seen him minus his gun and holster. Goosebumps pimpled her skin, thinking about later.

His deep voice aroused tingles. "Are you ready?"

Rebel stood on shaky legs, her red dress forming a circle of satin around her. Travis seemed to have trouble swallowing, and his eyes glowed with happiness.

"You're the most beautiful vision I've ever seen." He kissed the tender flesh behind her ear, leaving a trail of warmth, and her knees turned to pudding.

She slid an arm around his neck. "I'm glad I'm snatching you up while I can before the single women here push me aside. You're a handsome man, Travis Lassiter, and I'm proud to be yours."

With a growl, he swept her into his arms. "Ely, can you get the door?"

"Yes, Pa." Ely grinned, and Jenny stood beside him flicking her hands in excitement.

Two horses waited outside, and one had red ribbon decorating its bridle and saddle. Leading away from the house was a trail lit on each side with softly burning red candles.

Tears stung the back of Rebel's eyes. She put her hand to her mouth. "Oh, Travis."

"You like it?"

"It takes my breath. You're a very romantic man."

He chuckled and sat her on the decorated horse. "Please don't tell my wife, or she'll expect me to do things like this all the time."

"I think your secret is out." Rebel threw back her head and laughed, loving this life and this man who filled her whole world with such joy.

After lifting Ely and Jenny onto the second horse, he gathered the reins of both and walked toward the church, leading them. Rebel felt like a queen. She could hardly breathe because of sheer happiness. To think that she had almost missed this, and would have if not for Travis's voice full of anguish and love that had kept her anchored to this life.

The service that afternoon was everything Rebel had envisioned. Candles flickered along the walls and from every corner. The door to the packed church opened, and Eleanor slipped inside.

Rebel smiled. Baby steps led to bigger ones.

While organ music played, she walked toward Travis with Ely and Jenny on either side.

Then she took her place next to him, put her hand in his, and vowed to stand beside him in sickness and in health, forsaking all others.

As if she had eyes for anyone but Travis.

He was her future, her destiny, her one true love for all time.

∞

Darkness found her with Travis, his arm bracing her, watching the children dance around the Christmas tree, singing at the top of their lungs. Men raised their guns and fired into the midnight sky as the church bell tolled.

Hope's Crossing, the town of outlaws, was celebrating the birth of Jesus as only they knew how.

About the Author

Linda Broday resides in the Panhandle of Texas on the Llano Estacado. At a young age, she discovered a love for storytelling, history, and anything pertaining to the Old West. Cowboys fascinate her. There's something about Stetsons, boots, and tall, rugged cowboys that gets her fired up! A *New York Times* and *USA Today* bestselling author, Linda has won many awards, including the prestigious National Readers' Choice Award and the Texas Gold Award. Visit her at lindabroday.com.

A LOVE LETTER TO SANTA

❖•❖

Margaret Brownley

*Christmas is a great institution, especially
in time of trouble and disaster.*
—George Templeton Strong, 1862

One

WITH A NOD AT THE PIANIST, HOLLY SANDERS TURNED her attention back to the six elderly people staring at her in waiting silence. Wishing she could plug her ears, Holly braced herself with a quick breath and raised her baton. "One, two, three…"

As predicted, each singer started on a different beat. Slow as rising bread, their wobbly voices gradually grew louder, assaulting even the uppermost rafters of the old barn used for rehearsals. Unaware that they were singing off-key, the oldsters sang with such joyful abandon that Holly didn't have the heart to stop them and make them start over.

From a nearby stall, Romeo the donkey made no such allowances. Twitching his ears and stomping his foot, he drew back thick lips in protest and added to the dissonant sound with a loud *hee-haw*. Following his example, Molly the milk cow let out a low, though no less disapproving, *moo*.

Not that Holly could blame the barn's residents. Getting the six to sing in unison was harder than getting rain to fall on command. Forget about tonal deficiencies. If the oldsters would just learn to begin and end a song together, she would consider her job done.

Holly shot a look of apology to her pianist, Mrs. Brewster. The retired schoolmistress did her best to speed up or slow down on the whim of the singers, but she had the pinched look of a prune.

Feeling bad for putting the piano player through such an ordeal—not to mention the animals—Holly lowered her baton and groaned inwardly. Dear God. A group of yipping coyotes couldn't sound worse.

Still, it did her heart good to see her dear grandfather looking more like his old self. After Grandmama had died, he'd been so melancholy, Holly had feared losing him, too. It was only at Doc Avery's urging that she agreed to move her grandfather into the Oddfellows Home for the Aged. It turned out to be the right thing to do.

He now had friends his own age and had gained back some of his old spirit. Unlike the last three years, he also seemed to look forward to Christmas.

She only hoped that the good citizens of Haywire had a handy supply of cotton for their ears when the group took the stage at the annual Christmas pageant.

Though her baton remained motionless, the six oldsters seemed unaware that she had stopped directing.

As much as she liked seeing them have a good time, a body could take only so much discord, and hers had reached its limit. Signaling Mrs. Brewster to stop, Holly banged her baton against the music stand for attention.

Five singers mercifully fell silent. Oblivious to what was going on around him, her grandfather kept singing.

And singing.

It was the fifth night of rehearsal, but the group had shown little if any improvement. Whoever said that practice made perfect had never met her grandfather or his cronies.

Holly waved her hand to gain his attention, but it took a nudge by Mrs. Stone with her cane before her grandfather stopped singing. "Whatcha do that fer?" he asked, rubbing his side.

Mrs. Stone tossed a white-haired nod to the front of the barn, and Holly's grandfather's faded-gray eyes came to rest on her.

"We're singing 'Joy to the World,' Grandpapa," Holly explained, her calm voice belying her frustration. If the group didn't improve, her reputation as a teacher would be put in jeopardy. Since she was hoping to teach at the new school when it opened, that was a concern.

Certainly, she would never again be asked to direct the school pageant.

He lifted his hearing horn to his ear. "Aye? What did you say?"

Holly repeated herself, this time louder. Even with his hearing apparatus, Grandpapa couldn't hear worth a tinker's dam. She spoke louder. "We're singing 'Joy to the World,'" she repeated. "You were singing 'Deck the Halls.'"

Grandpapa smiled. Now, as always, his toothless grin made her forget her annoyance. That is, until he started singing off-key again, his grating voice hitting notes not found on any known musical scale. "Fa, la, la…"

Taking this as a cue, his elderly friends joined in, and for once their voices actually harmonized in a croaky sort of way. All except Mr. Carpenter's. The old veteran somehow managed to sing every Christmas carol to the tune of "John Brown's Body."

But John Brown's moldy body couldn't hold a candle to Miss Wright. In her younger days, the spinster had traveled to New York to hear Jenny Lind sing. Unfortunately, her imitation of the operatic singer sounded more like a screech owl than the Swedish Nightingale.

Holly waited for the last *fa, la, la* to fade away. "Let's sing 'Oh, Little Town of Bethlehem,'" she said. Heaven knows, they'd rehearsed it enough.

"Aye? Whatcha say?"

Raising her voice, Holly repeated the name of the carol for her grandfather's benefit. "All right, everyone." She raised her arms. On the count of three, she signaled the pianist with a nod of her head and dipped her baton. "Oh, little town...."

A screech owl was not part of the heavenly host on that very first Christmas, but it certainly was present tonight. And even John Brown's body couldn't compete with her grandfather's imitation of a pack of howling wolves. "Fa, la, la, la, la, laaaaaaaaaaa...."

Two

TOM CHANDLER STUCK HIS HEAD OUT OF THE SECOND-story window for a better look at the barn next door. For five nights, he'd been subjected to the worst possible noise and was at the end of his rope.

At first, he'd thought the wails emanating from the barn had been a dying bull. He'd also considered the possibility of someone practicing dentistry. Or maybe even a surgeon whose specialty was chopping off body parts. It took a while to figure out that the vociferous sounds were actually meant to be musical.

"Will they ever stop?" he muttered. It was nearly nine, and he was in dire need of peace and quiet.

Pulling his head inside, he slammed the window shut against the cool night air, but there was no glass thick enough to block out the god-awful howls.

The hardest part had been trying to keep his dog, Winston, from barking to show his disapproval.

Tonight was no different. After a series of low growls had failed to get the hoped-for results, Winston suddenly raced across the room in a black-and-white streak. The dog's jarring barks threatened to wake the dead.

Tom grabbed Winston by the collar. "Shh. Do you want to get me in trouble again?" Mrs. Greenfield had agreed to allow Winston to stay at the boardinghouse, but only if he didn't disturb the other guests.

The racket next door stopped, but if the past five nights were any indication, the reprieve would only be temporary.

Winston flopped down on the floor with a sigh and

crossed his front paws. Just as Tom had predicted, the loud groans—he refused to call it singing—started up again. Jumping up on all fours, Winston made a mad dash over the bed to the window. Paws on the sill, he did everything but yowl, and this time it was all Tom could do to pull him away.

"Quiet!"

Winston looked like he wanted to argue. Instead, he sat at Tom's command and laid his head down with a woebegone sigh.

Tom frowned. The dog had a disturbing way of making him feel guilty. "Do you want to get us both thrown out on the streets?"

Woeful, brown eyes looked up at him, and Tom's temper snapped. "Okay, that does it!" Pointing a finger at Winston and telling him to stay quiet, Tom stormed out of his room.

Moments later, he barreled into the barn next door and came to a skid in front of six elderly people, all bellowing as if their tongues were caught in a vise.

Whirling about, he turned to the young woman madly waving a stick.

"We need to talk." To be heard over the ruckus, it was necessary to raise his voice. The pianist stopped playing, but the old-timers kept going.

Eyes the color of spring grass peered at him from the music director's pretty, round face. It took several swipes of her stick against the music stand before blessed silence prevailed.

"Welcome," she said with a bright smile and an equally cheery voice. "My name is Holly. I'm so glad you decided to join us." Without giving him a chance to speak, she pointed to a spot next to a white-haired man holding a hearing horn to his ear. "If you would kindly stand over there…"

The old man must have misunderstood the gesture as

he immediately lowered the horn and opened his mouth to sing. "Deck the halls with boughs of—"

"Not yet, Grandpapa."

"Aye? Whatcha say?"

An elderly woman leaned on her cane and yelled in his ear. "She said not yet!"

The man looked affronted. "You don't have to yell!" he shouted back.

Tom's gaze traveled from one wizened face to the other before turning back to the woman named Holly. "I don't want to join your—" He stopped and began again in a voice he hoped would better solicit the lady's empathy. "I'm sorry, but I'm afraid I croak more than sing."

"Then you'll fit right in," she said in a conspiratorial voice meant for his ears only.

Glancing at the motley group of oldsters, he sincerely hoped she didn't mean that the way it sounded. "Actually, the reason I'm here is that your..."—he cleared his throat—"is causing me a problem."

Holly's eyes widened. "Oh?"

"You see, my dog has sensitive ears." He'd discovered quite by accident that mentioning his dog brought out a woman's soft maternal side. "As I'm sure you're aware, it's also late." As if to commiserate, the donkey let out a loud *hee-haw*.

Since the woman appeared confused, he explained. "I'm staying at the boardinghouse next door, and Mrs. Greenfield made it clear that if I don't keep my dog quiet, I'll have to leave. Do you have any idea how hard it is to find a place to live with a dog?"

Her eyes softened with sympathy. "Maybe...maybe your dog is lonely," she said, and quickly went on to explain. "Dogs tend to bark when they want company."

"Lonely?" Tom stared at her. "I don't think I made myself clear, ma'am—"

"Holly," she said.

"Sorry?"

"My name is Holly."

"Holly," he repeated, and wondered if her bright-red hair and sparkling green eyes had been the inspiration for her name. Since it appeared Holly didn't adhere to formalities, he introduced himself in kind.

"Name's Tom," he said and glanced at the oldsters staring at him. Not wanting to hurt their feelings, he decided it best not to mention dentistry, body parts, or even dying bulls.

"As I'm sure you're aware, it's late." He lowered his voice but was no less adamant. Her liquid eyes grew softer still, drawing his gaze ever deeper into their depths. "Unfortunately, the…the…"

"Singing," Holly said, her expression daring him to contradict.

"Singing," he said carefully, wanting to stay on her good side, "causes my dog's ears to—"

"Please accept my apology. I had no idea it had grown so late, and I certainly wouldn't want to do anything to harm your dog." She continued in a breathless voice. "I hold rehearsals in the barn so as not to bother the other residents. I didn't think the sound would carry next door. It was the only place we could find that had room enough for the piano."

Tom glanced at the upright piano that looked as bad as it sounded. The keys were yellow, and one crooked leg was propped up by a thick book.

"That's all right," he said, not wanting to make her feel bad. "No harm done."

She gave him a grateful smile. "Christmas is only a few weeks away. As I'm sure you noticed, we still have a lot of work to do."

He'd have to be deaf not to notice.

She bubbled on, words spilling from her lips like water down a mountainside. "You have my word. From now on, I'll keep rehearsals short so as not to bother your dog." This time, her brilliant smile almost made Tom forget his purpose in coming.

It wasn't until she looked at him all funny-like that he realized he was staring, but he couldn't seem to help himself. The combination of green eyes and red hair was only partly to blame. After spending the day amid the bleak walls of his blacksmith shop, he found her lively features and bright smiles a welcome relief. Her delicate, sweet fragrance didn't hurt, either, reminding him of violets in spring.

Catching himself still staring, he cleared his throat. "That would be a...start," he said, though he'd rather they stopped rehearsals altogether. But since she looked so eager to please, he added, "I'll be happy. Mrs. Greenfield will be happy. We'll all be happy."

"About your dog..." Holly began tentatively.

"My dog will be happy, too," he assured her.

"I was going to suggest perhaps finding your dog a playmate. You know, so it won't be lonely."

"Winston isn't lonely," he said, taking offense. The dog had more of a social life than he had. "The problem is my dog has sensitive ears and all that fa, la, la, la, la..."

Apparently taking Tom's words as a cue, Holly's grandfather opened his mouth and began to wail like a rabid wolf.

Holly waved her arms. "No more, Grandpapa. That's all for tonight."

The old man fell silent, and his partners glared at Tom as if he'd done something wrong.

Then Tom heard it: Winston in the distance, barking his head off.

"That's...that's my dog now," he said, backing toward the barn door. "I told you he has sensitive ears."

Turning on his heel, he dashed outside. The dang dog would be the death of him yet.

Even before he sped up the porch steps to the boardinghouse and raced up the stairs to the second floor, he could hear Mrs. Greenfield pounding on his door.

Three

STIFLING A YAWN, HOLLY STOOD BENEATH THE LAMPPOST on Main Street, watching men pile ladders onto the bed of a horse-drawn wagon. The crew supervisor waved as he drove away.

Nelson Parker had done her a huge favor by sending his workers to decorate the town. He offered to help only if she agreed to attend the Christmas Ball with him.

The invitation had come as no surprise, thanks to her matchmaking aunt. Aunt Daisy had invited him to Sunday dinner on several occasions in recent weeks and always made sure he and Holly had time alone.

Holly could hardly fault her aunt for her scheming ways. Nelson was everything a woman could want in a beau. He was educated, successful, and not bad to look at. His vast property holdings, including the Haywire Grande Hotel, made him one of the few who hadn't been adversely affected by the drought.

No question, she was one lucky woman. The problem was, she found him boring. She hated thinking of him that way, but she couldn't help it. All he ever talked about was business, business, business. Last week, he'd cornered her in Gordon's General Store and talked for a solid forty minutes about a real-estate deal in the making.

Maybe her aunt was right; maybe Holly was simply being too picky. But she had hoped that when the right man came along, he would make her heart sing, not glaze her eyes over.

Sighing, she breathed in the fresh morning air and

let her gaze wander. Main Street had been turned into a Christmas wonderland. So as not to interfere with business, Nelson had arranged for his men to work through the night. Now bright-red bows hung from every lamppost and decorated each shop door.

Bunting had been draped on the false-front buildings and homemade bells dangled from corner boards and cornices. Members of Holly's quilting bee had helped plaster paper snowflakes on storefront windows.

It had taken weeks of hard work to get ready. Just collecting supplies had taken more time than she cared to admit. The hardest job was having to beg for donations from merchants who could barely make ends meet.

Haywire had been hit by hard economic times. Holly hoped that making this the best Christmas ever would give the town's residents something to smile about.

Decorating and rehearsals were the least of it. There was still plenty of work to be done.

Monday, she planned to have her students write letters to Santa. Last year, some of her pupils had written letters on their own, and that had turned into a disaster. She felt a pain in her heart each time she recalled the disappointment on her pupils' faces as they stared at the sole child in her class whose Christmas wish had come true.

This year, Holly was determined that every child writing to Santa would get his or her wish. That was turning out to be a harder task than she'd imagined, but she had no intention of giving up.

Now, she felt a surge of excitement as the first light of dawn moved across the town like a rising tide. She could hardly wait till shop owners, businessmen, housewives, farmers, and ranchers arrived and spotted the bright decorations. If that didn't bring a smile to their grim faces, nothing would!

∽∾

Tom turned over and almost fell on the dirt floor. Again! The cot was too short, too narrow, too hard. Now that Mrs. Greenfield had tossed him and his dog out of the boardinghouse, he'd had no choice but to bed down at his blacksmith shop.

It was only the third night spent sleeping there, but already his body protested. His neck hurt, his shoulders ached, and his mood took another turn for the worse.

He flopped over on his back and stared at the dawn-lit ceiling. Morning had finally arrived.

He'd tried talking the stubborn landlady out of evicting him and had even offered to double his rent. Just as she'd looked about to give in, Holly's grandfather had started howling again, and Winston had gone wild. That got them both tossed out, bag and baggage.

It wasn't only the size of the cot that bothered him—or even that he was without a decent place to live—but that the town never slept. Somewhere around midnight, a group of rowdy cowboys had raced down Main Street shooting off pistols and yelling.

A little after 1:00 a.m., Tom had been awakened by a drunk singing at the top of his lungs. There were other sounds, too.

Wagon wheels, horses, and a persistent owl had kept him awake, as did a series of mysterious thumps that he couldn't for the life of him figure out.

Unfortunately, Winston thought it his responsibility to sound an alarm at the slightest disturbance. The dog needed a muzzle, earplugs, something...

A sliver of sunshine crept through the cracks of the double doors. Sitting up, Tom swung his feet to the floor. Winston lifted his head and looked all droopy-eyed.

"Serves you right for keeping me awake all night," Tom muttered. Groaning, he stood and rubbed his sore back. The only good thing was that he lacked a mirror and couldn't see how bad he looked.

He still hadn't made up his mind what to do about the shop. An uncle on his mother's side had suddenly died, leaving Tom the sole heir. He'd decided to check out the town before making a decision on whether to keep or sell the business. So far, he'd not been impressed with either Haywire or its residents. Still, owning his business, even with the inherent headaches, sure beat having to work for someone else.

He blinked the sleep out of his eyes and reached for his trousers. He needed coffee—the stronger the better. Following his usual morning trip to the Feedbag Café, he planned on stopping at the bathhouse and then the barber for a quick shave.

But first things first. After tugging on trousers, shirt, and boots, he called Winston to the door. "Come on, boy."

Winston jumped up, tail wagging. Nothing he liked more than his early-morning walks.

After slipping on Winston's leash, Tom opened one side of the double doors. Squinting against the bright morning sun, he stepped outside.

All at once he was ambushed—attacked more like it—and everything went black. Flailing his arms, he thrashed about, blindly.

"What the—?"

Yelping, Winston ran in circles, entangling them both in the leash. By the time Tom had managed to work his way free from the restraints, he was flat on his back, the dog practically on top of him.

Tom pushed Winston away, but it took longer to unravel himself from the leash and what seemed like an endless ream of fabric. The spooked dog just wouldn't stand still, and Tom was quickly losing his patience.

He finally escaped from what turned out to be red bunting—miles and miles of red bunting. Looking up to the roofline, Tom's jaw dropped. What in the name of Sam Hill had happened!

At first glance, it sure did seem like there had been an explosion. But a closer look revealed a method to the madness. Someone had gone to the trouble of decorating his blacksmith shop for Christmas. Bombarding it was more like it. That explained the mysterious thumps heard in the night.

A quick glance up Main Street made him cringe. Not a shop, business, or lamppost in town had escaped the onslaught.

Every false-front building was covered with bunting and dangling ornaments. Colored glass balls and shiny tin stars hung from weathered eaves. Doors were adorned with red-and-white-calico bows the size of wagon wheels.

Shaking his head in disbelief, Tom stared at the tumbleweeds dusted with flour stacked three high along the boardwalk to look like snowmen. Even the hitching posts hadn't escaped the blitz. Red ribbon was wrapped around the rails candy-cane style, matching the town's lampposts.

Fortunately for his horse, Blaze, the water troughs had been left unmolested. No doubt an oversight.

Muttering to himself, Tom jerked on Winston's leash, pulling him away from the tumbleweeds. The last thing he needed was to have to yank thorns out of Winston's coat.

He reached for the fabric wrapped around his feet. One end was still attached to the eaves. As he tried to untangle himself, the rest of the ornaments came tumbling down, burying him and his dog a second time.

Cursing beneath his breath, Tom battled a string of tin stars and silver bells. Next to him, Winston frantically jumped, barked, and tugged, making matters worse.

At last, Tom managed to pull the last of the decorations away from Winston. But somehow during the battle, the snowman had lost its head.

Winston looked at him with droopy ears, his tail between his legs. "You okay, boy?"

"*Woof!*" A tin star fell to the ground, and Winston jumped. Apparently, that was the last straw as Winston ran into the shop, dragging his leash behind him.

Sighing, Tom kicked the string of tin stars away from his feet. What an utter mess.

A gasp sounded from behind him, and Tom spun around.

A woman stared at him from the driver's seat of a horse and wagon, mouth and eyes rounded. Lifting her skirts and revealing a well-turned ankle, she jumped to the ground and stormed toward him. An advancing bull couldn't have packed more fury.

"Have you any idea how long it took to put up those decorations?" she demanded, hands at her waist. "How much work was involved?" She looked about to say more, but suddenly stopped and threw up her hands. "Oh! It's you. The man with the lonely dog."

"My dog is not—" He paused midsentence. Even discounting the red hair, he would have recognized those particular green eyes anywhere. "You're the…eh…" He stopped short of saying the woman who got him tossed out of the boardinghouse. "Music director." He indicated the heap of decorations at his feet. "Don't tell me you did this." It was hard to fathom that such a small package could cause such a disruption to his life.

She glared at him. "Me and a crew of hard-working men."

Tom drew in his breath and rubbed the back of his neck. Oh, boy. Now he'd done it.

Not giving him a chance to explain that he hadn't purposely ruined her work, she continued. "I thought it was just the singing you didn't like. But it's obvious you don't like Christmas. Period." As efficient as she was quick, she gathered up an armload of decorations and tossed them into the back of her wagon, muttering all the while.

Picking up the mountain of fabric at his feet, he tried folding it the best he could before handing it to her. "I like Christmas just fine—" he began, but she quickly cut him off before he could fully apologize.

"Never mind," she said. "I won't bother you again." Having collected the last of the decorations, she hopped into the driver's seat and drove away.

Tom watched her go. He didn't need the headless snowman to tell him that as far as the pretty miss was concerned, his name was mud.

Four

HOLLY PICKED UP A PIECE OF CHALK. "ALL RIGHT, BOYS and girls. Today, we're going to write letters to the North Pole, and I want you to use your best handwriting." She turned her back to the class and began writing on the blackboard. "This is the correct way to begin a letter."

She wrote *Dear Santa* on the board. The name Santa had grown in popularity in recent years and had replaced St. Nick. As she wrote the last sample on the board, she heard whispers behind her.

She dropped the chalk in the ledge and turned to face her class. "Is there something you wish to share, Bobby?"

Bobby Baker sat back in his seat, arms folded, his expression too hard and cynical for an eight-year-old. "Santa ain't gonna bring us any toys. He didn't bring us anything last year, and he ain't gonna bring anything this year."

Since hurt feelings were more important than grammar, Holly ignored the urge to correct his speech. There would be time enough later for that. Instead, she folded her hands together and surveyed her class. Fifteen pairs of eyes turned to her. Little Alice Harper looked close to tears, and she wasn't the only one.

Holly sighed. She'd hoped the English assignment would bring smiles, not tears. But then she could hardly blame Bobby for feeling the way he did.

"Last year was a bad year for everyone." She spoke in a calm voice that she hoped would both soothe and encourage. "Even Santa had a bad year. But this year will be different. Santa has a lot more helpers, and he promises to do his best to pay a visit to each and every one of you on Christmas Eve."

Her assurances brought a look of relief to some, but not Bobby. The poor boy had had too many disappointments in life to believe that things would be different. Bobby was the oldest of four. His mother had died in childbirth, and his father had his hands full keeping his business running and taking care of the children, the youngest being two.

"Any questions?" she asked.

Sandra Miller raised her hand and Holly called on her. "Can Santa bring me a baby brother or sister?"

Before Holly could answer, the minister's grandson, Jimmy Johnson piped up. "No, silly. That's God's department." Jimmy considered himself an authority on the subject.

Since Sandra seemed content, Holly let Jimmy's answer stand and called on Willie Tustin. "You have a question, Willie?"

"Can I ask for two things?"

"Only if you've been *very* good," Holly said. Since no one else raised a hand, she looked at her pendant watch. "You have twenty minutes to write your letters."

As her students began writing, she wandered from desk to desk, looking over each child's shoulder.

Some children asked after Santa's health. Others made sure to describe themselves in such saintly terms, Holly couldn't help but smile.

Jerry Maine wrote that he wanted a folding knife. This made Holly wonder whether the new blacksmith would be willing to donate one. Probably not, the old Scrooge.

Actually, the man wasn't that old. Probably not a day over thirty. Too bad he had such an aversion to Christmas.

Shaking the thought away, she stopped at Bobby's desk. His paper was still blank.

∞

Tom held the tongs over the fire to heat the metal until it was red. After the iron was sufficiently soft, he draped it over the anvil. Using various parts of the anvil, he shaped the heel of the horseshoe and gave it a couple of good whacks with the hammer.

The steel turned gray in color, but it was still hot enough to punch holes in. After repeatedly heating the metal and cooling it down, he inspected the newly forged horseshoe with a critical eye and tossed it into a wooden crate with the others.

He laid the hammer down and reached for Winston's leash. "Whatya say we take a break, buddy?"

Getting no response, he glanced around. The front door was open a crack, and there was no sign of Winston.

A chill raced through him. Like other towns, Haywire had no tolerance for stray dogs. Some folks feared rabies more than they feared rattlers—and pity the poor dog who got in the way.

Cursing himself for not noticing that the door hadn't closed properly, Tom whipped off his leather apron, grabbed his hat, and ran outside.

A playful bark followed by a woman's musical laughter made him spin around. The sounds came from across the street.

Tugging the brim of his hat lower to shade his eyes from the glaring sun, he scanned the opposite boardwalk. Winston was bouncing up and down like a rubber ball.

But it was the owner of the laugh who had Tom's full attention. He would recognize that bright-red hair anywhere.

Sitting on the edge of the boardwalk, Holly ran her hands through his dog's soft coat.

Winston jumped up to lick her face, and she giggled.

Not sure what kind of reception awaited him, Tom crossed the street. Since it appeared that Holly needed rescuing, he brought his hands together in a resounding clap. "Winston! Behave yourself."

Holly looked up. Today, her green eyes lacked the fiery sparks of their last encounter but were no less striking. "Oh, it's you."

Since she didn't sound especially happy to see him, Tom gave her a sheepish grin. "Sorry about Winston. He's usually only that friendly when he's wet."

He was hoping to make her smile, but instead she frowned. "Winston?" She blinked in disapproval. "Such a serious name for such a fun dog."

Tom shrugged. "Would you rather I called him Donner or Blitzen?" he asked, alluding to her obvious love of Christmas.

Winston jumped up and licked her on the cheek. "I think Cupid would be more appropriate," she said and laughed.

Since it looked like Holly was in danger of being slobbered to death, Tom grabbed Winston's collar and pulled him away. "Speaking of names, I don't believe we've properly introduced ourselves. Tom Chandler. And you're Holly…"

"Sanders," she said. "Holly Sanders."

"Sanders, uh?" He tilted his head. "Are you sure it's not Santa?"

"I'm pretty sure it's Sanders," she said, and this time her bright smile was solely for him.

Wishing he'd had time to shave, he ran a hand over his bristly chin. "I'm afraid we got off on the wrong foot the other day," he said. "I didn't pull the decorations down on purpose. I wouldn't do such a thing."

She narrowed her eyes as if to judge his sincerity. "I should be the one apologizing, Mr. Chandler," she said.

"Tom," he said. "Call me Tom."

"All right, then. Tom." She stood. "Actually, it was my fault. I thought the shop was empty. Had I known there was a new owner, I would have asked permission before letting the crew decorate."

"It all happened rather quickly," he said. "Did you… know the last owner?"

She made a face. "Unfortunately, yes. He didn't like Christmas, either."

Tom frowned. He felt like he should defend his uncle, but the truth was he'd only met him once and that was years ago.

Holly glanced at her pendant watch. "I'm sorry, I need to go. It's almost time for the school bell to ring. It won't do for the teacher to be tardy."

"You're also a schoolmarm?" He tilted his head. "Is there anything you don't do?"

The dimple in her cheek deepened. "Some might say that I'm not much of a music director."

"And they would be wrong."

She studied him a moment before bending to pet Winston and instinctively found the sweet spot behind his dog's ears. Tom never thought to be envious of Winston, but it sure did seem like he was having all the fun.

"Goodbye, Cupid. You be good now, you hear?" Holly said.

Watching her go with woeful eyes, Winston lowered his tail between his legs and whimpered. When she had vanished around a corner, the dog looked up at Tom as if he were to blame for the lady's departure.

Tom dropped on his haunches and ruffled Winston's fur. "You like her, too, eh?"

The dog cocked an ear as if he understood. "Okay, I forgive you for getting us tossed out of the boarding-house. Figure out a way that I can see the lady again, and I'll even let you off the hook for chewing up my boot."

Tom straightened with a sigh. What was he thinking? There was no place in his life for a woman right now. Least not till he found decent living quarters and decided whether to stay in Haywire.

"Come on, Winston."

Sitting, Winston refused to budge.

Tom slapped his hand against his thigh. "Come *on*, Winston."

Still no movement from Winston.

Tom groaned and slapped his forehead. Oh, no. Please no. "Don't tell me you now answer to the name Cupid!"

This time, the dog jumped up on all fours and followed him back to the blacksmith shop with a wagging tail.

Tom rolled his eyes. Somehow, Miss Holly Sanders had turned his life upside down in more ways than one.

Five

HOLLY STARED AT THE STACK OF LETTERS ON HER AUNT'S desk. In addition to what her pupils had written, the postmaster had sent over letters addressed to St. Nick, Santa, and Mr. Claus. A couple of envelopes were addressed to the North Pole.

Word had spread, and now the stack contained letters from the far corners of the county. That had added to the workload. How in the world would she ever get through the stack? Even more worrisome, how would she ever manage to fulfill each child's wishes?

One by one, she tore open the envelopes and read the letters inside. Each childish scrawl represented a heart filled with hope and expectations. For that reason, they were not to be taken lightly. Apparently having no paper, one child had written his wish list on a square of old fabric.

Feeling overwhelmed by the momentous task she had set for herself, Holly resisted the urge to correct spelling and punctuation—the curse of being a teacher.

She slit open an envelope that looked as if it had been run over by a wagon wheel. The writer's name was Kenny Howard, and he wanted fireworks and candy. *And don't forget this year*, he'd written.

"Santa won't," Holly murmured. She placed the letter in the basket marked *General store* and made a note for the owners of the candy shop.

Granting the wishes wouldn't have been possible had it not been for the generous donations from others. And they were generous, even though it took much in the way of bribery and begging to procure them.

Mr. Gordon, owner of the general store, had been among the hardest to convince to help. Not that she blamed him. Times were tough for everyone, including merchants. But he'd finally given in and agreed to provide fireworks. Though he'd insisted the donations would probably send him to the poorhouse.

The town craftsmen had been easier to recruit. The tinker was willing to provide tin soldiers. Kate and Brett Tucker, proprietors of the Haywire Book and Sweet Shop, agreed to donate books and sweets. Emily and Chase McKnight, owners of the largest cattle ranch in the area, had made a generous monetary donation.

Admittedly Holly was a bit nervous when Mr. Mason, the town coffin maker, volunteered his services. That is, until he explained he was also skilled in making wooden blocks and doll cradles.

She dropped a request for a slingshot into the coffin maker's basket and reached for the next letter in the pile, this one addressed to Mr. Claus.

❧

That morning, Tom stifled a yawn as he left the shop to take Winston for his morning walk. Dark clouds gathered like woolly sheep in the northern sky, and there was a definite chill in the air.

He still hadn't found new diggings. A recent rabies scare in town had put everyone on edge and all dogs were suspect, Winston more than others because of his size. One boardinghouse owner had slammed the door in his face the moment he set eyes on the dog by Tom's side.

At least there were some people who appreciated his dog. He caught the butcher just as he was opening his shop. The shop owner saved scraps of beef for Winston and refused to accept payment.

"Much obliged," Tom said. Winston jumped up to sniff the bag in his hand. "Down, boy. You don't get this till supper."

"*Woof!*"

Cutting his walk short, Tom hardly made it to the end of Main Street before icy-cold winds began sweeping through town. Wishing he'd thought to don gloves, he wrapped the leash around his wrist and shoved his one free hand into his coat pocket. *Brrr.*

Dust rose up in spirals, and shutters banged. Christmas decorations pulled loose, and a large, red bow flew over his head. Horses whinnied, and people ran for cover.

By the time Tom made it back to the blacksmith shop and battled the door shut, he and Winston were chilled to the bone.

He immediately set to work building a fire. Tossing dry kindling and green coal into the forge's firepot, he added balls of crumbled newspaper and struck a match. He gave the reluctant flames a blast of air from the bellows, and white smoke shot up the chimney. Warmth soon spread across the room. Winston flicked his tail back and forth as if in approval.

Tom needed coffee, but that meant going back outside. The need for a hot beverage, not to mention his still-sore back from lack of a decent mattress, added to his misery.

He peered out the window. The wind was blowing up a gale and showed no sign of stopping. The Christmas decorations flying around made him feel bad for Holly.

The clouds were now overhead and had completely blocked out the blue sky.

Just as he decided to chance a trip to the Feedbag Café, he spotted Holly. She was struggling against the wind with an armload of boxes. A sudden strong gust blew off her hat and caused her to drop the load she was carrying.

Turning to Winston, he said, "Stay," and dashed outside.

He found Holly frantically trying to corral the scattered boxes. Fearing the wind would blow her away, Tom battled dust, debris, and a sore back to help her.

They reached for a box at the same time, their fingers touching. Despite the cold, he felt a warm bolt shoot up his arms. Startled eyes met his before she pulled her hand away, and he wondered if she had felt it, too.

Even in the wind, she was a sight for sore eyes. Her hair had come loose and now blew around her head like red flames. The wind took liberties with her skirt, revealing intriguing glimpses of feminine lace.

"Oh, no," she cried as one box skittered across the street.

"I'll get it!" he yelled. Dodging a horse-drawn wagon, he chased after it.

After the last of the lot had been collected, she led the way along the boardwalk and turned up an alleyway. The wind was still blowing something fierce as he followed her up a winding path to a small, one-story adobe house.

Inside, he was greeted by a warm fire and pleasant surroundings. A fir Christmas tree stood on a table next to the window, its branches laden with shiny bulbs that reflected light from the crackling fire. Festive green garlands hung from the mantel and were draped over doorways and windowsills. Gold bells hung from the ceiling on shiny red ribbons.

A matronly woman sat in a rocking chair in front of the blazing fire, knitting, her white hair tucked beneath a ruffled white cap. She peered at Tom over her spectacles, her long needles clicking away.

Holly dumped the cartons on a table piled high with similar boxes and motioned him to do likewise. "Thank you," she said, pulling off her cape and warming her hands by the fireplace. Her cheeks were red from the cold, and her eyes sparkled like green glass. Tom couldn't recall seeing a more fetching sight. "You helped save Christmas," she said.

"I did?" He read the box labels, and his eyebrows shot up. "Fireworks?" He stared at her.

"If I didn't know better, I'd think you were trying to blow up the town."

His comment solicited a dimpled smile that quickened his pulse.

She rubbed her hands together and turned the palms toward the blazing logs. "Welcome to the North Pole."

"Sorry?"

She pointed to a corner desk stacked high with unopened mail and explained what she and a group of volunteers had set out to do. "Those are letters to Santa. Most little boys requested fireworks."

"Can't blame them there," Tom said and furrowed his brow. "Don't tell me you and a bunch of reindeer plan on riding around town on Christmas Eve delivering gifts."

The old lady looked up from her knitting. "Don't give her any ideas." Her knitting needles paused. "Where are your manners, Holly? Aren't you going to introduce us?"

"Sorry," Holly said and promptly made the introductions.

The woman Holly had introduced as Aunt Daisy had sharp eyes that he suspected missed nothing. "What made you decide to move to Haywire, Mr. Chandler?" she asked.

"Charley Watkins was my uncle."

Holly's aunt almost dropped her knitting. "Ole Ironsides was your uncle?" She scoffed. "Grouchiest man I ever met," she muttered. "The old coot."

"Now, Auntie," Holly said with an apologetic glance at Tom. "You'll have to forgive my aunt. Sometimes she forgets *her* manners, too."

She gave her aunt a meaningful look before directing his gaze to the boxes of toys in the corner. "To answer your question, the actual stocking-stuffing will be left for parents to do. The drought has hit the town hard, and most can't afford to celebrate Christmas. Thanks to a lot of volunteers, parents can come here and pick up gifts for their children, free of charge."

Intrigued, Tom studied her. "Sounds like a lot of work."

Holly's aunt nodded in agreement. "You can say that again."

"It *is* a lot of work," Holly agreed. "But the drought has driven many families into poverty. They can hardly afford food, let alone Christmas presents." She reached for a sheet of paper on the desk and handed it to him. "Last year, one of my students wrote this."

He read the title of the page and was confused. "April Ham Lincon?" he asked.

"Oh, sorry," she said. "Wrong pile." She took the essay from him and replaced it with another sheet of paper.

This time the childish scrawl read: *Deer Santa, how come you like some childrins moore than otters? I'm a good boy. Honest, but you skiped my house and gave the train I wanted to Timmy. I still like you.* The letter was signed Billy Hopps.

Tom handed the letter back, and he could see by the way she carefully folded it that it had moved her deeply.

She fell silent for a moment before adding, "This year, I aim to make sure that no child has to ask why he or she isn't liked by the man from the North Pole."

Tom's gaze traveled to the unopened mail on her desk. If the stack was any indication, she had her work cut out for her.

"Is there anything I can do to help?" he asked.

Her finely shaped eyebrows rose. "I thought you didn't like Christmas," she said with a tilt of her head.

Her aunt made a face. "Knowing who his uncle is, what do you expect?"

Tom rubbed his chin. "I like Christmas just fine," he said. Debating how much to say, he continued. "I was the youngest of twelve children. Growing up, Christmas was like any other day of the year. There were chores to be done, and my folks didn't have money to spend on anything that wasn't a necessity. I grew up thinking that only the rich celebrated Christmas."

Holly's eyes rounded in sympathy. "But Christmas isn't just another day," she said softly. "Jesus's birth is for everyone to celebrate."

"I know that now. But back then...." He shrugged. Funny thing was, he'd not felt deprived. As a child, he'd not known any better. It wasn't until he was older and heard the Christmas memories of others that he realized how much he'd missed out.

Holly moistened her lips, drawing his attention to the sweet curve of her mouth. "If you're still serious about helping...?"

He lifted his gaze to hers and was immediately drawn into the intriguing green depths. "Sure, I'll help. Long as you don't ask me to sing."

She laughed, and the pleasing sound made his heart flutter. "I could use some help with opening letters and collecting donations," she said. "That is, if you have time."

He didn't have time. He had work to do and needed to look for new diggings. "I'll make time," he said, surprising himself.

Her face lit up with a dimpled smile that practically spread from one shiny earbob to the other. Knowing that her smile was in response to something he'd said filled Tom with a warm glow.

"Could you come back later?" she asked.

He nodded. "Sure, but don't you have rehearsals?"

"We only have the dress rehearsal left. I'm afraid the group is as good as it'll ever be. So you and Cupid can relax."

He suddenly realized she thought he still lived at the boardinghouse, but before he could correct her, she asked, "Around six, okay?"

"Six is fine," he said. That would give him time to stop at the bathhouse and barber before returning. Maybe buy himself a new shirt. Or would that look too obvious?

She looked pleased. "I'll see you later, then."

He nodded and, after saying goodbye to the aunt, headed for the door. "Later."

Six

HOLLY HAD BARELY CLOSED THE DOOR AFTER TOM WHEN Aunt Daisy puckered her mouth. She set her knitting down on her lap, which was always a bad sign.

"It's just our luck that Ole Man Watkins had a nephew," she said.

Holly stooped to count the books Kate Tucker had sent from the Haywire Book and Sweet shop. "I don't know why you say that. He seems nice enough," Holly said, though admittedly they had gotten off on the wrong foot. But that had been more her fault than his.

"He did offer to help."

"Hmm." Aunt Daisy picked up her needles and resumed knitting, but for some reason she didn't look happy.

Sighing, Holly made a notation in her notebook, then closed it and stuck her pen in the penholder. "I've got to get ready for dress rehearsal. If Nelson stops by with more toys, have him put them over there." She pointed to the only place in the room that wasn't stacked high with donations.

The knitting needles stilled in Aunt Daisy's hands. "Speaking of Nelson, have you decided what you'll wear to the Christmas dance?"

Holly groaned. Normally, she looked forward to the dance, but this year she'd hardly had time to think about it. Collecting toys had taken up her every thought.

"I'll just wear…my green dress," she said.

Aunt Daisy frowned. "You wore that last year. And the year before that."

"You said you liked it on me."

"I do like it on you. The green brings out the color of your hair and adds sparkle to your eyes. I still think you should have had Mrs. Cuttwell make you something new."

Holly sighed. The town seamstress did fine work, but she didn't come cheap. "After what everyone has gone through these last two years, I wouldn't feel right throwing money away on a new dress."

"It would be for a good cause," her aunt argued. "It's not every day that a woman gets a marriage proposal."

"Now, Aunt Daisy. You don't know that Nelson means to propose."

"I most certainly do." She gazed at Holly over the rim of her spectacles. "I'd have to be blind not to notice the way that man looks at you. If he doesn't pop the question at the dance, that means he's waiting for Christmas." Her aunt gave a self-satisfied smile and held up her knitting to check her progress.

Holly knew it wasn't just wishful thinking on her aunt's part. She doubted a man would pay his crew to work all night decorating the town unless he had serious intentions.

"I just wish you'd be more excited about it," her aunt said.

"I am excited," Holly said. Only a fool would not be excited. Nelson was everything a woman could want in a husband. Once his ring was on her finger, she would be the envy of every single female in town.

"I am excited," Holly repeated for no good reason. Okay, so she wasn't exactly jumping up and down like her friend Janice had done when she sensed Jeff Myers was about to propose. But that didn't mean she wasn't excited. She just had a lot on her mind.

The wind had stopped by the time Tom left the shop with Winston in tow and walked the three blocks to Holly's house.

The sky was overcast, and it felt cold enough to snow. The lamplighter had already made his rounds, and moths darted around the flickering lights in a frenzied dance. Ornaments were scattered all about, and none of the tumbleweed snowmen had been left intact.

After all the work Holly had gone to, he felt bad for her. Bad for the town. Still, he was at a loss to explain what had made him volunteer to help. What he should be doing is looking for a place to live.

Holly certainly had a way about her. A very nice way.

Reaching Holly's house, he looked down at Winston. Earlier, the dog had refused to eat. Maybe Holly was right. Maybe Winston was lonely. Since so many locals feared rabies, Tom had to keep him chained in a corner during business hours. No doubt Winston missed the large yard back home in San Antonio, along with the neighbor's children.

"Now behave yourself, you hear?"

The dog lifted his ears and wagged his tail. Shaking his head, Tom started up the walkway to the door.

Holly answered on his first knock. Her face lit up upon seeing his dog, and she immediately dropped to her knees. Tom watched as Holly and Winston carried on like two long-lost friends. It wasn't just Winston's tail that wagged; his whole backside swung from side to side like a trainman's lantern.

Holly looked especially appealing tonight. She wore a white shirtwaist richly embroidered with green leaves over a red skirt. Her hair was piled on top of her head, with tendrils framing her face, and her eyes sparkled like newly polished emeralds.

Silver, bell-shaped earbobs swung from her ears as she laughed. Tom couldn't seem to hear enough of her laughter, which bubbled out of her like water from a spring.

Surprised to find himself wishing that she was as happy to see him as she had been to see his dog, he stepped into the room and unbuckled Winston's leash.

"Sorry," he said, and ordered Winston to sit. "He seems to forget his manners whenever he's around you."

She stood and gazed at him with sparkling eyes. "I seem to have that effect on people, but never before on a dog," she said.

"So…" He glanced around the small room, his gaze lingering on the blazing fire and comfortable-looking chairs and sofa. The small Christmas tree drew his gaze now, as it had earlier in the day. Once again, he regretted all the years that Christmas had been just another workday. Nothing special.

Staring at the bright ornaments, he made a silent vow that if he was ever lucky enough to have a home and family of his own, he would insist upon having the tallest Christmas tree he could find, even if it meant cutting a hole in his roof.

Surprised to find himself thinking such things, he cleared this throat. "What do you want me to do?"

Holly directed him over to the dining-room table that separated the parlor from the small kitchen. "I've got you all set up here," she said, and handed him a letter opener with a mother-of-pearl handle. "Read the letters and put them into the appropriate basket. The baskets are marked. Requests for fireworks go into Mr. Gordon's basket. Trains and blocks go here. As for dolls…"

After she'd explained the system, Tom tossed his hat on a chair and sat. Flopping down by his feet, Winston let out a contented sigh.

Holly took the chair opposite him, and they both set to work.

Conscious of her every move, Tom reached for an

envelope and tried to concentrate on the job at hand, but his gaze kept wandering across the table. The fire cast a golden glow across Holly's delicate features and turned her red hair into dazzling flames that begged to be tamed.

As if sensing his gaze, she looked up and regarded him through a ring of dark lashes. "Is there a problem?" she asked.

Embarrassed to be caught staring, he shrugged. "I was just wondering, what made you decide to be a teacher?"

A gentle smile curved her lips as if recalling the past brought her pleasure. "When I was in grammar school, we had a boy who couldn't talk. His name was Eddie Polk. Everyone thought him dumb and paid him little attention. But my teacher, Miss Bridget, took special interest in him and taught him how to read and write. Today he works for the *Washington Post*."

"That's pretty impressive," he said.

"To a ten-year-old, watching Eddie go from being the dumbest to the smartest kid in class seemed like magic. That's when I decided to be a teacher."

Tom studied her. "Your pupils are lucky to have you."

"And I'm lucky to have them." She slit the wax seal on another envelope. "What about you? What made you decide to be a blacksmith?"

"After my father died, I sold scrap iron to the local smithy. I'm not proud of this, but I stole rails from where track was being laid. The money I got helped feed the family. Watching that old smithy turn a piece of metal into something useful lit a fire in me. It seemed like..."

"Magic?" she said, and they both laughed.

For several moments, they worked in silence. Tom had expected to find lists of "I wants," but that turned out not to be the case.

Some children wrote asking after Santa's health or the health of his reindeer. One boy had gotten his mother to sign the letter proving that he had been good. A child named Artie explained the dime he'd sent in his letter to Santa.

I bursted my bank. Please give this to the poor little sick boy.

One letter made him laugh.

"What's so funny?" Holly asked.

He read the letter out loud. "'Dear Santa, please send a barrel of nuts, 14 pounds of candy, a small barrel of molasses, and chewing gum.'"

Holly laughed, too. "Why didn't he just ask for a tummy ache?"

He tossed the letter into the basket marked *Sweets* and reached for the next envelope. "Why do so many children ask after Santa's health?" he asked.

Holly looked up from the letter she was reading. "Parents unable to afford gifts last year told their children that Santa was sick and wasn't able to come."

"What you're doing here," he began slowly, locking her in his gaze, "is really great."

Her dimpled smile made his heart skip a beat. "I couldn't do it without a lot of help."

Fearing he was about to drown in the depth of her green eyes, he looked away. "You still deserve a lot of credit," he said and carefully pulled the letter out of the envelope in his hand. This one was from a boy who wrote that he was seven years old. Instead of wanting toys and candy, he asked for something far more difficult to provide. *Dear Santa,* he wrote. *All I want for Christmas is for you to move into my house so that Ma and me will feel safe again.*

"What do I do about this one?" Tom asked and read the letter aloud.

Holly stopped what she was doing. "Oh dear. Who wrote that?"

Tom checked the name on the bottom of the letter. "His name is Joe-Joe."

Nodding, Holly heaved a sigh. "Joe-Joe Adams is one of my pupils. His father died last year, and someone recently stole their horse and chickens."

Tom furrowed his brow. "Why would anyone do such a thing?"

"Like I said, times are tough. Fortunately, some of the other farmers got together and replaced what was stolen, but Joe-Joe's worried it will happen again." She slit open another envelope. "I'm afraid Joe-Joe's request might be because of something I said."

"Oh?"

"One of my students asked what would happen if a thief snuck into the North Pole. I said that would never happen. No one would ever steal from Santa because he's all about goodness and kindness and love, and those things can't be stolen."

"So, this boy…Joe-Joe…thinks that if Santa comes to live with him, he and his mother will be safe from future thefts."

"It appears that way," Holly said.

Tom rubbed his chin. "What do we do?"

Holly shook her head. "There's not much we can do," she said, and Tom could see how much it pained her to say it. She paused for a moment. "Put it in the empty basket. I'll talk to his ma."

Tom folded the letter ever so carefully and placed it in the basket. Having lost his own father when he was only twelve, he felt for the boy.

For several moments, Tom and Holly worked quietly, each in their own thoughts. Holly was the first to break the silence. "Do you like staying at Mrs. Greenfield's boardinghouse?" she asked.

"Holly, I've been meaning to tell you. I'm no longer stay—"

A knock sounded at the door, and Winston jumped up, barking.

While Tom calmed Winston, Holly rushed across the room to open the door. A man dressed in a frock coat, dark trousers, and a tall hat entered carrying a wooden crate. The man's impeccable dress made Tom wish he hadn't talked himself out of purchasing a new shirt.

"Mason asked me to drop off these wooden blocks," the visitor said.

Looking pleased, Holly pointed to a corner. "Set them over there."

After setting the crate on the floor, the man turned. Seeing Tom, his forehead creased with lines of curiosity. "Looks like you roped in another helper," he said.

Holly made the introductions. "Nelson owns the hotel," she said.

While Tom and Nelson shook hands, Winston growled. Not that Tom could blame him. Someone who spent as much time on appearances as Nelson had to have a character flaw somewhere. Tom just wished it was visible to more than just his dog.

If Nelson heard Winston's low growls, he chose to ignore them. "You must be new in town. Don't recall seeing you around."

"I've been here for two weeks. My uncle recently passed away and left me his blacksmith shop."

"Oh, so you're a smithy." Nelson somehow managed to make it sound like a lowly profession.

"Every town needs at least one," Tom said evenly. That wasn't necessarily true of hotels, but he bit down on his tongue to keep from saying it.

"And this," Holly said, stooping to pet Winston on the head, "is Cupid."

Ignoring the dog, Nelson turned his full attention on Holly. "The wind did a job on some of the decorations. But don't worry, I've already got my crew working on them."

Holly's smile was as bright as the midday sun, and

once again, Tom wished he had been the one to put it there.

"Thanks, Nel, you're the best."

Winston didn't seem to like Nelson any more than Tom did. Or maybe he just didn't like someone else getting all the attention. Whatever it was, Winston's throaty growls rolled across the room like thunder.

Since Nelson obviously intended to stay, Tom decided he and Winston had best leave.

Holly saw them to the door. "Thank you for your help," she said softly. "Do you have any free time tomorrow?"

Tom stepped out into the thin, cold air and turned. For some reason, her inquiry lifted his spirits. "After I close at six," he said, trying not to sound too eager.

She afforded him a grateful smile. "I'd like to offer you a proper supper, but the kitchen is piled high with toys. If you don't mind bread and cheese…"

The thought of sharing bread and cheese with Holly sounded like a meal made in heaven, but nevertheless he turned her offer down. "That's all right. I'll grab a bite at the Feedbag Café," he said, not wanting her to go to any trouble on his behalf. A thought occurred to him and he brightened. "But I can bring you and your aunt something to eat."

"That's very kind of you to offer, but we're fine," she said. "See you tomorrow."

"Tomorrow," he said.

She offered him a quick smile before closing the door.

Tom shoved his hands into his coat pockets. Winston looked up at him and whimpered.

"Don't blame me. You're part of the reason why we had to leave. But don't worry. We get to come back tomorrow."

Tom tugged gently on the leash and started down the walkway. A fancy carriage drawn by a fine horse was parked in front of Holly's house. Frowning, Tom headed back to the cold loneliness of his shop.

⌒⌒

For the next several days, Tom quit work, cleaned up and, after wolfing down a quick supper at the Feedbag Café, made a beeline to Holly's house to sort letters and toys.

Each night, the stacks of toys grew taller. The only chair safe from being taken over was Aunt Daisy's. By Wednesday night, there was no place for Winston to lie down.

"Oh, you poor dog," Holly said, and rearranged a pile of rag dolls to clear a spot for him.

After making Winston comfortable, she took her place opposite Tom.

"Where's your aunt tonight?" Tom asked.

"Aunt Daisy's literary group meets on Wednesday nights," she said.

"So, your aunt likes to read?" Tom asked. All he'd ever seen her do was knit.

"No. She just enjoys the company."

"She's lucky she has you," Tom said.

"Actually, I'm the lucky one. She and Grandpapa are the only family I have left. After my parents died, I was raised by my grandparents. When Grandpapa moved to the home, I invited her to come and live with me."

They worked in silence for several minutes before Tom asked, "What did you decide about Joe-Joe?"

"Nothing yet. I haven't had a chance to talk to his ma." She thought for a moment. "How do you make a child feel safe when his little world has been turned upside down?"

"I wish I knew," Tom said.

They spent the next two hours organizing the newly arrived toy donations. Finally, Holly clapped her hands to her chest and let out a happy little laugh. "That's the last of it," she announced. "All the children's wishes will be granted." She let out an audible sigh. "Except for Joe-Joe's."

Tom craned his head to look at her over the mountain-high stack of building blocks. He marveled at how she could do so much for so many and still bemoan the one child she couldn't help.

"I'm afraid that's out of Santa's hands," he said.

"I was hoping for a miracle."

He glanced around the room. "I'd say this is a roomful of miracles," he said. "I just wish there was something more I could do."

She smiled up at him. "You've done enough. The rest is up to Santa's elves, also known as parents."

"I…guess you won't be needing me anymore," Tom said. He watched her face, hoping the realization was as disappointing to her as it was to him.

"'Fraid not," she said, giving him no clue as to what she was thinking.

"Holly—"

He'd meant to ask her out, but before he had a chance, the door opened, and Aunt Daisy stepped inside, letting in a cold draft. "Are you two still at it?"

"We're finished," Holly announced.

Aunt Daisy pulled off her knitted gloves and scarf. "It's about time," she said.

Since Tom couldn't think of a legitimate reason to postpone his departure, he reached for Winston's leash and dropped to his haunches. "Come on, boy. Time to go."

Winston looked as reluctant to leave as Tom felt.

Seven

THE SCHOOL AUDITORIUM WAS PACKED THE NIGHT OF THE pageant. Normally, such a large turnout would have delighted Holly. Tonight, she'd rather that a snowstorm or something had kept people home.

So far, everything that could go wrong had. Holly thought that letting Joe-Joe play Joseph would make him feel important and give him much-needed confidence. Last year before his father died, he'd played one of the shepherds with no problems.

However, he now had a bad case of stage fright, and it required much in the way of persuasion to convince him to take his place. That was the least of it.

One of the wise men accidentally fell into the manger, overturning it and sending baby Jesus bouncing across the stage. The doll's head popped off, and its owner, Susie Whittaker, promptly burst into tears. It wouldn't have been so bad had Susie not been the same little girl who played Mary.

Not even Grandpapa's dissonant singing could distract the audience from Mary's sobs. Nor could anyone ignore the fact that the little boy who played Joseph had suddenly vanished. During the confusion with the doll, Joe-Joe had run offstage, and neither Holly nor his mother could convince him to return.

The moment the last *fa, la, la* faded away, Holly took center stage and faced now what were mostly empty seats. Even Nelson had sneaked out sometime midproduction. "Thank you all for coming tonight," she said, her voice sounding hollow in the near-deserted auditorium. "I wish you and your families a very merry Christmas."

Wondering if she only imagined the collective sigh of the few remaining people, she turned, only to be stopped by the sound of loud clapping. She glanced over her shoulder and was surprised to spot Tom at the back of the room. He was the only one clapping, and his encouraging smile and enthusiastic applause touched her heart. Suddenly, it was necessary to blink back tears.

"What do you think?" her grandfather asked, drawing her attention away from the lone figure at the back of the auditorium.

She gave Grandpapa a hug and stood on tiptoes to speak directly in his ear. "You did good," she said, not wanting to hurt his feelings.

"You did, too, Holly," he said.

A quick glance over her shoulder told her that Tom had left. Still, for her grandfather's sake, she forced a smile.

Looking pleased, he puffed out his chest. "We decided to give our singing group a name."

Mrs. Stone leaned on her cane and interjected. "We're calling ourselves the Ransom Notes."

Holly laughed. Since the group butchered every song they sang, the name certainly did fit the crime.

Her grandfather gave her a knowing look. "From what I hear, the Ransom Notes will soon be needed again."

"Oh?" Holly asked.

"Daisy said that wedding bells are about to ring."

"Nothing's definite," Holly said. It would have been nice if Nelson had stayed to the end of the program. Didn't he know that she could use a friendly shoulder to cry on? Had the roles been reversed, she would have been there for him.

Her grandfather nodded. "Let us know and we'll get to work."

Holly sighed. Her grandfather meant well, but the

thought of his singing at her wedding was enough to make her want to opt for spinsterhood.

"We gotta go," Grandpapa said. "Our chaperone is waiting." He slanted his head toward the man standing offstage.

"Mr. Evans is not a chaperone," Holly said. "He's just here to make sure you all get back safely."

"Yeah, like I said. A chaperone."

Watching her grandfather and his friends walk offstage, Holly felt very much alone. She picked up the headless doll and, sitting on a child-sized chair, laid it in the manger. Susie didn't know it, but Santa had a special gift in mind for her—a pretty porcelain doll.

If only she could think of a way to make Joe-Joe feel better. He used to be such a fun, outgoing child. Holly hated seeing him so insecure and fearful.

Elbows on her knees, she dropped her face in her hands. All she'd wanted was to make this Christmas a special one for a town that had gone through hard times. The decorations were pretty much destroyed, the pageant was a disaster, and at least two children had been traumatized. What more could possibly go wrong?

Hearing footsteps, she looked up. Tom stood on the other side of the manger holding two tin cups in his hand. "I have it on the best authority that in times like this, only hot cocoa will do." He handed her a cup over the manger. "Am I wrong?"

Sitting back in surprise, she took the steaming cup in both hands and shook her head. "Not at all."

He lowered himself onto the seat next to her, the chair so small his knees practically reached his shoulders.

She laughed.

He raised a dark brow. "What's so funny?"

"You," she said. "There are larger chairs backstage."

"I'm okay. Sometimes it's a good idea to view the world from a child's viewpoint."

Surprised at his answer, she looked at him intently. A pleasant whiff of his aftershave made her want to lean in closer. Funny, but she hadn't really noticed how handsome he was until tonight. It took a keen eye to look past his sharp features to the soft curve of his mouth; the gentle brown depths of his eyes.

"Where's Cupid?" she asked.

"Eh…home," he said. "I didn't think you needed a dog jumping all over you with everything else going on."

She blew on her cocoa and took a sip. The cocoa was just the right temperature, neither too hot nor too cold. "Delicious," she said, savoring the sweetness it left in her mouth. Valuing Tom's company even more.

"I asked for marshmallows, but the Feedbag Café was plumb out of them," he said.

"It's still good." Staring at the headless doll, she cringed. "It was awful, wasn't it?"

"I wouldn't say awful," he said. "Let's just say it was different. It's not every day that you see Jesus lose his head."

She shuddered. The more she thought about it, the worse the whole thing seemed. "Poor Susie. That was her favorite doll."

"Sounds like a problem that only Santa can fix."

She sighed. "I wish Joe-Joe's problem could be so easily remedied. I thought letting him play Joseph would make him feel better and bring him out of his shell. I was wrong."

Tom sat back. "Joe-Joe was Joseph?"

She nodded. "I'm afraid I only made things worse."

Sympathetic eyes met hers. "You can't solve all the problems of the world."

"It's not the world's problems I want to solve," she said. "Just the problem of one little boy."

"I wish there was something I could do to help," he said.

She smiled. "You being here helps," she said, surprised at how much she meant it. "And so does this," she added, raising her cup.

They sipped their cocoa in companionable silence for several moments, before Holly told him about her grandfather's singing group. "They're naming it the Ransom Notes."

His eyes twinkled with a glint of humor. "Maybe *Random* Notes would be more apt."

Holly laughed. It didn't seem possible that anyone could make her laugh after what had happened, but somehow that's exactly what Tom had done.

"The only good thing that could be said about tonight is that you'll never have to put up with another rehearsal."

He looked as if he wanted to say something, but hesitated.

She tilted her head in question. "Something wrong?"

"I've been meaning to tell you, but after I left the barn that night, Mrs. Greenfield kicked me out of the boardinghouse."

Holly gasped. "Oh, no! Because of Cupid's barking?"

Tom shrugged. "Like I said, he's got sensitive ears. I was warned what would happen if I didn't keep him quiet."

"It was all my fault…" She felt terrible. "I'm so sorry. Where are you staying?"

"For now, at the shop. I haven't had any luck in finding a place that will accept dogs."

"I'll talk to Nelson," she said. "He owns a lot of property. Maybe he can think of a place for you to stay."

Tom frowned but said nothing. Instead, he took the empty cup out of her hands and stood. "Come on. I'll walk you home. And if you're good, we can stop by and say hello to Winston."

"You mean Cupid," she said, and they both laughed.

Eight

THE MORNING AFTER THE PAGEANT, TOM BATTLED HIS way out of his cot with one thing in mind. He had to find a dog-friendly place to live. That's all there was to it.

The alternative was to buy his own place, but he still hadn't decided whether to make Haywire his permanent home. The town was smaller—a lot smaller—than San Antoine and that meant less business. On the other hand, Haywire had one very important thing in its favor, and her name was Holly Sanders.

Not that he thought he had a chance with her. But after what had happened last night...

He stopped himself. Nothing had happened last night. He and Holly had shared hot cocoa, and he'd walked the lady home. Period. He'd not even tried for a good-night kiss, though admittedly the thought had crossed his mind.

He was in no position to get involved with a woman. His life was too unsettled; too many obstacles loomed ahead. Romance would have to wait.

Still, there was no denying how much he liked spending time with her. He liked knowing he could make her smile even after a disastrous pageant. Make her laugh even after things had gone so wrong. But that was as far as it went. Had to be.

Besides, next to that dandy, Nelson Parker, Tom didn't have a snowball's chance in hell of winning the lady over. Given a choice between a real estate tycoon and the unsettled—make that homeless—owner of a blacksmith shop, a woman would have to be crazy to pick him.

But it wasn't just Holly on his mind. Since last night's pageant, he couldn't stop thinking about Joe-Joe. The boy's letter had been touching—no question. But seeing the fatherless seven-year-old onstage looking lost and scared made his plight seem that much more real. Tom wanted to do something, but what? If someone like Nelson Parker with all his resources and money couldn't help the boy, what possible chance did Tom have?

∽∽

Holly gave herself a critical look in the mirror. Her hair was arranged on top of her head in a fashionable bun. Tendrils coaxed into obedience by Aunt Daisy's curling iron fell gracefully around her face.

The emerald gown had been worn to prior dances, but she still loved it. The color enhanced the green of her eyes and brought a soft glow to her complexion.

The bustle was less generous than the current style, but only the most fashion-conscious woman would notice.

She applied pomade to her lips for color and dabbed perfume behind her ears.

Knowing that Nelson waited for her in the parlor, she reached for her purse and gloves. She was still upset with him for leaving the pageant early the other night, but he had apologized.

He'd also sent his crew to restore the decorations ruined by the wind, so she really had nothing to complain about.

Nelson was an expert at getting things fixed; he just wasn't any good at things that couldn't be manually repaired, like hurt feelings and disappointments. Never would it have occurred to him that she might have needed a sympathetic ear following the disastrous pageant. Or better yet, someone to ply her with hot cocoa and make her laugh. Like Tom.

She drew in her breath. It wasn't the first time she'd found herself comparing Nelson to Tom, and she felt bad for doing so. The men were as different as night and day, so there was no fair way of comparing the two. Still comparisons kept popping into her head, and that had her worried.

Determined not to let anything spoil the evening, she took a deep breath and left the room.

Nelson greeted her with a smile as she stepped into the parlor and brushed his lips across her forehead. In his dark frock coat and beaver top hat, he looked more like an easterner than a Texan.

"You look beautiful, as always," he said.

Aunt Daisy smiled up from her rocking chair. "I'd say she looks as pretty as a bride."

Holly rolled her eyes. Could her aunt be any more obvious?

Seeming not to notice her aunt's blatant hint, Nelson extended his elbow. "Ready?"

Holly slid her arm through his. "Ready," she murmured.

As she walked to the door by Nelson's side, the memory of hot cocoa and a warm, sympathetic smile came to mind. Startled by the vivid picture of soft brown eyes, she glanced over her shoulder at her aunt. Having no idea what Holly was thinking, her aunt stared back with a satisfied look and winked.

Tom slicked his hair back and looked down at his dog. "No, you can't go with me tonight."

Winston lifted his ears and looked up at him with his saddest expression. For added measure, the darn dog whimpered like a small child.

Normally, such tactics worked, but grim determination kept Tom from caving in. "Beg all you want, but you're not going with me," he said. Tonight, when he knocked on Holly's door, he wanted her full attention. "I'm asking the lady out, and I don't want you hogging her to yourself."

Woof!

Tom pointed his finger. "Stay."

He let himself out of the shop and rattled the door to make sure it was shut tight. Inhaling the cold night air, he shoved his hands in his coat pockets and started across the street. The lamplighter had just finished making his rounds, and Main Street was deserted. It was cold enough to snow, and Tom's breath left his mouth in white plumes.

Just as he reached Holly's street, he heard her voice. Stepping into the shadows of a sycamore tree, he spotted her with Nelson. Even in the dim glow of a gas streetlight, she looked beautiful. Her green gown shimmered, and her red hair looked like a fiery halo. But it was the radiant smile on her face as she looked up at her escort that caused Tom to back away even further, so as not to be seen.

Nelson helped her into the back of a fancy horse-drawn carriage, hung with gold kerosene lanterns. The vehicle came equipped with its own driver and the finest horse Tom had ever seen.

Standing in the shadows, he waited until the carriage had pulled away before walking back to Main Street. While walking to Holly's house, he'd felt like he was flying. Now he felt as if his feet had turned to lead.

Main Street had suddenly come alive with fancy-dressed couples, and that's when he remembered something about a Christmas Ball. Of course. That's where Holly and Nelson were headed. Clamping down on the disappointment that washed over him, he picked up his pace.

Though he'd left the shop only a few minutes earlier, all apparently was forgiven, as Winston greeted him with wagging tail.

Tom stooped to pet him and got his face washed. "It's just you and me tonight, buddy," he said.

Lonely, that's how he felt. As much as he loved his dog, no amount of tail-wagging or doggie kisses could fill the emptiness inside.

He glanced at his watch. It was only a little after seven o'clock; too early for bed. To pass the time, he cleaned his workbench and organized his orders. He tried not thinking of Holly dancing in the arms of another man, but the memory of her smile and big, green eyes kept popping into his head.

He pulled out a blank sheet of paper, intent on making a list of supplies he needed to order. Instead, he found himself writing, *Dear Santa…*

The next words flowed from his pen without conscious thought, dictated solely by stirrings of a lonely heart.

All I want for Christmas is to love and be loved by someone. She must have eyes that look like emeralds, hair as red as a summer rose, and a smile that takes the breath away. If by chance her name is Holly, I'd be the happiest man in the world.

He signed it and reread what he'd written. Feeling foolish, he threw down his pen. The only excuse he could think of for such childlike behavior was that he'd been reading too many letters to Santa. Joe-Joe wasn't the only one who wouldn't get his Christmas wish.

Scrunching the letter, he tossed it aside and pulled out a clean sheet of paper. He then made a list of needed supplies.

A sudden creaking of the building told him the wind had started up again, and he worried about Holly's decorations.

It was almost ten when he decided to call it a night. By then, the wind was blowing up a storm. Just as he was about to undress, the door blew open, and a gust of wind lifted the papers off his desk.

Winston jumped around, barking, as Tom rushed to shut the door. Bills, orders, and notes were scattered around the shop. His earlier attempt to organize his paperwork had all been for naught.

First thing tomorrow morning, he would fix that blasted door!

Nine

THE DANCE ENDED PROMPTLY AT MIDNIGHT, AND NELSON drove Holly home. The wind pulled at her wrap and tugged at the pins holding her hair in place. Cold air nipping at her flesh, she shivered and pulled her mantle closer.

The blacksmith shop looked dark and deserted as they drove by, but nonetheless made her think of hot cocoa and warm brown eyes. She was also reminded that she had promised Tom to query Nelson about a dog-friendly rental.

"I wonder if you could help Tom out," she said. "He's looking for a place to live."

Nelson frowned. "So why does he need my help?"

"As you might have noticed, he has a dog."

"I noticed," he muttered.

"I thought perhaps you could offer him a place to stay at one of your properties," she said.

"Sorry, but I can't take on that kind of responsibility. Not after the rabies scare we just had."

"But this isn't just any dog," Holly said. "He's friendly and loving and has a sweet disposition."

Nelson scoffed. "He didn't sound all that friendly and loving when I saw him. He looked like he wanted to bite my head off."

Holly moistened her lips. There was no denying that Nelson spoke the truth. "I'm sure that once you get to know him better—"

"I don't want to get to know him better," Nelson said, his tone telling her that the discussion was over.

The driver pulled the carriage up to the front of her house and stopped. "Thank you," she said, her voice breaking the awkward strain that had settled between them.

Nelson stepped out of the carriage and held out his hand to help her down. He then walked her to the porch. "I had a good time," he said.

"I did, too," she said. A tense silence followed, and she hastened to fill it in. "I better go in. It's late and—"

He stopped her with a hand to her arm. "Is something wrong?"

She looked up at him. "Wrong?"

"I had the feeling you were avoiding me all week. And tonight, you didn't seem like yourself."

"I just have a lot on my mind. You know, Christmas. Santa."

Nelson drew his hand away. "Are you sure that's all it is? You aren't still mad because I left the pageant early, are you?"

"You apologized," she said.

"You have to admit, it was pretty awful."

She was cold and tired and didn't want to talk about the pageant. Pulling her arm away, she said, "You don't have to remind me."

"The reason I brought it up is because you'd put the pageant before us. Just like you put everything before us."

She studied him. "That's not true."

"Isn't it? You think granting some kid's Christmas wish is more important than what you and I have."

Stunned that he could so easily discount something that was of prime importance to her, she stared at him. It wasn't the first time he'd disregarded her feelings, but this time it really stung.

In the past, she'd made allowances for him. Had even forgiven him for leaving the pageant early. Now she had neither the mind nor the heart to excuse or overlook his lack of understanding.

"What you and I have," she said evenly, "is friendship."

"Friendship?" he asked, his cold breath looking like icicles in the dark. "Is that all I am to you? A friend?"

He sounded hurt, but it couldn't be helped. "I'm just not ready for anything more than that right now," she said.

It was too dark to see his expression, but she sensed his withdrawal. "What can I do to help you get ready?" he asked.

She drew in her breath. Nelson was a brilliant businessman, but he didn't have a clue how to handle matters of the heart. At least he didn't offer to have his crew work on the problem, and for that, she was grateful. "Nothing," she said. "There's nothing you can do."

The damage had been done.

⚭

It was still windy the next morning when Tom took Winston for his morning walk. He tried not to think of Holly and how she had looked the previous night.

The problem was that every red bow and decorated shop window reminded him of her.

It was crazy. Made no sense. He'd only known her for a short while. Yet, the impression she'd made on him was undeniable. For some reason he couldn't understand, knowing her had made him even more aware of everything wrong with his life, starting with the fact that he was still without a decent place in which to hang his hat.

On the way back, he stopped at the butcher shop. Today, the owner included a bone along with the usual scraps. "Are you sure I can't pay you?" Tom asked. He didn't want to take advantage of the man's generosity.

"Nah," the butcher said. "Those scraps would only go to waste. Glad to see them put to good use."

Tom turned to leave, and that's when he noticed the little boy Joe-Joe was also in the shop. Winston, seeing someone his own size, wagged his tail and pattered up to him. The boy cried out and ran to his mother.

Tom pulled Winston back. "He won't hurt you," he said. "He's real friendly and just wants to say hello."

His mother tried persuading her son to pet the dog, but the boy would have none of it.

She shrugged an apology at Tom and turned to place her order over the counter.

Just as he left the shop, Tom was stopped by a matronly woman. Dressed in a divided skirt and checkered shirt, she peered at him from beneath a black, wide-brimmed hat. "You're the new smithy, right?"

"Yes, I am."

"I'm Mrs. Buttonwood. Welcome to Haywire."

A chatty woman, she managed to tell him the history of the town and her life story before he could get another word in edgewise.

Tom was trying to think how to make his escape when Winston took a sudden leap forward. Whipping the leash out of his hand, the dog bolted toward Joe-Joe, barking.

The boy cried out in fear and quickly backed away. Before Tom could grab the leash, the overhead sign crashed to the wooden sidewalk, falling where the boy had been standing seconds earlier.

Winston yelped and veered away from the sign. An instant of stunned silence was followed by pure bedlam. Joe-Joe's mother ran to her son and pulled him into her arms. Hiding his face in her skirts, the boy clung to her as if to never let go.

People rushed from the butcher shop, everyone talking at once. Mrs. Buttonwood took it upon herself to describe what had just happened. Passersby stopped and shook their heads.

One matronly woman tutted. "The boy could have been killed."

"The dog saved his life," Mrs. Buttonwood said.

Tom grabbed Winston by the leash. Dropping on his haunches, he rubbed his hands through his dog's fur. He could feel the dog tremble beneath his touch. "Good boy."

After calming her son, Joe-Joe's mother introduced herself to Tom. "I'm Mrs. Adams," she said.

"Tom Chandler," he said, standing.

"I don't know how to thank you." Glancing at the fallen sign, she shuddered. "How did your dog know it would fall?"

"I don't rightly know, ma'am. Dogs just know these things." He looked down at Joe-Joe, whose gaze was focused on Winston. "He'd like for you to pet him. Like I said, he's real friendly."

Joe-Joe shook his head but, with his mother's encouragement, finally extended a wary hand. Winston licked it, and Joe-Joe drew back.

"Told you he's friendly," Tom said, smiling.

Mrs. Adams gazed down at her son. "And he kept you safe from the falling sign."

Somehow that convinced Joe-Joe to pet Winston a second time, this time without any help. "You kept me safe," he said to the dog.

Winston jumped up to lick his face. Tom was about to pull the dog away, when Joe-Joe giggled in delight. Soon boy and dog were all over each other.

Tom was surprised to see Mrs. Adams wipe away a tear. "You all right?" he asked.

She nodded. "It's been a long time since I heard him laugh like that. Not since his father…" She forced a wan smile. "Thank you."

"I didn't do anything," Tom said. "My furry friend did all the work."

Mrs. Adams called to her son. "Come along, Joe-Joe, I have more errands to run."

"Ah, Ma. Can't I stay and play with the dog?"

"Maybe another time."

The boy reluctantly stood, his gaze fixed on Winston. "He saved me."

"Yes, yes, he did," his mother said. She flashed Tom a grateful smile before taking her son by the hand. "Come along now."

Watching the boy go, Winston's tail, ears, and head drooped, and he whined. Looking every bit as sad, Joe-Joe waved back.

"Come on," Tom said, tugging on Winston's leash, but the dog refused to move, and his gaze remained on the boy.

"Woof!"

Dogs tend to bark when they want company.

Tom stared down at his dog with more than a little guilt. Work had taken up most of his time, and he'd failed to give Winston the attention he needed. Even their morning walks had by necessity been cut short so Tom could get back to filling his orders. As much as he hated to admit it, what Winston needed was a playmate.

Tom swallowed the lump in his throat as he recalled the letter that had haunted him from the moment he'd first read it.

Dear Santa, All I want for Christmas is for you to move into my house so that Ma and me will feel safe again.

"Wait," he called. Not sure what he was doing, he hurried to catch up to mother and son. Joe-Joe threw his arms around Winston and buried his face in the dog's soft fur. Winston responded with wagging tail and licking tongue, bringing a look of pure joy to the young boy's face.

It was then that Tom knew exactly what he must do. Not just for Joe-Joe's sake, but for Winston's, too.

He pulled Winston away and told him to sit. He needed the boy's full attention. "Would you like to take my dog home?"

Joe-Joe's eyes widened. "You mean I can keep him?"

"Only if it's okay with your ma."

Joe-Joe gave his mother an anxious look. "Please, Mama, can I? Can I?"

Mrs. Adams looked like she didn't know what to say. "Well—"

Taking that as a yes, Joe-Joe flung his arms around Winston.

Since Mrs. Adams still looked uncertain, Tom wiggled the package in his hands. "It won't cost to feed him. The butcher saves him scraps, and he doesn't charge for them."

Mrs. Adams regarded Tom with a puzzled look. "Why would you part with your dog?"

Tom tossed a nod at the smiling boy. Heck, even Winston was grinning. "Doesn't look like I have much of a choice," he said.

Tom dropped down on one knee and looked Joe-Joe square in the eye. "I just want to make sure you'll take good care of him. You need to feed him and take him for walks. More than anything, he needs you to keep him safe. Just like he will keep you and your ma safe. Do we have a deal?"

Joe-Joe's expression grew solemn, but his arms stayed firmly around Winston's neck. "Yes, sir."

Tom ran his hands through Winston's fur. The dog, seeming to sense something, gazed up at him. "Do you promise to take care of Joe-Joe and keep him safe?"

Winston wagged his tail. "*Woof!*"

"That's dog talk for yes," Joe-Joe said.

"Yeah, I guess you can say that." Tom stood and handed the boy the leash. He knew in his heart it was the right thing to do, but it sure did hurt. Hurt like hell. "He's all yours," he said, barely able to get the words out.

Taking the leash in his hands, Joe-Joe was all smiles. "What's his name?"

The name Winston was on the tip of Tom's tongue, but he couldn't bring himself to say it. Somehow it was easier to say Cupid than Winston, but not by much.

"His name is Cupid," he said, the lump in his throat strangling his words. He cleared his throat. "Just like Santa's reindeer."

Ten

THE GENERAL STORE WAS ABUZZ THAT AFTERNOON WHEN Holly walked in. A small crowd gathered in front of the counter and appeared to be hanging onto Mrs. Buttonwood's every word.

Never one to be shy, Mrs. Buttonwood made the most of the attention. Her speech was punctuated with dramatic pauses and exaggerated hand motions.

"And then do you know what he did?" she asked, surveying her audience before she answered her own question.

Holly moved closer to the others, not sure that she'd heard right. "Excuse me. Did you say Tom gave his dog to Joe-Joe?"

"Yes, indeed," Mrs. Buttonwood said.

Holly couldn't imagine Tom parting with his dog. "Why…why would he do such a thing?"

"I asked him that very same question, and he said it had something to do with a letter Joe-Joe had written to Santa. Said the dog would keep him safe…"

Mrs. Buttonwood said more, but Holly didn't stay around long enough to hear the rest. Tom had thought of a way to make a little boy's wish come true. Clutching at her skirts, she dashed out of the shop and ran all the way to the blacksmith shop.

The double doors of the blacksmith shop stood open, and the sound of clanking iron rang through the air.

Holly paused at the door to catch her breath. "Tom!"

He turned his head in her direction. Greeting her with a crooked smile, he set his hammer down. "Holly—"

Before he could say another word, she quickly closed the distance between them. Flinging her arms around his neck and looking into his startled eyes, she kissed him on the cheek. It was a kiss of heartfelt gratitude that would have been over in an instant had he not wrapped her in his arms and pulled her close.

"What was that for?" he whispered.

Heart pounding, she gazed up at him and savored the feel of his warm, masculine embrace. "What you did for Joe-Joe..." She moistened her lips, drawing his gaze to them. Pressing her hand against his cheek, she smiled. "I can't thank you enough."

He took her hand in his and, holding her gaze, dropped a kiss into her palm. "No need to thank me," he said, his voice husky.

They stared at each other for a heart-stopping moment before he lowered his mouth to hers. His lips brushed against hers tenderly at first—like a whisper—awakening feelings within her that were new and exciting. Never had she experienced anything so pleasurable or sweet.

When she offered no resistance, his strong arms tightened around her waist, and he pulled her closer. She gazed into his heated eyes, and her heart pounded. It beat even harder when his mouth swooped down to capture hers, this time with more intensity. Never had she felt more desirable or needed than she did at that moment.

Working her arms around his neck, she melted against him and returned his kiss with equal ardor and need. Nothing seemed to exist outside his powerful arms or beyond his enticing lips.

Lost in the moment, she was shocked when he suddenly pulled away.

"I'm sorry," he said. "I didn't mean... I should never have..."

An awkward silence followed, and she drew in her breath. Her lips still burning with the memory of his kiss, she felt strangely disoriented, as if he had taken part of her with him.

Still shaken, she stared at him in confusion. "T-there's no need to apologize," she stammered. "What you did for Joe-Joe... I know how much Winston meant to you."

"It helps knowing that he has a good home with Joe-Joe."

She managed a smile. "Santa couldn't have done better."

He smiled, too, but all too quickly his somber expression returned.

"I'll let you get back to work," she said, not knowing what to say. What to think. Before turning to leave, she tried to read the look in his eyes but couldn't.

At the door, she glanced over her shoulder. His back was turned, his shoulders rigid.

He hadn't meant—? What would it have felt like, she wondered, had he really meant to kiss her? Could his kiss have been any more passionate, any more encompassing? Any more complete? With that burning thought, she walked outside.

∞

Long after Holly had left, Tom stood frozen in place. He was afraid to move for fear he'd wake up and find that kissing Holly had been but a dream.

When at last he got up the courage to move, he stared at the spot where he'd held her, kissed her. He certainly hadn't been prepared for the feel of her, the scent of her, the sensation of her breath next to his.

He'd kissed other women, but none had affected him as much as Holly.

He'd known all along that he was attracted to her. Intrigued by her. But when he'd held her in his arms and tasted her sweet lips, it wasn't just attraction he'd felt. It was something far stronger, more portent. It felt like the first stirrings of love.

True, she'd kissed him back. But as much as he wanted to believe her kisses had meant the same to her as they had to him, he knew otherwise. She had kissed him out of gratitude. Nothing more. Due to an act of fate, he had been able to grant Joe-Joe's wish, and Holly had simply been showing appreciation.

No woman would be foolish enough to choose him over Nelson. The man owned half the town and could give Holly everything she ever wanted. While he was but a lowly smithy, fighting to eke out a living from a town hard hit by the economy.

It didn't take a genius to know that his chances with her were nil.

Eleven

IT WAS CHRISTMAS EVE, AND A STEADY STREAM OF parents had tracked to Holly's door to collect toys for their young.

Mrs. Whittaker was one of the last ones to show up. Holly handed her a porcelain doll, along with a little wooden crib. "I think little Susie will really like this," she said.

Mrs. Whittaker gazed at Holly with tear-filled eyes. "I can't tell you how much I appreciate what you've done."

"I was happy to do it," Holly said. "I just want you and your family to have a merry Christmas."

"Thanks to you, the whole town will have a merry Christmas." After giving Holly a hug, Mrs. Whittaker drew a handkerchief from her sleeve. Dabbing at her eyes, she left.

Bobby Baker's father arrived soon after. Upon seeing the toys for all four of his children, he was practically speechless. "Bobby doesn't think Santa will come."

"I would say he's in for a big surprise," Holly said.

"This...this is the nicest thing that happened since my wife—" Voice choking, he fell silent for a moment. "I don't know how to thank you."

"You can thank me by having a very merry Christmas." Holly said.

After Mr. Baker left, she glanced around. Now that all the toys were gone, the room seemed empty, just like her heart.

"You done good, Holly," her aunt said from her

chair. "When you first told me what you planned, I thought you were crazy."

"You weren't alone," Holly said. She reached for her cloak.

"How come I haven't seen Nelson around?"

Holly bit her lower lip. She hated to disappoint her aunt, but it couldn't be helped. "We've both been busy," she said, not wanting to spoil her aunt's Christmas. "Are you sure you don't want to join us for caroling?"

Her aunt narrowed her eyes. "Is Harold gonna be there?"

Holly nodded. "Yes, Grandpapa will be there, along with the rest of the Random…eh…Ransom Notes."

"Then I'll pass. I heard enough screeching at the school pageant."

Wrapping her cloak around her shoulders, Holly kissed her aunt on the forehead. "I won't be late."

"Are you sure you don't want cotton for your ears?"

Holly laughed. "Don't tempt me."

Outside, the wind had stopped, and a full moon smiled down on her. It was a perfect night for Santa to make his rounds. Thinking about the squeals of happy children, she hurried toward Main Street.

The carolers had decided to meet in front of the Haywire Book and Sweet Shop, the most centrally located place in town.

Holly's breath caught in her chest as she passed the blacksmith shop. She hadn't seen Tom since the day they'd kissed. Had he purposely avoided her? She debated on whether to ask him to join in the singing, but no lights shone in the window. There was, however, a sign that read *For Sale*.

Holly froze. Tom was selling the business? A searing pain shot through her, and her knees threatened to buckle. That could mean only one thing: he was leaving town.

Shaken by the realization, Holly started down the

wooden sidewalk toward the sweet shop. She understood her surprise, but not the depth of her sadness. She had known Tom for such a short while, but his kindness and gentleness of spirit had captured her heart.

She and Tom had shared a kiss only the one time, but the memory had left its mark and she'd hardly been able to think of anything else since.

She joined the little knot of people waiting for her in front of the sweet shop and tried to hide her pain and confusion beneath an overbright smile.

The owners of the candy shop, Kate and Brett Tucker, were there, along with the Ramsom Notes and some of Holly's friends from church. Joe-Joe and his mother arrived just after Holly, with the boy's dog in tow. The dog greeted her with wagging tail, and Holly bent to pet him.

"Hi, Winston," she said, scratching him behind both ears. "How are you doing?"

Joe-Joe frowned. "His name is Cupid. Like Santa's reindeer."

Holly looked up. "Cupid? Did you name him that?"

"That was already his name. When the nice man let me have him."

Her heart thudded. Why would Tom—

"I'm keeping him safe," Joe-Joe said, his voice earnest. "And he's keeping Ma and me safe, too."

Holly straightened. "I'm glad you have such a loyal friend."

"Come on, let's go," her grandfather called. He and the others started down the street, singing on the top of their lungs. "Deck the halls with boughs of holly…"

Holly fell in step behind them, and Joe-Joe walked by her side, holding Cupid's leash.

Cupid barked and whined, and Joe-Joe was certain his dog was singing. Holly didn't have the heart to tell him that Cupid was more likely barking in protest.

It did Holly's heart good to hear Joe-Joe singing his little heart out. Even Grandpapa was impressed. "If you ever want to join the Ransom Notes, let me know," he said.

They were just about ready to call it a night when Joe-Joe's mother noticed something in Cupid's mouth. "What's that?" she asked.

"I don't know." Joe-Joe tried grabbing the thing away from the dog, with no luck. "He won't let me have it."

Holly patted her thigh. "Come here, boy." Cupid trotted up to her. "What do you have there, eh?"

Much to her surprise, Cupid dropped the thing at her feet. It was a paper ball. "Good boy," she said, shoving it in her pocket to be discarded later.

Cupid wagged his tail and barked.

"Maybe he wants you to throw the ball," Joe-Joe said.

Holly smiled. "Maybe Santa will bring him a real ball to play with," she said in a conspiratorial whisper. Fortunately, she had included a ball in the box his mother had picked up earlier.

Joe-Joe's mother called. "Come along, Joe-Joe. It's time to go home and get ready for Santa."

Joe-Joe waved. "Good night, Miss Sanders."

"Good night, Joe-Joe."

The rest of the group scattered, and Holly walked home alone. She tried not to look at Tom's shop, but the *For Sale* sign in the window was like a beacon. She reached home feeling more depressed than ever.

Her aunt had already gone to bed, and the fire was almost out. Since Holly wanted to read before turning in, she reached for the poker and stabbed at the dying flames.

Needing paper, she glanced around the room. What had Aunt Daisy done with the morning newspaper? Recalling the paper ball retrieved from Cupid's mouth, Holly reached in her pocket. She was about to toss the wadded paper into the fire when the words *Dear Santa* caught her eye. Worried that a child's letter had gone astray, she moved closer to the gas lamp and carefully unfolded the paper. Just as she'd expected, it was a letter to Santa. As she read the masculine scrawl, her mouth dropped.

All I want for Christmas is to love and be loved by someone. She must have eyes that look like emeralds, hair as red as a summer rose, and a smile that takes the breath away. If by chance her name is Holly, I'd be the happiest man in the world.

It was signed *Tom.* She ran her fingers over his name and clutched the letter to her chest. How in the world had Cupid known the letter was from Tom? Unless, of course, everything she'd ever heard about a dog's sense of smell was true.

Rereading the letter again and again, she could no longer deny what was in her heart. She was definitely attracted to Tom Chandler and, crazy as it seemed, maybe even more than a little bit in love with him.

Twelve

TOM STARED AT HIMSELF IN THE MIRROR OVER THE DRY sink. He was now staying at Mrs. Gray's boardinghouse. It was better than the shop by far. The bed was comfortable, the food good, and the surroundings pleasant.

But it was still lonely.

It was Christmas Day, but he didn't feel like celebrating. Nelson had made him an offer on the shop, contingent on him staying until another smithy could be found to take his place.

He didn't want to stay. He wished to God he'd never come to Haywire. He'd lost his best friend, Winston, but that was the least of it. He now knew he'd also lost a big piece of his heart to Holly.

If only he hadn't tasted her sweet lips. If only the memory of her smile didn't continue to haunt him. If only…

Clamping down on his thoughts, he turned from the mirror and reached for his leather vest. While everyone else was celebrating, it was a good day to go to the shop and work.

It's just another day, his father had said every Christmas during Tom's early growing-up years. But it wasn't until he'd met Holly that he realized how special Christmas could be, especially when doing for others. He only wished he could hear the happy squeals of delighted youngers that morning as they found what Santa had left for them.

A knock sounded at the door, interrupting his

thoughts. It was the boardinghouse owner, Mrs. Gray. "Merry Christmas," she said.

"Merry Christmas."

"You have something waiting for you under the tree."

Tom lifted an eyebrow. "You shouldn't have. I mean…"

She discounted his protests with a wave of her hands. "Don't thank me. I believe it's from Santa." Laughing, she turned her bulky form and lumbered away.

Curious, he quickly finished dressing and left the room. The smell of coffee greeted him as he jogged down the stairs and crossed the hall into the parlor.

He stopped in the open doorway. Afraid to believe his eyes, he blinked. "Holly?"

She sat by the tall Christmas tree, looking more beautiful than anyone had the right to look. The skirt of her pretty green dress formed a circle around her. Her hair was pulled up and cascaded down her back in soft, luxurious curls.

He moved across the room to where she sat. "What… what are you doing here?" he asked when at last he found his voice.

She unfolded a piece of wrinkled paper in her hand. "'Dear Santa,'" she read softly. "'All I want for Christmas is to love and be loved by someone.'" She lifted her gaze to his. "That's funny. That's all I want, too."

Feeling utterly foolish, he shook his head. "Where?"

She smiled. "Winston found it and brought it to me," she said.

"You mean Cupid," he said.

"No, I'm pretty sure that the dog that found your letter was Winston," she said and stood. "Cupid is looking after Joe-Joe, but Winston is still looking out for you."

Tom tilted his head, not sure what to think. "Are you saying that you're here because of that letter?"

Her mouth curved. "No letter to Santa should ever go unanswered."

His heart practically turned over. Was she saying what he'd hoped she was saying? "But…what about Nelson?"

"Well, you see, it's like this," Holly said with a mischievous glint in her eyes. "Winston/Cupid isn't only looking out for you and Joe-Joe. He was also looking out for me. And he told me in no uncertain terms that he didn't approve of Nelson."

Tom shook his head in disbelief. *Don't let this be a dream.* "You do know that anything Santa leaves under the tree is meant to be kept."

"I wouldn't have it any other way," she said, and was suddenly in his arms. "But, of course, that would mean you'll have to stay in Haywire."

At that moment, Tom felt as if he could hear the happy squeals of every child in the county. In the world. "I'm staying, I'm staying." His heart bursting with happiness, he sprinkled loving kisses on her forehead, her nose and, finally, her mouth.

Gazing into her eyes, he was already planning his next letter to Santa, and it had to do with wedding bells.

"This is the best Christmas I've ever had," he said. "It's…" He tried to think of the right word and couldn't.

"Magic?" she said.

He smiled. "Magic."

She laughed. "Wait till you see what I have in store for you next Christmas."

He arched an eyebrow. "I won't have to sing, will I?"

Her eyes twinkled. "You'll just have to wait and see."

"I have a feeling I'm in trouble." He kissed her again and again. "I don't know how it happened, but sometime between you getting me tossed from the boardinghouse and bombarding me with Christmas ornaments, I seem to have fallen head over heels in love."

She giggled. "Like I said. Magic."

About the Author

New York Times bestselling author Margaret Brownley has penned more than forty-five novels and novellas. She's a two-time Romance Writers of American RITA finalist and has written for a TV soap. She is also a recipient of the Romantic Times Pioneer Award. Margaret makes her home in Southern California and wrote this story during a hundred-degree heat wave. You can find Margaret at margaret-brownley.com.

Author's Note

Dear Readers,

I hope you enjoyed Tom and Holly's story.

I thought you might be interested to know that this particular tale was inspired by the following letter from A. Z. Salomon printed in the Greeley Tribune, December 19, 1877: "If there be any person or family in this community too poor to buy Christmas presents for their young children, I would like them to call on me personally for aid. All communications of this nature considered strictly confidential. Also, if there be persons in this community in need of provisions, who are unable to purchase them, I would like to know."

Wishing you and your family a Merry Christmas.

Until next time,
Margaret

ONE SNOWY CHRISTMAS EVE

---•◦•---

Anna Schmidt

One

THE TIN SHINGLE OUTSIDE THE WEATHERWORN STORE-front rocked in the wind, squealing in protest at each blast of the frigid air. Colin Foster leaned against the building and looked up at it.

Evelyn Prescott, MD.

Part of her name had been damaged—looked like somebody had tried to scratch it off. Even so, Evie had done it. She'd actually gone and gotten herself a medical degree. He noted that even though the shingle displayed her name, the window had Doc Williams's name on it. Maybe she was still working for Doc—or maybe she was working *with* him.

Colin turned up the collar of his wool-lined jacket and stuffed his bare hands in his pockets. The cold cut through him like a sharp knife slicing a ripe tomato as he stood there staring at the sign. Small icicles hung off the bottom edge, little daggers poised to strike some unsuspecting passerby. He'd ridden into town hoping to catch Doc before the old man and his wife headed off to Christmas Eve services at the church across the street. He'd left his horse at the livery out of the weather in case this took some time. He was sure Doc could fix him up with some concoction that would allow him to get back to work.

For a cowhand like him—a man who drifted from ranch to ranch working the herds from spring through fall—finding something in the middle of winter wasn't easy. He'd finally landed this job with Tom Madison, a rancher he'd worked for years earlier—a rancher who was offering him a chance to stay on permanently as foreman. His plan was to get some medicine from Doc and then take to his bunk. By the day after tomorrow, he should be good as new.

Still he hesitated before knocking on the frosted-glass panel of the door. Seeing Evie's name on the shingle was unexpected. They'd spent a season together five years ago when Doc and his wife took her in after she'd run away from home. Colin had been a seasonal hire at the Madison ranch then. Through the summer and fall, he and Evie had spent every moment they could find to be together.

She was always talking about what she planned on doing once she'd saved enough money. He was always more interested in what they might do that afternoon. Their parting late that December had not been pretty. They'd argued—him wanting to get married and settle down, and her determined to get her medical degree even if she had to leave Sagebrush, and him, to do it. She'd assured him she would come back to him, but Colin was a man who lived in the moment. He didn't trust such promises, having had them broken before when jobs that might have given him the stability he sought never panned out.

Last time he'd come through this way a year or so ago, he'd stopped to see Doc. The two of them had sat down for a beer at the Paradise Saloon, and Doc hadn't said a word about planning to close up shop. He for sure hadn't mentioned turning his practice over to Evie Prescott. He *had* mentioned that Evie was head of her class in medical school and might even be hired to teach once she finished her degree. He'd told Colin what a waste he thought that would be.

"She's got a gift for healing. That don't belong in no classroom," Doc had said.

Now Colin was in need of medical attention, but Evie? She'd more likely kill him than cure him. Besides if the fellas back at the ranch found out he'd gone to see a female doctor, he'd never hear the end of it.

He cupped his hands around his face to ward off the sting of the icy snow blowing around him and peered in through the front window, hoping to see Doc bent over his desk. Between the weather and a fever that was worsening, he was having trouble focusing. But everything looked pretty much as it had last time he'd stopped by.

Through an open doorway at the back of the office, a lamp threw shadows across the rough, whitewashed plaster walls. A figure passed between the light and shadow, moving into the office—moving toward him. A woman who moved too briskly to be Doc's wife. Colin shrank back into the dark of the deserted street, inching around the corner and down a side alley to huddle in the doorway that led to Doc's living quarters.

As the church bells sounded the call for early evening services and the citizens of Sagebrush left their homes and shops and headed for the church, Colin surrendered to a coughing jag that felt as if his insides might end up on the dirty snow piled against the building. He wrapped his arms around his gut and doubled over. The coughing and gagging went on and on, weakening him to the point that when it finally passed, he pressed against the cold wood of the building, gasping for air.

"You should come inside, sir." He knew that voice as well as he knew his own. It had haunted his dreams for five long years. He also knew she hadn't recognized him. He lowered his head so his hat gave him cover.

"I'll be all right." His voice was raw, his chest still burning. She was dressed for church—in a shawl and a perky little hat that did nothing to protect her golden hair.

"I am a doctor, sir. Please come inside so I can help you." She placed her hand on his shoulder.

He shook her off. "Said I was fine," he mumbled, realizing at the same time that he had no strength and if he took a step, he'd likely end up facedown in the snow. "Give me a minute," he said, and then added, "Thanks," hoping she'd give up and go on to church.

But this was Evie, and Evie did not give up. She had always been mulish, always so sure she was right. She'd also been the only woman ever to set his heart—and body—on fire. "Come on, cowboy," she said, hooking his arm over her shoulders and wrapping hers around his waist. "If you're determined to let what is probably a simple chest infection kill you, let's at least get you warmed up enough to go on your way and not die within sight of my front stoop. That would be bad for business, and business is bad enough."

She delivered this through gritted teeth and huffs of breath as she struggled to move his six-foot frame back around the corner and through the open door of her office. Once inside, she kicked the door shut with one foot and then helped him to a chair near the potbelly stove.

"Stay," she ordered as she bustled around, shaking the fresh snow from her shawl before hanging it on a hook, unpinning the silly hat, and setting it on the desk. She lit a lamp, then filled a tin cup with water from a kettle on the stove. "Drink."

He kept his head lowered as he wrapped his trembling hands around the cup. The way she snapped out orders annoyed him. He wasn't a dog after all. If this was the way she handled patients, no wonder she had no business. He took a couple small sips of the water and felt the tension in his body relax slightly as the warmth from the liquid spread through him.

Evie sat at the desk and opened a notebook. He realized he was seeing two of her and shook his head in a failed attempt to clear his vision. He clutched the edge of the chair, determined not to give in to a wave of dizziness. She licked the tip of a pencil and said, "How long have you had this cough, Mister...?"

"Couple of days." He ignored her request for his name.

She snorted and turned to him. "Couple of weeks is more like it. If you refuse to be truthful with me, I can't help you."

"Don't recall asking for your help, and..." He started coughing again. The cup shook in his hand, the water sloshing over the edges. Pain shot through his chest and torso.

"All right, that's quite enough," Evie muttered. "Let's have a look and a listen." Once again, with the strength of a man twice her size, she maneuvered him from the chair and onto the examining table. In the process his hat came off, and when she had him on the table and was sure he wasn't going to fall, she stood back, her breathing ragged, her hands on her slim hips.

Colin knew the exact moment she recognized him. He'd thought maybe the fact that it had been years and he hadn't shaved for several days would keep her from realizing who he was, but when her eyes went wide and her mouth opened and closed a couple of times with no sound coming out, he knew the game was up.

"Hello, Evie," he managed.

∞

Colin Foster.

Evie swallowed around the sudden lump in her throat that threatened to make her breathing as much a challenge as his. From the first time she'd seen him striding across Sagebrush's small plaza, he'd had that effect on her. Colin had always had a way of sucking the oxygen out of a room. "You," she croaked.

He managed a weak grin that turned to a grimace as the coughing overtook him again. Unable to see anyone—even Colin Foster—in pain, Evie went to work.

She wrestled with the exam table to raise the head so that he was in a half-reclined position. "Needs a good oiling," she muttered as if he cared. It had been five years since she and Colin had parted. Things had changed for both of them. She felt self-conscious seeing him again after all this time.

Finally, the rods snapped into place. "All right," she said more to herself than him. She covered his head and shoulders with a towel and then poured steaming water from the kettle into a pan and held it beneath the tent of the towel. "Breathe," she instructed. "Deep breaths."

The fact that he didn't argue told her just how sick he was. Colin Foster always argued with her, especially when she was trying to get him to do something— especially when he was sure he knew better—which was always.

"Just give me some tonic and—"

"Shush," she ordered.

After several minutes had passed, his breathing steadied, and she saw the tension leave his body as he relaxed. She set the pan of now-tepid water on a side table and removed the towel. His eyes were closed.

"You need to remove your jacket and unbutton your shirt so I can examine you," she said, hoping her tone was professional when the very idea of seeing Colin's muscled body—a body she knew all too well—beneath the tight knit of the long johns he surely wore brought heat to her cheeks that had nothing to do with the warmth of the room.

He opened his eyes and looked at her. "You first," he

said with a hint of the devilish grin that had always been her undoing.

"Be serious," she snapped. "The way you've been coughing just since I found you, you could have cracked a rib." She began pulling his jacket over his shoulders and knew her diagnosis could be right by the way he stiffened and bit down on his lip.

"I can manage." He shrugged out of the jacket and managed to open two buttons of his shirt before lying back exhausted.

"No need to completely remove your shirt," she said as she finished undoing the buttons, pulling it free of his trousers and spreading the flaps. She gently pressed her hands onto his chest, moving slowly over his body as she watched his expression.

He met her gaze with bleary-eyed defiance, clearly determined not to reveal what her touch was doing to him. But he could not disguise the way his body jerked in pain when she pressed his right side. Without saying anything, she reached for her stethoscope and listened to the thunder of his heart—strong beats but too fast. "Lean forward and take deep breaths," she murmured, moving to listen to his lungs—lungs that gurgled with fluid. She frowned as she eased him back onto the raised table.

"So, Doc, what's the verdict? Will I live through the night?" He tried a laugh that ended up another crackling cough.

She realized he had no idea how ill he was—how if he had not decided to come to town tonight, this might have turned into pneumonia and he might have died. "I'll do my best to make sure you're still here by morning," she said.

He frowned. "Bad for business, is it?"

"Something like that." She thrust a thermometer between his open lips and lifted his wrist to count his pulse—also too fast. She did not allow herself to even consider that his rapid pulse might have something to do with being here with her.

When she removed the thermometer and checked the reading—too high—he shuddered and reached for his jacket. "You need to stoke that fire, Evie. It's freezing in here, and if you're gonna insist on having me strip down…"

The room was so warm Evie had resisted the urge to open the high, tight collar of her shirtwaist, but Colin was shivering. She considered her options. She had already prepared her bed, thinking after she returned from early services, she would get under the covers and read until sleep overcame her.

Her bedroom was steps away from the examining table, and a fire in the fireplace there plus the three quilts piled on her bed would help break his fever. "Come on," she said as she eased his legs over the side of the table and once again draped his arm over her shoulders.

"Where we going?"

"I need to get you to bed," she replied.

He choked out half a laugh. "Thought you'd never ask."

"Just shut up and try putting one foot in front of the other," she snapped as they stumbled forward.

Somehow they managed to make it from one room to the other, and once they were near enough, she dropped him onto the bed. As he curled onto his side, she pulled off his boots before lifting his long legs onto the bed and reaching for the covers. His shirt was wet with perspiration, and his breathing was rapid and shallow from the exertion. She pushed an extra pillow beneath his head and shoulders, and when she realized he wasn't objecting—or helping—she knew he was a lot sicker than even she had suspected. He was still conscious, but just barely.

"Colin." She whispered his name as she stroked his

dark hair back from his forehead. How she had loved this man!

And how badly he had shattered her fragile heart the day he walked away without so much as a backward look. All because he was a man who wanted what he wanted when he wanted it, and she had dared suggest marriage could wait while she got her medical degree.

Not that she hadn't wanted to marry him—spend every night lying in his arms, waking to his kiss every morning. But there were practicalities to consider. If they were going to settle down, one of them needed steady work. His job required moving from place to place, following a herd as it was driven from high country to grazing lands to market—and then it was on to another ranch in another place to do the same. Even if she couldn't get accepted to medical school, she had the promise of steady work with Doc. That meant he could take a job at a ranch or even in town and stop his drifting from one place to another, never knowing for sure if there would be work or not.

And then on the afternoon of Christmas Eve the letter had arrived—her acceptance to medical school in Kansas City. She'd thought Colin would be so happy for her. But before she could share her news, he had proposed—not only proposed but insisted they marry at once. He'd worked everything out already, so when she handed him the letter, he read it and then looked at her. "What about us, Evie?"

"We'll be fine, Colin," she'd replied, still caught up in the thrill of the news. "I'm going to be a doctor."

"Evie, I know you've dreamed of this and worked hard for it, but I don't think you've thought it through. Who do you think will be your patients? Certainly no cowboy I know would ever let a woman so much as bandage a simple cut, much less treat a broken bone or snakebite."

It was the first time he'd shown doubt in her. Before,

he had been the one to assure her she could do anything she set her mind to.

"They have wives and children who will need treatment. I'll start with them, and in time, once I earn their trust…"

"And how are you gonna pay for all this?" He tapped the letter with two fingers.

"I've been saving my wages from Doc, and the school is offering me a scholarship and…"

They'd gone back and forth, their arguments escalating as each sought to win. He'd fought for marriage, a family, postponing medical school. She'd debated that was putting the cart well before the horse and might indeed prevent her from ever achieving her dream.

She recalled how Colin had sucked in a breath and stared hard at the sky before looking back down at her. "Why, Evie? Why aren't I enough?"

She'd tried to explain. As a girl whose father was a drunk and whose mother had died, leaving Evie to fend for herself, she'd been determined she would not depend on anyone ever again. Her love for Colin had tested that resolve. But that night when he'd turned his back on her, she'd renewed her vow of independence. She would make her way in the world with or without this man she loved. "People die, Colin," she'd told him, "and they leave."

"I'm not gonna die," Colin had said through gritted teeth.

She remembered she had stroked his cheek. "Everyone dies, Colin. It's part of life."

"Then if we're all dying, why would you waste your time heading off to school when we could be together, starting a family, and living whatever time we've got?"

She'd tried reasoning with him but knew they both had quick tempers. He'd triggered hers with those three words: *waste your time.* "I'm going," she'd said, snatching back the letter and waving it in his face.

He'd hesitated a moment and then said softly, "Then I guess I am, too." He'd left, and she hadn't seen him since.

Until now.

"Evie?" His voice was raw and husky. He licked his dry lips. "So cold," he mumbled as he clutched the covers closer.

"It's the fever," she told him, feeling helpless in the face of his suffering in spite of her training. She stuffed rags around the window to block the draft and put another log on the fire. She'd need to restock the woodpile.

She felt his forehead. It was hot against the back of her hand. His temperature was rising. She went to the front door and filled a pan with fresh snow. By the time she returned to his bedside, he had thrown aside the covers and was thrashing about on the bed, mumbling gibberish.

Scooping some snow into her palm, she kneaded it into a small ball and pressed it against his lips. He licked at it hungrily. When it had all melted and the last drops dribbled down his chin, Evie soaked a cloth in the melting snow remaining in the pan and placed it across his forehead. His face relaxed, but his breathing was still shallow. She covered him again and then went into her office to prepare a poultice that she hoped would help break up the congestion in his chest. Beyond that, she was at a loss.

Some doctor you are, Evie Prescott. Treating patients had been so much easier when she was in medical school. She had trained in a hospital where she had access to the latest equipment and drugs. Here in Sagebrush, she had to rely on her own concoctions and the herbal treatments she'd picked up from the native tribes in the area. Right now, bringing down Colin's fever and alleviating the fluid in his chest were her main priorities.

Think, she commanded herself as she studied a row

of powders and herbs lining one shelf. She chose several containers, took down her mortar and pestle, and carefully measured out the ingredients for the poultice. From the bedroom she could hear Colin moan.

"I'm coming, Colin," she called. She also needed to wrap his chest to support what she believed could be a cracked rib. And none of that did anything to address the fever.

When she hurried back to his bedside, he was delirious, his eyes closed, muttering incoherently and sometimes crying out. She opened the buttons on his long johns and applied the poultice, slapping his hands away when he tried to cover himself. "Stop that," she muttered as she concentrated on her work. Sweat dotted her forehead, and her hands shook. She was being ridiculous. Colin was a patient, just like anyone else she might treat.

Of course, since hanging her shingle three months earlier, the fact was she'd seen only three patients—a girl with a cut foot, a woman suffering from morning sickness, and a surly boy with a broken wrist. Doc had left in September to take his wife for treatment at a tuberculosis sanitarium, and a recent letter had informed her he would not be returning until spring—if then.

Mentally, she pictured the words and diagrams in her medical texts. *Cool the body to bring down fever.* Of course, she had acted instinctively, wanting to relieve Colin's discomfort by covering him and blocking the windows, trying to warm him. She opened the window as wide as it would go and shivered as snow stung her face. She pulled the covers off him and out of his reach. She let the fire burn down without adding logs.

Over time as the temperature in the room dropped several degrees, she wrapped her shawl around her shoulders and tied it in front so her hands were free. She continued wiping the sweat from Colin's face with cloths soaked in melted snow. Then she remembered Doc had left her a small container of the so-called miracle drug—aspirin. While in medical school, Evie had learned of the discovery by a German chemist of this compound. She had seen it work on many patients. Now, it had become available even out here in New Mexico.

"Nothing like it for bringing down a fever, but use it sparingly," Doc had advised. "Not as easy to come by way out here as it might be in the city." She hurried to her office to retrieve the precious supply.

"Open," she instructed Colin when she returned to his bedside. She forced the powder she'd mixed in water between his chapped lips and held his mouth closed until he swallowed. "One more spoon," she murmured, repeating the process. He choked and coughed, and she watched to be sure he didn't spit up the medicine. When he collapsed back onto the pillows, she set the glass and spoon aside and gently wiped his face.

From outside, she heard the church bells at the same time the clock Doc Williams had given her chimed in the office. She heard the jingle of harnesses as sleighs passed on the street, and the occasional call of one neighbor to another. Early services letting out—laughter and squeals from the children excited to head home and wait for Santa.

Christmas Eve. Her first Christmas back in Sagebrush. Her first Christmas as a doctor. And here was Colin—her first real adult male patient.

She pulled the only chair in the room closer and sat. It was going to be a long night.

Two

A CAROUSEL OF COLORS AND IMAGES FILLED COLIN'S mind. He saw Evie, all dressed in yellow, her hair the color of sunshine, falling down her back as she ran to him. She was laughing and so beautiful, and he reached for her, but she wasn't there. He tried to call out to her, but no words came. He felt a weight on his chest, then hands pressing something foul-smelling and sticky onto his skin. He swatted at the offending touch, and finally it stopped. He wanted to complain about the heat—the heaviness of the air—but no words came. Then he felt a blast of cool air and had an image of Evie and him on a summer day, lying on the tall, soft grass next to the river, in the shade of a cottonwood tree.

He unbuttoned her dress and traced the rise of her breasts above the lace on her undergarment, all the time watching her face. If she had shown fear or anger, he would have stopped, but what he saw in those deep-blue eyes was something he could only describe as wonder. She reached for him, her mouth an inch from his. But then someone was grabbing his jaw—hard, forcing his lips open and shoving something metal inside before withdrawing it and holding his mouth closed until he had no choice but to swallow.

Her father had found them that day. He'd called Evie a whore and quoted Scripture to her as he dragged her back to the shanty they called home. Later he'd warned Colin that if he ever caught him anywhere near his girl again, he would kill him. Neither he nor Evie had heeded the warning. Two nights later, she'd slipped away, walked the three miles to the ranch where he was working that season, and waited for him outside the bunkhouse. When he stumbled out before dawn to splash water on his face before heading to the high country to start his shift, she told him she'd come for that kiss.

He'd been more than happy to oblige.

⚬∞⚬

Colin was smiling, his eyelids fluttering with whatever dream he was seeing. Evie hoped that was a good sign. She was so tired and would like nothing better than to stretch out next to him and get some sleep. But she wasn't fooled by this seeming reprieve in his condition. She needed to stay alert.

An hour passed, and he slept while Evie gave in to the need to close her eyes—just for a minute. Then she would take care of restocking the woodpile. She dozed, dreamed, and was vaguely aware of people arriving for eleven o'clock services at the small adobe church across the street.

The next thing she knew, church bells rang out with the news that Christmas Day had just arrived. How was that possible? She hurried to the front window, saw people leaving the church, and then everything outside her office was quiet—snow falling on a deserted street. It was almost as if she and Colin were the only two people around. There had been a time when that had been all she wanted.

As she returned to the bedroom, stirred the fire, and added the last of the logs, she thought of the day her father had caught them by the river. That was the day she had realized all she would ever want or need was Colin. She'd just turned eighteen years old. But her father had dragged her away, had called her unspeakable names, had hit her repeatedly as he continued to shout Scripture at her.

Knowing that fighting back would only prolong

the agony, she'd blocked out the pain of his blows and
planned her escape. Ever since her mother's death, her
father had deteriorated into this monster who thought
of her as nothing more than property—someone he
expected to cook and scrub and clean him up when he
stumbled back from town drunk and bloodied from some
fight she knew he'd started.

That was the day she'd decided depending on a
man—any man, no matter how good he was or how
much she loved him—would not be enough. The very
next night, she'd packed her belongings in a carpetbag
and slipped away. She'd walked to the ranch where
Colin worked and waited for him. The first thing she
needed to do was erase the nightmare of her father's
abuse, and she figured Colin could do that.

"What are you doing here, Evie?" Colin had been
half-asleep when he came out of the bunkhouse to splash
water on his face and saddle his horse.

"I came for that kiss," she told him.

They'd kissed before, but that day by the river she'd
had the sense their kisses were about to move to another
level, and she wanted to know what that meant.

"Teach me," she'd pleaded, and he'd been more than
happy to oblige.

Taking her hand, he'd led her into the barn and up
the ladder to the loft. There he'd helped her recline on a
bed of fresh straw—she could still smell the sweet aroma
of hay and leather and horses.

"I can't stay long," he'd told her, stretching out next
to her.

"I know." She touched his face.

"He hurt you," he whispered, running his fingers over
her swollen cheek.

"Yes, but that's the past."

Frowning, Colin stroked her hair. "What are we
going to do?"

"I'm doing it. Are you going to kiss me or not?"

He grinned. "Yes, ma'am."

The kiss was everything she had hoped and more. He was gentle and tender. He tested her willingness by pressing the tip of his tongue to her teeth. Opening to him was another way of saying yes. And suddenly it had been as if she couldn't be close enough to him. She huddled her body to his, wanting him to take her in, to protect her against any pain or harm that might come. He pulled back, and she tugged him closer. She tried to speak, and he swallowed her words with his mouth and tongue.

All too soon he pulled away, his breath coming in heaves. "I have to go, but…"

"I'm never going back there," she told him.

"Evie, think. Where can you go?"

He was right. For a man, coming and going was different. He could just leave, find work, bed down in a barn or field or bunkhouse. For her—for a woman—there were no such options.

"Maybe Doc and Mrs. Williams will take me in," she said. "I could earn my keep cleaning and cooking and…"

A sliver of the first light of day cut through the shadows. In the stalls beneath them, a horse whinnied. Colin glanced toward the ladder, then back at her.

"Come on," he whispered, standing and holding his hand out to her. They climbed down from the loft. He saddled a horse, tied her carpetbag to the back and mounted, stretching out his hand to pull her up to ride sidesaddle in front of him.

Now as she sponged the sweat from his face and neck, she remembered how she had nestled against him that morning, her face resting in the curve of his neck, his pulse beating steadily against her cheek, their bodies fitting together like pieces of a puzzle.

She was tempted to see if they still fit, or if time and distance and the different paths they'd traveled had changed all that. She'd missed him every day…every night…but she could not regret her decision to follow her dream of becoming a doctor. Still, her journey had been such a lonely one. Surely there was no harm. He would never know. No one would ever know.

Stretching out next to him, she rested her head lightly against his back. When he didn't move or make any protest, she inched closer and rested one hand on his neck. Beneath her fingertips, she felt the rapid beat of his pulse and closed her eyes. Instinctively, he reached up and covered her hand with his. She smiled and relaxed.

They still fit.

His shivering woke her. He had shifted and was clutching her closer, seeking any warmth he could, mumbling incoherently. She sprang into action, shutting the window, feeding the fire, and covering him with every quilt within reach. This would be the pattern— fever that felt as if he were on fire, alternating with chills so severe they made his body writhe and twitch. The cycle could go on for hours or perhaps days—if it didn't kill him first.

She wished Doc was still in town, but he had his own problems. She sat by Colin's bedside, trying to decide what else she might do to relieve his suffering. His clothing was twisted and soaked with sweat. The least she could do was make him as comfortable as possible. He appeared to be resting a bit easier—probably exhaustion—so she slid the straps of his suspenders over his shoulders and down his arms. Then she studied his trousers. They should come off as well.

It wasn't as if she hadn't had to undress a male patient. During her training there had been any number of emergencies where some poor man was brought in bleeding or with a broken leg in need of setting or…

"You're a doctor," she muttered and set about opening the buttons on the front of Colin's trousers.

She lifted his hips as she eased the trousers down and off and hurriedly covered him with the blankets, and still he thrashed about, kicking the blankets off with his feet before reaching for them again. She didn't want to remember another night under very different circumstances when they'd clung to each other in the loft of that barn. He'd covered her with his coat, and she had covered him with her body.

The fire! Need more wood.

She started for the door, but Colin cried out, clearly delirious with fever. She was afraid to leave him even for a moment. Instead, she grabbed his wrists and fell back with him onto the bed. For a second, neither of them moved, and then his arms came around her, pinning her to him.

∞

Colin fought to hang on to the dream. Evie and him down by the river, her hair spilling over his bare chest, her mouth an inch from his. He reached for her. She wasn't there. He was so cold, as if winter had come in an instant. Somewhere a window slammed shut, rattling the glass. He had no strength—weak as a newborn calf, Evie would say. He had no choice but to surrender to whatever was there to overpower him. And then she was back. He smelled the pine soap she used, remembering how she was always washing up, scrubbing her hands and telling him cleanliness—hygiene, she called it—was important for a doctor, even before she was one. He felt her nearness, and when she slipped one suspender strap off his shoulder, he relaxed. The dream was back.

Him, Evie—in the loft where they'd taken to meeting once she'd settled in with Doc in town.

It was not their first time. They'd spent many an hour kissing…touching…but today was the day they'd both decided would go beyond kissing and touching. Today they would become lovers in every sense of that word. As the late-afternoon sun played over them between the gaps in the slats of the barn, he'd opened the buttons on her shirtwaist to give him access to her perfect skin, the swell of her small breasts pressing against the lace border of her camisole. He'd bent to kiss her there.

She'd nipped his ear and whispered, "My turn," as she wriggled from beneath him and straddled him to tug at his suspenders. They had continued the game until both were naked from the waist up. "Your turn," he'd challenged, knowing all that was left of his clothing were his trousers and underwear.

"Not fair," she'd muttered. "Women have all these layers you have to get through."

He'd laughed at that. "Tell me about it," he'd said and immediately realized his mistake. "Not that I'm all that experienced. I mean, Evie, you're…"

"Do not lie, Colin Foster," she'd said, then given him a devilish grin. "Truth is, it's probably best if one of us knows what to do." Then she placed her hand on the swell of his fly. "For instance, does this help?"

"Evie," he'd moaned as she opened the buttons, one by one, exposing his thin cotton drawers that could barely contain his erection.

"Oh my," she'd whispered.

He'd kicked himself free of the rest of his clothes and run his hands up and under her skirt and petticoat until he touched her pantaloons. He cupped her, and she bucked. "Does this help, Evie?" he whispered, repeating her challenge.

"Get them off," she'd growled, and he'd been more than happy to oblige. Once she was naked under her skirt and petticoat, he rolled with her in the warm, sweet hay until she straddled him, her clothing puddled around them. Once his erection touched her, it was all he could do to hold on.

"Evie, love," he'd whispered as she bent over him, her hair falling like a curtain around them, her hands pressing into his bare chest as she…

A shot of pain ricocheted through him so sharply that he cried out. He squinted into the unfamiliar surroundings, trying to get his bearings. He tried to sit up, but strong hands held him back.

"Shhh," a woman whispered. "You need to lie still, Colin."

And then he remembered—the shingle, the voice too familiar, the sudden warmth of a fire and covers to stop his shivering.

Evie.

He collapsed back onto pillows, remembering everything. "You should send for Doc Williams," he croaked.

ᔥᴔᴓᔐ

Evie stepped back, her fists clenched. How dare he! She was a doctor—there was a piece of paper hanging on the wall above her desk and a shingle outside the door to prove it. All the struggle she'd faced trying to get her practice started roiled through her, firing her fury—and her defeat. Who was she kidding? No man—even this one—would ever accept that she could possibly know what she was doing.

She had excelled in her studies, determined to earn the respect of her fellow students and the doctors who had taught her—all of them male. At her graduation she'd been offered a teaching post at the school, but she had turned that down in favor of coming back to Sagebrush where she felt she was needed, given Doc's age and his wife's poor health.

She stood next to Colin as the tears of frustration she'd held at bay for months burst like a dam. They fell unchecked onto the covers he clutched as once again a fit of chills overtook him. She tucked the quilts tight around his shoulders and neck, and finally he relaxed into sleep.

This was a man she had once loved—had never stopped loving. This was a man who had wanted her to give up on her dreams, and when she didn't, he'd walked away. And this man's life was possibly now in her hands. She would show him. She would show them all.

She leaned close, her hand resting on his cheek and then forehead. His fever was down. The next time he woke, she would take his temperature. "Don't you dare die on me, Colin Foster. You owe me that much." She swiped away her tears with the backs of her hands and tended to the fire before going to stand at the window. It was snowing harder now, covering the empty streets. At this rate, nothing would be moving by sunup. Hers was the only lamp still burning as the rest of the town slept.

She went over the pattern of Colin's symptoms since she'd brought him inside, taking pencil and paper from her pocket to make notes. Three hours had passed. Fever, then chills, then raging fever that bordered on delirium. When had she administered the first dose of aspirin? She recalled the church bells and wrote *midnight* on the paper. Given that he seemed calmer and was sleeping, maybe the aspirin had eased things for him. If she set up a timetable for dosing him, maybe that would help break the fever. She went to her examining room and measured the remaining powder. Half a dozen doses maybe. Every four hours? And he would need to eat something—some broth at least. Yes, liquids. He was seriously dehydrated, of that she was certain. She rested her hands on the windowsill and her forehead against the coolness of the glass.

She could do this. She *would* do this.

Three

COLIN SQUINTED. HIS EYELIDS FELT AS IF THEY WERE crusted shut. He smelled the putrid odor of whatever covered his chest. He heard only silence and the occasional shifting of a log. He saw the glow of a dying fire—and Evie.

She was asleep on a hard wooden chair, her shawl pulled close around her shoulders, her hair coming free of the pins and combs she used to control it. Even through his blurred vision, she was beautiful.

The room was cold—the remaining heat of the fire unable to keep pace with the falling temperatures. Outside it was dark and yet light, the snow creating a glow of its own. Colin pushed himself up to rest on one elbow and forced his eyes fully open. His breathing was shallow, and yet, he had to do something about the fire or they would both freeze to death. He shoved back the quilts Evie had used to cover him.

Had he imagined her also covering him with her body?

He shook off the thought and eased his legs over the side of the bed, taking a moment to overcome a wave of dizziness and noting the woodpile was empty. No doubt Evie had meant to bring in more wood but had exhausted herself hauling him around instead. Colin placed his stocking feet firmly on the floor and reached for the bedpost to pull himself upright. Recalling he'd seen wood stacked near the side door when he'd tried to hide from her in the alley, he held on to the doorframe and furniture pieces as he made his way from the bedroom, around the corner, and into the kitchen.

As he passed through the short hallway, wind howled and rattled the glass in the front entrance to the office. He could see the silhouette of snow mounded against the front window and hear the squeal of the shingle with her name on it. Gripping the kitchen doorframe, he mentally measured the distance from there to the back door and the woodpile.

And just as it came to him that he hadn't the strength to open the door, much less carry logs, his knees buckled and he slid to the floor and rolled to his side.

∽∞∾

Evie woke in a panic. How could she have allowed herself to sleep—again? There was so much to do—refill the wood bin, prepare the next dose of medicine for Colin, try to get him to eat something or at least swallow some broth. She scrambled to her feet, knocking over the chair she'd moved closer to the bed as she pulled free of the shawl she'd wrapped herself in. Locks of her hair had come undone and now blocked her vision, but she felt the chill and knew the fire was almost out. Gathering her hair, she pulled it away from her face and over one shoulder as she looked first to the bed.

Empty.

"No," she whispered, hurrying to the far side, expecting to see Colin huddled on the floor. He wasn't there.

Panicked, she turned in a circle. Where would he have gone? She spotted his boots. Surely that was a good sign.

A low moan. Was it the wind? No—it was human.

"Colin?" She rounded the corner to the kitchen and saw him, lying on the floor, shivering violently. "Oh my stars," she muttered, racing back to the bed and grabbing as many quilts as she could. "What were you thinking?"

she demanded as she covered him, rolled him to his back so he was lying on the quilts instead of the bare floor, and then wrapped them tight around him.

"Wood," he murmured. "Fire."

"You could simply have called for me—wakened me." She fumed as she struggled to haul him to a sitting position, thinking the less he was in contact with the cold floor, the better. Once she had him propped against the doorframe, she continued mummifying him with the covers.

He smiled a goofy smile. "Angel," he whispered. "Beautiful angel."

Some angel.

The truth was, Evie was not upset with Colin, but with herself. What if he'd made it outside and wandered off? What if she hadn't wakened? She'd fallen asleep and put her patient at risk in more ways than one. Satisfied that for the time being he was as protected as possible, she began heating broth. It seemed only logical that getting something warm down him might help.

"Drink this," she instructed, holding the cup to his lips. He slurped in a mouthful and swallowed. "More," she said, tilting the tin cup higher.

Unable to swat her away with his hands trapped in the covers, he swung his head side to side. "No," he protested. "Hot!"

Evie was aware of the beverage burning her hand through the cup. She'd made it too hot and caused him even more pain.

"Sorry," she muttered as she set the cup aside and opened the kitchen window. Snow tumbled into the dry sink. She dropped some in the hot liquid and the rest in a bowl. "Try this," she urged. "Better?"

He didn't turn his head so she figured she had her answer. "Now stay here while I rebuild the fire and stock wood."

Colin leaned back and closed his eyes. From the office, Evie heard the chime of her clock and kept count. Four bells.

Aspirin.

Forgetting all about the need to get wood and rebuild the fire, she rushed to her office and measured out a dose of the miracle powder. Mixing it in the leftover melted snow, she fed it to him as she had before, clamping his mouth shut until he swallowed.

"Dang it, woman," he sputtered.

Evie allowed herself a moment of pleasure. His temper was a good sign. Colin had always been frustrated by her determination to overcome his objections and do things her way.

But then his eyes drifted shut and he clutched at the covers, shivering so much his teeth actually chattered. Evie wrestled the kitchen door open and hurried to the woodpile, where she removed the tarpaulin that kept the fuel dry and loaded four logs in her arms, even as the blowing, icy snow stung her cheeks and hands. Once back inside, she kicked the door shut so hard the glass rattled. She hurried to the fireplace in the bedroom. In minutes, she had the fire going again. Now the problem was to get Colin closer, then get more fuel, then make sure there was wood for the stove in the kitchen, then…

"Evie?"

His voice was weak, but how many times had she lain awake nights wishing just once she could hear him calling?

"Right here," she assured him as she knelt by his side. "We have to get you back to my bed," she added.

It was a measure of how sick he was that he didn't smile at the double meaning of her words. "Yeah," he whispered.

She eased him down so that he was fully resting on top of the quilts. He fought her at first, protesting the loss of warmth when she spread them flat. But she needed those covers to move him. "Lie still," she ordered as she grabbed the corners above his head and began pulling him slowly toward the bedroom.

Mentally, she calculated the difference in their size. He was over six feet and probably close to a hundred and seventy-five pounds—most of it muscle. She was strong, but she was also a good eight inches shorter and probably fifty pounds lighter. On top of that, there was no way he could lighten the load for her, so getting him off the floor and onto the bed would be impossible. Inch by inch, she tugged the covers, stopping to get a better grip as she made it through the doorway and on toward the fireplace. Finally, she gave one last tug and settled him in front of the fire.

Sweat lined her forehead, and her breath came in short, urgent gasps as she stood over him, hands on hips, deciding whether he was too close to the hearth or not close enough.

Now for the wood.

Making sure he was covered again and pushing an extra pillow under his head and shoulders, she hurried back outside, returned with a stack, and added two fresh logs to the fire. Then back again and again until she had enough wood to not only see them through the rest of the night, but the following day as well. The storm showed no signs of letting up, and that meant getting out to do normal chores or errands would not be possible. Evie sat on the edge of the bed to catch her breath.

As the wind howled around the building, rattling doors and windows as if trying to find its way inside, she studied her hands—fingertips numb and nearly blue. Her hair lay in snow-soaked strands plastered to her cheeks and forehead. It felt as if she might never be warm again. Given the way the snow had settled in piles and drifts, she wondered if it would ever stop, or if by morning the doors to the office and her living quarters would be iced over and nearly impossible to open.

She moved closer to the fire, stretching her hands toward the warmth. She was exhausted. Colin finally seemed to be breathing more easily. She sat cross-legged near the hearth, waiting for her breathing to slow and allowing the fire to warm her. They would both need to eat. Fortunately, she had stocks of food thanks to local townspeople who had welcomed her return to Sagebrush with baskets filled with food supplies, although they would travel miles to see a male doctor in another town rather than allow her to treat them or their families. The few patients she had seen had also paid her with food.

Sitting on the floor with her damp skirt spread around her, she studied Colin. He'd changed since she'd first set eyes on him that June day, now six years ago. He'd come to town to buy supplies for the ranch where he worked. She'd just left Doc's office on her way to Gibson's mercantile, a list clutched in her hand. She was still living with her pa, but came to town every day to help Doc and Mrs. Williams, using the money they paid her to buy food for her father's supper.

She and Colin had arrived at the entrance to the store at the same time. He'd opened the door for her, offering her a small bow and a devastating smile.

Was that the moment she had realized there would never be anyone else for her but Colin? If so, he'd seemed equally smitten. He'd completed his business in the store and waited outside for her. He'd introduced himself, stumbling over the words and further endearing himself to her with his lack of brashness—a trait most men in the West seemed to have in abundance. He'd invited her to take a buggy ride with him the following Sunday, and without hesitation she had agreed. And they had been inseparable from that day until she'd received her acceptance to medical school—the night Colin had proposed.

That Christmas Eve he'd looked especially handsome—his dark hair tamed from its usual tousled nest of waves, his face clean-shaven, and his eyes sparkling as he drew her into the shadows outside the church just as the bells tolled the dawn of Christmas Day.

"Evie, let's get married. Let's not have another year begin without us being together as man and wife."

For reasons she could never explain, his choice of words had given her pause, her quick and always questioning mind examining their true meaning.

Man and wife.

Had he said *husband and wife*, there would have been the flavor of equality—a partnership in life. Somehow, man and wife posed a hierarchy where decisions would not be shared.

When she hesitated, Colin continued to make matters worse. "I've decided this is the best way forward, Evie."

I...I...I...

She remembered how he'd held her hand and smiled, sure of himself and her agreement.

"We can't." She'd felt his grip loosen as she handed him the letter announcing her acceptance to medical school in Kansas City. Colin had always taken her ambition to become a doctor seriously, unlike most others in town. "We'll need to wait. I'm to begin classes on the second."

To this day, she could still vividly recall the look that had crossed his face. It began with an uncertain smile as if he thought she might be pulling a joke that he didn't quite get. Then he'd stepped closer to the light still spilling through the open church doors and studied the letter. His smile wavered. "It's the news you've waited to hear, Evie," he said slowly. "Still, if they have a place in January, it'll be there in spring as well. I can look for work closer to Kansas City, and we can find a little place and..."

"That's not how things work, Colin. There are schedules to be kept, and if I turn this down, then they will question the seriousness of my intent."

Carefully, Colin had refolded the letter—its thick parchment crackling in the cold. "And what of our schedule, Evie?" He hadn't looked at her.

"Don't you see, Colin? With a medical degree, we can make a solid start. We can…"

She'd seen his shoulders tense. "You're doubting that I can provide properly for you?"

"No! It's just once I find a position, it will come with housing—a place of our own where we can start a family and…"

He was quiet for so long that Evie realized everyone had left the church and the priest had closed the doors. The darkness that surrounded them suddenly felt like much more than a deserted street at midnight. She felt something slipping away.

"Nothing's really changed, Colin," she'd said, knowing that everything had.

"It's late. I'll see you back to Doc's." He'd taken a light hold on her arm—a stranger's polite hold—and started walking.

"Can't we talk about…"

"Seems to me you've made up your mind," he muttered.

She'd jerked free of him, snatched the letter from his hand, and stood at the end of the lane that led to her room above Doc's office and living quarters.

They'd argued, him telling her no one would take her seriously as a doctor, while she accused him of not truly loving her. They'd said things they didn't mean but could not take back.

"I'm going," she'd said defiantly.

She had never forgotten the look he gave her—his eyes narrowing, his smile gone. He'd turned his back to her, tugging his hat lower. "Then I guess I am too," he'd said, adding, "I hope you get everything you want, Evie." He'd walked away, shoulders hunched against the wind, his footprints a lonely trail in the fresh snow.

Now as she watched him sleep, she realized his wish for her that Christmas had only been half-fulfilled. She had gotten everything she wanted—except him.

⌒⌒

Christmas…

They'd been so young—not yet twenty. He and his friends had rented a wagon and called for Evie and her friends. Together they boarded that sled wagon filled with hay and blankets, and all evening they rode around the countryside serenading neighbors with carols. They ended up back at the church by eleven, in time for midnight services, and just as the church bells rang in a new Christmas Day, Colin was planning to propose. Not only that, but he was planning to suggest they marry one week later on New Year's Eve. He saw not one single reason for delay. Starting a new year together was the perfect plan.

He'd had no doubt of the outcome. He'd imagined it all in detail—Evie all bundled up in that red-plaid coat worn over a solid wool dress of green as deep as a forest of evergreens at twilight, her cheeks rosy with the cold, her laughter competing with the bells the team of horses wore to announce their coming. She would rest her head on his shoulder, snuggled into the curve of his arm as the group made their way back to town.

In church they would squeeze into one of the pews, thankful for the need to sit so close without old Mrs. Dobbins glaring at them disapprovingly. Under the cover of Evie's full skirt, they would hold hands. When they shared a hymnal for the responsive reading or a hymn, she would look up at him and smile. His heart would beat so fast and hard, he'd have trouble getting out the song. And then as everyone lit a candle and silently filed outside, he would pull Evie away from the others and propose. She would squeal with delight, fling her arms around him, and hand in hand they would hurry to tell their friends the good news.

Yep, it was gonna be just about perfect.

Except it wasn't.

Colin opened his eyes and took stock of his surroundings. The small room was filled with light—a combination of the snow-covered landscape outside the window and the coming dawn. He was lying on a mattress of quilts on the floor near the hearth and could feel the heat of the fire on his face.

His fever had broken. His breathing had eased. He was weak as a newborn calf, but definitely much improved. He smelled bacon frying and coffee boiling and realized he was hungry. Pushing himself to a sitting position, he rested his back against the foot of the bed—Evie's bed.

"Evie?" His voice was just above a raspy whisper. He coughed and tried again. "Evie?"

In an instant she was there, spatula in hand, eyes wide with concern.

He grinned up at her. "Happy Christmas," he managed before a coughing jag that threatened to rip out his insides overwhelmed him. She knelt next to him, her small hand flat on his back as she urged him to lean forward, to breathe. Very professional, except he wanted her tenderness, not her proficiency. He gulped in air.

"Better?"

He nodded, unable to speak. When she made a move to stand, he took hold of her hand. "I've missed you, Evie," he managed.

Slowly she laced her fingers with his, her eyes lowered, her cheeks a rosy pink. In that moment they were the boy and girl lying together in the field—lovers basking in the aftermath of a passion just shared. He reached for her, but she was gone.

"The bacon!" she cried as she ran to the kitchen.

The scent of charred meat and the thick smoke of a small grease fire filled the room. Using the bedpost as leverage, Colin pulled himself to his feet. He was wearing only his long johns. He saw his trousers folded neatly with his shirt on a nearby chair, but when he tried to retrieve them, weakness overcame him, and he was forced to sit on the edge of the bed.

"Just what do you think you're doing?" Evie demanded, setting a tray loaded with food and two steaming cups of coffee on top of a dresser as once again she hurried to his side.

He patted the bed. "Sit, Evie. I've got something to say."

He saw resistance flash across her features, and as usual she ignored his request. Instead she brought the tray to him and handed him a glass. "Drink this down, and then try to eat something."

He swallowed the gray liquid in the glass, made a face, and reached for the coffee to kill the bitter taste. Meanwhile, she busied herself adding another log to the fire and straightening the covers.

"Evie, will you please stop flitting about and come sit with me?" He held up the second cup she'd left on the tray, and to his relief, she accepted it.

"Eat," she instructed, wrapping her hands around the sides of the cup to warm them.

He took a bite of a biscuit. "No bacon?" He gave her a teasing smile, and that earned him the first twitch of her mouth.

"I never was much of a cook," she admitted shyly.

"As I recall, we'd worked it out that I would handle the cooking. Remember?"

She nodded. "Try the broth. There's not much I can do to ruin broth, and it will soothe your throat."

He filled a spoon and slurped it down.

She stood and turned toward the window. "After you finish eating, you should rest as much as possible. Your fever is down, but you are in no condition to go anywhere. Not that anyone alive should venture out in this weather."

He ate more of the broth, watching her.

"Did you make the right choice, Evie?"

He saw her spine straighten, but she did not turn around. "As I recall," she said, "I wasn't the one who walked away. The choice was not mine to make."

"Wasn't it?" He set the tray aside, stood, and reached for his trousers. This was not a conversation he wanted to have while wearing nothing but his undergarments. "Seems to me…"

He had one leg of his trousers pulled on when she whirled to face him. "And that's the root of it, Colin. 'Seems to you' this or that. Did you once stop to consider how things might seem to me? How I might have seen our future? We could have made it work."

He buttoned his fly and hooked his suspenders over his shoulders. "I thought we wanted the same thing, Evie."

Her eyes filled with tears. "So did I," she admitted.

He took half a step toward her, watching her as if she were a wild mustang easily spooked. When she didn't back away, he took the full step that brought him near enough so that he could run his knuckles over the smooth skin of her cheek. "Evie," he said, his voice husky with longing.

Tears balanced a moment on her lashes and then dropped to her cheeks. His reaction was as instinctive as breathing. He closed the remaining distance between them and folded her in his arms. "Let it out," he said as he kissed her hair, inhaling the sweet scent of pine soap.

"It's been so hard, Colin," she blubbered. "So very lonely."

He felt her arms come around him, completing the circle of their embrace. It was like coming home.

"And what if we could change that? What if it's not too late, Evie? For us, I mean?"

She looked up at him, her eyes wide with what he could only describe as hope.

"I was a danged fool back then, Evie," he admitted. "And not a day or night has passed when I didn't know that."

"Then why not write or come find me?"

"Pride—stupid pride."

"And now?" she asked.

"I reckon that's up to you."

She shook her head. "It's up to us, Colin. I mean, I'm here and so are you. We'll have to find a way to respect the choices each of us made back then."

"Or start again? As partners this time?" He ran his fingertip along her cheek.

"Equal partners?"

"We can try," he said. "Of course, I might trip up now and again."

She smiled. "Lucky for you, I'm pretty good at setting folks right when they trip."

He leaned in closer, and still she did not turn away.

Their kiss was everything he remembered of those summer days in the grass—those cold winter nights in the loft of his employer's barn. Their mouths fit perfectly, and neither hesitated to open to the other. He felt the outline of her breasts pressed to his chest and recalled the times they had lain together, unencumbered by clothes. He felt his passion swell as it always had whenever he and Evie were together—as it had countless lonely nights as he lay awake out on the range thinking of her.

The bed was less than a foot behind them. If he lifted

her, would she refuse? Her fingers were tangled in his hair, urging him closer. Their breath came in a duet of syncopation as if they were one. There was an insistent pounding that he at first thought was the twin beating of their hearts.

Suddenly, Evie pulled back, her head turned toward the kitchen and the side door. "Someone's here," she whispered.

He tightened his hold on her. "They'll leave."

"Evelyn!" The pounding grew more intense.

"It's Father Whitestone," she whispered. She pulled free of Colin and was fixing her hair as she hurried past him to the kitchen. "Coming," she called out.

Colin heard her wrestle with the door, apparently frozen shut by the snow and ice piled outside it. It banged back on its hinges, sending a wave of frigid air through the house that made the fire shimmy. "Happy Christmas, Father," he heard Evie say as the door slammed shut again.

"And to you, child. You weren't at services last night, and I was concerned. Is everything all right?"

"I had a patient—a local cowboy who was in a bad way when I found him. Blessedly, he has made it through the night and…"

"He's still here? He stayed the night?"

Colin bit back a hoot of laughter, knowing exactly how Evie would react to that comment. "If I were a man," she would begin.

But instead he heard Evie say, "He was deathly ill. What would you have me do?"

"Still…a woman, alone…"

"His fever broke just before dawn," Evie continued, her voice tight. "He's resting comfortably, and I am sure by day's end…"

Colin heard the priest grunt and the scrape of a chair being pulled away from the table as Evie apparently set a place for him.

"No service today?" Evie asked as she served coffee.

"The storm has everyone trapped wherever they are," Whitestone replied, slurping his coffee and then stirring it. "The worst of it has passed, but the drifting makes travel—even on foot—quite treacherous."

More sounds of a kettle's whistle, then a spoon stirring, the priest shifting on his chair as Evie served him. "This patient, Evie—a local man, you say?"

"Yes. I believe he works…"

Colin had heard more than enough. Evie was right. Had the doctor been a man, this conversation—this probing for information—would not be happening. He cleared his throat and stepped into the kitchen, extending his hand to the preacher.

"Colin Foster, sir. I'm foreman for the Madison ranch." He pulled out the second chair and sat. "Truth is, Doc here gave me quite the Christmas present in that it's more than likely she saved my life." He paused for the threat of a coughing jag to pass, then took a swallow of the water Evie handed him. "I just hope the people of Sagebrush have the good sense to know what a treasure they've got in her."

Father Whitestone's bushy, gray eyebrows lifted and fell and lifted again as he looked from Colin to Evie. "You seem to have indeed made quite the recovery, young man. Miss Prescott gave me to understand…"

"*Doctor* Prescott has quite the healing touch," Colin said with a grin at Evie.

Four

EVIE HAD HOPED COLIN WOULD HAVE SENSE ENOUGH TO get back in bed and stay there. Instead here he sat—barefoot, wearing trousers over long johns, and looking far healthier than the picture she'd described to the priest.

"More tea, Father?" She lifted the kettle and tried to keep her hand from shaking as she refilled the priest's proffered cup. His eyes were fixed on Colin.

"Forgive me, but why do I have the sense the two of you are more than doctor and patient?" he asked.

Colin met his gaze. "Evie and I are old friends. Imagine our mutual surprise when I showed up last night looking for Doc Williams and found her instead."

"Indeed." Father Whitestone seemed inclined to linger. "I don't mean to pry, but…"

"Mr. Foster and I met several years ago when I was living with Doc and his wife and he was working at the Madison ranch."

"I see."

"Then I went off to medical school, and Mr. Foster followed his work moving cattle to market and such. We lost touch. It's been five years since…" She was babbling.

"We were sweethearts, Father," Colin said quietly. "Sweethearts who came to a parting of the ways, sadly. Biggest mistake I ever made." He turned his gaze to Evie.

Father Whitestone cleared his throat, drawing her attention back to him. He studied her for a long moment. "I see." He sipped his tea. "We all do things we regret. Sometimes, however, God blesses us with the opportunity to rectify those regrets."

She turned away, busying herself with clearing dishes and refilling the kettle. "It was a long time ago, Father. We were young."

The priest turned his attention back to Colin. "Your current position with the Madison outfit—it's secure?" Evie let out a breath of relief at the change in subject.

"I'm the foreman. I reckon in my line of work, that's about as secure as it gets." Colin's tone took on an edge of defensiveness.

Father Whitestone tapped his fingernails on the wooden tabletop. "Life in this part of the country can be quite difficult—and lonely. I have worried about Evelyn. She has taken on quite a challenge."

"Yes, sir," Colin replied.

Once again, the men in the room were talking about her as if she weren't there. "There was a time when Colin and I thought we might marry," she blurted out, taking perverse pleasure in the way both men snapped to attention and faced her. "Of course, that didn't work out, but it's nice to have the chance to renew a friendship."

She turned to Colin. "You need to rest," she instructed. "Father, if you would be so kind…"

The priest immediately stood and came around the table, offering his support. While Evie moved the breakfast tray, Father Whitestone got Colin settled under the covers. He stoked the fire while Evie took Colin's temperature.

"Much better," she murmured as Colin collapsed back against the pillows.

He looked exhausted, and Evie could not resist pushing a lock of his hair away from his forehead before turning to find the priest studying the two of them. She led the way back to the kitchen. "He'll sleep for much of the day," she said, setting the breakfast tray on the table.

Father Whitestone picked up his tea and stood at the window. "Will he be all right?"

"He's much improved," Evie said. "He needs rest more than anything."

The priest nodded. "As do you, my dear. Why don't I sit with Mr. Foster while you get some sleep?"

"I couldn't…"

Father Whitestone smiled. "I have nowhere else to be, Evelyn, and frankly, given the choice between sitting here in your warm home or going back out into that bitter cold…"

"If you're sure."

He pulled a leather-bound Bible from the pocket of his sack coat. "I have good company right here. You take some time for yourself—maybe curl up in your office there. I'll come get you should there be a need."

"Thank you," she said softly and returned to her office where she took a blanket and lay down on the examination table. Her last thoughts before she drifted off were of the kiss she and Colin had shared and of what Father Whitestone had said about God sometimes offering the opportunity to correct the past.

I still love him—I will always love him, her heart murmured.

∞

Colin had no sense of time. All he knew was that the sky outside the window was bright blue and cloudless, and light streamed through the lace curtains, leaving a shifting pattern on the floor. He pushed himself higher on the pillows and looked around.

The priest smiled at him. "Well, did you have a good rest, young man?"

"Where's Evie?"

"Sleeping." He nodded in the direction of the office. "You're still here."

"Nowhere else to be at the moment." Whitestone stood and stretched. "Can I get you anything? A glass of water, perhaps?"

Colin cleared his throat. "Sure. Thanks." He watched the priest fill a glass from the pitcher Evie had left by the bed. "I'm curious. Would you have stayed if Evie was a man?" he asked.

"Probably not. Evelyn is perfectly capable of managing any patient—male or female—without my help. However, given the past you two have shared, I thought it best…"

"I love her," Colin blurted out.

"Yes, I believe you do. There is a certain…energy that passes between the two of you. Would it surprise you to know I believe she returns those feelings?"

"For all the good that does," Colin muttered.

"Nevertheless, for those reasons—and others—I felt it best to stay. You and Evelyn are at a time in your lives when the clock tends to speed up. That can lead to challenges. Perhaps God brought me here to help you navigate those challenges?"

Colin smiled. "I'm not exactly a believer in such things, Father."

Whitestone shrugged. "Fortunately, I am. Doc Williams and I have been concerned for Evelyn. Since returning to Sagebrush and setting up her practice, rather than becoming engaged in the larger community, she has increasingly shut herself away. She is a fine doctor to be sure, but beyond that she has much to offer as a friend and neighbor. The truth is, when she did not attend either service last night, I was determined to have a serious talk with her."

"Evie's always been able to take care of herself," Colin said.

"That's true, but perhaps the more pressing question is: Should she have that burden to bear? Is not life more fulfilling when shared with another?"

Colin couldn't believe what the priest was suggesting. "You think me and Evie…"

Again, the slight shrug. "It is not my choice to make. Still it occurs to me the two of you were once well on your way to a shared life when you hit a patch of rough road."

"You might say that."

"Well, you're both past that now, and somehow your paths have reconnected. Whether you believe it or not, I believe that God is offering you a chance to reexamine that."

"Meaning?"

"Will you walk forward together, or is it too late?"

"The truth is, Father, Evie has more cause than me not to trust men. Her father…"

"I know all about her father, Colin. I also have no reason to believe you are anything like that man."

"But I was—not the beating and such, but I sure wanted things my way and saw it as my responsibility to be the provider. So when Evie got that letter accepting her to medical school, it scared me."

"In what way?"

"Why would she need me? What would I ever have to offer her?"

"Love? A safe haven after a long day? The simple joys of raising a family? In short, the very things you were looking to her to provide for you."

"I think we might have gotten past what happened before, but she may not…"

"And then again, she may. The question is whether or not you have the courage to find out."

Colin ran his palm over the stubble of his beard. "Now? Today?"

Again the slight lift of his shoulders as the priest replied, "You're here, and so is she… Will there be another time?"

Colin considered the idea. "I'm not at my best—I stink and I need a shave."

"I could help with that."

Colin could not believe he was buying into this idea. "Not sure Evie keeps a straight razor around."

"Ah, good point. Still we could do something about washing up." The older man picked up the tin basin Evie had used to collect snow to cool Colin's fever and headed for the kitchen.

"Is Colin...?" he heard Evie ask, her voice groggy with sleep.

"He's fine. Just having a bit of a wash-up. You rest, my dear."

Returning to the bedroom, the priest set a pan of water on the side table, along with a bar of soap and a towel. "Can you manage?"

"Yeah. Thanks."

"I'll be just outside the door." Whitestone stepped into the hall and closed the door.

Colin stripped naked, knowing his long johns held the bulk of his foul scent. He washed and dried himself, then instead of putting the undergarments back on, pulled on his trousers and shirt. On Evie's dresser he saw a comb and used it to tame his hair. He stepped back, studying himself in the mirror over Evie's dresser. *Not great but definitely better.* He studied the room reflected in the mirror—Evie's room, but could it one day be their room? Or maybe the foreman's quarters at the ranch? She could ride to and from town and do her rounds—once people started to realize she was the doctor—*their* doctor.

He saw a life for them and felt his heart swell. Maybe Whitestone was right. Maybe it wasn't too late after all.

∞

Evie found Father Whitestone sitting at the table in the kitchen just outside the closed door of her bedroom. "Is he all right?"

"I think he's much improved."

"I'm sure by tomorrow he'll be able to be on his way." She pulled out a chair and sat across from him. "Father, I don't want you to think anything untoward happened here. He's a patient and…"

"And a friend. Once upon a time he was more than a friend, was he not?"

She nodded.

"Evelyn, I cannot help but wonder what you might be feeling now."

Evie folded her hands, twisting her fingers and not looking at him. "It was all so unexpected, seeing him again after so many years had passed."

"And yet?"

"It was as if we had spoken yesterday," she whispered, surprised at the truth of that statement.

"So, you still have feelings for him—feelings that go beyond the renewal of a friendship."

Evie looked up at the kind face watching her carefully. "I loved him. I have never stopped loving him."

"Ah." He reached across the table and covered her hands with one of his. "Then heal yourself, Doctor Prescott."

"How?"

"Open your heart to the possibilities God may have brought you on this blessed day."

Evie laughed as she withdrew her hand and stood. "I doubt God has time to be concerned with bringing me special gifts, Father." She stood and ran her palms over her apron. "I should…" She looked around and realized there was nothing to be done.

"Perhaps I should see how Mr. Foster is faring," Father Whitestone said.

As Evie stood staring out at the empty street, she heard the murmur of conversation coming from the bedroom.

"Ridiculous. So much time. We've both changed," she muttered, turning from the window. She should ask the priest to stay for lunch. She wiped out the skillet, then set the table for three. Colin would be hungry. In the months they had spent together, it seemed he was always hungry. She considered what she might put together for a Christmas lunch. With little else to keep her busy these last several days, she'd made a wheat bread stuffed with nuts and raisins. She was an excellent baker, if a terrible cook. And there was the marmalade the patient with morning sickness had sent her. Both seemed festive enough for the occasion. She set the bread on a cutting board and placed it on the table with the marmalade and a dish of butter.

What else? She sliced cheese and hard salami onto a plate, all the while keeping an ear cocked toward the closed door of the bedroom. What could they be talking about for so long?

The door squeaked open.

"Looks awfully good," Colin said as he and the priest returned to the kitchen.

"A Christmas feast," Father Whitestone announced. "I'll bring the extra chair from your office, Evelyn."

"Can I help?" Colin asked. He'd dressed, and Evie could smell the scent of her pine soap when he came nearer.

"You're not well enough to head back to the ranch," she said, ignoring his question as she studied him from head to foot. "In this weather…"

"Not intending to," he said. "Just thought I might make myself a little more presentable."

The priest returned with the chair and set it at the table. "You have no tree or decorations, Evelyn?"

"I thought of adding some greens, but then the storm started and…" She shrugged and filled their plates. "Not much of a Christmas dinner," she said softly.

"Looks great to me," Colin assured her. He stood and pulled out her chair. "Sit, Evie."

They bowed their heads as Father Whitestone blessed the meal. She noticed Colin's appetite had improved and smiled. The aspirin had worked. He would be all right. Surely that was a Christmas gift worth celebrating.

"When I was a girl—before Mama died," she said, "we always took turns stating our blessings on Christmas Day. Shall we?"

"A fine idea. I'll begin," Father said. "I am blessed to have settled here in Sagebrush as I come to the end of my career as a pastor." He made the sign of the cross. "Colin?"

"I am blessed to have made my way back to these parts and found steady work to sustain me—and with any luck a family someday." He glanced shyly at Evie, and she felt a blush climb her neck to her cheeks.

"Evelyn?" The priest prompted.

"I am blessed to be doing the work I love," she said and then grinned. "Even if others have not yet seen fit to take advantage of my skills."

Colin and the priest laughed. They continued taking turns, interspersing their blessings with bites of the meal Evie had prepared. "My turn again?" Father Whitestone asked. "I am blessed to have brought countless couples together in holy matrimony and witnessed their journey through the years of that marriage as they walked side by side every day—their love and strength sustaining each other through the years."

There was a long silence while they ate their food. "Colin?" Father Whitestone said after the silence became uncomfortable.

"I am blessed..." he began, focusing on his plate, now cleared of food. "I am blessed to have found Evie again." He glanced up at her.

She swallowed the last bits of cheese and took a long swallow of water, fighting the tears that threatened. "And I am blessed," she whispered, "to have the chance to tell Colin I have thought of him with...fondness...so often since the day we parted all those years ago."

Father Whitestone, seated between them, took hold of Colin's hand and then Evie's and joined them. "And I am so very blessed to bear witness to this reunion of two hearts split apart and rejoined by God's divine providence." He closed his eyes in silent prayer. He wiped his mouth with the cloth napkin. "I should return to the church in case anyone decides to stop by," he announced, pushing away from the table and standing. "Thank you, Evelyn, for a lovely Christmas repast." He turned to Colin and shook his hand before heading to the door, where he hesitated. "Should the two of you decide you have need of my counseling—or other services—do not hesitate to come to me."

Evie was so confused by the priest's cryptic offer and her own feelings. Was the priest offering his blessing? And did Colin understand? And was this what he wanted, or was he embarrassed by Father Whitestone's obvious—and clumsy—attempt to reunite them?

"Thank you," Colin murmured, his eyes on their joined hands.

As the door closed behind the priest, Evie stood and began clearing the table. She was aware of Colin watching her.

"I could make us snow creams," he offered.

She was assailed by another memory of an early December snowstorm when they had gathered fresh snow and combined it with eggs and vanilla and eaten the cold, sweet concoction while sitting before a fire.

She smiled. "That would be nice, but you are not going out in this weather." She wiped her hands on a towel and took a tin pan down from a hook above the dry sink. "I'll collect the snow."

"Put on a coat," he called.

She was back in less than a minute, holding up the pan of snow.

"I need eggs and vanilla," he announced.

She pointed to the egg basket and took down a bottle of vanilla from the shelf above the dry sink. He took down a large mixing bowl, cracked eggs into it, and beat them with the vanilla. Then he added the snow and slowly stirred the mixture, watching as it solidified into the dessert of their youth. He scooped a spoonful and fed it to her.

Evie closed her eyes as she savored the cold and sweetness. "Heaven," she murmured.

"Yeah," he said, but he was looking at her. "Evie, do you think maybe—I mean, Whitestone seems to think maybe we could try again."

"We're not the same people we were before," she said.

He took a bite of the snow cream and moved away. "It was just a thought. I mean, with me working at the ranch and you here in town, we're bound to run into each other from time to time."

"You think it will be awkward?"

He stared at her. "I think it will be painful," he said softly. "At least for me. A reminder of what we could have had and I walked away from."

"We both walked away, Colin. And you're right. We were young and not ready."

He tucked a lock of her hair behind her ear. "And now? Would you allow me to call on you, Evie? Court you again?"

Evie closed her eyes, remembering all the lonely nights she'd lain awake missing him—wanting him. Remembering the times they'd made love, wondering if memories would ever be enough.

"I don't want courtship, Colin." They'd moved well beyond those days—years when their lives had traveled separate paths. And now that they had found each other again and he'd admitted his mistakes of the past and shown his pride and belief in her as a doctor, she was ready to move forward instead of always looking back.

His eyes clouded with disappointment, and he looked away. She cupped his jaw and kissed him softly.

"I know you, Colin, and you know me. Why waste time?"

"It's just I think we might get beyond the past and find our way again."

"I've found my way, Colin, and I do not want to waste another day. Marry me?"

⁓⁓

Colin could not have been more surprised if she'd suddenly taken up the freshly wiped skillet and slugged him with it.

"Marry you?" he managed in a strangled voice.

She turned away, her back stiffening as she cleared the eggshells and put the stopper back in the bottle of vanilla. "Or walk away again," she muttered as she dumped the melting snow cream into a pail and carried it to the door.

He stopped her before she could open the door, relieved her of the pail, set it down, and held out his arms to her. "Come here, Evie."

She hesitated, and he took the half step that separated them and wrapped his arms around her. "We need to think this through… You need to think this through. A lot of time has passed, and I'll admit there hasn't been a day I haven't regretted walking away. But for you, Evie… I mean, you're a doctor. I'm just a cowboy. You deserve…"

"You're doing it again, Colin. Always telling me what you think I need or want as if I haven't the sense to think for myself. If you don't want this, I accept that, but do not tell me what I want."

He pulled her closer. "Evie, I want you—us. Have done so since the day I first laid eyes on you coming across the plaza. I'd never met a girl like you—so strong and deter-mined and willful. So damned maddening and lovable."

He felt the tension ease from her body, felt her hands soften as they held him in return. She turned her face so her cheek rested against his chest, and he took all that as a good sign that he hadn't lost her—again. And in that moment, he understood her thinking. There was no need to waste any more time. They were not getting any younger. Their time for being together and raising a family and sharing their lives was finite. As a doctor, she understood that more than most. She wasn't being impulsive in suggesting they wed at once.

As usual, Evie was simply being practical.

"Let me finish dressing, and we'll go to the church," he whispered.

Her head shot up, her eyes boring into his. "Right now?" She stepped back, put her hands to her hair, then to her soiled apron. "I can't go like this."

"I thought…"

"You finish dressing while I clean up the rest of the mess here. After that, I'll change, and then we'll go to the church." But instead of turning back to the kitchen, she began rummaging through a trunk that sat near the back door, pulling out woolen scarves and a man's mackintosh. "You'll need these. Or maybe I could go and ask Father Whitestone to come back here. You're still…"

Colin took hold of her shoulders and turned her to face him. "I'm as ready as I'm going to be, other than putting on my boots and jacket, so go change if that's what you want, or let's go to the church."

"I can't be married in this," she said, and when she reached the bedroom, she looked back at him. They were both smiling—the easy smiles they'd shared in their youth. And then slowly her smile faded into something far more serious.

"I love you, Colin Foster," she said softly and stepped into the bedroom and closed the door.

Five

CHRISTMAS DAY. HER WEDDING DAY.

It was all beyond belief, so much so that Evie stood paralyzed into inaction in the middle of her bedroom. The bedcovers were rumpled from where Colin had fought his way back to her. She picked up a pillow and inhaled the male scent of him. Realizing they would return here after they were married, she quickly straightened the covers, sprinkling a bit of rosewater to freshen the linens.

Then she stripped to her undergarments and washed herself with snow she gathered from the windowsill, shivering as she breathed in the cold air of a bright, sunny day. She shut the window, dried herself, and turned to her wardrobe. Her collection of clothing was meager and utilitarian, but in a chest lined with cedar was a dress she had been unable to part with through all the years since that other Christmas Eve.

She pulled out the solid-green wool dress she'd worn that night. Colin had said it reminded him of the forest. She wondered if he would remember. Not likely. Men did not take much stock in such things. The important thing was that she remembered—that in choosing this dress to be married in, she was completing the circle they had broken that night.

She brushed out her long hair and left it hanging free, pinning the sides back with a pair of combs before turning to the mirror. She looked younger—happier. They were taking a risk, of course. Time and changes they had both experienced might stand in their way. But surely a love that had lasted through all that would sustain them. Still, if he had doubts…

"Evie?" Colin knocked and then opened the door and stepped into the room. He had put on his boots, and he filled the doorway with his height and breadth.

When he saw her, he sucked in a long breath. "You look so…" He shook his head and grinned. "You take my breath away, Evie, and we both know right now I don't have a lot of breath to spare." He offered her his arm. "Shall we?"

"You're sure?"

"I think I've been sure pretty much since I saw that shingle swinging in the wind with your name on it."

In her office, he held her coat for her and put on his jacket and hat while she pulled on her gloves and wrapped her shawl around her head and shoulders. Side by side, they walked out into the cold, clear day and arm in arm crossed the deserted street. They entered the courtyard of the adobe church and stepped inside the sanctuary.

Father Whitestone sat in the front pew, his Bible open. He was wearing the robes he wore to conduct services, and when he heard the door open and close, he stood and faced them. "Ah, you came." He motioned to the altar. "Have you come to a decision?"

"Yes," Colin said. "We've come to be married."

"Colin," Evie whispered, suddenly shy.

"Better late than never," the priest said and motioned them forward as he took his position. "Tomorrow you can make arrangements to secure the official documents, but this ceremony before God is the important part."

Evie savored the exchange of words she and Colin repeated to each other—promises and time-honored vows binding them together for a future they had both longed for and would now share. She had never been happier.

As Father Whitestone gave him their blessing, Colin held both her hands in his, and the way he looked at her told her they shared the joy of this moment.

"I'll get you a ring," he said.

"I don't need a ring." She stroked his cheek. "Just you."

The priest cleared his throat. "Well, now, my young friends, in the absence of music or guests to cheer you on your way, I have an idea. Follow me."

He led the way up the aisle and out into the courtyard to the bell tower. "It's a doubly blessed day," he said, handing Colin the rope pull and then placing Evie's hands on it as well. "Let the bells ring out," he said and stepped back to give them room to pull the rope together.

At one point, Colin let go so that the rope pulled Evie into the air, and she laughed as he caught her and pulled her safely back to her feet. While in the air, she saw doors open along the street and people coming out from their houses as they headed for the church, called by the bell.

When several had gathered, Father Whitestone led Colin and Evie forward and announced, "My friends, on this holy day we have just celebrated the wedding of Doctor Evelyn Prescott to Mr. Colin Foster. Please join me in prayer as together we bless this holy union and wish them much happiness."

Everyone gathered closer, forming a circle around Evie and Colin. They held hands and bowed their heads as Father Whitestone placed his hands on Colin and Evie's bowed heads.

"Holy Father, spirit of life and love, we ask all blessings upon Colin and Evelyn as they begin their life together. Bless them with patience in times of trial and tension; with kindness as they nurture and care for one another in times of joy or sorrow; and bless them with humor and the joy of appreciating all that will come their way.

Finally let love be their guide—love they share with each other and with all they meet in their life's journey. In the name of the Father, the Son, and the Holy Spirit. Amen."

There was a moment of silence, and then everyone started to cheer. They broke the circle and stepped forward to congratulate Colin and hug Evie. A few picked up a handful of the dry powdery snow and tossed it at them in the absence of rice or confetti. Before they knew what was happening, they were being ushered back inside the church, while the women hurried back to their houses to get whatever they could to make a proper wedding meal. The owner of the Paradise Saloon brought three bottles of elderberry wine he claimed to have been holding for just such an occasion, and everyone raised a glass in a toast to the happy couple.

Evie had never felt more like a part of this community. For the first time since she'd taken over Doc's practice, she felt she could make a real difference for the families of Sagebrush. Oh, it would take time, but she was nothing if not patient.

As the meal and toasts gradually came to an end, Colin and Evie moved to the door, ready to offer their thanks and say their good nights. The sun was setting, and the sky was clear enough to expose the promise of a full moon. Someone pulled out a harmonica and played a carol, and others sang along.

They continued to stand gathered in the church courtyard, singing favorite carols until only the moon and the candles inside the church gave them light. Evie clung to Colin's arm, loving the sound of his voice raised in song. But then she realized he was trying to suppress a coughing spell.

"Good night, all," she said as she gently tugged his arm and started to cross the street to her office and living quarters. "The night air, you know. Thank you so much."

Colin came willingly, and that told her he was exhausted and needed to rest. All he could manage as he covered his coughing was a hand raised in appreciation.

Once inside, Evie dropped any pretense that everything was fine. "Come on," she urged as she led him to the bedroom, her arm around his waist supporting him. "Sit," she instructed when they reached the bed. She threw off her coat and shawl and bent to remove his boots.

"Evie?"

"Take your jacket off," she said, "and get under the covers. You're shivering."

"Not unless you get in here with me," he managed through coughs.

"Stop talking." She tossed his boots aside and helped him out of his coat. "Lie down." She covered him. "I'll be right back."

In the kitchen she put the kettle on to heat, then went to her office for the last precious dose of aspirin. She was stirring the medicine into water when she returned to the bedroom.

"Some wedding night, huh?" Colin joked.

"Take this," she said, holding the spoon of medicine to his lips. "Swallow. Good."

"Did I ever know you were this bossy?" He lay back against the pillows.

"If you didn't, you weren't paying attention." She fussed with the covers, pulling them up to his chin.

He caught her hand. "Stop playing doctor, Evie, and just be my wife."

She hesitated, then set aside the glass and spoon and crawled under the covers next to him.

"You're overdressed," he whispered.

"So are you," she replied.

He chuckled. "Seems like all along we've gotten things backward, Evie. In a perfect world..."

"In a perfect world, you would never have gotten so

sick, and then you would never have shown up outside my office door and we wouldn't be here at all. If that's getting everything backward, then count me in."

She snuggled closer to him, resting her face in the curve of his shoulder.

He kissed her temple. "Do you have any idea how many nights I dreamed of you being here next to me like this?"

"I'm here, Colin, and not going anywhere."

He pulled her close so that she was curled in to him, and moments later she heard his even breathing. Once she was certain he was sleeping soundly, she slipped out of bed and removed her dress. When he woke, she hoped maybe the medicine would have taken effect and the wedding night they had both dreamed of would finally become a reality. She closed her eyes and slept.

∽∾

Colin thought he must be dreaming. Evie was lying close to him the way she always had when they lay together by the creek or in the loft. Only now the warmth they shared came from the piles of bedcovers and not the sun. Outside it was dark. A log that was reduced mostly to ash crackled and shifted in the fireplace. He eased free of Evie's embrace and sat on the side of the bed. In the firelight he saw her green dress draped over a bedpost and looked back at her. She was wearing only her undergarments, and that made him smile.

He stood and lowered his suspenders, then pulled his shirt over his head and removed his trousers. He hung both on the bedpost opposite the one where she'd hung her dress. He paused, taking in the sight of something shared—this bed. For the first time not a field of grass and wildflowers or a hayloft, but a real bed. They were married. From this day forward, they would share whatever the day might bring.

From her office, he heard the clock chime ten times and realized it was still Christmas Day. There was still time to seal their vows. He shut his eyes and imagined them as one and felt the stirring of desire.

"Colin?"

Her voice was foggy with sleep. She rose up on one elbow and looked at him, a slight frown marring her lovely face in the ebbing light of the fire.

"Just putting another log on the fire," he said as he made his way unsteadily to the woodpile next to the hearth. He was so damned weak. For a minute he wondered if he'd even be able to perform his part in the consummation of their marriage.

"Let me…" She was out of bed and next to him, barefoot and wearing only her chemise and pantaloons.

"I can…"

"We'll do it together," she said softly, taking the log he held and kneeling to place it on the fire before reaching out for another. She dusted off her hands, then stood. "Come back to bed," she said, holding out her hand in invitation.

He stepped closer and cradled her face in his hands. "My wife," he whispered, and then he kissed her—a long, tender kiss absent the rushed, frantic passion they had found so necessary in the past, lest they be caught. Finally, they had time—all the time in the world.

He finished undressing. She watched, chewing her lower lip. "Maybe it's too…" He undid the ribbons and buttons that held her undergarments in place.

She pressed her body to his, then pulled her lips free and smiled. "Well," she said, "seems like maybe you're feeling better—stronger. Perhaps a little light exertion would not be…"

"Shut up, Doc," he said as he half carried, half dragged her back to the bed.

She giggled as she fell backward and he fell on top of

her. He knew the sound of that laughter—it came from the girl he'd fallen in love with five years earlier. And as if there had not been years of loneliness and regret between them, they rediscovered all the hidden places each knew would bring pleasure to the other. And when he entered her and at long last they were one again, he let out a ragged sigh of pure relief and pleasure.

Slowly he moved within her, watching her expression as her features softened and her eyes drifted shut. She rose to meet each thrust, clinging to his shoulders as she urged him deeper. When he exploded within her and cried out, she held him until his breathing calmed, then gently pushed him away so that he was lying next to her.

"Rest," she whispered, kissing his ear.

But that wasn't the way he and Evie did things. Once in a while they shared the miracle of coming at the same time, but he knew she hadn't yet gotten there. So he rolled to face her and began stroking her inner thighs.

"You have a short memory, Mrs. Foster," he whispered and grinned as he felt her tense beneath his probing fingers. "I guess we're a little out of practice. Let's see if I can fix that."

"Colin, really I... You..."

She gasped, telling him she was so close, and when she arched and cried out, her fingers digging into his shoulder, he wrapped her in the warmth of his embrace—his love.

"Merry Christmas, Evie," he whispered and feathered kisses along her face as he added, "My wife. My one true love."

About the Author

Award-winning author Anna Schmidt resides in Wisconsin. She delights in creating stories where her characters must wrestle with the challenges of their times. Critics have consistently praised Schmidt for her ability to seamlessly integrate actual events with her fictional characters to produce strong tales of hope and love in the face of seemingly insurmountable obstacles. Visit her at booksbyanna.com.

THROUGH THE STORM

—◦•◦—

Amy Sandas

One

EDMUND ALISTAIR GEORGE LINWOOD—KNOWN IN America's western territories as Gentleman George— tipped his chair onto its two back legs as he eyed the cards in his hand. They were pretty good cards, but that didn't mean a whole lot when playing with this bunch. He lifted his gaze to study the other players.

To his left was Hewett Durand, the town's under- taker, who was rarely seen without a whiskey in hand after 10:00 a.m. Across the table sat Tad Perry, who owned the saloon they were sitting in as well as the tobacco shop next door. And lastly, to George's right was Perry's friend and hanger-on, Joe Turnbull.

Cheats. All of them.

As the game continued, George noted an occasional sleight of hand or wandering eye, but he kept his mouth shut and kept playing. He enjoyed the challenge of pitting his skill against unfair odds.

"Well, I'll be shit-damned."

George looked up to see Perry standing half out of his seat, craning his short neck to look out the smoky saloon window. The saloon owner was a man who possessed a healthy appetite for women and spirits, which gave him a florid complexion and made him a frequent visitor to the whorehouse. He was also one of those men who believed anything he wanted should be his and happened to have the kind of money that usually made it so.

George followed the man's avid gaze across the narrow main street of Chester Springs to a wagon that had just pulled to a stop. A slim figure dressed in various animal furs hopped gracefully down from the driver's seat and went into the general store.

"What's so damn interesting?" Durand asked, his eyes glued to his cards.

"That there was the daughter of old Mountain Man Jones."

George's eye twitched at Perry's disdainful yet covetous tone. The man was a toad.

"So what," Durand grumbled. "We've got a game to play here."

"I fold," Perry declared as he swept his coat off the back of his chair and placed his hat on his balding head. "I've been waiting for that pretty half-breed to come to town. Now that her pa is gone, she's all alone up on that mountain." He gave the men at the table a lascivious grin. "She's likely to be hankering for a little company."

"And you plan to give it to her," Turnbull declared with a gleeful cackle.

"Damn right," Perry said as he headed out the door with Turnbull tight on his heels.

"Well, shit." Durand tossed his cards down and pushed to his feet. "I'm getting another drink."

George set his cards facedown on the table and watched out the window as the two men made their way across the main road through town. An uneasy feeling settled in his gut. Perry and Turnbull were menaces to the small town of Chester Springs. Wealthy, profligate, and in possession of dubious moral compasses, they took pleasure in throwing their weight around to get what they wanted regardless of how it affected anyone else.

George knew better than to get involved. It was crucial he keep a low profile whenever he was in town.

Still…he found himself scraping his chair back and rising to his feet. The sound of his boots on the wooden floor echoed as he strode to the saloon door. When he stepped out onto the boardwalk, the snow swirled in a gust that had him tucking his coat closer about his large frame.

It was less than a week until Christmas, and despite the winter chill that cut through the air and the dark-gray skies overhead, plenty of townsfolk were out and about, completing their errands in preparation for the holiday. George paused to smile and nod politely as a couple of older ladies bustled past.

There was no sign of Perry.

Maybe the man had decided not to cause trouble after all.

As George hesitated under the upper-floor balcony of the saloon, a bell rang above the door to the general store across the road. The fur-covered figure stepped out carrying a weighted load of supplies packed in a wooden crate and topped by brown-paper-wrapped parcels.

The deep hood of her furs concealed her face, but it was likely Perry had been right in guessing her identity.

The man known as Mountain Man Jones had lived on an isolated mountaintop not far from the valley where George had been making his home the last several years. Despite their proximity, George had never encountered Jones or his daughter, not in the mountains and not in town. The two were known for being extremely reclusive and only rarely left the mountains until it was time to sell their furs in the spring.

The fur-clad woman secured the supplies in the back of the wagon before pulling a canvas tarp over everything and tying it down with some rope. With her focus on the task, she didn't notice the two men stepping from the alley beside the mercantile. Turnbull hung back a bit while Perry came up behind her to wrap a thick arm around the woman's upper body, pressing himself against her backside. George was too far away to hear what Perry was saying, but he figured it couldn't be anything good.

Muttering a stiff curse beneath his breath, he started across the road in long, easy strides, opening his coat to tuck the edges behind his two holstered Colts. He got to within a few steps of the assault when Perry let out a yelp of pain and stumbled back a step. The woman calmly but swiftly turned to face him, a wicked-looking hunting knife in her hand.

Her hood had slipped back in the brief struggle, and a jolt of appreciation shot through George's system as he caught sight of her face. Smooth, black hair was parted in the center with its length tucked into the back of her coat. Dark eyes flashed from a round face accented by straight black brows, strong cheekbones, and a wide, lush mouth.

As was to be expected in a small town like Chester Springs, a mystery like the mountain man and his half-Shoshone daughter caused a lot of talk among folks. But George was pretty sure no one had ever mentioned how bloody beautiful the woman was.

"You ever think to touch me again, you disgusting pig," she declared in a firm and even tone, "I'll gut you so fast your innards will be on the ground before you even feel the slice of my blade."

Perry's eyes bulged, and his face went bright red in his fury. "You can't talk to me like that, you filthy slut." He made as if to lunge for her, but she countered with a lunge of her own that had Perry scrambling back a few steps as his feet slid on the frozen ground.

"Insult me again." The woman's voice was lightly challenging, as if she almost wished he would.

Turnbull, who had been giving his friend hoots of encouragement just moments ago, backed up until his retreat was stopped by the building behind him. The man was only brave when he had Perry's influence holding him up.

And Perry could barely hold *himself* up at the moment.

George chuckled at Perry's incredulous expression— not unlike a trout that had been pulled from a river and tossed straight onto the fire. The flush of temper coloring Perry's face darkened to near purple as he charged the woman again.

The man's idiocy was astounding. He was obviously no match for his intended victim. It took less than a minute for her to deflect his attack and execute a retaliatory move. The woman wielded her knife with more speed and grace than George had ever seen.

With a shout and a snarl, Perry stumbled back yet again, making a grab for his pants so they wouldn't end up around his ankles. She'd sliced through his coat and his suspenders with a couple easy arcs of her blade.

George whistled his admiration.

She didn't even glance his way. Her steady gaze remained trained on Perry.

"You idiot," Perry shouted to Turnbull, fumbling to maintain his modesty. "Do something."

Turnbull reached for his gun but didn't get it halfway clear of the holster before George had his own gun drawn. "I wouldn't," he said with a grin.

Turnbull immediately put his hands up in surrender.

"Coward," Perry accused before he turned his attention back to the woman. "You're gonna regret trying to make a fool of me."

George couldn't resist commenting. "A fool? You managed that all on your own, Perry. And I wouldn't be tossing threats around so freely. Someone might take exception."

Perry sneered. "You? A man who talks all fancy and proper and calls himself Gentleman George?"

George grinned. "If we're listing my finer qualities, please don't forget to include my impeccable manners and irresistible charm."

Perry's florid expression hardened. "You'd best watch your back," he threatened. "And you," Perry added, looking back to the woman who hadn't lowered her blade or shifted her gaze. "Someday, I'll find you without that knife in easy reach."

George had hit his limit.

He reached Perry in two long strides to shove him back against a post supporting the short roof that extended over the general store doorway. Keeping his gun pointed at Turnbull, in case the man decided to show some balls, George pressed his forearm to Perry's throat. "You know something, Perry?" George noted conversationally. "You're as ignorant a fool as everyone says you are."

Fury burned in Perry's eyes as his face flushed red with rising temper and lack of air.

"If I hear of you threatening this woman by word or action ever again, I'm gonna come calling." George smiled with a flash of teeth. "I promise... You don't want me to come calling. Are we clear?"

Perry looked at him as if he wanted shove a knife up beneath George's ribs, but after a moment, he gave a short nod. George released the pressure of his arm and took a step back, keeping himself between the two men and the woman who stood still and silent behind him.

Perry stumbled, grasping his throat and coughing between sharp inhales. Turnbull stepped toward him, but Perry shrugged him off. He cast a rage-filled glance at George before his shifty gaze started jumping around to notice the little crowd that had gathered to watch the show.

His flesh grew more livid in color. It appeared he didn't like being the center of attention unless he was the one in control. After sending a sneering glare at the curious onlookers, he turned back to George and spit a disgusting glob to the snow at his feet. "This ain't over," he declared. Casting a fury-filled glance toward the woman, he added, "You can count on that."

Holding his pants up with a tight fist and cursing at Turnbull under his breath, Perry made a face of disgust, then turned and walked away.

A sudden gust of wind swept down the road, causing a murmur of discomfort among the curious townsfolk still hovering about. One by one, they turned to continue about their day, anxious to finish their errands and get out of the cold.

George waited to be sure the two wastrels were truly gone before he turned back to see that the woman in furs had already leaped up onto the seat of her wagon. She gave a flick of her wrists and the horses started off, leaving George standing in the road feeling rather bemused and disappointed.

Most damsels in distress George had been fortunate enough to assist over the years offered up a sweet little thank-you or a smile or a flutter of lashes…something.

But then, this one hadn't really been in much distress and probably would have handled the situation just fine without George's interference.

If what had just happened was an example of what she experienced whenever she came to town, it was no wonder she preferred to keep to the mountains.

Still, he figured as he watched her ride away, it would've been nice to discover her name.

Then another gust of wind swept past him—this one even fiercer than the last. He tugged his coat close against the blast of frigid air and glanced up at the darkening sky, hoping it wasn't a forewarning of more extreme weather to come.

Two

SNOW SWIRLED WITH BLINDING FORCE AS GEORGE huddled atop his buckskin mustang, head bowed and hands tucked inside his sheepskin coat.

He cursed his boredom for luring him into town for a diverting game of cards.

He cursed Tad Perry for being an arse and delaying his departure.

And he cursed the whiteout conditions for getting him so lost.

If he'd been smart, he'd have stayed in Chester Springs to wait out the storm. Instead, he'd been distracted by thoughts of brown eyes and the loveliest mouth he'd ever seen.

He lifted his face and peered through the worsening deluge of snow. Surely, he should have gotten to the pass that would take him to the hidden valley by now.

Or perhaps the wind and deepening snow had slowed his progress enough that he hadn't yet reached the concealed trail. The trouble was that he couldn't see a foot or two in front of him to identify any landmarks to get his bearings. And the turnoff was difficult to spot in clear weather.

He imagined his mates were probably sitting all toasty and warm in front of the bunkhouse hearth. What he wouldn't give to be there with them right now!

He lowered his head against a fierce gust of wind that cut like ice through his winter layers. He tried to wriggle his toes, but he couldn't feel them. They had gone completely numb in his boots despite the woolen stockings he wore.

Another blast of driving snow set his teeth to chattering. His heart broke at the thought of not reaching the valley and the welcoming hearth, but if he didn't hunker down and get out of the blizzard, there was a chance he wouldn't make it through the storm at all.

Lifting his chin, he squinted against the icy wind that beat his face and scanned for anything that might provide some shelter. Thank God, Gabe had seen fit to show him how to build a makeshift shelter a few winters ago when they'd been traveling through a similar storm.

George figured he remembered the gist of it.

Locating a grouping of three trees tucked in close together, he stiffly dismounted and trudged through the snow. With his knife, he cut down saplings and trimmed pine boughs. After about an hour of doing his best to ignore the creeping numbness that had now reached his thighs, he had his mustang tied to a tree behind his shelter where the animal would be protected from the worst of the wind as George took up a spot inside. He sat on pine boughs to keep the snow underneath him from freezing his arse, with his arms wrapped around his bent legs.

The wind whipped snow in through every little crack, and he still couldn't feel his fingers or toes, but at least he had a chance of making it until the storm passed. As long as it didn't last too long. Or get much worse.

He had no idea how long he'd been sitting there when his mustang snorted. A second later, one carefully constructed wall of his shelter was swept away to reveal a figure dressed in furs, holding a shotgun aimed at his head. "Don't move." The voice was female, rich and warm though the words were spoken in a sharp tone.

Even if he *could* still move his frozen limbs, he wasn't going to. Though her face was concealed by the deep hood of her coat, he recognized her as the mountain man's daughter. He was sure that at any moment, she'd realize he was the man who'd defended her against Perry and would lower her weapon.

Except, she didn't. "Why are you following me?"

Though his jaw was sore from all the chattering his teeth had been doing the last few hours, he managed a somewhat coherent reply. "Since I couldn't see two feet past my nose, I sure as hell wouldn't have been able to follow anyone, even if I'd intended to."

"What're you doing up here?"

"I happen to live in these mountains, though I suspect I missed my trail."

"The pass to the valley is blocked by a fallen tree."

How did she know about the pass?

It was one of only two ways into the hidden valley he called home. The reason their gang had lasted so long was because no one had ever been able to find their hideout unless they'd wanted to be found.

"That explains why I missed it," he replied.

"So you thought you'd hole up here? In this?" she asked with a suspicious thread of amusement running through her voice.

George frowned and glanced about the shelter he'd been rather proud of until that moment. "I thought I did a fair job."

She shook her head. "You must have a death wish."

"Not at all. Hence, the shelter."

"This storm is gonna go on through the night and into tomorrow at least. You won't last more than another couple hours out here." She sighed, then lowered the gun. "I suppose you'd better come with me."

Not waiting for his agreement, she turned and disappeared from sight.

George scrambled from his hut as quickly as he could, fearing she'd disappear into the swirling whiteout he crawled into. But she had just gone around to untie his horse. Without even sparing a glance over her shoulder to ensure he followed, she started off into the blizzard.

He trudged after her, and no more than ten minutes later, the dark shape of a small cabin started to emerge out of the white.

If he hadn't stopped to make a shelter, he would have ridden right into it. He had been far more lost than he'd imagined. That or the mountain man and his daughter lived a lot closer to the valley than he'd realized.

"Go inside. I'll see to your horse." Not waiting for a reply, she veered to the left, and soon she and his horse both disappeared from sight.

George considered waiting for her before going inside. It just didn't seem proper to enter the woman's home without her. But the cold had gotten to him. He needed to thaw out.

He stumbled up two shallow steps to a small, uneven porch. Another two steps with his frozen feet, and he reached for the door's latch. It swung easily inward, and George bustled himself inside.

Warmth.

It enveloped him as soon as the door closed behind him. For a moment he noticed nothing about the cabin interior beyond the healthy fire blazing in a stone fireplace that took up half of the wall opposite where he stood. He kicked off his boots near the door, then crossed the small cabin to get nearer to the roaring heat of the fire.

He'd never been so cold in his life. Even the couple winters he'd spent in northern Scotland couldn't compare. Back home, he'd preferred to enjoy the colder months tucked safely in the comfort of his Lowland manor with a brandy in his hand or a warm woman in his bed.

Standing as close to the fire as he could get without crawling into it, he took a look around.

The cabin was comprised of a single room with a loft built in the rafters above and a ladder for access. The windows had been tightly shuttered, and the only light was created by the fire itself, but it was enough to see that the place was very sparsely furnished with only two overstuffed chairs set before the fire with a small table between. Cupboards lined the wall on either side of the door, and a little, black iron stove nestled in one corner. An enormous bear pelt was nailed to one wall, and the space beneath the loft held a couple trunks and some shelves that were overflowing with books.

The books surprised him, and he almost wandered over to see what sort of reading material he'd find in this rustic little mountain cabin. Before he could do so, the front door opened. The woman who'd likely saved him from being buried alive in the snow secured the door with a cross board and propped her rifle beside it before turning around and pushing her hood back.

Warm, dark eyes, thick black lashes, broad bone structure, and a lush, generous mouth.

Though his teeth still chattered and his hands and feet were beginning to ache as they thawed, George was amazed to discover that his blood was still capable of rushing quick and hot through his veins with the right inspiration.

And the woman wrapped in all those furs was stunning.

When she caught sight of him standing before the fire, her straight black brows furrowed over her coffee-colored gaze. "Why are you still dressed?"

The flames inside him leaped in reaction to her husky tone, not to mention the very suggestive words. But he quickly stomped them down. Though a man could surely hope, it was unlikely she'd meant the words in the way his suddenly unruly libido interpreted.

"Pardon," he said with lifted brows.

"Strip down," she ordered. "Once the snow on your clothes starts melting, you're not only going to be freezing cold, you're going to be *wet* and freezing cold. And I sure as hell am not going to nurse you though an illness."

She removed her coat and hung it on a hook next to the door. Underneath it, she wore a flannel button-down shirt tucked into buckskin breeches with a hunting knife strapped high on her thigh. Her thick, black hair was tied back at her nape and brushed the small of her back as she turned to face him.

Her expression furrowed as she noted that he hadn't moved to do as she said. Propping her hands on her hips, she repeated sharply, "Clothes off. Now."

Three

LUCY STARED THE MAN DOWN UNTIL HE FINALLY LIFTED his hands to release the buttons of his coat. Then she turned to lift the bucket she'd filled with snow just before heading out to drag the man from his shelter. Pouring some of the melted snow into an old dented teapot on her stove, she focused on getting her heart rate down and her thoughts back in order.

Involving herself in other people's problems was not something she did as a rule, and she wondered why she hadn't left him to fend for himself.

Because the storm would have turned his shelter into a scattered pile of branches within hours and the man likely would've been dead by morning.

Just because he'd stepped in on her behalf in town didn't make him her responsibility. She could have handled those two idiots just fine on her own. If there was one lesson her father had instilled in her, it was that she couldn't trust anyone, men least of all. At the tender age of eleven, she was assured in a gruff and serious tone that if anyone tried to take something from her she wasn't willing to give, she had her father's full permission to gut the bastard.

That fumbling pig in town hadn't been the first to mistakenly assume that just because she was alone, she was vulnerable and ripe for the picking. He was lucky the tall, handsome red-haired man had interfered when he did, or he might have lost more than his limited dignity.

Handsome? Is that why you brought him to the cabin?

Of course not, she mentally insisted as she mixed some

tea leaves with an assortment of dried herbs that were helpful in chasing a chill from the body.

Maybe you just like the way he talks.

There is that, she acknowledged. His accent was quite enjoyable to listen to, even when he'd been berating the man who'd accosted her.

Or maybe your loneliness has gotten the better of you.

Lucy frowned. Her father had always valued solitude over all else. Lucy, on the other hand, enjoyed a good conversation when she could find it, which was usually only in the spring when she traveled around to the various trading posts she and her father had always done business with. Though she accepted her more social nature, she still didn't like to admit that she might be in need of anything she couldn't provide for herself.

Leaving the water to boil, she turned back to see if the man was removing his wet clothing as she'd instructed. The sight of his progress had her freezing in place as a rush of awareness rolled through her from head to toe.

He'd managed to strip down much faster than she'd expected and currently stood facing the fire in nothing but his britches, which were damp and plastered to long, thickly muscled legs. His bare arms were roped with more muscle, as were his shoulders and back.

It had been hard to miss the fact that he stood at least six inches taller than her, but she hadn't thought he'd be so well formed.

As his hands went to the fly of his britches, he paused and looked back over his shoulder.

His gaze slammed into hers.

Russet-colored brows gathered for a brief moment at the sight of her watching him. Then a twinkle entered his gaze, and one corner of his mouth tilted upward into a crooked smile that sparked an odd weakness in her knees. "Shall I turn around and give you something worth ogling?" he asked. Humor thickened his voice.

She probably should have been embarrassed for having been caught staring, but it wasn't often—all right, it was *never*—that she had an opportunity to observe such a fine example of the male form. And she was far too fascinated by what she saw to feel anything but pleasure in the sight of him.

She lifted her brows. "You're pretty sure of yourself."

"I've never had a woman complain."

His arrogance was likely not misplaced. What she could already see of his body was strong and large and well defined. She imagined he was equally impressive everywhere.

She started across the room, walking toward him with her eyes locked on his.

As she neared, the half grin slid from his lips and he slowly turned to face her full on. Surprise and something else—something mysterious…and wicked—flickered in his eyes.

She wouldn't have been able to stop herself from looking at the wonderfully defined ridges of his muscled chest and abdomen even if she'd tried. When she noticed the lines angling across his hips to disappear beneath the waistband of his britches, her lower belly drew taut with a delicious ache.

Breathing deeply to clear the sudden haze she'd drifted into, she reached for the blanket that was draped over the back of her reading chair and tossed it to him.

He caught it against his chest with one hand.

"Wrap yourself in that until your clothes dry," she said before turning her back to him and returning to the stove. Steeping the herbs gave her a much-needed distraction. It probably wouldn't have been considered proper for her to blatantly observe him as he stripped the rest of the way down. No matter how badly she wanted to.

"Are you hungry?" she asked without turning around.

"If you're offering to share whatever is creating that

wonderful aroma, I would be thrilled to accept," he replied.

Though her body wound tighter and tighter as she sensed him coming near, she did her best not to show it. He stepped up beside her, his great height making it easy for him to lean over her shoulder and get a peek at what she was doing. "Are you brewing tea?" His rich, velvety voice deepened with a hopeful note.

Glancing at him, she was immediately distracted by a broad expanse of naked male torso.

She'd expected him to wrap the blanket around his shoulders, holding it together in front of him. But it appeared he'd opted for wrapping the blanket around his waist instead. To be fair, the man was so tall and large, there was a good chance the blanket wouldn't have covered much if he'd tried it the other way. Still, having to endure his company while he stood in all his half-naked glory—and it *was* glorious—was not going to be easy on her nerves.

Maybe she should have saved some of her father's clothes after he'd died. There hadn't seemed to be any reason to keep them at the time, but now that there was a nearly naked man in her cabin…some extra clothes would have come in handy.

She shifted her gaze back up to his, noticing just then that his eyes were a surprisingly dark shade of gray. Like the summer storm clouds that rolled powerfully over the mountains in August. Dark gray with nearly black outer rims and tiny silver flecks throughout. He had breathtaking eyes…

Eyes that were currently staring at her rather closely. "I haven't had a decent cup of tea in ages."

The anticipation of pleasure was evident in the velvety texture of his voice, which in turn gave rise to the delicate hairs on the nape of her neck and down her arms. As a direct response to the sudden assault on her senses, her next words came out sharper than she'd intended. "It'll be a while longer before you do. This tea includes herbs that will help fight onset of fever, but it won't exactly be pleasing to taste."

"Pity," he replied, his voice lowering with disappointment.

She stepped away from him to reach into an upper cupboard for two large tin bowls and a couple eating utensils. Earlier, while he'd been fumbling through his construction of a shelter, she'd brought up some onions, potatoes, and wild garlic from the cellar dug out beneath the cabin and had thrown it all together with fresh rabbit from one of her snares.

Turning back to hand him one of the bowls and a spoon, she nodded toward the stew pot hanging over the fire. "You can help yourself."

His lips spread in a charming smile as he took the bowl in one hand while extending his other. "Since we'll be sharing a meal, it seems only proper that I introduce myself. Most people around here like to call me Gentleman George."

She waited for him to continue, then realized he wasn't planning on offering her anything more.

She wiped her hands on the cloth beside her, then matched her palm to his. "Lucy."

His fingers wrapped firmly around hers as his smile widened. "Charmed," he replied, his voice low and lovely.

Doing her best not to be affected by the way his focused attention made her insides tingle, she replied, "I get the sense I'm the one who is supposed to be charmed."

His chuckle was swift and rich, rolling from his chest. "Only if you want to be."

A heavy gust of wind rattled the cabin despite the heavy wooden covers she'd latched tight to protect the glass, effectively chasing away her physical reaction to that rich-textured rumble.

Thank goodness she'd had the foresight to head to town today for a few extra supplies. The storm was shaping up to be one helluva blizzard.

"I should check on Thistle," the man beside her murmured.

"Thistle?" she asked.

"My horse."

"Your mare is fine," she replied, turning away from the warmth in his eyes. "Go on and eat."

Fortunately, he did as she said.

Once the herbal brew was sufficiently steeped, she poured it into her father's old mug and turned back toward the hearth to see that her guest had taken a seat in her father's reading chair. She and her father had never made use of the small table and chairs they used to have for dining, so they'd ended up throwing them on the fire one cold winter.

As she reached his side, the man who'd called himself Gentleman George rose to his feet. It was unexpected and resulted in much closer proximity than she'd intended as she handed him the tea.

"Thank you," he said smoothly with another one of his ready smiles.

She frowned in response and took her bowl to the stew pot, dishing up some supper before turning toward her own chair.

Except...he was still standing...in front of his chair, one hand cupping the bowl, the other wrapped around the hot mug. "What are you doing?" she asked.

"Waiting for you to be seated."

Lucy gave a quiet snort. "That's ridiculous. Sit down."

George smiled and gave a shallow bow. "After you."

She tensed, wondering if he was mocking her. "You don't have to bring out your pretty manners for me."

"Sometimes pretty manners are all a gentleman has left," he replied with a telling glance at the blanket around his waist.

Lucy's lips twitched, but she chose to let the matter drop as she took a seat.

For a good length of time they sat in awkward silence, side by side, watching the fire burn as they ate their stew.

Lucy wished she could say it was reminiscent of her meals with her father, but eating beside this man was anything but familiar. She'd never been so aware of another person in her life. She seemed to feel every shift of his body in her father's old chair, every turn of his head when he looked in her direction. Despite her hyperawareness, it jolted her a little when his voice broke the extended silence.

"I'm surprised we haven't previously encountered each other since we live so close," he said with a slight tilt of his burnished head.

"I make it a point to avoid outlaws," she replied without looking up from her bowl.

He chuckled. "That's probably a good policy."

Lucy gave him a curious glance. "You don't deny it?"

"Being an outlaw?" he asked. Then he shrugged, drawing Lucy's attention to his shoulders before she could regain control of her wayward gaze. "I'm not generally one to be bothered by other people's opinions of me."

"Being an outlaw isn't exactly a matter of opinion."

"Isn't it?" he asked. "The truth is, we're about far more than just robbing stagecoaches and kidnapping wealthy ladies."

"Kidnapping?" She had known the gang that had taken up residence in the nearby valley had committed various robberies of stagecoaches and train cargos over the years, but this was the first she'd heard of kidnapping.

He tilted one corner of his mouth. "More like rescued, actually."

"They're hardly the same thing," she argued.

He grinned broadly. The action caused a flutter in her belly. "In this case they were. I assure you, the lady is quite content with her new circumstances."

"If that's what you have to tell yourself..." she replied, allowing her voice to trail off.

"For a woman who'd prefer to avoid outlaws, you were rather quick to offer shelter to one. Why is that?"

Lucy refused to look at him. She couldn't exactly tell him it was because she liked the rolling cadence of his accent, or—God forbid—that she was lonely and thought having a handsome man sharing her fire might be a nice change. "Maybe I just didn't want to deal with a frozen corpse so close to my cabin," she suggested before spooning a mouthful of food past her lips.

"Hmm, I suppose that could be the reason," he said in a lowered tone. "Or perhaps you have a secret desire to lure a big, ginger half-Scotsman into your lair where you can order him to strip off his clothes and have your way with him."

She knew he'd said it just to get a reaction out of her. She hoped the uncertain firelight wouldn't reveal anything in her expression as she met his mischievous gaze with a narrowed look. "No."

His eyes crinkled, and his lips tipped in a half grin. "Just wanted to be sure."

The timbre of his words caused her belly to flop like a fish just pulled from the river. "You're awfully bold for a man who claims to be a gentleman," she observed.

He gave a shrug. "Gentlemen *outlaws* are allowed a slightly different set of rules."

"Well, I have only one rule," she replied. "Any man who dares touch me without an express invitation to do so becomes intimately acquainted with my knife. If you hadn't interfered in town, you'd have witnessed an example firsthand."

His russet brows arched in surprise. "I wasn't sure you'd recognized me."

"If I hadn't," she answered, "you'd still be freezing to death in your nest of twigs."

"Whoa, now just a moment," he exclaimed, sitting straight in his chair. "I was rather proud of that place. It was the very first house I ever built for myself."

Lucy couldn't stop the corner of her lips from twitching at his exaggerated indignation. "I suggest it be your last."

He pressed his hand over his heart as he dropped his head back against the chair. Firelight reflected off his masculine forehead, straight nose, and square jaw, casting his features in a strong, almost medieval light as his stormy gray eyes peered at her from beneath lowered eyelids. The tone of his voice dipped even lower, as though he were in pain. "You wound me, lass."

The heavy drama in his voice had Lucy chuckling despite herself.

Something in her laugh seemed to trigger a shift in the man beside her. The muscles in his large body tensed, and his eyes darkened despite the silver flame that sparked to life in their depths. Lucy's momentary burst of humor was swiftly replaced by a very different sensation.

It was not the first time she'd seen such a look in a man's eyes, but it was the first time it inspired something inside her beyond wary trepidation or flat annoyance.

Heat roared through her body, melting her insides and weakening her resistance. Her breath came short, and her belly twisted in a delicious fashion.

It was desire.

The only problem was…she had no idea what to do with it.

She rose swiftly to her feet. "Not yet," she finally replied, her voice curt as she turned back toward the kitchen, "but keep up your nonsense and I might."

Four

GEORGE CLEARED HIS THROAT, FORCING HIMSELF TO STARE at the fire rather than watch her walk away.

The sound of the woman's soft laugh had nearly done him in. He'd never heard anything so sultry and rich. It soaked into his body like warm honey into freshly baked bread. It was the kind of sound that put him in mind of kisses exchanged before a glowing hearth and sensual secrets shared beneath an oversize quilt. He hadn't been able to hide his thoughts when she'd looked at him.

He hadn't wanted to, to be honest.

But her reaction was exactly as it should have been—as he should have expected.

George was an accomplished flirt. It was something he'd been practicing since he was a boy in Berwickshire. He'd discovered early that females liked his boyish grin and irreverent charm. And he'd made the most of it, in a hedonistic search for endless pleasures as a young man, and more recently in service to the gang of outlaws of which he counted himself a member. His rakish manner was his specialty, and he'd learned to employ it well.

He wouldn't deny that he found Lucy very desirable indeed. She was a beautiful, capable, fascinating woman. Whether she'd admit it or not, by taking him in, she'd allowed herself to be in a vulnerable position.

He'd never do anything to dishonor that trust.

"I didn't keep Pa's bed after he died, but I can get you some furs to make a pallet on the floor in front of the fire," she said as she crossed from the kitchen behind him to the ladder that went up to the loft.

George knew he probably shouldn't find so much pleasure in watching her lithe, slim-muscled form climb the ladder. He was dedicated to being a gentleman, but he was still a *man*. To keep himself from indecently admiring her lovely, curved backside, he asked, "How long has your father been gone?"

"A few winters now."

There was just a hint of melancholy in her voice, but George picked up on it. "You miss him?" he asked as she disappeared into the shadows of the loft.

"Sometimes," she admitted from the darkness. "But more often, I forget that he isn't coming back. When he was alive, he was always out trekking the mountains on his own. I grew accustomed to his absences... It's the lack of an anticipated return that strikes the hardest at times."

She returned to the edge of the loft, leaning her head out over the edge. "Here. Catch."

George rose to his feet just in time to catch a heap of soft furs she tossed down.

"That should be enough to keep you warm," she said as she ambled back down the ladder.

George looked at her over the armful of various furs. "Where do you sleep?" She lifted a brow, and he clarified with a smile. "I mean, I wouldn't want to put you out by taking anything you might be in need of."

"I'll be fine. Go ahead and get settled. I'm just going to take care of a few things before I turn in."

George watched her cross the cabin to retrieve her heavy layered coat from where it hung by the door. "You're going outside?" he asked incredulously.

"Just for a few moments. Don't worry," she said with a glance from beneath her shadowed hood. "You'll be perfectly safe while I'm gone."

She paused to grab a couple wooden buckets, then reached for the door. As soon as she opened it, a billow of wind and swirling snow forced the door wide before she caught it again and drew it shut tight behind her.

George stood in indecision. The rules of gentlemanly behavior that had been instilled in him from a young age urged him to throw on his clothes and boots and go after her. It was full night outside, and the blizzard sounded even fiercer than it had earlier.

But he was pretty sure he'd only be a hindrance, so he did as she instructed and started laying out the furs in front of the fire. By the time he finished, his temporary bed looked more luxurious than anything he'd slept in since he'd left home as young man.

Perhaps even longer than that.

The manor had certainly never had furs on the beds. Or at least not for the last few centuries.

Checking his clothes, he found that although they had been warmed by the fire, they were still damp. He did not relish the idea of sleeping in wet clothes, so he left them where they were and wrapped the blanket more securely around his hips before he went about cleaning the dishes they'd used for dinner and stacking them neatly on the counter before laying down in his furs to await sweet Lucy's return.

His lips quirked in humor at the thought of how the woman would likely react to being called *sweet*. Her dynamic temperament suggested she wouldn't be flattered by the adjective. But George couldn't help imagining that her kiss would be rather sweet indeed.

Just keep any thoughts of kissing to yourself, you cad.

It was quite some time before he heard a muffled stomping on the small wooden porch. A moment later, a furious gust of wind swept through the cabin before Lucy could slam the door shut again.

George propped himself up on his elbows to see her

better and found himself entranced by the flush of cold on her cheeks and the icicles that were swiftly melting on her thick, black lashes.

"Whoo," she breathed audibly as she set down the two buckets filled with snow, then gave a fierce stomp of her feet before unfastening her coat and hanging it on a peg beside the door. "It's as bad as I've ever seen it out there," she said as she turned around.

Catching sight of him, her eyes went wide for a moment and her lips parted as though she'd been about to say something but lost all the words. After a poignant moment as her warm gaze swept over his lounging form, her breath started up again with an audible inhale.

Bloody hell, he sure hoped he wasn't imagining that smoldering heat in her gaze.

Not that he'd do anything about it, but it was nice to think his intense attraction wasn't totally one-sided.

"You look…comfortable," she said in a voice that seemed to tremble just a bit.

"I am." His own voice was rather unsteady. "Quite."

"Well, then." She took another heavy breath. "Sleep tight." Then she strode swiftly to the ladder leading up to the loft and ascended into the shadows without another glance in George's direction.

He lay back down with a sigh that seemed to travel through his entire body, forcing its way past the sexual tension that rode him high and hard after that odd yet stimulating interaction.

He doubted he'd get much sleep.

❧

Lucy crawled onto her bed and rolled over to lie flat on her back. Staring at the darkened ceiling that flickered with a golden glow from the fire below, she pressed both hands to her lower stomach. As if she could force the trembling away by her will alone.

It didn't work.

She remained flushed and warm. Her muscles felt weak and her nerves too sensitive.

Then she heard his low, melting sigh, and she nearly whimpered at the flush of heat that angled down between her legs. It was not right that she should be so physically affected by just the sight of the man.

Even though the sight of him is so wondrously masculine? And don't forget that burning, knowing look his eyes and the wicked-yet-boyish tilt of his lips…

As if she could.

With a grunt of annoyance at her wayward thoughts, she rolled onto her side, only then realizing she still had her boots on. And they were dripping all over her bedding. Muttering a curse, she sat up to tug the boots off and set them in a corner of the loft before lying back down again.

With the fire burning strongly in the hearth, her loft benefited from a constant waft of warmth. Typically, she undressed to just her flannel underwear for sleeping.

She had no intention of doing that tonight.

Not that she suspected the man below would do anything untoward—and even if he did, there was always her father's old knife tucked under her pillow and the one she always kept tucked in the lining of her boot. It just didn't seem like a very good idea for *both* of them to be half-naked.

She remained wide awake long into the night, listening until the blustering wind that swirled beyond the sturdy logs of her cabin eventually calmed to an occasional gust and the roaring fire slowly died to a quiet crackle. She considered getting up to add more wood to the fireplace to prevent the naked man on her floor from waking up with chattering teeth in the morning, but before she could drag herself to the ladder to do just that, she finally slipped into an uneasy sleep.

Five

THE SOUND OF SIZZLING MEAT TUGGED LUCY FROM HER slumber with a brief tingle of nostalgia. But as her brain fully awakened, she realized with a start that it couldn't possibly be her father cooking.

Blinking the sleep from her eyes, she crawled to the edge of the loft so she could look down into the cabin below.

Her guest was crouched in front of her fire, tending the coals. Lucy experienced a wave of disappointment at seeing that he was once again dressed in his shirt and britches. His sleeves were rolled up to his elbows, and he was humming to himself—something low and pleasant that put her in mind of dark, green places surrounded by misty mountains.

A quick glance around showed that he had hung his now-dry coat on a peg next to hers and had stacked his bed furs in a neat pile off to one side. Her coffeepot hung from a hook near the hearth, and her frying pan sat on her little stove, sizzling away.

He'd apparently found her cellar and the freshly cured ham she'd brought back from town yesterday, which explained the wonderful smell filling the sleepy cabin.

Doing her best to tame the anticipation in her belly that had nothing to do with the scent of the frying meat or the promise of steaming hot coffee, she made her way to the ladder, grabbing her boots along the way. She tried to be quiet, hoping to make it to common ground before he realized she was awake, but as soon as her feet touched the floorboards and she turned around, he was there.

She gave a little start at his unexpected proximity and blinked at the mug he held out to her. Anything she might have said got stuck in her throat as she caught sight of his crooked smile.

"Coffee?" he asked with a lift of his brows.

"Uh, thank you," she said as she tried to reach for the mug with her boots still in hand.

"Here. Allow me to take those while you take this," he said, taking her boots in one of his large hands while handing over the coffee. He crossed the cabin to set the boots beside the door. When he turned back, she still stood at the base of the ladder, feeling overwhelmed and out of place.

"What is it?" he asked, a note of concern in his voice.

Lucy tried to shake off her sleepy confusion. "I just didn't expect you to be so…ambitious in the morning."

He shrugged and glanced about the cabin. "I had a hard time sleeping and figured I may as well get up and make myself useful." He winked. "I wouldn't want you to regret dragging me in out of the cold last night."

"There's still time for that," she muttered, feeling thrown off-kilter by his amiability and how it made her feel all soft and warm inside.

"Och, you aim straight for my heart, lass," he said in an exaggerated burr.

She raised her brows. "Should I aim lower?"

He chuckled. "Your tongue is as sharp as your blade."

"And I'm not afraid to use either."

"I've no doubt of that," he said with an elegant bow. The courtly gesture was made slightly less effective by the fact that he stood in his stockings.

"Were your boots not dry this morning?" she asked.

He grimaced. "No. They are still a sogging mess."

She walked over to where they had been set on the

hearth. Picking one up, she noted that the leather had broken down in places from the wet and cold and ceaseless wear. "These are useless for winter."

"I believe I noticed that yesterday."

She lifted her head. "Have you taken a look outside?"

"Not yet," he replied.

The cold air stole her breath when she opened the door. Snow had drifted toward the cabin, covering her porch and rising above hip height beyond that. Everything was hidden beneath a thick blanket of white, and though the wind had calmed, snow continued to fall from the sky in thick, fluffy flakes.

"Bloody hell," George whispered behind her.

Too close behind her.

Sparks of awareness ran through her body at his proximity. With the cold in front of her and his warmth behind her, she felt locked in place, unsure where to go.

"That's a lot of snow," he muttered in amazement.

"We'll have to venture out to see how bad it really is."

"Well, that sounds like something that can wait until after breakfast. And another cup of hot coffee wouldn't hurt. Unless you have a spot of brandy to warm the blood?"

His hopeful tone had Lucy turning around. He was exactly as close as she'd thought he'd be. As she tipped her head back to meet his beautiful eyes, she forgot for a second what they were discussing.

Everything inside her grew still and quiet. Everything except her heart, which beat at a swift and furious pace. She could smell the warmth on his skin like woodsmoke and caramel molasses.

His eyelids grew heavy, and his gaze dropped to rest on her mouth as a ragged breath passed between his lips. Her own lips tingled in response. The odd sensation recalled her wits.

He had asked a question… About what?

Snow?

Boots?

Oh yes, brandy.

"No brandy, I'm afraid," she stated quickly.

His gaze was locked on her mouth, the muscles in his jaw bunching and releasing. His tone was gravelly and low as he acknowledged her response with a sound that didn't quite manage to be a word.

It looked as though he wanted to touch her—kiss her maybe.

And for a moment, she wasn't sure she would stop him if he did.

Then the space between his brows furrowed, and he lowered his gaze to the floor as he stepped back. The sudden loss of his nearness and warmth drew Lucy from the odd little trance, but it did not dispel the hum of anticipation in her blood.

"No matter," he said as he flashed her a quick smile. "We'd better eat while it's still warm."

Lucy released a slow and heavy sigh as he walked back to the fire.

Breakfast was delicious. In addition to the ham, he'd also fried some potatoes that he kept warm by the fire. This time, as they sat side by side in the chairs, it wasn't quite as awkward as it had been the night before. And though she would have liked to take her time to enjoy it, they needed to assess the snowfall and check on the horses.

The blast of cold as they stepped outside seized her breath for a second. Two snow shovels were propped beside the door. She took one and handed the larger one her father had always used to George. Stepping past her porch, she started shoveling a path through the snow. George followed suit beside her.

It took a while to get past the worst of the drift, but once they did, they paused to look around. The average height of snow was easily past their knees. It was heavy

and thick and continued to fall from the pale-gray sky,
weighing down tree branches and covering the trails that
led to her snares. It was going to take days to dig out all
her traps and reset them.

But that wasn't the most worrisome thought.

She looked to the man standing beside her. His gaze,
several shades darker than the sky above, scanned the
white-covered land around them before coming to rest
on her face.

With the amount of snow they'd gotten through
the night—not to mention what continued to fall—the
narrow pass into his valley was not going to be available,
even if a fallen tree hadn't blocked the path. Lucy knew
there was another way into the valley, but it was nearly
a full day's ride, and there was nothing to guarantee that
way would be open either. The truth was, trying to go
anywhere under the current conditions would be foolish.

The smile he gave her might have been apologetic, if
the sparkle in his eyes hadn't killed the attempt. "Looks
like you're stuck with me for a spell."

"Lucky me," she replied in a tone of dread despite the
fact that dread wasn't at all what she was feeling.

Elation tempered by a good dose of uncertainty was
much closer to the truth. There was also a hint of wary
excitement for having the opportunity to more carefully
explore the way he made her feel jittery and melty at the
same time.

∞

Over the next few hours, they cleared a good path from
the cabin door and continued around to check on the
horses.

At first, all George saw was the rocky face of the
mountain as it rose up beyond the cabin. But as they
neared, he noticed a wooden barn door set into the rock.

He glanced at the woman trudging through the snow

beside him, but he couldn't see beyond her furred hood
to her face.

They had to shovel more snow away to make way for
the barn door to swing open, but once they did, Lucy
tugged it wide enough for them to pass through. George
grabbed the door to keep it from being forced shut again
by the wind that had picked up over the last couple hours
and gestured for her to precede him.

She looked up at him with a questioning glance.

George just smiled and gave a small bow of his head.
"Ladies first."

She snorted softly. "Haven't you figured out yet that
I don't fit that category?"

He tried to hold back, he really did, but George just
couldn't stop himself from sweeping an appreciative
gaze over the bold feminine lines and curves of her face.
Focusing on her lips for longer than he should—long
enough to cause a stirring sensation below the belt—he
met her gaze again. It was a good thing she was covered
head to toe in furs, or his hungry gaze would have
continued over every enticing dip, curve, and valley he
could find. "Seems to me you fit quite well."

Rueful annoyance flashed in her eyes. "Being female
doesn't equate to being a lady."

"It does in my book," he replied gently.

Something fleeting and curious flickered across her
face before she glanced to the side. "Fine, then. It's
certainly not worth standing in the snow to argue about."

She slipped into the barn, and George followed behind
her, an odd tightness invading his chest. No woman
should believe herself undeserving of basic courtesies, no
matter how she chose to live.

The barn door closed behind them, shutting out a
great deal of the daylight. But as his eyes accustomed to
the darkness, he realized there was still a steady source of
light coming from above where holes and niches in the

mountain allowed streams of light and fresh air to filter into the cave without allowing much of the weather to follow.

The cave itself was not exceptionally large, but it was certainly big enough for the four stalls that were built into the space. The hardy workhorse he'd seen pulling her wagon in town stood in the first stall, with Thistle tucked into the one beside him. The water troughs were full and unfrozen, and buckets of half-eaten grain stood in each stall. Glancing into the two empty stalls, he saw a pile of hay, the wagon from town, and some additional tack and supplies.

"This is quite a place," George said.

He turned back to watch as Lucy offered her draft horse a few friendly strokes along his muscled neck. She gazed into the animal's eyes with true affection. "We didn't have any animals for the earliest years of my memory. Pa would pull his furs to the trading posts on a sleigh he'd fashioned to drag easily over rock or grass or snow. But when Mother left and he had to start bringing me along, he traded for old Rupert, here, and later built this for him. I think he expected to eventually get another horse, but we never did."

"Impressive," George replied, watching her as intently as her horse did, and likely with nearly as much admiration. "Why did your mother leave?"

She slid a narrow glance at him from the corner of her eyes. "Most folks try *not* to pry into other people's personal business."

George shrugged. "When I discover something interesting, I like to know more about it."

She scoffed. "I'm not that interesting."

"I disagree. Your past makes up part of who you are. And you are just about the most interesting person I've ever had the pleasure to meet."

She turned her attention back to her horse, but not

before George noticed the blush of color warming her cheeks and the wary shadow in her eyes. "Pa met my mother one spring when he was trading with her tribe. He says he fell in love with her on sight. I don't know if the feeling was mutual, but she agreed to marry him when he asked. They lived together up here for a few years. They might have been happy, or maybe not. On a return trip to her people when I was barely more than a babe, she decided she wanted to stay. Pa wouldn't leave me behind, and she wasn't against letting me go, so..."

"Did you ever see her again?" George asked, though he already suspected the answer by the raw note she struggled to keep from her voice.

"Pa never went back."

"But you did," George said, hearing what she didn't say.

She gave her horse a final pat before turning to George. "After Pa died, I went to find her. She'd died several years before, but I met a few members of her family."

George instinctively stepped toward her, his only desire in that moment to assuage the hard edge of loss in her voice. "I'm sorry, lass."

Her brown eyes reflected her sadness, though she forced a smile to her lips. "Don't be. It's more family than I ever had before."

"Do you visit them?"

"I've been back a couple times." Before George could reply, she took a deep breath and a swift glance around. "Are you satisfied with your mare's well-being? Shall we head back to the cabin before your feet freeze in those boots?"

"Too late," George said, accepting her need to change the direction of the conversation. "My toes were sufficiently numbed an hour ago."

She shook her head. "I can't believe you've lived in

the mountains as long as you have and you don't have better boots."

"Well, considering I typically stay where it's warm and cozy, preferably with a hot cup of tea or a brandy rather than venturing outside in blizzards, I've never really worried about it."

She turned to lead the way back out into the cold. "I get the sense there are a lot of things you don't worry about."

He flashed a smile. "I bloody hell try not to."

Six

GEORGE WAS WORRIED.

If the snow continued to fall and the trails remained impassable, there was no telling how long he would be holed up in the cozy little cabin with the extremely fascinating and highly desirable Lucy. Considering how intense his attraction was to the woman and how swiftly it was growing, he reckoned it was going to be a torturous duration.

Her competence as a woman living on her own in an extremely challenging and unforgiving environment was astonishing. If he were any less of a man, her proficiency in so many tasks would likely make him feel…well, less of a man. But he simply found himself in awe of her skills.

Her slightly jaded, yet totally sheltered view of the world made him want to offer his services as protector and partner in exploring all the things she might have been kept from while living such an isolated life.

Her occasional sarcasm made his skin tingle. Her laugh made him ache. And the way she slipped him subtle looks of curiosity and unexpected yearning drove him nearly mad.

He was damned worried all right—worried he wouldn't make it through another night.

Especially after they spent nearly an hour dancing around each other in the kitchen as they worked together in readying the evening meal. Her warmth and female scent cornered him at every turn.

And then there was the intense little moment when they both turned in unison with the intention of going in opposite directions—only to slam into each other. Their bodies met with full force from chest to knee. When he instinctively brought his hands to her hips to keep them from losing their balance, she released a weighted exhale that slid into a soft moan. Even the very brief contact was enough to give George a clear impression of her full breasts, taut belly, rounded hips, and firm thighs.

The memory of how she felt pressed against him would likely haunt his lonely nights for weeks. As would the flickering heat in her eyes when she'd looked up at him.

By the time they had finished their meal and were settled in the cozy chairs they'd occupied the night before, George was fighting to keep the tension from his muscles.

"Do you wanna go to bed?"

Lust flared hot and bright in his blood as his gaze flew to hers.

What did she just ask him?

Seeing his confusion, she nodded toward the floor where he'd made his bed the night before. "Were you planning to go to bed right away? I don't usually retire so early, but I wouldn't want to keep you awake."

Oh. Of course. "Not at all," George replied with a vigorous nod. "I'm a bit of a night owl myself."

"Great," she replied.

George forced his blood to cool as he watched her cross the cabin to kneel in front of a large wooden trunk tucked in the shadows beneath the loft. Opening the trunk, she sat back on her heels to sort through various scraps of furs and tanned hides and large patches of oiled leather, carefully selecting the right pieces for whatever project she intended to work on. His position in the chair allowed him a perfect view of her gorgeously curved backside, narrow waist, and strong shoulders.

He could practically feel the softness of her buckskin breeches beneath his palms as he imagined sliding his hands up her firm thighs to the lush curve of her bottom.

Dammit, George. Think of something else.

He quickly shifted his gaze and tried to focus on the next nearest thing, which happened to be the shelves of books lining the low wall beside her. Perfect.

Rising to his feet, he asked, "Do you mind if I look for something to read?"

She paused to look back at him as he approached the shadowed corner. "I, ah…" She glanced from him to the books, then back to him again. "You can look, but I doubt you'll find anything."

He'd take his chances. It was the only distraction he could come up with at the moment. "I'm a gentleman of varied tastes and experiences. I imagine I'll find something…" he replied as he crouched down beside her to scan the titles on the worn spines of the books.

He noted a copy of *Moby-Dick*, Thackeray's *Vanity Fair*, a couple titles by Dickens, a well-worn copy of *Jane Eyre*, *Uncle Tom's Cabin*, *Nature* by Emerson, and nearly a dozen others. In addition to the novels, there were at least three plays by Shakespeare and a large tome of British history.

"How did you acquire all these?" he asked.

"Pa was a man of letters before he came west and took to trapping. He made sure I had a proper education, mainly supported by whatever books he came across at the trading posts. Every year, I'd have a new stack to read. Most of them were eventually traded back for something else." She gestured to the books in front of them. "These are the ones I couldn't bear to part with."

George skimmed the titles once again, and a smile curved his lips. The selection revealed a bit more about the intriguing woman beside him.

"I said you wouldn't find anything," she noted as she pushed to her feet.

"On the contrary," he replied, "there are a number of books I'd enjoy." He leaned forward and withdrew a copy of Sir Walter Scott's *Rob Roy*, then stood to full height. "Now, this is a worthy tale."

He didn't realize she had paused before walking away, and it surprised him—in a wonderful, wickedly inappropriate way—to find himself suddenly standing quite close to her. Close enough to hear her swift inhale and see the jump of her pulse in her throat. Close enough to see the black centers of her eyes dilate as she looked up from the book in his hand to meet his gaze.

"That one? Really?" she asked in surprise.

"Why not?" he asked. "It's got adventure, history, romance, *outlaws*," he added with a wink.

She smiled, and George was pretty sure his heart stopped for a moment. "It's the romance part I wasn't expecting."

He lifted his brows. "And why not?"

Her features shifted into a jaded expression. "I suppose I should have considered that with your…reputation, you would make it a point to be well versed in *romance*."

Her tone and the stress she put on the last word suggested an attempt at flippancy, but he didn't quite believe it. "It's true. I have some experience, lass." His voice lowered as he dipped his head closer to hers. "But it might not be in the way you're imagining."

"I'm not imagining anything," she denied rather quickly.

"You can if you want to," he said, a smile lifting his mouth. "I don't mind."

Her eyes darkened, and her lips parted as though she was doing exactly as he suggested. In that moment, he would have given up all worldly possessions to know what went through her mind. Then she furrowed her brow. "Don't tell me you're gonna try to say you've never lain with a woman."

He chuckled at the thought. "Of course not. But being in love and making love are two separate things," he explained. "One I've done plenty. The other's been as elusive as the farthest star."

A moment of silence fell between them. Then she murmured, "It's hard to believe an outlaw has much time for stargazing."

"You'd be surprised," George replied, surprising *himself* at the admission.

Her expression suggested she wasn't quite prepared to take his words as truth. She was wary of him, and he could understand why. He was a charmer, a ladies' man, a self-indulgent scoundrel. But he'd been completely honest in suggesting he'd prefer something more real and lasting than the quick tumbles of his past.

He just wished she'd believe him.

He looked down at the book in his hand, then turned to place it back on the shelf. "You know," he said thoughtfully, "with Christmas only days away, I find myself in the mood for something a wee bit more festive. Do you have anything befitting the holiday season?"

There was a lengthy pause following his request before she stepped up beside him. Shifting some books aside, she reached into a shadowed corner and withdrew a slim volume.

"I haven't thought of this book in years," she noted softly as she smoothed her hand over the worn cover. "It enchanted me as a child. A mysterious stranger, a guardian angel in the form of a cricket, a selfish old miser transformed by the spirit of Christmas… I loved it, but my father would never have let me keep it if he knew what it was about." Looking up, she gave George a rueful smile. "Pa didn't believe in traditions or holidays or anything like that. And for some reason, he especially hated Christmas."

George was stunned. "How can anyone hate Christmas?"

She shrugged. "I don't know. I just grew up knowing

it was not something to discuss or celebrate. I used to imagine what it might be like to celebrate the holiday as it is portrayed in the story: family and friends, food and warmth and laughter. I guess I'd forgotten about it in the last years," she added in a voice that faded away.

"So, you've never celebrated Christmas?"

She shook her head.

George held out his hand. After a very brief pause, she handed the book to him. Turning it over in his hands, he read the title out loud. "*The Cricket on the Hearth: A Fairy Tale of Home*, by Charles Dickens. I don't think I've read this one."

Glancing upward, he met her dark gaze and something warm and urgent flowed through him. For some reason, it felt imperative that he share this story with her as she had been unable to share it with her father. "Do you mind if I read it aloud?" he asked.

There was a flash of something unreadable in her eyes before she glanced away and took an abrupt step back. "If you wish. I doubt it will bother me."

George hadn't realized the amount of heat that had surrounded them until a waft of cool air rushed in to fill the sudden space she left behind.

As she took a seat and arranged the various scraps of fur and sewing materials across her lap and the arms of her chair, George claimed his spot in the chair beside her. Then he opened the book and began to read. It was not long before he became lost in the words he spoke aloud over the quiet crackle of the fireplace. He didn't even notice when her hands stilled, ceasing their work, and her head fell back against the tall back of her chair. When he first realized that her eyes had closed, he wondered if she'd fallen asleep, but then her lips curled into a smile as he read over an amusing passage. It was not a very long story, but by the time he reached the uplifting conclusion, George knew what he wanted to do.

Seven

LUCY WOKE WITH A START THE NEXT MORNING AS A GUST of cold air swept through the cabin. Bolting to the edge of the loft, she looked down to see George coming in from outside with his arms overflowing with tree branches.

"What on earth are you doing?" she asked in sleepy shock.

He glanced upward with a wide grin as he kicked the door shut behind him. "Decorating."

He'd lost his mind.

She scrambled down the ladder, reaching him just as he set the pine boughs on the floor where he'd made his bed the last two nights.

"Decorating?" she asked with her hands planted firmly on her hips. "With those?"

His eyes were bright and twinkling, and he gave a hearty nod. "Aye, with these."

She reached up to press her palm to his forehead. "Are you feeling all right?"

His laugh was warm and rich as he grasped her wrist and brought her hand down to hold it gently in his. "There's nothing like the smell of fresh pine over a crackling hearth to put one in the spirit for Christmas. Trust me," he added in an earnest tone before giving her a jaunty wink.

He wanted to decorate her cabin for the holiday.

Lucy was speechless as he moved about, locating a hammer and some nails. Then he carefully sorted through the fresh-cut boughs and formed them into a sort of garland that he tacked to the logs above the fireplace.

It was amazing how the minimal effort managed to transform the space. And he was right; the smell of warming pine filled the cabin and inspired Lucy to add her own touch to the festive arrangement. It took a bit to find what she was looking for, but when she approached George with the scraps of old cloth, his wide smile made her feel self-conscious and a little giddy.

Together, they tied the pieces of cloth to the branches, and when they were finished and stepped back to get a look at the full effect, Lucy was amazed as how beautifully it had come together.

"What d'ya think?" he asked.

Lucy smiled. "I think it's wonderful."

"Aye. 'Tis, indeed."

"Thank you," she added quietly.

His voice was low and warm as he replied, "You're very welcome."

∞

The snow continued to fall over the next few days. Sometimes it came down in sweeping gusts of wind, and other times it was in quiet, thick flakes. Either way, the trails remained impassable.

A few times a day, Lucy would head out to assess the status of the blizzard, fetch fresh water, and check on the horses.

And George would accompany her.

There was no reason for him to do so. On more than one occasion, it had been on the tip of her tongue to tell him to stay in the cabin, but she appreciated his company. And he seemed to enjoy getting out as much as she did. With the shutters still tight over the windows to keep out the frigid drafts, the cabin existed in a perpetual state of night.

They'd fallen into an oddly cozy routine. George was often the first to rise, and he set right about getting coffee on and breakfast started. Each evening, they'd settle in front of the fire. Lucy would work on her furs while George read out loud from *Rob Roy*. She had read the story at least a half dozen times, but just as when he'd read *The Cricket on the Hearth*, it had never been so richly woven and densely satisfying as it was when spoken in George's rolling Scottish burr.

On the morning of the fourth day of being snowed in, they went outside to find a clear sky. And not only that, but the air had lost its chilly edge and the trees dripped with melting ice and snow. Neither of them commented on the shift in the weather that day or the next as the warmer temperatures continued, but it seemed to inspire a strange sort of tension between them.

She wasn't sure what George was thinking, but to Lucy, it felt like something lovely was coming to its inevitable end.

She'd spent her entire life in that cabin and the last couple years of it alone. Though she loved a great many aspects of her life, she had never been able to fully accept the sense of isolation that came with it. It had been easier to ignore when her father had been alive. But in the time since his death, she'd started to feel…trapped in the way of life she'd always known.

The changing weather would soon allow George to be on his way again while she remained.

Unless she left, too…

But where would she go? And what would she do?

The only life she knew was to live off what the mountain provided. And she enjoyed it. She just wished it wasn't such a solitary existence.

After George finished reading that night and closed the book on another chapter, Lucy found herself asking something she'd been curious about for a while. "It's

clear by the way you read that story how much you love
your homeland. Why did you leave?"

He'd stood up to tend the fire as she started speaking
and didn't turn around right away.

Lucy studied the sturdy width of his shoulders and
the long line of his muscled back. His tousled hair was
a deep shade of burnished auburn in the flickering light,
and his forearms tensed beneath his rolled-up sleeves as
he shifted the logs to make room for a couple more to
keep the cabin cozy through the night, though not nearly
as much wood had been needed lately.

She waited patiently for him to answer, knowing he
would despite how prying the question might have been.
She'd come to expect his openness.

At first it had thrown her off balance—his willingness
to offer up his thoughts on just about anything. It was
the exact opposite of her father, who had been able to
go days without really speaking. But she found that she
rather enjoyed speaking with someone who answered in
more than monosyllables.

The fact that George paused so long before answering
told her the topic was more intimate than she'd realized.
She almost wished she could take the question back even
as the yearning to know grew stronger.

He rolled his shoulders and cast his gaze up to the
rafters before he shrugged. "I was young and stupid. I
had to leave, or I would've ruined my entire family."

Lucy set aside the furs she was working on and asked
pointedly, "What did you do?"

"You want the sordid details, lass?" he asked with a
jaded, teasing look tossed over his shoulder.

She didn't give in to his flippancy and nodded.

With a sigh that chased away his half-hearted attempt
at humor, he turned to face her. "I was a young man
with more wealth and freedom than I knew what to
do with. As a younger son, I was quite happy to forget

that along with my privilege came a responsibility to my family and my station. One night—or very early morning, rather—my mate and I were racing our horses through the narrow streets of Edinburgh. We were foxed out of our minds and could barely keep our seats in the saddles, but we thought it was glorious fun to dodge the street vendors that were starting to set up for the day to come." His brow darkened and heavy lines of regret scarred his handsome features. "I misjudged the space needed to get around an apple cart and sent it toppling to the cobblestones. Right in front of my mate."

George met her gaze with a haunted look in his eyes. "His horse took a tumble. He fell from the saddle and broke his neck, dying instantly."

Lucy took a breath before speaking in an even tone. "It was a terrible accident. No one was at fault."

He laughed, but it was a painful sound. "Not so, lass. When the heir to a dukedom dies, someone is most definitely at fault. The scandal cast a long and heavy shadow. With my brother and sister's futures and a grand estate to think about, my father had no choice but to ask me to leave, hoping that in my absence, the scandal would die a quick death."

"Did it?" Lucy asked.

He lifted his brows. "I've no idea. I haven't been back."

"You received no letters over the years?"

He shoved his hand back through his burnished locks. "I never told them where I was going."

"That sounds rather cowardly."

He smiled. "I should have known I could count on you to be blunt and honest with my faults."

"We all have faults, George. I don't see how a letter to your family, letting them know you still live, could cause any harm to anything but your own pride. We all make mistakes."

"I bet you don't," he teased, and Lucy was grateful to see a bit of his usual humor return.

She narrowed her gaze in mock severity. "I can't say I've ever done anything so drastic as join a gang of outlaws, but I've certainly experienced moments of poor judgment."

"Like when you dragged one of those outlaws out of a blizzard?"

"No," she replied in earnest. "Not that."

His eyes warmed, making Lucy's belly tighten. She tried to ignore how the subtle evidence of his pleasure made her feel all soft and tingly, but she couldn't quite manage it. Clearing her throat, she asked, "So how did you end up joining the men in the valley?"

"It was mostly luck that brought me to Luke and the gang, but once it did, I knew it was a good fit. We watch out for each other. In a way, it's like a family. After wandering for years, the gang gives my life purpose."

"Stealing is your purpose?" she asked skeptically.

He smiled. "It's a little more complicated than that. We're not just a bunch of criminals stealing for greed or the selfish pleasure of it. You may not believe it, but we often manage to help people who have no option but to trust in strangers." He lowered his voice. "In a lawless land, sometimes the outlaw becomes the hero."

Lucy lifted her brows. "Don't tell me you're likening yourself to Rob Roy now."

"Och, of course not, lass," he exclaimed in mock horror. "I'm far more handsome than that goat."

Lucy laughed. She couldn't help it. And as her laughter filled the room, his expression shifted.

Intensified.

Smoldered.

Heat rolled through Lucy as she met his stormy gaze where hunger burned like a bonfire in the dark. She wasn't just going to let it pass this time. "Why are you looking at me like that?"

He lowered his chin and gave a rueful smile. "Sorry, lass. It's the sound of your laughter. It gets me in here." He rubbed a hand across his chest.

The heat inside her gathered to create a gentle pulsing pressure in the apex of her thighs. "What do you mean?" she asked in a rough murmur.

He looked at her for a few moments. The wanting in his eyes made the ache more poignant.

Then he shook his head and replied. "Forgive me. I should have kept that to myself."

He wanted her. She could see it—feel it—as a force that was equal and opposite to her own desire. Like the resistance of two magnets. If they just repositioned themselves…it'd be an inevitable joining.

She was tempted to tell him that she welcomed the pull between them. But she couldn't bring herself to do it.

What if all she'd be to him was another passing fancy? A woman to warm his bed and chase away his boredom until he could return to the rest of his life?

What if that could be enough?

She wanted him. She admired him and trusted him. Would it be so bad to indulge in a love affair with such a man, even if it was fleeting?

When he finally glanced away, the ache of their inevitable parting invaded her marrow. She'd never considered herself a coward, but then, she'd never expected to yearn for a man as she did for George. If she accepted her desire for him and followed the urging inside her, would she be able to keep her heart from being damaged in the process?

It was some time later, as they each lay in their respective furs—his on the floor before the fire, hers up in the dark loft—that she wondered more at her reluctance.

Perhaps it was because she had gone all her life in opposition to such things. When her father had been alive, their existence had been about avoiding personal connections at all costs. She'd never really understood his reasons, but it was the only life she'd known.

Since she'd been on her own, her perceived vulnerability had brought out the worst in some men who thought she was available for claiming whether she wanted it or not. Fighting such things had been second nature for so long.

And now, she had a man living alongside her, sleeping in front of her fire, joining her in the daily tasks of life, reading to her from one of her own books each night.

And she found herself craving more. Something deeper, more intense. She wanted to give in to the magnetic pull she felt every day. Wasn't it better to experience such a gift—even if it was only for a short time—than to never embrace it at all because of fear?

Lucy believed it was, and she didn't want to waste the time she had left with him. But she was awkward and inexperienced with such things. She had no idea how to initiate a more intimate arrangement.

He did. But he resisted.

Oh, why does he have to be such a gentleman?

She didn't realize she'd groaned out loud at the thought until George spoke up from below. "What is it?"

"Nothing. I'm sorry," she muttered quickly.

"Do you plan on settling in anytime soon?" he asked. "It sounds like a grizzly bear rolling around up there."

She snorted. "Have you ever heard a grizzly?"

"Of course not. Have you?" George asked, a note of shock in his voice.

Lucy was almost pleased to retort, "Many times, and I assure you I sound nothing like one."

"What's got you so restless, then?"

"I'm too hot," she finally admitted.

∞

George ground his teeth against the burst of heat her words sent raging through his blood.

Surely, she hadn't meant for them to come out sounding so sultry and sensual. It had to be his wayward imagination creating what he *wanted* to hear rather than what was true.

Each day and night he'd been in her company had added fuel to a fire that had been growing inside him. It now appeared to have reached a point that it was affecting his hearing.

George sat up. "Should I take a log or two off the fire?" The last couple nights had been warmer. He'd actually been thinking the cabin was getting too warm himself and had already removed his shirt for greater comfort. He hadn't wanted to touch the fire, thinking she might be chilled.

There was a long pause before she answered in a tone that was another half groan, half sigh. "It won't help."

George nearly groaned himself. To keep from thinking of her thrashing about in her bed, sweat glistening on her skin, he rolled to his back and threw an arm over his eyes, then counted to five. But still, his words came out sounding tight and unnatural. "What can I do?"

There was no answer. Just more shifting movement that had him imagining her removing layer after layer of clothing until her body slid against the furs…

He couldn't hold back the groan any longer. It was a low, tortured sound that came from deep inside where his body craved and hungered and yearned.

"George?"

He tensed from head to toe because the sound of his name, softly spoken, was way too close. He was almost afraid to lift his arm away from his eyes, but his desire was far stronger than any fear.

She stood beside him, dressed in nothing but red cotton long johns that outlined every curve and hollow of her toned female form. Her thick, black hair rested over her shoulder in a long, loose braid. Her features—lit by the flickering orange glow of fire—were drawn into an expression of hopeful determination while her eyes burned with fierce longing.

George held his breath. The muscles across his chest and abdomen tightened as he fought to keep his attraction from revealing itself in a very obvious aspect of his anatomy.

But then her gaze swept over the exposed surface of his torso, and her lips softly parted.

He exhaled in a rush, then sucked in another swift breath.

And when she lifted her hand to start releasing the buttons of her long johns, he could do nothing but stare in rapt wonder and stunned anticipation.

She was gorgeous. A goddess. A queen. A living dream in the flesh. And he was a mortal man resisting a sensual hunger unlike anything he'd ever experienced before.

He should stop her.

He should figure out how to breathe first. Then he should stop her.

She slipped the buttons free one after another until a swath of skin was exposed spanning her collarbone. Continuing down the row of buttons, she revealed her sternum and the inner curves of her breasts, providing just a narrow glimpse of her toned stomach and shadowed navel.

George's breath expelled in a ragged, groaning sigh. He made a gallant effort. "Lucy," he said in a tone that he meant to sound like a warning, but came out more like a plea.

She drew the red cotton off her shoulders, exposing her upper body—her full breasts and slim waist. Then she pushed the cotton down past the lovely swell of her hips. When she bent forward to tug the garment off her feet, her braid swung toward George, and he was oh-so-tempted to grasp it and wind it about his hand until she was forced down atop him.

He didn't and was infinitely grateful for his restraint when she straightened again, fully naked, totally proud, and stunningly beautiful. Her skin glowed a warm bronze in the firelight as she bowed just her chin to look down at where he lay stiff and prone on the floor at her feet.

After a bit, he realized she was waiting.

For him.

She had so bravely offered herself, and now she waited for his response.

He blamed his desire-softened brain for not recognizing the gentle dip of inquiry in her brow.

She didn't know if he would accept.

How could he possibly refuse? She was everything he'd ever dreamed of. Even if all they could have was this night, he'd be a fool to turn away such a gift.

And George was no fool.

His stomach tightened as he lifted his hand to her.

She slid her fingers in his almost immediately and lowered to her knees beside him as he flipped back the edge of his furs to invite her beneath them.

Stretching out on her side, she curled one arm beneath her head and rested the other on his chest. As her smooth, soft skin came in contact with his, he gave a roughened moan of pleasure. He covered them both with the fur, enclosing them in warmth. Then he turned to his side and propped his head in his hand so he could meet her tempting gaze.

Unable to keep from touching her, he brushed the backs of his fingers over the curve of her jaw, then down the slim line of her throat. "Why?" he asked.

He allowed his fingers to drift along the crest of her collarbone to her shoulder, and her lashes fluttered in response. "Because we both want this," she answered in a husky voice, "and I knew you wouldn't."

"Are you certain?" He turned his hand to cover the plump curve of her breast with his broad palm before brushing his thumb over the peak. So soft. So perfectly full.

She gasped and held her breath. Her body shifted beside him—arching, seeking greater contact.

His stomach tightened. His cock hardened and throbbed with need. He was grateful he still wore his britches, or she'd discover quickly just how bad he wanted this.

She met his gaze. Her gorgeous dark eyes were soft and dreamy. The light of desire in their depths was undeniable. "Do I appear uncertain?"

George could only shake his head as he leaned forward, aching for a taste of her.

Finally.

The press of his mouth on hers was an initiation, an awakening. A swift and sudden ignition of the sparks between them.

Her lips felt like the finest satin, and she tasted like paradise. Sweet, sultry, rich.

He'd never experienced anything so perfectly decadent. He wanted more.

Sliding his hand from her breast to brace against her midback, he pulled her toward him. More warmth, smooth silkiness, softness and curves pressed to his chest and belly.

She sighed, and he groaned low in his throat. It was wonderful, but he still wanted more.

He rolled toward her, over her, laying her back on the furs as he rose above. He shifted his legs to settle between hers, pressing his hips between her thighs.

It was a *helluva* good thing he still had his britches on. She slid her hands up and down the broad surface of his back. Her touch was insistent and needful as she lifted her mouth to his, claiming more of his kiss. Giving more of her own.

When her hands lowered and she gripped his buttocks to pull him more firmly to her core, he gave a guttural sound and thrust his tongue past her gasping lips. She met it immediately with her own. The velvety glide stoked the flames in them both.

She arched beneath him, pressing herself to his body, angling her head for a deeper kiss while she bent her legs to hook over his hips. A demanding hum sounded in her throat.

George adjusted to prop himself on his elbows so he could gently frame her face in between his hands. Lifting his head, he murmured roughly, "Slow down, lass. There's no need to rush."

"Are you sure?" she asked with a shuddering breath. "Because I feel like I need to rush."

George chuckled, and her lashes swept open. The hunger in her eyes hit him hard in the gut, sending a stab of aching need to his groin.

He took her lips again in a hot, wet, openmouthed kiss that had her rolling her hips beneath him. Breaking from the kiss, he gave a ragged sigh. "Ah…I think I'm sure." He sought her mouth again, unable to resist the lush sweetness there. "Maybe," he murmured before indulging in a languorous sweep of his tongue. "No… Yes. Yes, we should slow down," he insisted, lifting his head.

She chuckled softly as she slid her hands down his sides to rest on the waistband of his britches.

"We've got all night." He flashed a grin. "Let's make it last a while."

She gave a nod and tipped her lips back up to meet his, but this time it was a soft, sweet kiss.

He was astounded by how perfect a single, ordinary

kiss could be. The simplicity. The heat and comfort. The veil of serenity over fiercely banked fire. His heart thundered in his chest, and pangs of deep sexual hunger speared through his blood.

He wanted the moment to last forever.

He wanted a thousand—a million—more moments just like this one.

With this woman.

He loved the way she challenged him.

She filled the spaces inside him he hadn't even realized were empty. The spaces that longed for peace and warmth and companionship. When he looked into her eyes and saw her smile, he could see a future filled with things he'd left behind long ago. He hadn't dreamed of such things in ages. But in the last several days it had become astoundingly easy.

And although the kiss—or the silky feel of her body beneath his—didn't promise forever, he couldn't help but believe this was only the beginning.

Eight

LUCY HAD NEVER FELT ANYTHING MORE WONDERFUL than George's kiss. The touch of his mouth, the glide of his tongue, the taste of his intoxicating desire. It was *everything*.

Then he lightly brushed his lips back and forth across hers, and it was somehow *more*.

Tingling chills danced over her skin with every touch of his lips. From her jaw to her shoulder. From the pulse at the base of her throat to the center of her sternum. Light, teasing kisses. A direct contrast to the pressure and heat and hardness of his body where it pressed between her thighs.

She was about to ask him to remove the last of his clothes so she could feel his bare skin against hers…but at that moment, he brought his lips to the peak of her breast in another teasing brush of his mouth.

Lucy had had enough teasing. She slid her hands up his back to hook over his shoulders as she arched her back and lifted her breasts, seeking a deeper caress.

The sound he made reverberated straight to the sensitive flesh of her sex.

He took her breast deep into his mouth.

It was hot and wet. The twirl of his tongue was a pleasure she never could have imagined existed, and she told him so.

His laugh was a rich rumble. Turning his head to flick his tongue against the nipple of her other breast, he said, "If you think *this* is a pleasure beyond imagining, I can't wait to hear what you think about the rest."

"You're assuming I'll like the rest," she challenged.

"Oh, you'll like it," he replied with a growl. "I'd wager on you loving it."

Lucy gasped as he flicked and circled his tongue, but she still managed a quick retort, "Your arrogance is astounding."

"With good reason, lass," he replied, rising up to kiss her in a deep and fiery joining of mouths and tongues and breath. When he lifted his head again, it was to offer her a wicked wink before he slid down the length of her body beneath the furs to lift her legs over his shoulders, putting his face right in line with—

"What are you doing?" she gasped, reaching down to grasp at his arms in an attempt to pull him back up.

His breath fanned over her belly, making her insides quiver. "I promised unimaginable pleasure," he answered in a voice that had gone rough and thick. "It's time to pay up."

The heat of his breath slid against her inner thighs, and she possessed just enough mindfulness to gasp a breath before she felt his tongue glide in a long and languid stroke along her sex. She thought she'd die from the pleasure of it.

Then he used his fingers to gently part her flesh and gave another melting stroke of his tongue.

The breath she took escaped on a heavy moan. Her fingers curled into the muscles of his arms like talons.

He continued to torment her with twirls and flicks of his tongue followed by tugging nips of his lips and the delicious draw of his mouth as he suckled her sensitive flesh. His efforts slowly increased in intensity, the pleasure tumbling over itself until she was at a loss for words, for thought, for anything at all except the sensation spiraling from where he made love to her with his mouth.

And he didn't seem to have any intention of stopping.

The pleasure continued to crest without breaking, creating a growing sense of anticipation she didn't quite understand. Carrying her higher and higher until she felt certain she would not survive another minute. She writhed beneath him, gasping for breath and moaning as her hands fisted and released in the furs.

While his mouth continued its magic, he pressed a long, blunt finger inside her. It was a slow, insistent possession. Beautiful in how it seemed to complete the circle of sensations her body was riding. First the liquid attention of his tongue, then the firm thrust and withdrawal of his finger.

When he added a second finger, her legs tensed involuntarily, and she wasn't sure if it was to halt his progress or urge him on to more. The additional width and steady rhythm finally pushed her over the edge.

Pleasure burst inside her, expanding to every nerve in her body. Glittering, gasping, astounding pleasure that left her trembling.

While she slowly recovered from the stunning experience, she noted George's attentive kisses on her inner thighs and the steady pressure of his fingers in her body. It was comforting and disconcerting as her awareness slowly returned.

Before she could start to feel awkward, he removed his fingers and pressed another kiss to her still-pulsing flesh. Then he crawled up the length of her body until his sweat-glistened shoulders loomed over her. His hips settled between hers with his hard, thick erection pressing intimately to her sex, and his stormy gray gaze met hers.

Framing her face in his hands, he pressed the flat of his thumb to the center of her lower lip. Desire still burned bright and hot in his eyes. "Are you all right?" he asked in a voice that was heavily laced with hunger.

On impulse, she parted her lips and brought his thumb into her mouth. Closing her lips over it, she swirled her tongue around the tip.

He closed his eyes. A heavy groan sounded in his throat.

With another teasing swirl of her tongue, she parted her lips. He withdrew his thumb slowly, dragging it over the edge of her teeth before swiping it across her lower lip. The action cause a tingling thread of sensation to wind through her center.

"I concede," she murmured. "Your arrogance is warranted."

His lopsided smile went straight to her heart, and his deep chuckle warmed her from head to toe. "That's just the beginning. There's so much more to come."

She shifted beneath him. "Show me."

Lowering his head beside hers, he whispered darkly into her ear. "I promised we'd have all night." He shifted to settle beside her. With a large hand splayed on her belly, he gently urged her to her side facing away from him, then he pulled her toward him until her back curved against his chest and her buttocks pressed firmly to his still-hard length. "Rest now, lass. I'm not going anywhere."

"You couldn't even if you wanted to," she replied sleepily as her eyes fell closed without her full consent. The warmth of the furs and the fire and the secure comfort of his body embracing hers were too much to resist, and she drifted off to sleep.

It couldn't have been much later that she woke again.

The fire still blazed, and her body retained a subtle hum of sensual awareness—though it was possible the hum was a reawakening, since George was pressing delicate little kisses across the back of her shoulders and along her nape. Tingling sparked over the surface of her skin, and her womb tensed with delicious yearning. She rolled her hips back, seeking a more intimate connection with his body, and he responded by sliding his hand over her hip to flatten against her stomach. When she rolled her hips again, he pressed with his palm, creating a wonderful balance of pressure from the front and from behind.

It was a heady, intoxicating sensation, the sense of being held—surrounded—but not contained.

She rolled her hips again.

He gently scraped his teeth across the muscle of her shoulder, drawing a swift gasp. "Are you ready for more?" he murmured thickly.

Yes. More.

She couldn't speak and instead replied by arching her head back, exposing her throat to more attention. The wet heat of his mouth slid up the column of her neck until his teeth closed over her earlobe. He held the soft flesh between his teeth as he slid his hand down between her thighs.

His touch was gentle and insistent as he slid his middle finger along her crease and then between. Delving into her heated moisture. Circling the apex in teasing strokes. Triggering a deep, aching sweetness.

She gasped and moaned.

He reduced her so easily to primitive sounds and thoughtless feeling.

She loved it. She craved it. She embraced the power it gave her to explore the full depths of the experience.

When he pushed his muscled thigh between hers, parting her legs to allow him better access, she was more than ready. And when he inserted first one finger, then two into her body, she welcomed the taut anticipation that infused her muscles. Encircling his wrist with her hand, she urged him to a slow, possessive rhythm of thrust and retreat.

As she rocked her hips against his hand, she felt the growing, hardening length of his erection against her buttocks.

More.

With a low sound, she eased his hand from between her legs and turned in his arms. Grasping his head in her hands, she brought his mouth to hers for a deep, wet kiss. His tongue tangled with hers, and his hands gripped her rear.

Drawing back, she accused, "You've still got your britches on."

"Should I take them off?"

"You'd better," she replied roughly.

He chuckled. Rolling to his back, he quickly shucked the pants beneath the furs and tossed them aside before turning toward her again and drawing her back into his arms.

She gasped at the heat of his skin as it came in contact with hers, and the full length of his erection throbbed between them. Hooking her leg over his hip, she leveraged herself against him until his smooth tip pressed firmly to her entrance.

Then she stopped. Gasping for breath against his lips, she opened her eyes and met his heavy-lidded gaze. The moment was suddenly poised on a precipice.

"Do you want to stop?"

Lucy gave a short shake of her head.

"I'll be wanting to hear the words." His Scottish burr had thickened with his desire.

She closed her eyes and drew a long breath that filled her with light and hope and something so much more than any feeling she'd ever imagined before. "I don't want to stop. Ever, I think," she added with a smile as she opened her eyes again.

"It seems we're in perfect agreement," he replied roughly before he took her mouth in a kiss, grasped her firmly around the waist and rolled her to her back.

This time, when he settled between her legs, there was nothing between them.

The smooth tip of his erection pressed more fully to her core. In a rush of impatience, she bent her legs alongside his hips to create a deeper cradle. The increased pressure was satisfying, but it wasn't quite enough. Yet, he didn't move to enter her. In fact, he seemed to stop completely; his breath heavy and rough, his eyes tightly closed.

She slid her hands up and down his tensely muscled back. His skin was heated and slicked with sweat. Everywhere she touched, he felt wonderful. Masculine, strong...*hers*.

Oh, how she wanted that to be true. Not just for tonight, but for always.

She could imagine spending the rest of her life with him taking up the chair beside her, making her laugh with his teasing smile, getting up early to make her breakfast.

She didn't realize she'd stopped caressing him and now clung to him with her face tucked to the curve of his throat until he eased back in her arms to look down at her.

Though she would have preferred to hide the emotions rising high in her chest, pressing through her throat, she didn't. She couldn't find it in herself to be anything but completely honest with him in that moment, so she left herself exposed to his gaze.

The flash of concern in his eyes darkened as he took in the sight of her. His brows lowered, and his lips pressed together. When a tear escaped from the corner of her eye, he caught it with a swipe of his thumb across her temple.

Her stomach tightened with the fear that he wouldn't like what he saw. But then one corner of his mouth ticked upward. "It's a lot to manage, isn't it, lass?"

And then she knew. He was feeling it, too.

It was there in the storm of his eyes, in the control he exerted over his body and in the care he gave hers.

Perhaps he was like that with all his prior lovers. But at least right now, it was just for her.

"We can wait," he said gruffly as he started to lift himself off her.

"No," she cried in a burst of panic, reaching down between them to wrap her hand around his hard length.

He groaned.

He was much larger than she'd expected. And smoother. And hotter.

Once she had him in her hand, she couldn't help but explore as she slid her hand down to the base and then back up to his blunt tip. He was magnificent.

He held himself rigid and still, supporting his weight on straight arms roped with muscle. As she stroked him up and down, then circled her fingers around the ridge at the top, he bowed his head and breathed heavy through his nose.

"You make me weak," he muttered.

The words gave her a rush of power and purpose.

Taking him in hand, she guided him to her entrance. She rolled her hips against him, coating his tip in her moisture, coaxing him with her heat.

He groaned again—a deep, rich sound. And she smiled. "I'm going to need your help with this part," she said.

He lifted his head and pinned her with a wicked stare. "I don't think you need my help with anything, but I'm more than happy to join you in this…if you're certain."

"I am. Very. I honestly don't think I can handle this ache inside me much longer." She squeezed him, enjoying the way his gaze unfocused as she did so. Seeing his pleasure fueled her own. "I need you to fill me," she whispered huskily.

He lowered his mouth swiftly to hers, claiming her lips and tongue in a possessive, passionate kiss. The he braced his weight on one elbow as he reached between them and took himself from her hand. "Hold on to me, lass."

She did as he said, grasping hard to his upper arms as he began to press into her body.

His size and her inexperience made the way difficult and slow.

She arched her head back and tightened her legs

around his hips as the burning sensation of his possession took over her awareness. It wasn't exactly painful… just totally consuming. The pressure and stretching and inescapable fullness; the odd sense of invasion and surrender. She wanted it desperately, and yet she fought it at the same time.

"Kiss me," he murmured against the side of her throat.

She turned her head and met his mouth. His tongue invaded with a luxurious glide, and his gaze bored into hers. As he sucked her tongue into his mouth, he withdrew. Not by much, but it was enough for her to feel a shift inside her from the altered friction. Then he pressed forward again, going deeper.

She gasped into his mouth.

He withdrew and thrust forward again; slowly, patiently claiming a deeper connection.

Sweat slicked his skin and dripped from his brow, yet he maintained a steady, careful rhythm. A rhythm that glided along sensitive inner nerves she didn't know existed until they were wide awake and yearning. A rhythm that slid thick and hard over the bud of her sex with every stroke until she felt that delicious building of tension inside her once again. Except it originated from such a deeper place this time.

She curled against him—sliding her arms around his neck and wrapping her legs around his hips—and kept fierce contact with his mouth. She wanted to taste him as he consumed her body with his. She wanted to breathe him in with every breath.

She held tight as something began to break inside her. It was like the burst of pleasure from earlier, but more. It pulsed into being with a deep and gorgeous song, igniting sparks along the way as it spread through her.

"Lucy." Her name on his lips anchored her to him as he gave a hoarse cry and thrust deep. His release pulsed in her core.

She'd never felt so perfectly content in all her life as she did in that moment.

∽∞∾

Later, they lay on their sides, facing each other before the slowly fading fire. They'd both dressed some time ago and now lay tucked beneath the furs as the flickering light danced about the room.

George swept his hand up and down her arm. He couldn't seem to stop touching her, as though he needed to assure himself she was real and not some dream he'd conjured up. He'd never felt so complete after being with a woman. So complete and yet insatiably hungry and deeply moved.

Lucy had curled around his heart, filling the empty spaces in his soul with her lovely, sarcastic, generous self.

How had he existed before her?

How could he imagine ever existing without her again?

Something of his thoughts must have shown in his eyes because her brows dipped subtly over her gaze. Reaching her hand to caress his jaw, she lifted her face and brought her lips to his.

The kiss was sweet and sleepy. Perfect.

He closed his eyes and wrapped his arm around her waist to tug her in closer. Her lips slid to his cheek and then the side of his throat as she tucked her head beneath his chin.

Within seconds, they were both asleep.

Nine

LUCY WOKE WITH A START. HER HEART WAS BEATING A fierce rhythm as she sucked in a deep breath that seared a choking path to her lungs. Her ragged coughing startled George, bringing him to full wakefulness in an instant. He immediately leapt to his feet, dragging Lucy up with him.

"Fire! Lucy, the cabin's on fire."

She looked around and noticed that the reddish glow around them didn't come from the fireplace, but from the corner of the cabin near the door. As she spun in place, more flames leaped to life around them, dancing up the walls until they were quickly surrounded.

Despite the rapidly rising heat around them, her blood ran ice cold and her heart froze in shock at the realization of what was happening.

"We've gotta get out of here."

George's words finally spurred her into movement, and they rushed to the door as smoke unfurled, thick and black in the air. Bending low, they stuffed their feet in their boots. George's expression was grim as he threw her coat around her shoulders, then grabbed his own before reaching for the door.

It wouldn't budge.

"What in bloody hell?" He shoved again.

It was stuck. Panic rushed through Lucy's body, tightening her lungs against the invading smoke.

They had to get out. Now.

With a low growl of fury, George took two long steps back, then charged at the door with all his strength and momentum, splitting the wood and propelling him out into the winter night.

Lucy charged after him, gasping for breath as soon as the crisp winter air hit her face.

The snow crunched under their feet as they ran from the cabin. The night was still dark, but the full moon illuminated the snow and cast an eerie orange glow all around. Through the crackle and snap of the heated inferno, she heard the distressed call of the horses.

"Stay here," George shouted as he took off running toward the cave.

Still sucking in great gulps of clean air, Lucy was too stunned to do anything more than turn around to look back at the fiery destruction being wrought on her home. Billows of black smoke rolled from her chimney and doorway. Roaring flames climbed the outer walls and danced along her roof.

Everything inside her clenched tight. A sob that wouldn't release threatened to choke her as her eyes burned from smoke and emotion.

The cabin wasn't going to last much more than another few minutes.

The cabin and everything in it; a lifetime of personal treasures.

Her heart gave a sudden jolt as she realized there was one thing in particular she could not leave to be destroyed along with everything else.

She had to go back.

Without considering the risk—or anything at all—she charged across the snow and into the cabin. The smoke was so thick she could barely see and the flames were everywhere—bright and hot and furious. But she charged forward. It took her only a minute to grab what she'd wanted and stuff it under her coat, but by the time she stumbled back outside, her eyes were stinging and her lungs felt like they were trapped in a heated vise.

The heat at her back kept her stumbling across the snow as she hastily wiped the burning tears from her eyes.

Suddenly, an arm came around her from behind, drawing her up short as a disgusting cackle sounded in her ear. "I'd've been happy to know you roasted alive in there, but I can't say I'm disappointed for the chance for a little sport before you die. How does it feel, knowing your man just ran off and left you to burn?"

It was the man who'd assaulted her in town. Lucy snarled and twisted in his grip. She kicked back with one foot, connecting with his knee and causing him to loosen his hold just enough that she could bend forward and withdraw the knife she had stashed in the lining of her boot. She didn't hesitate to slash at the arm around her waist.

He let her go with a howl of pain.

Lucy whirled to face him, her knife raised and ready.

Her attacker glared at her. Then he smiled as he lifted a pistol from under his coat. "You're probably a shit lay anyway," he sneered as he pulled back on the hammer of the gun.

Lucy flipped the knife in her hand and lifted her arm to throw it.

Before she could, George came flying out of the darkness at a full run. He tackled the other man to the ground, sending the gun flying from his hand to land nearly at Lucy's feet. She quickly dove to scoop up the weapon while the two men tumbled across the snow. Her attacker somehow scrambled free and gained his feet first. But George leaped up swiftly after and immediately sidestepped to put himself between the crazed man and Lucy.

Dammit. She appreciated his intention to protect her, but she couldn't throw her knife if she couldn't see her target past George's wide shoulders.

"You shoulda minded your own business back in town," the smaller man sneered. "Now you're both gonna die."

"Not tonight, mate," George replied.

Before she could get into better position, their attacker charged with a murderous yell. He was outmatched by George's superior size and strength, but he didn't seem to care.

One swing of George's great fist to his midsection doubled him over. But he refused to back down. He charged again; his lips drawn back in a snarl, madness bright in his glaring gaze.

Another punch to the jaw sent him stumbling back. As he tried to regain purchase in the deep and shifting snow, he tripped over something on the ground and twisted to avoid losing his balance even more, but the added impetus sent him careening straight toward the cabin.

Lucy's body froze in place as she watched the scene unfolding as if in slow motion. For an odd moment, she almost stepped forward to reach for him—to stop his fall. But there was nothing she could do.

He crashed into the fiery cabin with a shrill cry before the wall gave way. His scream was swallowed by a deafening crash as the roof collapsed and the cabin fell in around him.

It happened in an instant.

"Holy shite," George muttered.

Lucy rushed to his side, wrapping her arms tight around his middle as she buried her face in his chest. Breathing deeply of his scent and pressing her ear to the rapid beat of his heart, she stood enclosed securely in his arms while the fire raged beside them and the snow melted at their feet. Her entire life before this moment was being consumed by the relentless flames, but at least they were both alive. After a while, she lifted her face to the sky and dragged in a few raw breaths of the chill night air before meeting his concerned gaze.

"Are you all right, lass?" His voice was rough and ragged.

Lucy nodded and blinked to clear the blurring tears from her eyes. "The horses?" she asked.

He nodded. "They're fine."

"I think he started the fire."

"He did," George replied, tipping his head toward the empty oil cans the man had left behind to trip over.

Lucy shook her head, stunned by the destruction wrought by one man. Perhaps it was fitting that his avarice resulted in his own death, but Lucy couldn't help but feel the utter waste of it all.

As she watched the only home she'd ever known disintegrate beneath the raging hunger of the flames, she slowly began to feel an odd sort of acceptance. Everything she'd ever cared about had been inside. Her books, mementos of her father, the basic elements of her existence. But they were just possessions. None of those things could really define a life.

Shortly after her father's death, she'd come to the realization that the solitude and isolation her father had created on this mountain had been for *him*. It was the life *he* had wanted, not her.

Now…there was nothing left to keep her here.

Within a short time, the cabin was reduced to a skeletal structure with only the hardiest beam and supports still standing. But even they would fall eventually.

"You can rebuild," George said beside her. "You're alive. That's what matters."

She looked at him and saw the compassion and support in his steady gaze. "I know."

At the moment, she didn't know if she'd want to build another home here or somewhere else. The fact was that she was free to decide that for herself. One thing she knew for certain—she didn't want to be alone anymore.

"The pass to the valley is likely open by now," George noted gently. "We can take shelter there."

Lucy nodded.

Not long ago, she never would have considered entering that valley, under any circumstances.

But now…

At least George would be with her, and unless she wanted to take up residence in the cave, she had nowhere else to go. The ride was solemn, but it did not take long to reach the hidden pass. The tree that had fallen across the way at the start of the blizzard had already been dragged away, and there was evidence of others having passed that way since the heavy snowfall.

Sunrise was still hours away when they reached the end of the winding trail, but the sky was clear, allowing the stars and moon to illuminate the valley that opened up at the end of the pass.

Lucy had never really imagined what an outlaw hideout might look like, but she certainly wouldn't have guessed it would appear so peaceful.

The valley was wide and long, extending farther into the distance than she could see in the night, and it was covered in thick, white snow that glistened under the moonlight. Protective pines rose up the slopes on each side, creating a natural haven. A log bunkhouse with a long covered porch running along the front was the most prominent building. No lights shone from inside, but a thin thread of smoke drifted up from the chimney as though an earlier fire had only just burned down to the glow of coals. Beyond the bunkhouse, Lucy could make out a large barn outlined in the darkness, and she thought she could see a small cabin tucked in among the trees off to the right some distance up the mountainside, but she couldn't be sure.

It was a beautiful scene.

The still and quiet hush of the winter valley seemed to whisper to Lucy of hope and warmth and other things she wasn't quite ready to name.

A smile tickled her lips as they neared the bunkhouse and she noticed evergreen garland looped along the porch railing with red bows tied to each post.

Not at all what she would have expected of outlaws.

But then, hadn't George surprised her from the start?

With only the sound of their horses' steps in the snow breaking the serene silence of the winter night, he led her around back to the barn. They quickly saw their horses settled with water and grain before George took her hand and led her toward the bunkhouse.

All was quiet and dark inside, but he didn't need a light to make his way through the familiar space. Lucy was more grateful than ever for his presence. Tonight, she needed him to take care of her. Tomorrow, she would be capable again. Tomorrow, she would address her new circumstances.

But for now, all she had to do was follow the man in front of her.

He brought her to a small room tucked halfway down a dark and narrow hallway. After closing the door quietly behind them, he turned to release the ties on her coat. Tugging it free, he laid it over a chair in the corner of the room. Then he placed his hands on her shoulders and walked her back to the bed, indicating she should sit.

Kneeling before her, he silently removed her boots, then looked up at her with a quiet smile that warmed her in the dusky darkness. "Rest a bit, lass," he whispered hoarsely.

She did as he said, and he pulled the blankets over her. "Lie with me," she said.

"Of course," he replied as he shrugged off his coat and removed his boots to climb into the bed behind her. Curling around her back, he whispered against her nape. "The morn brings a new day."

Ten

LUCY OPENED HER EYES TO A ROOM FLOODED WITH morning light.

She immediately recalled the events of the prior night. Her throat still burned from the smoke, and her chest ached with loss and fury.

Then she remembered George's words. She was still alive. And life meant hope.

She rolled to her back and reached an arm out beside her, seeking his warmth. She encountered an expanse of cool, empty mattress. A very grand expanse.

Sitting up, she realized she lay on one side of a bed that was bigger than any she'd ever seen before. It was nearly too big for the room it was in and allowed very little space for anything else.

As she grew more alert, she became aware of a significant amount of noise coming from beyond the closed door of the room. A cacophony of voices and activity.

But one of the voices was definitely George's. She'd recognize his great roaring laugh anywhere. A smile widened her lips at the sound, and her body warmed with something like joy.

Her father had instilled a hard core of independence in her. She'd been resentful at times about the isolated life he'd created for them, but she understood he'd been motivated by a desire to protect her. And she'd become confident in her belief that she didn't need anyone. And then she'd gone and dragged a ridiculous, handsome, considerate, wonderful man out of the blizzard, and she could no longer imagine her life without him.

She'd gone and fallen in love with him.

Her heart leapt in her chest at the sudden realization. Oh my God, she loved him!

It was true. Love was the cause of the sensation that swept through her whenever his gray eyes met hers. Love made her chest ache with the thought that they'd someday part ways. And love gave her the strength and hope to think maybe parting wasn't so inevitable after all.

Suddenly anxious to be in his company, despite knowing she would be stepping into what sounded like a crowd of strangers, she slipped from the bed and crept from the room. She made her way down the narrow hallway toward what appeared to be a large common area.

Lucy enjoyed people even if she'd never really had an opportunity to be around very many at once, but as she stepped from the hall and looked around at the activity spread before her, she felt more than a little out of her element.

The first thing she noticed was that there weren't quite so many people as she'd expected by the level of noise they made, though over half a dozen were still more than she was accustomed to.

The second was that the large great room and open kitchen area were decorated for Christmas.

Pine boughs and droopy red bows graced the wooden mantel of the large fireplace, which was a centerpiece to the room.

A Christmas tree stood in the corner of the room. A boy of two or three with a shock of honey-gold hair and vivid blue eyes was decorating the branches with colorful ribbons and scraps of cloth shaped into angels. A man with black hair but those same blue eyes was on hand to lift the boy up so he could reach the higher branches.

Lucy realized with a shock of surprise that the man was none other than the doctor from Chester Springs.

What on earth would he be doing here?

Laughter erupted from the group seated around a long table set in front of a row of windows to Lucy's far right. On one end of the table stood a girl of about eleven with the same blue eyes as the boy but the black hair of their father. She was covered in flour up to her elbows and was rolling dough out on the tabletop while grinning at the antics of the three rough-looking men seated around the table threading popcorn and dried cranberries onto string. The outlaws jostled and elbowed each other in their attempts to find the best pieces for their garlands. They were clearly the cause of most of the noise.

The kitchen took up the far corner and was open to the rest of the great room. A lanky young man was chopping vegetables at the counter, while another stood in front of a very large, black iron stove, slowly stirring something in an oversize pot. Overseeing them both was a beautiful woman who possessed a firm air of command and honey-gold hair just like the boy.

It looked for all the world like a large family gathering.

Or rather, what Lucy would imagine a family gathering looked like.

Hearing a door open, she turned to see two newcomers entering from outside.

The first was a small and graceful woman with pale hair and elegant features surrounding the softest blue eyes Lucy had ever seen. She walked just a step ahead of the man behind her, and her hand was reached back and linked with his. Before he came into full view, they released each other's hands, and he stepped up beside her.

Lucy recognized him as Gabriel Sloan, a Cheyenne with long, black braids and a still gaze. Gabriel who was the only member of the gang that had ever come to the cabin—before George, that is. He and Lucy's father had been acquaintances of a sort and had come to the agreement that allowed them to live so close to the outlaw gang without any trouble.

After hanging their coats on hooks, Gabriel scanned the room in an efficient glance. When his dark gaze fell on Lucy, still tucked into the shadows of the hallway, his only response was an abbreviated nod. The woman beside him noticed his focus and looked toward Lucy curiously before giving a gentle smile.

Seeing the woman's fine and natural elegance suddenly made Lucy painfully aware of how disheveled she must look in her red flannel long johns covered only by her buckskin breeches with her hair twisted into a tangled braid. She was relieved when the woman shifted her attention to the boy who had noticed her entrance and came running forward with a shout of delight to greet her. After a quick and energetic embrace, the boy tugged at the woman's hand and led her toward the tree. Gabriel followed behind her.

As Lucy soaked in the festive scene, she realized with a sinking feeling that George wasn't present.

But she swore she'd heard his laugh only moments ago.

And then she heard it again. She breathed a sigh of relief as he emerged from the hallway extending from the great room directly across from her.

He was talking to the man who had followed him down the hall—a handsome enough fellow with a striking golden gaze and brows that were drawn at a serious angle. The other man said something Lucy couldn't quite make out, but before George could reply, he caught sight of Lucy across the room. His lips spread into a wide grin, and his companion was all but forgotten as George crossed the room toward her.

As soon as her eyes met his, Lucy didn't give another thought to anyone else. Suddenly, she was excited, emboldened, and infinitely aware of the pull that was still there between them as he came to stand before her. Looking down at her from his impressive height, his wide grin turned into that half-crooked smile she adored as he took her hand and brought it to his lips. The brief brush of his mouth across her knuckles sent her senses into a tailspin.

"Are you feeling better this morning?" he asked in a low tone.

"I'm still a bit...off, I guess," she admitted, "but definitely better."

He nodded.

"Are you going to introduce us to your friend there, George?"

Lucy looked toward the kitchen to see the lanky young man with amused brown eyes staring boldly in their direction.

George didn't bother to turn his head; he just shouted back. "Not at the moment, so just go right on back to whatever you're doing."

The young outlaw guffawed, apparently not at all put off by George's curt reply.

Lucy, on the other hand, lifted a brow. "That was rude. What happened to your renowned charm?"

His smile was heated and intimate. "I'm saving all my charm for you, lass."

Lucy had to glance away from the smolder in his eyes, or she'd end up dragging him back to his bed. It was only then that she noticed he carried something in his hand. "What is that?"

George glanced down. "Oh shite. You weren't supposed to see this yet."

"Why not?" she asked, her curiosity growing.

"Och, what the hell. Come on." He tugged on her hand and led her back down the hall to his bedroom.

Once the door was closed, he gestured for her to take

a seat on the bed before he crouched down in front of her and offered her the parcel. "This is for you. From me."

Lucy took the small rectangular package and looked at it pensively. It was wrapped in brown paper and tied off with a festive red bow. "What? Why?"

He chuckled. "Because it's Christmas Eve and because I wanted to. Usually we all wait until tomorrow morning for such things, but I reckon we don't have to follow those rules if we don't want to."

"A Christmas present?" Lucy asked, her throat suddenly tightening up.

George took a seat on the bed beside her and laid his large hand on her thigh. "What's the matter, lass?"

"I'm sorry, it's just…this is all a little unexpected."

George lifted his hand to cradle her face, turning her head until she met his gaze. "I know and I'm sorry. I'd forgotten today was Christmas Eve, but if you'd like to join the festivities, you'll be in for a treat. No one puts on a better Christmas Eve feast than Honey. And after we eat, there'll be music and dancing. You'll probably hear a few wild tales from Old Pete…" Something of her astonishment must have shown in her face because he paused. "But that'll be later, and if it sounds like too much, I understand. This, anyway, is just between us," he added gently as he glanced down at the parcel still clutched in her hands. "Open it."

Lucy willed her racing heart to a slower pace as she untied the ribbon and removed the paper to reveal a lovely book bound in faded red leather that had been softened and worn from frequent handling. She opened it to the title page, which read The Works of Robert Burns Complete in One Volume with Life by Allan Cunningham.

"A collection of poems from the Scottish bard. It was my favorite when I was lad," George explained. "It's one of the few things I brought with me when I left."

She looked up in surprise. "Then why are you giving it to me? It means too much to you."

He placed his hands over hers, forcing her to hold the book more securely. "That's exactly why I want you to have it. You lost everything last night," he said in a roughened tone. "I'd like you to consider it the start of your new collection."

"I don't know what to say." She'd never received anything so thoughtful...so perfect. "Thank you. It's an amazing gift. I'm...overwhelmed."

His smile was jaunty as he replied, "That's what I was going for."

Lucy pressed the book to her chest as her heart welled with emotion. Intense and bright and a little bit terrifying.

And wonderful, she added as she looked into George's beautiful, stormy eyes. Last night she'd lost everything that had made up her life before meeting him. Today, she'd awoken in his bedroom, in a lodge filled with strangers. Yet, when their gazes met and held, she felt safe and happy and...home.

"Oh my God," she exclaimed, leaping to her feet. "I almost forgot."

"What? What's wrong?"

"Nothing," she said quickly as she tugged on her boots. Handing him the book, she said, "Just stay here. I'll be right back."

She dashed from the room and down the hall. Ignoring everyone in the great room, she let herself out the back door and ran across the snow to the barn.

She found Rupert snug in a stall beside Thistle, and she quickly untied the bundle of fur she'd secured to his saddle before they'd left the cave. Holding it to her chest, she ran back into the bunkhouse and to George's room.

He stood beside the bed, looking bemused and slightly worried. "What is it, lass?"

Lucy pressed her hand to her chest as she caught her breath. "I have something for you too."

She'd never given anyone a gift before. She didn't realize how anxiety-ridden the experience could be.

Would he like them?

Would he wear them?

Would he even know what they were?

He took the odd bundle with a raised brow and unwrapped it to reveal a pair of boots that were similar to hers but in a much larger size.

"So your feet don't freeze," she explained unnecessarily.

"Are these what you've been making every night?" he asked with an odd look in his eyes.

Lucy nodded, feeling foolish.

"But the fire…" he said, a frown deepening between his eyes. "You didn't have them when we came out."

"I went back for them."

"You did what?" he shouted, his eyes going wide before he stepped toward her and wrapped her up in a hug that lifted her off her feet so he could plant a heavy kiss on her mouth. Easing back just a bit, he murmured roughly, "You brave, unbelievable woman. It's the best gift I've ever gotten. Thank you."

Lucy's cheeks grew warm as she accepted another heated kiss.

When they drew apart, she could see a light in his eyes unlike anything she'd ever seen before. It was beautiful and profound. She tipped her head in question and a reddish hue spread across his cheeks.

"The book is more than just an old favorite. There's a passage inside I'd like to read to you, if you don't mind."

Lucy nodded, feeling a strange tightening in her chest and a wild flutter in her belly.

He flipped through the well-worn pages until he found the one he wanted. Looking at her from beneath surprisingly earnest brows, he said, "Would you sit? Please?"

She did, and he lowered himself to one knee before

her. Then he cleared his throat, and the words of Robert Burns flowed from his lips in rich, lyrical Scots.

> *Ithers seek they ken na what,*
> *Features, carriage, and a' that;*
> *Gie me love in her I court,*
> *Love to love makes a' the sport.*
> *Let love sparkle in her e'e;*
> *Let her lo'e nae man but me;*
> *That's the tocher-gude I prize,*
> *There the luver's treasure lies.*

By the end, Lucy's eyes burned with tears. She didn't recognize more than half of the words, but she'd have felt the meaning in the roughened burr of his voice even if one word in particular hadn't stood out above the rest.

George closed the book and lifted his head to look into her face. Seeing her tears, he sighed and reached to brush his thumb across her cheek. "Och, lass. I didn't mean to make you cry," he muttered softly. "I just want you to know how I feel. I was hoping you might consider staying here. With me," he added with a hopeful note. "Forever."

Lucy's thoughts were reeling, and her heart was filled near to bursting. But she couldn't pull up any words through the thickness in her throat. All she could manage was a rapid shake of her head.

Seeing the gesture, a slight look of panic tightened his features. "It doesn't have to be forever. We could just try it out. You need a place to stay for a while anyway, so why not with me?" He looked down at their joined hands, continuing roughly, "Ol' Robbie Burns says it far better than I, but the truth is…" He paused to take a deep breath. "I've fallen in love with you, lass. And I just can't fathom spending even a day of my life without you."

Realizing he thought she was refusing him, Lucy

forcefully cleared her throat and reached up to cup his face in her hands. Urging him to meet her gaze, she said, "I love you too. But I am not going to stay forever in a bunkhouse with who knows how many other people. We will wait until the spring thaw, and then we'll build a cabin of our own. Close by...but not too close."

George started grinning wildly halfway through her declaration, and by the end, his full-bodied laughter filled the room. Then with a heavy sigh, he wrapped his arms around her and tackled her back onto the mattress of his oversize bed.

A wicked gleam flashed in his gray gaze. "Just promise me the cabin will have a loft so I can have the pleasure of watching you climb the ladder every night."

Lucy gave him a wicked look in return. "Only if you climb up every night to join me. *And* you have to make breakfast every morning," she added quickly.

His laughter was warm and rich. "With pleasure, lass."

About the Author

Amy Sandas's love of romance began one summer when she stumbled across one of her mother's Barbara Cartland books. Her affinity for writing began with sappy preteen poems and led to a bachelor's degree with an emphasis on creative writing from the University of Minnesota Twin Cities. She lives with her husband and children in northern Wisconsin. Visit her website at amysandas.com.